THE CHAOS CHRONICLES
by Jeffrey A. Carver

"A *2001* for the nineties."—John E. Stith

Book 2: *Strange Attractors*

"Carver is at his rousing best in this wild ride into the heart of an enigmatic world beyond the Milky Way. This is science fiction out at the frontier. Maybe beyond the frontier."

—Jack McDevitt

"Full of wonders and adventures."

—*Science Fiction Chronicle*

"Carver's latest novel showcases his own fertile imagination and his talent for creating a host of engagingly sympathetic characters." —*Library Journal*

"Has all the ingredients for a well-deserved popularity: an original creative angle using the budding science of chaos theory; an intriguing alien life-form in the symbiotic quarx, Charlie; and an irresistibly readable story line reinforced by fascinating speculative science." —*Booklist*

Book 1: *Neptune Crossing*
A *Science Fiction Chronicle*
Best SF Novel of the Year

"This book reveals an alien encounter brushing hard against a soul, and takes us from there to the far reaches of the cosmos, all with the sure touch of a writer who knows his science. Jeff Carver has done it again!" —David Brin

"One of the very best things Carver has written, a traditional adventure filled with mystery and wonder."

—*Science Fiction Chronicle*

"Those who read this one will surely return for a second helping. . . . Carver has a fascinating vehicle here, he's going someplace interesting, and there are still seats available. Grab one." —Thomas A. Easton, *Analog*

Books by Jeffrey A. Carver

Seas of Ernathe
*Star Rigger's Way
‡Panglor
*The Infinity Link
*The Rapture Effect
Roger Zelazny's Alien Speedway: Clypsis
From a Changeling Star
Down the Stream of Stars
*Dragons in the Stars
*Dragon Rigger

THE CHAOS CHRONICLES
*Neptune Crossing
*Strange Attractors
‡The Infinite Sea

*denotes a Tor book
‡forthcoming in a Tor Books edition

STRANGE ATTRACTORS

JEFFREY A. CARVER

A TOM DOHERTY ASSOCIATES BOOK
NEW YORK

STRANGE ATTRACTORS

Copyright © 1995 by Jeffrey A. Carver

Cover art by Alan Gutierrez

A Tor Book
Published by Tom Doherty Associates, Inc.
175 Fifth Avenue
New York, N.Y. 10010

Tor Books on the World Wide Web:
http://www.tor.com

Tor® is a registered trademark of Tom Doherty Associates, Inc.

ISBN: 0-812-53516-2
Library of Congress Card Catalog Number: 94-47206

First edition: April 1995
First mass market edition: April 1996

Printed in the United States of America

0 9 8 7 6 5 4 3 2 1

For Nancy and Fred Lorey

and

For those Palmers:
Fay and Phil,
and Andrew and Suzanne

"I have not yet spoken of the esthetic appeal of strange attractors. These systems of curves, these clouds of points, suggest sometimes fireworks or galaxies . . . A realm lies here to be explored and harmonies to be discovered."

—David Ruel, "Strange Attractors"

Strange attractors . . .

. . . n. 1. *Chaos theory*. Patterns of turbulence; harmonies underlying disorder. 2. In phase-space, channels of order emerging from uncertainty; paths of transformation. 3. *Shipworld sociology*. Unseen forces tending to bring disparate energies and intelligences into convergence. Purposefulness of intent remains conjectural.

PRELUDE

JOURNAL ENTRY BY JOHN BANDICUT:
(EARTH DATE UNKNOWN)

 AS I RECORD this, I find myself wondering, just who am I addressing? Julie? Krackey? Dakota? I feel as if I want to write a letter . . . but I am thousands of light-years from you now. I can only imagine all of you as you were before I left. You've probably all been dead for centuries. But really, I have no way of knowing.

How much time has passed? I can only guess.

All I can do, then, is speak my thoughts into these stones and pray that they will one day be heard by someone who cares—though I have little hope that it will be anyone human. Still, I must not abandon whatever hope I have. There is so much I don't know. So very much.

Have you ever heard voices in your head, voices that could lead you to do stranger things than you could imagine? It's a trick question, really; if the answer is yes, you're either a neurolinker, or crazy. If you neurolink, you just go to the nearest datajack to hear voices. I had to go to Neptune and Triton to find the voice that changed my life—but then, that trip turned out to be the shortest leg of the journey.

If you're a neurolinker, the datanet practically defines your existence. I know that even without knowing who you are; I was one of you once. But if you've ever lost your neuro, then you know the emptiness of never again having that sea of awareness lapping at your mind, offering you every sort of *connection imaginable. It is* almost *the most terrifying loss I* can think of. Almost.

I faced that loss, and it scared me as much as deafness and blindness rolled into one. But even that wasn't half as frightening as what came later—when the inner silence broke, and a voice told me to sacrifice everything I had, to save a world I barely knew anymore.

And that, of course, is what got me where I am now. Somewhere out here on the edge of eternity, friendless—at least in the beginning. Fine friendships have come to me since, of course, but nothing can erase the terror, the stark loneliness *of what I faced, in that first view of the galaxy.*

Am I being melodramatic? Probably. If Charlie were in my head now, I am sure he would chide me for it. But Charlie's not here; he's dead right now.

I'm sure he'll speak his piece later, when he rejoins me . . .

1

AT ETERNITY'S EDGE

 HE HAD SURVIVED. John Bandicut knew that, and little more. What he did know didn't reassure him. He was trapped inside a structure of immense proportion and unknown nature, somewhere outside the galaxy of his birth. The image still blazed in his mind, long after it was blocked from his view: the vast spiral ocean of the Milky Way splayed across the sky before him, with its glittering stars and its dust lanes and its luminous core. Not *around* him or overhead in the sky, but *before* him, spread out in all of its awesome glory. He was marooned half a universe from home, in a survey craft built for leisurely orbits around the planet Neptune.

Neptune. Solar system. Earth. For all practical purposes, they were gone now, along with everyone he had ever known or cared for. Charlie, Julie, Krackey, Dakota . . . all gone. He had saved Earth from destruction. But he hadn't saved himself, not in any way that gave him comfort. He was alone now, except for a pair of simple robots, and left with the haunting question: *Who has done this to me—and why?* No one had come knocking since his ship had docked, so it seemed if he wanted to learn what sort of place he had been taken aboard, he would have to go out and see for himself.

He zipped up the utility backpack and dropped it on the deck. It was stuffed full of rations, a recorder, some spare clothes, and a few simple tools. After a last check of the ship's bridge, he called the robots to the airlock. He reached for his spacesuit—or rather, the spacesuit he had stolen from Triton Station just before he had stolen the spaceship.

You didn't steal it, he reminded himself. You borrowed it, to save the Earth. He sighed, weary of the memory, and began to unfasten the front seam.

You will not need a spacesuit.

He started at the voice in his head. The translator-stone in his right wrist flickered diamond-white, as it spoke for the first time in several hours. It was a daughter-stone of the alien "translator" that he had found in a cavern on Triton, and a component of the incomprehensible mechanism that had brought him to this place. It was also the closest thing he had to a guide since Charlie the quarx had died, just before impact with the comet. The translator-stone seemed to have some knowledge of this place, but it parceled that knowledge out in exceedingly small doses. When it spoke at all, it displayed little interest in answering Bandicut's questions.

Bandicut frowned. /How sure are you about that?/ he asked silently, reluctant to hang the spacesuit back up.

You will not need a spacesuit.

Bandicut grunted and left the spacesuit hanging. Beside him, the two mining robots that had accompanied him from Triton whirred and clicked quietly. "Ready, boys?" he asked. "Fully charged?" Copernicus, a low-slung tunnel surveyor on wheels shaped like fat, horizontal ice cream cones, replied with a light drumtap. "Aye, Cap'n." Napoleon, shaped like a cross between a monkey and a chest-high grasshopper, and built for walking rather than rolling, flexed its knees in a quick plié and said, "Ready, John Bandicut."

Bandicut hefted one strap of the bag over his shoulder, took a deep breath, and hit the airlock button.

The outer door thunked open. He blinked, facing a featureless, meter-deep boarding passageway—ending in a purplish bulkhead. "So." He frowned. An instant later, the bulkhead dissolved, revealing a long, smooth-walled corridor, gloomily lit. At its far end, the corridor bent to the right.

Bandicut swallowed, twice. Then he took his first step

onto an alien world. It didn't feel like much, as his foot touched the floor. The gravity felt the same—a little heavy, for one recently accustomed to the one-thirteenth gee of Triton—but that change had occurred earlier, at the moment of docking. He stepped into the corridor and paused to see if his hosts would appear, or maybe just strike him dead.

Proceed.

He blinked. Was the translator-stone receiving messages, or did it already know what Bandicut was about to encounter? He had no idea what world the translator was from; could this place be its home? He didn't bother asking. /Okay,/ he said, and glanced back at the robots. "Let's go, boys." He started down the passageway. The robots clicked and thrummed behind him.

The walls of the corridor gave off a satiny sheen. The violet light seemed stronger ahead; it flickered with an erratic, strobelike intensity that soon made him feel a little dizzy. He put out a steadying hand. The wall was cool to the touch and finely textured. There was something more to the touch, though; he felt a momentary mental dizziness, and a sudden urgency to keep moving, not quite an encouragement and not quite a threat. It was more like a sense of *need,* like the urgency that might have been conveyed by an approaching siren.

/Do you know what that is?/ he asked nervously.

The stones did not answer.

He rounded the bend, and the passageway widened. On the left wall were a number of indecipherable panels, with strangely fuzzy, flickering lights that didn't seem to illuminate anything. Bandicut clicked on a handheld lantern and flashed it around briefly, before continuing onward. The passage narrowed again, but the violet strobe was growing brighter. Followed by the whirring robots, Bandicut rounded a second bend, to the left, and entered a large, oval chamber.

It looked a little like the lobby of a theater, darkened, but with pools and flashes of light radiating into the darkness. It was roughly circular, with dark panels lining most of the outer wall. To his right, a pool of violet light flickered, apparently created by shifting, sparkling patterns in the adjacent walls and ceiling. This was the source of the strobe. It looked almost as if it were intended to spotlight some object—a sculpture perhaps, some absent work of art.

Dropping his backpack, Bandicut squinted at a broad glass partition that appeared to bisect the chamber. On the far side of the glass was what looked like a control room, though he quickly saw that it was, in fact, a wide hallway that swept out of view in both directions. Directly opposite, on the far wall of the control room, were four panels with screens and controls, shaped and indented in ways that clearly suggested nonhuman users. "Anyone there?" he murmured, rapping softly on the partition with his knuckles. His rapping was silent, at least to his ears. There was no one visible.

On his side of the room, a series of lights came on. He turned. The wall panels were glowing now—perhaps in response to his voice. They looked like video or holo screens. Images came into focus, different images in each one. They were all landscapes: desert, forest, lake, shattered moonscape; and they were changing—*blink*—every second or so. He scanned the panels in bewilderment. Marsh—*blink*—glacier—*blink*—red sun—city structures—vast rooms—*blink blink*—incomprehensible mechanical structures—*blink blink blink*—at an accelerating rate.

"What is this?" he whispered.

The robots clicked and whirred, and Napoleon strode toward him. "We are in a flattened oval chamber, approximately twelve meters in diameter, three meters in height—"

"Yes, Nappy, I can see that. I was hoping for more useful insight."

Napoleon fell silent. But Copernicus rolled toward the glass partition. "Cap'n, movement beyond the pane."

Bandicut whirled.

"Your ten o'clock, Cap'n."

Bandicut peered through the glass and finally saw a small machine gliding along the base of the far wall, just coming into the control-room area. It looked like a tiny robot, casting a faint sideways swath of light across the floor. Something looked odd about that light; it was dim, but sparkling. As the little machine passed in front of him, Bandicut realized that within the fan of light, myriad particles were gleaming, rising into the robot.

"It's vacuuming. The damn thing is *vacuuming*." He glanced at Copernicus. "Isn't that what it looks like to you?"

Copernicus whirred. "Uncertain of the reference, Cap'n."

Bandicut knocked on the partition again, but the little robot ignored him, passed the length of the control area, and disappeared down the hallway to the right. Bandicut pressed his fingers in frustration against the glass, and was startled to realize that it was perfectly smooth: no dirt, no grit, no sensation of it being a *material* surface. He remembered an impassable barrier that he had encountered once, on Triton, surrounding the alien translator.

He sighed and spoke silently to the translator-stones in his wrists. /What is this place? Does anyone live here? What am I supposed to be doing? Damn it—/

Step under the lights.

He blinked. /Lights?/

Behind you.

He turned, frowning toward the pool of light in the corner. /And do what?/

Communicate. We will translate.

Bandicut stared at the strobing light. Communicate with whom? he wondered. And if someone wanted to communicate with him, why didn't they come out in person?

Copernicus rolled toward the lights, as if it had heard Bandicut's inner dialogue. It paused at the edge of the light, rotating its sensor array. "Electromagnetic fields, Cap'n. Shall I attempt measurements?"

Bandicut was about to reply in the affirmative, when the translator-stones urged him forward with a sharp tingle in both wrists.

Step under the lights. Without delay, please. Bring your possessions.

He blinked in confusion, but felt a faint tingle of confirmation as he picked up his bag and stepped forward. "Coppy, would you mind carrying this?" He set the bag on the robot's back, and Copernicus closed a manipulator-arm to secure it. "Thanks. You two keep a sharp eye out, and stay close to me." He felt another tingle of confirmation. But he also recalled his very first encounter with the alien translator—years ago it seemed, in the cavern on Triton—and how useless his suit scanners had been in gathering any real information. "Stay *real* close," he murmured.

Napoleon stepped beside him with the delicacy of an oversized granddaddy longlegs. Bandicut took a deep breath, comforted by the presence of the robots. As he stepped into the violet pool, a ray of light strobed in his eyes. He flinched. "Hello? Anyone here?"

For an instant, nothing. Then the strobes splintered, and shards of light flashed around him like rain. In an instant, he was enveloped in a coruscating cocoon of light, colors changing at a dizzying speed. He wanted to flee, but the floor had turned to fire beneath him. He could not move.

The light brightened, until it seemed not so much like dazzling rays in his eyes as an inner light . . . and something else, a presence of something vaster and more powerful. Something aware. Something intelligent. It stirred in his mind, just beyond the limits of his own consciousness. It knew he was here; it was interested in him.

And then it blossomed, transforming itself into something that was color and sound and smell, and none of those things . . . and then the bottom fell out of it all, and he felt his consciousness slipping away.

To his surprise, he did not actually lose consciousness. With a heartstopping shift, he felt his consciousness *expanding* . . . not in size or space, but in dimension. He felt his mind unfolding like a vast, convoluted paper fan, his memories separating and opening . . .

The presence moved in silence through his thoughts, exploring memories that were sorting themselves out into the open. It was an oddly familiar sensation. It reminded him of the probing that he had once endured from the translator, but this felt more methodical, in a certain way gentler, yet if anything more powerful than the translator's probe. He felt a useless impulse to guard his memories. He no longer had Charlie here protecting him, or trying to justify what was happening.

/// Charlie . . . ///

sighed a faint voice, and then something folded again, and the memory shifted away. How he wished that voice were more than a memory! If only Charlie hadn't died! The first time it had happened, the quarx had come back to life within hours. But now . . . all Bandicut seemed to have were the memories.

This thing felt quite different from the quarx. Stranger. Potentially more threatening.

/Who . . . are . . . you . . . ?/ His whisper of thought emerged in slow motion.

He sensed a glimmer of awareness in reply.

***. . . *wish to perceive and understand* . . . ***

He blinked, inwardly. Then he heard another whisper, in a voice like Charlie's.

/// You must listen . . . ///

He drew a sharp breath. Had he imagined those words? /Charlie?/ he called out.

Instead of Charlie, though, he felt that other presence deepen its touch, scalpel sharp. This time it didn't stop at brushing open the folds of his memories; it began taking them apart, illuminating them with its own darkly flickering inner light, as he remembered . . .

>>>

. . . silence-fugue, as if it had happened just moments ago—the madness that had driven him across the silent emptiness of the Triton landscape, under Neptune's frown, veering his survey rover off the assigned course. The madness that was soon to take him into the presence of the mysterious translator.

>>>

. . . the shocking appearance of the quarx in his mind, placed there by the translator—and the revelation that he had been chosen to sacrifice everything to save the Earth from an invisible danger. Which was harder to accept—the uninvited presence of the alien, or the mission being thrust upon him? Or the quarx's own uncertainty about what, exactly, the mission *was?*

>>>

. . . the absurd figure of a talking holographic dinosaur, explaining why they were to steal a spaceship, and then cross the solar system in an impossible race to collide headlong with a comet.

>>>

. . . the quick, attractive movements of Julie Stone as she played EineySteiney, knocking planets into the gravity wells of the 3D pool table.

>>>

. . . the warm, whispering movements of Julie as she made love to him; the shudders of pleasure that he would never know again, because he was going to steal a spaceship and fly to his certain death.

>>>

. . . or *almost* certain death, because when he actually careened into the comet, releasing more energy than a million hydrogen bombs, he was somehow *translated* across space and perhaps time as well, to a place thousands of light-years from home, on the outside of his own galaxy. And not just marooned, but *alone,* because the quarx had died, instead of him.

>>>

. . . and only a little later, approaching a vast structure floating somewhere above the disk of the Milky Way, until the structure silently drew him and his ship into itself . . .

>>>

Why?
    Why?

>>>

And a whispering voice answered:
    *** . . . *because you are needed* . . . ***

>>>

And before he could assimilate that, the memories abruptly shifted and whirled to earlier times, and in a dizzying rush, he saw his childhood replayed, in glimpses too fast to focus upon . . . the loneliness and struggle . . . the family he loved, but always at a strained distance . . . his discovery that his family had been taken from him in a terrible accident . . . his niece Dakota, the only remaining relative he cared for . . .

>>>

Why?

—he murmured, struggling to put meaning to all this.

>>>

And he thought he heard two voices trying to be heard. And then one whispered:

✳✳✳ . . . *because you are needed . . .*
    that is all . . . ✳✳✳

>>>

And he wasn't a bit sure that it had answered the same question he had meant to ask.

>>>

The images changed abruptly, and it was no longer anything familiar, but memories of places he had never seen. Alien landscapes. Alien suns. Alien creatures. Tall. Stooping. Billowing. Floating in gaseous seas. Creeping in frozen wastes. Floating in the dark of space. Faster, flickering, the visions came too fast to comprehend . . .

>>>

And then *everything* changed—and he began spinning, twisting in space and time, turning inside out—and not just twisting, but changing—not his soul or his being, but something in his body being altered profoundly—

>>>

Then light and dark collided, and splinters of light shot through darkness, and he was aware of a dazzlingly bright fire in the middle of it all, and he sensed without understanding that he could not possibly approach that fire without dying . . .

>>>

But then he tumbled—not just toward it, but *through* it . . .

2

SNOW AND ICE

 HE FLAILED, TRYING to gain control. He staggered, and realized that he was neither floating nor falling, but standing—on a hillside. It was cold, and a bright sun blazed in his eyes. The room and the pool of light were gone, and his ears were ringing with the sound of fading voices. In their places, he heard a whistling wind, and a low, continuous thunder. He gasped, trying to focus.

Through a blur, he thought he saw a landscape covered with snow. And ice. *Snow and ice?* That explained why he felt a brisk chill through his thin jumpsuit.

His thoughts were interrupted by an urgent tapping. Metallic. He looked down. He was on some sort of path, with Copernicus parked beside him. At his glance, Copernicus stopped tapping. Napoleon was on his other flank. He felt an abrupt sense of relief. "Record everything," he whispered. *"Everything."* He raised his eyes, shading them against the glare. "Where the mokin' foke are we?" They were on the side of an icy hill, under what appeared to be a bright sun, peering out over a slope covered with snow-capped trees. Forest stretched as far as he could see.

Mokin' foke . . .

His head was still ringing, and for an instant, he thought he heard that voice again, like a haunting echo. /Charlie? Is that you?/ He heard nothing except the wind, and the low thunder.

What was this? A bizarre hallucination? He had passed

through some sort of transformational process . . . and it was possible that all of this had been implanted in his mind. But he didn't think so. He felt the weight of gravity under him, he was definitely cold, and his head was starting to clear. He rubbed his arms and hugged himself.

No, he was pretty sure that he was really standing on a snow-and-ice covered hillside. He squinted, but couldn't see the sun too clearly. The sky was a pale, featureless blue-grey. Every sense told him that he was standing on the surface of a planet. "But that," he murmured, "is ridiculous."

He was answered by Copernicus's metallic tapping. The two robots looked like a pair of metal dogs at his side. Copernicus's sensor-array was rotating; Napoleon was beeping softly to itself, shifting its head, as though to gain understanding. "What are you two seeing?"

The robots spoke at once: "Ranging exceeds design parameters—" "Loss of continuity—" "—cannot reconcile conflicting input—"

"One at a time! Nappy?"

Copernicus clicked and became still. Napoleon bobbed. "John Bandicut. I experienced a loss of continuity, with conflicting data. I observed a bright influx of visible light, then a period of . . . numerous error interrupts, lasting approximately nine minutes. The time measurement is uncertain."

Bandicut rubbed his arms again, rapidly. "Do you have any idea what happened?" He could see his breath against the wintry landscape. He opened his bag on Copernicus's back and rummaged for a lightweight jacket, the closest thing he had to exposure garb.

"Uncertain," said Napoleon. "I also noted a fluctuation in gravitational readings. Those data may be corrupted. Negative correlation with norms in the Triton database."

Bandicut shrugged into his jacket. "Nappy, we're not on Triton anymore."

"Acknowledged, John Bandicut." The robot's sensor eyes looked almost thoughtful for a moment. "But that is the only database at my disposal."

"You might want to start compiling a new one." Bandicut gazed upslope. Not far above them, overlooking the path, was a smooth stone wall, slick with ice.

"I also detected certain changes in my internal systems," Napoleon continued. "However, I am unable to characterize those changes. My internal perceptions were themselves undergoing alteration."

Bandicut glanced back. "You too, Coppy?"

Copernicus drumtapped acknowledgment. "Yes, Cap'n. Cannot elaborate. However, I am now registering a significantly altered environment. I cannot account for its appearance."

"That much we can agree upon. What else about the *transition?*"

Copernicus ticked softly. "I show a chronology lapse and . . . damaged analysis. Was there a change in programming?"

Bandicut blinked out over the snow-covered trees. "Yeah, I guess you could say that. I wonder how the hell *far* we were transported from—" his voice caught suddenly "—our ship." Their last piece of Earth. The closest thing they had to a home.

Napoleon stretched to its full height of about a meter. "I can provide no information. Inertial alignment was lost during the transition."

Bandicut nodded and squinted at the sky. It looked odd to him, in a way he couldn't put his finger on. "Well, whatever the hell happened, I have a feeling we're *still* not on a planet." He wondered if he had been transported into something like the Earth-orbiting L5 City, a habitat complete with inner landscaping and active ecologies. But if that were so, this bit of wilderness made L5 look like a backyard garden.

He hoisted his backpack over his shoulders. "Let's see what's along this path. Maybe we can get a better view from up here." He trudged up the path, stepping carefully with his sneakers on the crusted snow. There were no tracks visible; nonetheless, it did look like a *path*. The view above the ice-glazed wall was blocked by trees. However, just below the wall the path appeared to level off on an open ledge.

He glanced back. Napoleon was following; but Copernicus's wheel base was a little large for the path and it was still trying to get itself turned around, with short back and forth movements. "Coppy!" he shouted. "Why don't you just stay there a minute! We'll be right back." He resumed hiking, with Napoleon close behind. "Can you make anything out up there?" he asked, indicating the wall.

"Rock and ice with uncertain spectrographic signatures," Napoleon rasped.

"Mm." No reason to be surprised by that.

The path petered out, but the ledge afforded a clearer view below. "Take a look here, Nappy." There seemed to be a river. He couldn't see much of it, but here and there through the forest cover, he glimpsed water. Maybe that was what the thundering noise was: rapids in the river. He felt better, having even that bit of knowledge about his surroundings.

"What do you make of these plants?" He puffed through his hands as he bent to examine the underbrush and trees. He resisted an impulse to touch the dark, shiny green leaves of the underbrush. Thoughts of poison ivy, and worse, went through his mind. The plants were totally unfamiliar, which helped dispel any notion that this whole scene had somehow been created out of his own memories and imagination.

The location is real.

He started. /You still here? Can you give me some useful information?/ The thought came out with an edge of annoyance; he'd gotten pretty tired of the stones' terse manner.

We can only provide such information as we have.

Bandicut grunted. He continued his inspection of the nearby trees. The branch structure was similar to Earth-trees, except that the branches stuck out horizontally, then curved upward like scimitars. The leaves were pointy-clawed, like the outstretched hands of an old crone—purplish on top, and on the underside, like coarse black cloth. "Nappy, what do you get on these leaves?"

The robot waved flickering sensors. "These objects? I detect metallic traces, but less than required to meet current mining criteria."

"Uh-huh. What else? Coppy! What are you doing here? I thought I told you to wait."

The wheeled robot ground to a stop on the ice. "I thought you might need me, Cap'n."

Bandicut squinted at Copernicus. Since when had this machine become such an independent thinker? Between Charlie's reprogramming efforts and whatever they'd just been through, he wondered how much these robots of his had changed. "I see. Well, do you have any data on plant life?"

Copernicus made a buzzing sound like a stalled motor. "Don't think so, Cap'n."

"Nappy?"

"Negative, John Bandicut. Please define *plant life*."

"You're looking at it. That's a tree. It's a form of plant life. So is this underbrush. And—" he pointed "—the foliage growing on this wall."

"Unfamiliar with those forms, Cap'n," said Copernicus.

Nappy turned its head one way, then another, like a large bird taking in its surroundings. Bandicut frowned, wondering whether his robots were going to be any help at all here. Or were they too far out of their league? He shook his head, shivering at the thought of having only himself to depend on. "Well, never mind. Let's head down toward that river. If nothing else, we might be able to find drinkable water. And maybe then—" His voice trailed off. He had no idea where he wanted to go from here. The realization had just hit him all over again that he was now stranded in an alien world, separated even from his spacecraft. He had better find food, water, and shelter. Soon.

Agreed.

/Thanks,/ he thought sarcastically. And then maybe he could start worrying about who had brought him here, and why.

His hands and feet were growing numb as he headed down the slope, but at least by moving around he was generating some heat. The path switched back and forth, giving him the occasional fresh glimpse of the band of water below. Across the river, the land rose again, completing a gentle canyon of rock and forest. Everything seemed capped with snow and ice. Across the river, the slopes were backed up against more hills. And the horizon . . . as he looked at it now, it seemed more bandlike than he had realized before. A wall? He felt more certain than ever that this was an astonishingly sophisticated, closed habitat, not a planetary surface. He could not escape a feeling of awe at the power that had created this place. But how eager was he to meet its creators in person?

He peered again at the sun. It was too bright to focus on, but he thought it looked a little small. Was it really a sun, or some other kind of light source? He wasn't sure whether it had moved in the sky or not.

Downslope, the path grew uneven, which made it difficult for the robots. They were having trouble with traction on the ice and snow, which was far more slippery than the cryogenic ices they had been built for on Triton. He kept glancing back at them. As a result, he almost didn't see the spot where the path dropped and twisted sharply to the right. He caught himself in midstride. For a frightening instant, he felt his body warring between his one-thirteenth-gee reflexes from Triton, and the one gee that was about to tumble him over. He swayed, arms out, then brought his weight back around onto the path.

With a gasp, he looked up at the robots, Copernicus churning up a small cloud of snow particles with his conical wheels, and Napoleon goosestepping behind. "Slow down, you two! There's a steep drop right—"

Copernicus slewed to a stop, teetering at the edge. How the hell was it going to nose down over that dip and make the right-angle turn? "Steep drop here, Cap'n," the robot remarked. "Shall I give it a try?"

"Hold on a sec. Napoleon, can you help Coppy around that?" Bandicut remembered, far too clearly, how the robots—because they weren't programmed for higher-gravity gradients—had once knocked loose a set of heavy tanks, back on the spaceship, and nearly killed him.

The legged robot edged up beside its partner and peered

over. Without speaking, it braced its upper arms on Copernicus and swung its lower legs around to back down the drop-off, like a small child negotiating stairs. Backing partway around, it groped for a secure handhold on Copernicus and said, "Proceed slowly. I will apply leverage."

Bandicut tugged nervously at his backpack straps, watching.

Copernicus inched forward, until its front wheels hung out over the drop-off and its belly rasped on the ice. It ground for purchase with its rear wheels, pushing itself out, until the front wheels suddenly dropped, whirring for traction. Napoleon strained to lever the wheeled robot around the bend.

"You got him, Nappy?"

"Attempting—" Napoleon began, just as Copernicus lost traction in its back wheels. All four wheels spun in a cloud of ice particles. It slid sideways. There was no way Napoleon could stop it as it teetered at the corner, then toppled over the edge. "Stop, Copernicus!" Napoleon rasped. It was no use; Copernicus was tumbling, and Napoleon went over with it, down the slope.

"Wait!" Bandicut yelled futilely. He winced as the two machines bounced apart, slamming through snow and foliage, and disappeared through the trees. "Are you all right?" he shouted. There was no answer, just the continuous rumble of the river. "Damn!"

For an instant, he considered following them down the slope. But that would be dumb; better to run on ahead and hope the path switched back again. He hurried, slipping a little on the crusty snow.

The path wound through a dense thicket of shrubs, all brittle with ice crystals, then cut back left, descending sharply into the stand of trees where the robots had vanished. Ahead, almost at his level now, he glimpsed the silver ribbon of water. But he saw no sign of either robot. "Napoleon! Copernicus!" he yelled.

Over the thunder of the river, he heard a *snap*. He squinted, casting his gaze around. *Snap*. He saw nothing moving. But it sounded like branches breaking. "Nappy! Coppy!"

He peered up through the trees, trying to gauge where the two must have fallen. He couldn't be sure. He hurried on.

Not much farther ahead, the trees opened up to reveal the riverbank. He must have missed the robots or their trail, somehow. Perhaps the smartest thing would be to reconnoiter along the bank, then backtrack if he didn't find them. He continued out of the trees, where the path snaked along a narrow strip beside the water. He paused to catch his breath.

It was a stunningly beautiful panorama. The river was about twenty meters wide—shallow, fast moving, glistening over icy boulders. The water was clear, and he could see numerous, large flat rocks both above and below the surface. To his right, the river swept into sight from around a large elbow of land on his side. To his left, the water rushed over the boulder-strewn bed and crooked away around a massive outcropping on the far shore. The thundering was coming from that direction.

Bandicut tucked his hands under his armpits, shivering. It was beautiful, yes—but just now he was starting to think more about freezing to death.

We can help.

He blinked. /What's that?/

He felt a sudden twinge of heat in both wrists, and a flush of warmth in his torso. /Thanks,/ he thought with a shiver of relief. /Why'd you wait so long?/

Our reserves are limited.

He grunted, gazing down into the river. He wondered if it would kill him to drink the water. He wondered if there was some way to test it, other than the hard way.

Crack-k-k-k!

He turned back toward the woods. That had sounded more like breaking ice than branches. "Hello!" he shouted. "Coppy? Nappy?"

A moment later, he heard a crash and a whir of motors. Copernicus tumbled out of the trees, a short distance downriver from where Bandicut stood. It landed on its wheels, then spun for traction as it slid over sloping ice toward the water. Its motors whined, reversing futilely. "Oh, moke—" Bandicut breathed. At that instant, Napoleon crashed out of the trees, as well, curled up in a protective ball. It bounced across the ice after Copernicus, kicking up puffs of ice-dust. Bandicut watched in horror as the robots careened toward the water.

Whirrrrrr! Copernicus's wheels picked up some traction, but it was moving too fast, and it tumbled over the bank and crashed into the water. Napoleon slammed into the rocky bank, bounced over Copernicus, and hit the water with an even bigger splash. Bandicut cursed and ran to the edge of the bank. He had no idea if the robots were waterproof, and half expected them to short out before his eyes.

He dropped his backpack, then hesitated. What the hell did he think he was going to do? He could freeze if he went into that water—and for all he knew it could be full of poisons, or God knew what else. For that matter, he didn't even know for sure that it was water, and not some other clear liquid. He blinked, waiting to see if the robots could get out by themselves. Copernicus had landed on its back, half submerged, its wheels spinning just above the surface. Napoleon had uncurled and was struggling futilely to get to its feet. *Look at them,* he thought—*they're dinosaurs in this goddamn place. There's no way to recharge them, and they're going to run down in a couple of days anyway, and that will be that. Don't be an idiot. Leave them.*

He swallowed.

Don't be a jerk, he thought. *They're your* friends.

"Hang on, you two!" he yelled. And he took a deep breath and strode into the swirling, icy waters.

3

ICESTORM

THE WATER HIT him with a frigid shock. He gasped, struggling to stay upright on the treacherous bottom.

He reached Copernicus first. All four wheels were spinning uselessly, reversing direction at random. Bandicut shuddered and leaned into the freezing water to see if he could turn the robot over; but it was impossible to get a handhold anywhere, except maybe on the wheels. *"Coppy—stop spinning!"* he gasped.

There was no way the robot could hear him. He straightened, trembling from the cold, and moved around to see if he could help Napoleon. The other robot had managed to sit up, and was trying to stand. Its metal feet found some purchase on a submerged rock. But as it rose, it flailed suddenly, lost its balance, and toppled back into the water.

"Napoleon! Are you all right?"

Its next attempt was more successful. Whirring and splashing, it rose to a crouch and turned toward Bandicut's voice. Its sensor-eyes blinked; it seemed to be having some trouble finding him. Its mechanical hands stretched out, as though groping blindly.

Bandicut shuffled closer. "Right here!"

Napoleon made a sputtering sound, venting water. "Re-setting—" it croaked. "One moment—" Its sensors flickered, then brightened and seemed to focus on Bandicut. "John—Bandicut—we must remove ourselves—"

"Help me with Copernicus!" Bandicut shouted.

Napoleon shifted its eyes, as though seeing Copernicus in the water for the first time. It seemed about to say something, then abruptly raised a metal hand and pointed toward the shore. "John Bandicut! Hazard alert! Hazard alert! Objects approaching!"

"What—?" Bandicut twisted to look, nearly losing his footing. He blinked in disbelief.

The riverbank had come alive.

The ice and snow were fragmenting into chunks as if broken by a silent earthquake. The pieces were vibrating and dancing into the air like drops of water on a hot griddle. Above the path, the slope was erupting almost volcanically, with chunks of snow and ice bouncing up and down out of the trees. Some pieces were not just airborne, but buzzing straight toward Bandicut and the robots.

Bandicut threw up a protective arm, just as the first pieces of ice hit him. A few fragments glanced off his arm and shoulder, and one off the side of his head. He reeled in pain. *"Jeez—!"* he grunted and crouched in the freezing water, trying to shield himself.

"John Bandicut! You are in danger!" cried Napoleon.

A new fusillade of ice hit him. The robot was being pummeled, as well. It rocked, ice ringing off its metal skin, and toppled back into the water with a crash. Mokin' A. What had they done—triggered an environmental defense mechanism? /Stones!/ he cried silently. /If you know what's happening, help me!/

The black stone in his left wrist burned with momentary heat, and he became aware of a shimmer of light around him. The next pieces of ice hit with less energy. It seemed to be a protective field; it didn't stop the chunks, but slowed them. In the air above the shore, more pieces of ice were buzzing like an angry swarm of bees.

We are limited, without more energy.

/Uh—/ Bandicut saw Napoleon struggling to get up again. The water around them was erupting with splashes, like old movies of a naval battle.

"Hraaaiieeeeeee!"

Hearing a loud whistle, and a strangled-sounding cry, Bandicut looked back toward the shore. A tall, lanky humanoid creature was striding along the riverbank—shouting indecipherably and whirling some kind of rope through the air. Was Bandicut about to meet an enemy?

A ululating groan came from higher on the slope. The ground was beginning to look like a nightmarish strip mine. The snow cover was half gone, revealing wounded, trembling earth. *"Hraaahh!"* cried the humanoid. It appeared to be running toward Bandicut.

As it approached, the angry ice-swarm actually settled a little. Bandicut stared at the humanoid. It ceased twirling its length of rope and stood on the riverbank, peering out at him. Had it *stopped* the attack?

"Hel-l-l-lo!" Bandicut called, shivering. The being cocked its head. How could he make himself understood? He had to get out of here before the exposure killed him. The glow around him was slowly fading, as the stones conserved energy. His feet were numb.

The being swayed from side to side, as though trying to determine what Bandicut was doing out there in the river. Bandicut gestured helplessly to his robots, trembling with urgency. He would have to abandon them soon, if he couldn't get them out of the water.

Napoleon whistled and shrieked and jerked erect, spraying Bandicut with freezing water. "John Bandicut! John Bandicut! I am still at your side. Why have you sent Copernicus under the water?"

"I d-didn't! Help me get him upright!"

Napoleon stumbled toward its fellow robot. "L-lift that end and tr-try to turn him toward shore!" Napoleon obeyed, bending to avoid the slowly spinning wheels, and found a grip on the end of Copernicus's body. "Now!" Bandicut yelled. "T-turn him!"

Whirring and grunting, they both strained, and Copernicus slowly rolled. It also began to slide, not toward shore, but toward Bandicut—and deeper water. *"Toward you!"* Bandicut yelled. But Napoleon too was losing traction, and Bandicut could feel himself slipping under Copernicus now, unable to stop the slide. His foot had somehow gotten caught under the robot, and he couldn't get out of the way, even to let go. He was now up to his waist in the frigid water—and going down—and as water rushed over his chest, he was stunned to realize that he was in real danger of drowning under the robot. "Nappy—" he choked, taking a mouthful of water. "Pull—him—back—"

There was a splash alongside him. Coughing through the spray, Bandicut saw the tall creature from the riverbank at his side. "Unh—" he struggled to say, but then he slipped backwards. Water lapped over his face.

He was aware of the alien creature reaching under Copernicus. An instant later, he felt the weight lift from his leg and body, and he struggled to scramble out from under the robot. He staggered, choking, to his feet.

He shuddered and pushed weakly against Copernicus, and realized that the alien was already helping Napoleon to roll Copernicus. "That-t-t's it-t-t!" he gasped, as Copernicus crashed into the water rightside up, a meter closer to the river-bank. His teeth chattered as he looked up at his rescuer. The tall being peered back at him from a blue-white face, then gestured toward shore.

"Th-thanks—" Bandicut wheezed, and pushed on Copernicus's nose to steer it back toward the bank. It seemed to be having trouble orienting itself. "Get *g-going!*" Bandicut yelled, hitting it weakly on the back.

Copernicus finally got traction under its wheels, and lumbered over the submerged rocks and up over the short incline onto the riverbank. Napoleon and Bandicut staggered along-side, following their alien rescuer out of the water. Bandicut's legs were completely numb, and he was unable to walk in a straight line. He felt a bony hand on his arm, and gasped in gratitude as the alien helped him up the last few steps onto the bank. He sank to his knees.

"Hrahh! Awauk!" cried the alien, and Bandicut blinked

up at him. "Awauk!" The voice of the being was rough and strong, and unmistakably urgent.

"Wh-what?" he panted.

"Urrr—awauk!" The being gestured toward the slope, where the chunks of ice had risen to assault them. Bandicut squinted and realized that the snow and ice were still vibrating up and down. He looked back at the being. It was gesturing urgently downriver.

Bandicut's breath escaped convulsively. "I don't—know —if I can—m-move!" He shuddered, feeling a new rush of warmth driving back some of the numbing chill. The black stone in his left wrist was glowing a dull red.

"Heikka?"

Bandicut saw the creature staring at his wrist and the glowing stone. "Uh—" he grunted, wondering if the stone looked frightening—or maybe desirable. He gazed into his rescuer's sculpted blue face. A glint of light seemed to come from within its smallish, deep-set black eyes. It emitted a low rumble, then pointed with a long, articulated finger to the side of its own head, to a spot roughly equivalent to the human temple.

"Uhh—?"

A gemlike stone was embedded in the creature's temple, and it flickered with a diamond sparkle as the being said, "Heikka . . . y-yarrrr?"

"You—have one—too?" Bandicut gasped.

The being's eyes blazed with an inner light. "Yarrrr . . . *ye-e-e-sss*," it grunted. Its voice seemed sharper, clearer than a moment ago.

Bandicut stumbled to his feet, his right wrist tingling sharply. "Mokin' foke," he whispered. "What'd you just say?"

"Ye-e-e-ss," said the being again, cocking its head the other way. But before Bandicut could reply, it jerked around and pointed urgently back at the slope where the ice and snow were shaking, rising into the air. "Moo-sst rooo-n! *Alei-kaaa!*" It pointed downriver. "Moo-ust . . . roo-un!"

Bandicut coughed at the robots, "Can you guys—run?"

Napoleon rose creakily. "I am . . . functional."

Copernicus jerked violently forward and backward, as though trying to gauge the traction. "With you, Cap'n!"

"Hrrr—*aleika!*"

Bandicut nodded. "Let's go!" He saw a flicker on the other's temple, and the alien strode off down the riverbank.

Bandicut suddenly remembered his backpack. He scrambled back for it, slung it over his shoulder, and hurried after the alien, with the two robots grinding along behind. A moment later, he was pelted from behind with clods of ice and dirt, and he staggered on his stiff legs, trying to move faster. "C'mon, you two!" he shouted to the robots.

A cloud of snow and ice was rushing toward them.

"Hiiieee!" shrieked the alien. *"H-hurrrrry!"*

Bandicut ran, throbbing legs or no.

The alien was trotting along the riverbank with a surefooted gait. It probably could easily have outrun them, but it held to a pace that Bandicut could just barely keep up with.

The river bent to the right, past a stand of trees. With luck, once they got past the bend, they would be out of danger. But the background thunder was growing louder. The alien yelled, "Don't-t . . . stop-p-p!"

He saw why. The riverbank ahead of them was becoming as riled as the slope behind them. The alien veered into the water with a splash.

"Oh, no—wait!" he panted. But the alien appeared to be crossing at a shallow point, trotting through ankle-deep water, with a glance back every few seconds. Bandicut hesitated at the water's edge, but a chunk of ice slammed into his shoulder blades and convinced him to keep moving. "C'mon, you two!" he yelled. *"Don't roll over!"*

The robots trundled after him, and this time kept upright, plowing through the water close behind him. The numbing cold flashed up Bandicut's legs again; it took all of his strength not to collapse back into the water. He staggered, but kept moving.

Where was the alien going?

The thundering grew louder. He hoped they weren't going to wade downstream through whitewater rapids. The view beyond the bend was blocked by a large outcropping with overhanging trees, but the alien was heading that way, apparently in an effort to stay close to the far bank. The creature waved them on, and disappeared around the bend.

As Bandicut hurried around the outcropping, he glanced nervously up at the overhanging trees, praying that nothing would fall down on them. Then he rounded the bend and saw the source of the thundering: a waterfall cascading down a cliff face, into the river. And the alien was striding directly toward it.

"What—" he panted "—are you—?"

It was too far away to hear. Bandicut glanced back at the robots. "Oh, Christ!" Napoleon had gone down, and Copernicus had paused beside it. Napoleon clambered back to its feet, leaning on its more compact companion. "Can you keep going?" Bandicut yelled. He ducked as a fusillade of ice scattered into the water around him.

Napoleon was up, squawking, "Coming, John Bandicut!" Copernicus revved its wheels, shooting back a stream of water as it surged forward. Bandicut turned and kept moving. The alien was standing in the spray at the base of the waterfall.

"Hraaahhh!" it cried, waving its arms. *"Be-hiiind!"*

Bandicut heard a new rumble. He looked over his shoulder and gasped.

The riverbed itself was coming alive. The surface of the water was dancing in agitation, as if coming to a boil. Several large boulders were shaking, almost lifting out of the water. Bandicut gasped in disbelief. Farther upstream, the river itself was rising in a large wave.

"NAPOLEON! COPERNICUS!" he screamed. *"FASTER!"*

The robots rushed in an eruption of spray.

Bandicut charged toward the falls—then stumbled to a halt. The alien was gone. Bandicut blinked, half blinded by spray. "HELLOOOO!" he shouted in a hoarse voice. *"WHERE ARE YOU?"* He looked around frantically. The boulders were dancing forward, and behind them, the wave was engorging itself into a thunderous wall of water. Directly in front of the wave, the barren riverbed was exposed, where the water was being drawn up like an indrawn breath.

"Hii-i-e-e-e!" The alien dashed out of the waterfall, gesturing wildly, then turned and vanished back into it.

Bandicut gaped at the falls, thundering before him, its spray drenching him. *"What are you doing?"* he cried. Was he supposed to run into the wall of water, and the cliff face behind it?

"Run, John Bandicut!" rasped Napoleon, behind him.

The water around him exploded with a shotgun blast of rocks. One caught him in the back of the head, and he staggered, half blinded with pain. The wave was looming, almost upon him.

A hand grabbed him and yanked him straight into the falls. Water crashed over his head, stunning him senseless. He was aware of shouting and mechanical clanking, and a great crash of rock upon rock. He pitched forward, tumbling into silence.

BANDICUT GROANED AND sat up painfully, his head spinning. He must have lost consciousness for a few moments. He was chilled to the bone—but he was no longer under the waterfall, or in water of any sort. Where the hell was he? He blinked his eyes back into focus. There was a sun low on the horizon, and a warmish breeze blowing over his skin, and not a snowflake in sight. He was sitting on some sort of . . . grass. "What the—?"

He heard a crash, and turned to see Napoleon tumbling out of what looked like a shadow in a stone wall. Napoleon toppled over on the soft footing, almost landing on top of Bandicut. A minute later, Copernicus appeared. It rolled a few meters, then shuddered to a halt, tapping like a cooling engine. "Cap'n—we appear to have passed through another transition boundary," it announced.

"Yeah," Bandicut sighed, overcome with joy at seeing the two intact. He was still shivering from the frigid drenching, warm breeze or not, but at least he had hope now of recovery. But what had happened to their rescuer? "Hey!" he yelled. "Hello! Friend!" Shrugging off his backpack, he clambered to his feet, squishing in soggy shoes. A small meadow lay before him, and there was a low cliff wall to his back. "*Halloooooooo!*" he called, cupping his hands.

He thought he heard a distant call, but couldn't quite locate its direction.

"Where is the other?" Copernicus asked haltingly. Its sensor-array looked a little bent.

"I don't know," Bandicut said. "Scan for him, will you? Nappy? You okay?"

The robot stood with a creak. "I seem unharmed by the immersion, John Bandicut." Stretching to its full height, it peered one way and then another, and finally sank back to a crouch with a sound remarkably like a sigh.

Bandicut echoed the sentiment. "I want to thank that guy for saving our hides. But first I guess we'd better look for some shelter. I don't know about you two, but I need to dry out and warm up." He hoisted his wet bag onto Copernicus's back. "That okay, Coppy?"

"Of course, Cap'n."

Of course. Loyal servant, never complained. "How are you two doing, power-wise?" He almost hesitated to ask. Away from the ship, once their batteries ran down . . .

"I read my charge at ninety-four percent, John Bandicut," said Napoleon.

"Eh?" That was much higher than he would have guessed. They had been running hard for some time now. "Coppy?"

"Ah—Cap'n, somewhere between eighty-nine and ninety-two percent. I must run some diagnostics to interpret the uncertainty."

Bandicut blinked in surprise. "Okay, but first let's find our friend—or at least a place to camp." He started walking, waving them to follow. What could give the robots such endurance? he wondered. Had their hardware, as well as their programming, been altered during the "transition" into this place? He supposed there was no point in worrying about it right now.

"Anyone know a song?" he asked.

Neither of the robots answered.

The sky was quickly taking on a twilight cast, as they crossed the small meadow. Beyond it, a stand of trees half-enclosed a rocky knoll. Bandicut moved cautiously, and passed under the trees. They looked a bit more Earthlike than the ones he had seen in the previous place. A couple of them looked like copper beeches, and several others reminded him of pine or fir. "Take note of the trees, the grass, anything you can put in your databases, guys. You never know what information we might need later."

Napoleon, in response, began to zigzag, inspecting the foliage.

Bandicut rubbed his arms, thinking that he would be smart to get a fire going. He glanced around for pieces of deadwood, and found one half-fallen branch hanging off one of the trees. He tugged on it and it came loose in his hand. As a sudden thought crossed his mind, he dropped it and stared at his palm to see if the contact was going to make his skin curl up and die. His hand looked okay, felt okay.

Your body chemistry has been normalized to metaship standard.

/Huh? What's that?/

There was no elaboration. But he wondered: Did that mean he could eat the local food? That would be a great relief.

He heard a snapping sound, and then "Glleeeer—" *rasp* "—com-m-me!" He turned toward the outcropping of rock. Their alien rescuer had emerged from a sheltered alcove in the rock, and was beckoning with a wave.

Bandicut sighed gratefully. A sudden shiver went through him, and he shook like a wet dog. He needed to get out of his wet clothes; with luck, some clothes in his backpack might still be dry. If he was luckier still, they could build a fire and *both* warm up. He suddenly realized that the alien was pointing toward a small, flickering pile of wood—a fire, already burning.

Bandicut waved to the robots to follow, picked up the dry branch—his contribution—and walked to join the alien. He paused at the entrance to the sheltered area, and the alien gestured toward the fire. "Come."

Yes . . . this is right, whispered a small voice in Bandicut's head, a familiar voice.

He started.

The alien cocked its head.

Bandicut swallowed, thinking, dear God this is no time to start in with the haunting memories—or, worse yet, silence-fugue. The alien stepped aside to let him kneel by the fire. It was small—the flames licking out of what was little more than a pile of twigs—but he sighed over and over in gratitude as he reached out to it, wishing he could drink its warmth through his hands and wrists.

"Hrrr—" *rasp* "—c-c-cold?" said the alien, crouching on the other side of the fire. The stone in the alien's right temple glimmered as it spoke.

Bandicut stared at the tingling stone in his own wrist. He sensed that it was working hard to translate the sense of the being's various words; except for the rasp of uncertainty, the sounds of the translation were indistinguishable from the alien's own voice. He looked up earnestly into the alien's sculpted, blue face, and felt the sudden full impact of what was happening. An *alien*. His life had just been saved by a flesh-and-blood being from another world. His mind reeled at the thought. "Yes," he whispered, answering the question at last. "Very cold."

The two robots lumbered alongside and parked themselves. Bandicut got up with a grunt and lifted his sodden backpack off Copernicus. "My, uh, supplies," he explained.

The alien, whose face was shadowed now in the dimming twilight, angled its head for a better look. Bandicut opened the bag and tilted it so that his host could see into it—or least feel that the gesture had been made. He reached in, groping for dry clothes, and pulled out a jumpsuit and some underwear. They were damp in spots, but a lot drier than what he was wearing now. The air was cooling quickly as the daylight faded, lending urgency to his actions.

He shook out the clothes and held them up for the alien to see. He tugged at the wet fabric clinging to his body. *"Dry clothes,"* he said, as distinctly as he could, through the quaver in his voice. "I'm going to change."

The alien remained silent, perhaps waiting for him to demonstrate.

He hesitated, feeling a sense of absurdity. Here he was, in a historic encounter with an alien species, and the first thing he was going to do was undress. It couldn't be helped, of course—and there was a certain logic to it, beyond the necessity. He might as well let the creature see what he looked like, and perhaps reassure it that he wore no weapons. He took a breath and quickly unzipped his soaked jacket and jumpsuit, stripping naked. He grabbed his spare clothes—then hesitated a moment, though he was trembling and covered with goosebumps.

The alien studied him with interest, and spoke again in that tongue-rolling tone. "Cl-l-l-ooooothes?"

"Yes." Bandicut starting dressing, hurriedly, then hunkered back down by the fire. It was faltering a bit, and he puffed gently on it. He picked up his dry branch, cracked it over his knee, and propped the pieces over the tiny, flickering flames.

The alien responded by picking up something from the grass on its side—another piece of deadwood. Snapping it in two, the alien placed the pieces of wood carefully beside the fire—not on it, but beside it. Saving it for later.

Bandicut nodded, rubbing his hands together. The alien, too, crouched close to the small flames, extending its own hands. They were larger than Bandicut's hands, with three long, articulated fingers—bony, but powerful looking—and two opposing thumbs per hand, giving them the look of strong mechanical grippers.

"Warrrmmm."

"Warm," Bandicut repeated. He looked up into the alien's eyes and realized suddenly that he was not the only one who had gotten soaked in the frigid waters. Was the alien suffering from the cold, too? It was wearing a smooth body covering that looked like leather, and was probably as wet as Bandicut's clothes. Maybe that was why it had vanished after pulling Bandicut to safety—to hurry and get a fire going.

Bandicut tried to read its expression, but couldn't. The being's face was angular, and rather high and narrow. It had a horny-looking mouth that protruded slightly and appeared to have a fixed curve to it. There was no visible nose, but its eyes were close enough to being humanlike, though smallish and deep-set in bone-ridged sockets. Its gaze was intense; there was a diamondlike sparkle deep in its eyes that seemed to be more than just reflection. Its head was hairless, and sculpted with smooth indentations and bulges.

"Are you cold, too?" Bandicut asked. The stones pulsed in his wrists as he posed the question.

"C-cold. Ik-k-k c-cold," the alien agreed. After a moment, it cast a sidelong glance at the robots.

"They won't bother you," Bandicut said hastily. "I—" He hesitated. "My name is—*Bandicut.*" He pointed his hands back in at himself. "John Bandicut."

The alien sat back a little, eyes flickering. It seemed to consider this for a moment. "Ik," it said finally, pointing a finger at its forehead.

"Your *name* is Ik?"

"*Ik!*" the alien repeated, with a sharp emphasis, as though to clarify the pronunciation.

"Ik," Bandicut repeated.

The alien grunted, perhaps in satisfaction. It—or *he,* Bandicut decided, based on nothing more than intuition—made a small sweeping gesture toward Bandicut. "J-John . . . B-Band—"

"Bandicut. John Bandicut."

Ik raised his head slightly, then lowered it. "John Bandicut."

/// John Bandicut.
Do I . . . know you? ///

There was a whispering movement in his thoughts, like a breeze fluttering around loose papers in an old attic. Bandicut felt a sudden upwelling of sadness, mingled with hope. /Charlie?/ But there was no further sound. He wanted to believe it was Charlie's voice he had just heard, but there had been too many echoes of memory haunting him lately. Charlie had returned to life once before, after dying—but much more quickly. Best not to hope, or believe. He felt tears welling in his eyes. At that moment, a waft of smoke from the fire caught him in the face, and he coughed violently.

Ik sat back in a crouch, hands raised a little, in what looked like a defensive posture. He was undoubtedly uncertain about Bandicut; it would only be natural. What could Bandicut say to explain himself? The alien's eyes flickered with a glint of blue.

"Ik," Bandicut whispered, thinking, *I know I should be excited, but I'm cold. Tired. Confused.* The warmth from the fire was ever so slowly seeping into him. "Where are we, Ik? This is all new to me. Do you live here? Do you know this place?"

"No. No." Ik rose suddenly. "Not my—place. Cannot—stay." He took three steps from the fire and surveyed the copse that lay outside their little shelter. Daylight was fading fast. "Must leave—" *rasp* "—at first light."

Bandicut rose, too, his legs protesting with a sharp ache. "Why? Is there danger?"

Napoleon suddenly beeped. "Danger, John Bandicut? Please specify."

Ik stared at the robot for a moment, then returned to hunch close to the fire.

Bandicut sat crosslegged again, feeling more uncertain than ever. "Ik, are we in danger here?"

The alien reached out with his hands until they were almost in the flames. He looked at Bandicut with a sharp gaze. "D-danger? No. But I have . . . need." Ik stared into the fire.

"Then, we can stay here for the night?"

"Yes," Ik said to the fire. "It seems a good place to stay."

Bandicut sighed. "Thank God. And Ik?"

The alien's gaze did not shift.

"Thanks. For saving me—us—back there."

Ik looked up. "Th-thank?"

"For what you did. I appreciate it." Bandicut made a gesture, pointing from his heart toward the other.

The alien's eyes flickered.

Bandicut took that as acknowledgment. "I would really like to know," he said, "just exactly what happened back there. Why were we attacked?"

Ik cocked his head, then made a gesture toward the two robots.

Bandicut blinked, and remembered the way they had tumbled down the slope into the river. Had some defensive mechanism taken *that* as an attack?

"Disturbed—" *rasp* "—frightened—the ice," said Ik.

"Uh?" Bandicut's right wrist tingled as the translator-stone struggled with the words. "Frightened the *ice*?"

"Hraaahh," said the alien, looking sideways again at the robots. "Yes. In a manner of speaking."

"You're saying the ice back there was *alive*?" Bandicut swallowed, remembering the tidal wave that had nearly swept him under. "And the riverbed, too?"

The alien rubbed his chest, peering at Bandicut. "Rii-ight." He leaned closer to the fire, which was snapping and darting taller. In its flickering light, his face looked eerily like a wind-carved stone formation.

Bandicut frowned, wondering if they were communicating accurately. The stone in his wrist seemed to be tingling still, inconclusively.

Ik stirred, as though disturbed by something. "The ice, the—" *rasp* "—life-water, the—"

Bandicut's wrist buzzed; the stone flickered and flared.

"—river—heart—slope." The alien scratched at the grass with a long finger. "One." He looked up again. "Do you under-s-stand?"

Bandicut stared. "They're *all* alive?" he whispered.

"It!" said Ik. "*It.*"

"All of it? One being? Alive?"

"Yah!" Ik clacked his hard mouth shut. He sat back. After a few moments, he drew a hand, uncomfortably it seemed, over his clothing.

Ik probably had nothing dry to change into, Bandicut thought. He poked nervously at his own wet clothes, spread out on the ground, and thought of a riverbed, river, bank, and icy slope all being one enormous organism. The idea frightened him, not so much in principle—even though he couldn't understand how such a thing could be—as because he had just witnessed the temperament of one such being. "Hostile," he murmured, more to himself than to Ik.

"Urrrm?" Ik closed his eyes, and opened them again. "Perhaps so. Perhaps not. There have been—problems, in this portion of the—" *rasp rasp* "—world."

Bandicut sensed that there was something incomplete about that translation. "What do you mean—problems?"

"Hrrrr." Ik seemed to have trouble choosing words. "Unusual events. Problems. Lands, beings not—behaving as they should."

Bandicut stared at him. "I don't understand."

Ik rubbed his chest for a moment. "I do not, exactly, either. But we were fortunate that the . . . ice . . . gave way before my—" *rasp rasp* "—rahhh." The translator seemed befuddled by his choice of words, but Ik lifted his coiled rope—or what looked like a rope—high enough to see.

Bandicut remembered how the ice-attack had faltered briefly when the alien had twirled his rope in the air. "You mean, it was *frightened* of your rope?"

"*Rope,*" Ik echoed with a slight shift of his head. "Not—frightened, exactly, but—" He murmured something in a low growl, which once more the stones could not translate. Then he spoke again. "It seems there is a kind of—" *rasp* "—contamination, affecting everything." Ik snapped his mouth shut and bowed his head, apparently disinclined to speak further of it.

Bandicut's thoughts spun in useless circles, as he reflected silently on how far he had come, in such a short time—to him, anyway—and how little he knew of where he was to go from here. His encounter with Ik was the first promising thing that had happened to him here. Perhaps Ik could help him understand this new world a little.

Ik placed another piece of deadwood on the fire, muttering something that Bandicut didn't quite catch. Then he settled back into a pose that looked like a lotus position, gazing somberly into the flames. Bandicut was reluctant to disturb him, but finally the need to understand overcame his reluctance.

"Ik?"

The alien raised his eyes.

"Do you—is this where—you live? Where you come from?" Bandicut made a gesture with his arm toward the open meadow. "Is this your . . . home? This world?" As he said *world,* he realized he meant not so much this local environment as the great structure that had swallowed him and his ship, and presumably still contained them.

The alien made a clicking sound. "No," he said. Then a moment later, he turned the question around. "Is this—" and he made a similar gesture "—*your* home?"

Bandicut shook his head and laughed bitterly. "Hardly. No, I come from a *long* way away."

"Indeed," said Ik. "L-long way away." He clacked his mouth shut. Then he looked up, reached up with his arm, and made a sweeping arc across the sky. Bandicut followed his gesture, and drew a startled breath. He suddenly realized, for the first time, that he was sitting beneath a sky full of stars. *Stars!* And he wondered, with heartstopping astonishment, if Ik meant that *he* was from the stars, too.

Ik did not elaborate, however. "Now," he said, "must rest." He uttered a sound like a sigh and stared, motionless, into the fire.

Bandicut blinked at Ik, then back up at the stars. There was nothing recognizable in the stars' pattern. The ache of loneliness returned. But he realized one other thing: there was no sign of the sprawling, swirling view of the galaxy that he had seen before entering this world. How could that be?

He shook his head, and finally stretched out on the ground, trying to find a restful position while still huddling close to the fire. When he peered across the flames at Ik, he saw that the alien's eyes were closed, giving his face a look of stone. "Good night, Ik," he murmured. "And thanks again."

There was no answer from the alien.

Bandicut rolled onto his back, crossing his arms over his chest. He gazed up into the sky, if that was what it was, and fell into a reverie, reflecting back on his entry into this world. He finally fell asleep just as he was recalling, in puzzlement, the words that had been spoken to him by the translator-stones: "*. . . because you are needed.*"

5

QUESTIONS AND QUARX

FRACTAL IMAGES ERUPTED and coalesced in his dreams: infinitely unfolding flower petals, spreading through a landscape of tortured helixes. Those faded, but in their place appeared chaotic attractors: spun-silk traceries of overlapping dragonfly wings, and tenuous clouds of colored vapors contracting into spinning balls of fire representing unknown mysteries of memory and being . . .

And voices whispering,

/// John Bandicut.

Is it you, John Bandicut? ///

Bandicut rolled toward the fire, huddling for warmth. But there didn't seem to be any warmth any longer—just disturbing, disjointed dreams . . . dreams of chaos captured in a spoon and stirred into the world like cream into coffee . . . dreams of a quarx.

/// Quarx.

Is that what I was called? ///

whispered a voice within the dream.

Bandicut shuddered, could not get warm. The fractals splintered like shards of glass, the attractors bifurcated into great elongated loops of glowing gas . . .

/// Please—what is our situation? ///

Bandicut sat up in the dark. "Charlie!" he cried. He looked around in confusion. "Charlie? Was that you, for

God's sake?'' He was shivering. More than shivering: crying. He had been dreaming vividly, intensely, remembering the quarx, who had died. "Charlie, you bastard," he hissed into the night. "Don't haunt me like this! Come back if you're going to come back!" He hugged himself, in a vain attempt to get warm. /Please come back,/he pleaded silently.

For a moment, he listened to a soft clicking somewhere off in the distance, which startled him by its resemblance to the sound of crickets. Then he felt a rustling in his thoughts, and heard:

/// I'm just . . . trying to understand . . . ///

He squeezed his eyes shut, and for a moment saw exploding rosette patterns. "Is it really you?" he whispered. "Because I can't take much more of this. I really can't."

/// I am . . . quarx. ///

Bandicut pressed his face into his hands, shuddering with pain, with joy.

"John Bandicut, are you in distress?" queried a metal voice out of the darkness.

"What?" he croaked. *"Who is that?* Oh—Nappy!" And with a terrible start, he remembered where he was, and who he was with. "No—I'm fine," he choked, and rubbed his eyes, peering around the campsite. The fire had smoldered down; only a thin wisp of smoke curled up from it, and it was giving off no heat to speak of. There was just enough starlight to make out the shapes of rocks, and the two robots nearby. And, silhouetted against the starry sky, the statuesque form of Ik, seated crosslegged.

Ik's eyes gleamed like starlight, staring at him.

Bandicut let out a long breath. He had undoubtedly awakened Ik, who could only have seen him talking to invisible beings in the night. He cleared his throat. "Ik, I—sorry. I didn't mean to wake you."

"Urrrr," said Ik, motionless.

"I was talking to . . . someone, uh . . ."

"Hreeeeuhh?" *Rasp.*

Bandicut swallowed. "There's a, uh, *quarx*—an alien, uh,

being—" he hesitated and pointed to his right temple "—in here. It just came back to life. I think."

Ik's eyes flared.

"It's not—I mean, it's a *friend.*" Bandicut knew he wasn't making much sense.

"You s-speak to—"

"Quarx," said Bandicut. "A being that is . . . invisible . . . in my—" he tapped his head again "—mind. A friend."

Ik shifted position, and rubbed his chest.

/// You called me "friend." ///

Bandicut closed his eyes with a sigh. /Yes, you idiot, you stupid moking goak. What did you think? Of course you're my friend!/ Tears were welling up in his eyes again, tears of joy.

/// And . . . "Charlie."
Is that what you called me? ///

Bandicut squeezed his eyes shut against the tears. /Yes./ He tried not to tremble. /That's right. Charlie./ At least, the first two incarnations of the quarx had been named Charlie. But each time it came back to life, it seemed to have a different set of memories.

The answering voice seemed thoughtful.

/// Who is this other person you're talking to? ///
/Him? Ik./

/// And what is . . . Ik? ///

Bandicut blinked his eyes open, to find the alien gazing at him under the stars. /I don't know, actually./

/// ??? ///

/We just met. Charlie, how much do you remember?/

Ik's alien eyes were glowing steadily, as he tilted his head, perhaps in an attempt to decipher Bandicut's strained expression. "This quarx—" he began.

/// There was . . .
a close encounter with death,
was there not? ///

/Oh yes. Indeed. Which one are you remembering?/

"Does it speak through your—?" *Rasp.*

/// I remember being cold,
and wet. ///

Bandicut blinked at Ik, aware that Ik was trying to ask something. /That just happened. Ik saved my life./

Ik pointed to his own temples, then toward Bandicut's wrists. The translator-stones.

Bandicut shook his head. "No. Not exactly." He rubbed the tiny bump of the gemlike mechanism embedded in his right wrist. "But I do *hear* him, in the same way I hear the stones. He lives in my—" Bandicut waved his hands along-side his head "—thoughts."

Ik clacked his mouth shut with a rumble.

/// Daughter-stones?
Is that what you're talking about? ///
the quarx whispered.

/// From the translator?
I seem to remember a translator.
It was very important, wasn't it? ///

/You could say that,/ Bandicut murmured, and nearly fell over with a sudden rush of memories, released by the quarx. A cascade of memories . . . friends, days at work, home . . . and deep mourning, for all he had lost. But as he struggled to sur-face from the passing wave, he thought—at least he had re-gained his friend, the quarx. /Welcome back, Charlie! Do you remember helping me save the Earth? Do you remember sav-ing my skin, so we could finish the mission?/

/// Saving your skin? ///

/A long time ago. When the robots dropped some heavy tanks and nearly killed me./ The pain of the broken ribs was still present. It had not actually been such a long time.

He felt the quarx's thoughts stirring in the musty attic of his mind.

/// I'm . . . uncertain about these things.
I must reflect. ///

And with that, the quarx seemed to fade away, as if retreating into another room to study what he had been told.

Bandicut sighed, breathing warm air into his cupped

hands. He didn't mind the quarx going off by himself, just as long as he was *here,* alive. Bandicut leaned forward to see if he could breathe some life back into the fire. There were still some unburned pieces of wood among the ashes. He poked at them, trying to coax them into burning. A minute later, he had succeeded only in extinguishing what fire remained. He peered ruefully up at the alien in the darkness. "I'm not much of a woodsman," he apologized. "But I think I have a lighter in my bag."

Ik raised a hand and Bandicut paused. The alien rubbed at his abdomen with one hand. He leaned over the ashes and carefully readjusted the remnants of wood. Something sparkled under his hand, and when he sat back, tiny flames licked up out of the pile. He groped in the dark grass, found another piece of wood, and broke it and placed it gingerly on the bit of fire. Within seconds, the flames flickered higher and Bandicut could feel their warmth. He leaned close, shivering with the sensation of heat.

"I have had . . . practice," Ik remarked. He clacked his mouth shut and watched the fire with glimmering eyes. He said nothing further about Bandicut's invisible friend, but after a time, murmured, "R-r-rest again?"

Bandicut nodded, but sat motionless. Though exhausted, he was also wide awake, and he wanted to huddle close to this fire as long as he could.

"Yes?" asked the alien.

Bandicut sighed and finally lay down again. "Yes. Let's rest."

Sleep did not come again for a long time. The alien sat like a silent statue, while Bandicut tried unsuccessfully to get comfortable. He spent half an eternity shifting positions, waiting for his thoughts to wind down. But the ground was cold and damp with dew, and finally he gave up trying, and sat up again, huddling and staring at the shrinking embers of their fire.

If this was a taste of what he had to look forward to . . . He shook his head. The question kept ringing back to him: Who had brought him here, and why? *"Because you are needed . . ."* Which was almost worse than no answer at all. What need could possibly explain this? As for the "who," he assumed it was the builders, or owners, of the translator that he had encountered on Triton; but he didn't even know that for certain. Surely he hadn't been brought all this way just to bring the daughter-stones home. Or worse yet, to begin some new mission. Jesus, he hoped not. He shook his head and closed his eyes again, remembering . . .

The solar system . . . Triton . . . Julie Stone . . . .

Especially Julie Stone.

Julie probably never did understand why he had stolen the spaceship from Triton, and fled across the solar system, mere hours after their intimacy together. *Could* she have understood it? Had she heard—or believed—the messages he had broadcast from *Neptune Explorer*? He desperately wanted to think she had—to believe that he had somehow redeemed himself in her eyes. But he knew that it was a lot to hope for. He sighed, and tried not to think about those wants and hurts, tried just to remember her eyes, her laugh, the way she'd looked and felt when they'd made love . . . and then he started to tremble, as those memories rushed back to him.

No, no. If he started dwelling on that, he would go mad.

Remember the flight instead. The crazy dive past the sun that he had made because somebody had to do it, and it was just his bad luck to be the somebody.

He had tried to explain, but he didn't know if anyone had believed his explanation—that he was saving Earth from an impending catastrophe. Maybe they saw the flash when he hit the planet-killer comet; maybe they didn't. And during his space-threading transit from the solar system to the edge of the galaxy, who knew how much time had passed—generations, probably. Or centuries. Or even millennia. Not that it mattered much in a practical sense. He was never going home again. How could he? And if he was going to be marooned thousands of light-years from Earth, what difference did it make what year it was back home? Except, it *did* matter, to think that Julie was alive, still—or dead.

He felt a voice whispering in his thoughts.

/// Somehow,
I feel that these questions
are my questions, also. ///

Bandicut half closed his eyes, rocking forward and back. /What do you mean, Charlie?/

/// I'm not precisely sure. ///

The quarx seemed to be trying to frame something in his own mind. When he spoke again, it was with a mixture of puzzlement and grief.

/// I don't remember my own world,
John Bandicut.
It's . . . not the same as yours,
is it? ///

Bandicut shook his head, remembering Charlie-One, or maybe it was Charlie-Two, telling him that he was completely isolated from his own people; he didn't even know if there were any other living quarx in the universe. It saddened Bandicut to remember that. And yet, it was strangely comforting not to be the only one living in cosmic exile.

Perhaps noting his thoughts, Charlie whispered,

/// Do you have
memories of mine that you could
share with me?
I seem to have so few of my own. ///

/Feel free to look around. But that feeling may pass. It took you a while to remember things, the last time you came back to life./

/// ??? ///

/You do remember that you've had past lives? That you've died, and come back to life before? And your memories were . . . incomplete?/ He shook his head and stopped trying to put it into words. A quarx, reborn, seemed to share some of its predecessors' memories, but not all of them. It was an inconvenient trait.

He chuckled suddenly. /Charlie?/

/// Yes? ///

/What are you going to be like this time? A practical joker? A brilliant artist? A con man?/

/// ??? ///

He sighed. /Don't mind me, I'm just giving you a hard time. You don't remember that you come with a new personality each time?/

/// No.
I think I must
study this a while longer. ///

/Good idea,/ Bandicut whispered, yawning. He lay down, huddling close to the fire. /Help yourself to any memories you find in the cupboard. I need to get some sleep now./

He closed his eyes, and slept at last.

Ik woke before the first light of dawn. He sat motionless, letting his eyes focus on the curled up form of his new companion, on the other side of the fire's ashes. A most interesting being, this John Bandicut, with its robots and its inside alien! Ik wasn't quite sure what to make of it. But one thing he did know was that in his half-dozen seasons here on Shipworld (as nearly as he could judge the passage of time), he had met very few other beings who had voice-stones. He thought the appearance of a new one was likely to be important. Ik touched his own stones, on both sides of his head, and decided that he wished to learn more about John Bandicut.

Unfortunately, he did not have the luxury of time. He needed to keep moving. Li-Jared had missed their scheduled rendezvous, and Ik was worried. His friend never missed a rendezvous unless something was wrong. But there was a possible trail: he had seen a few footprints that looked like Li-Jared's, back in the last region, and the disturbance of the ice-river bore all the signs of an environment troubled by the passage of someone like his friend. John Bandicut's robots probably had set off the immediate attack; but unless the contamination had grown worse than Ik imagined, the ice-river must already have been irritated.

Ik hated rushing off—on this chase or any other. It was the sort of thing that precluded thoughtfulness and caution. Ik believed in thoughtfulness, in taking the long view. But when boldness was called for, there was no point in hesitation. If only he knew what sort of boldness was appropriate! If only he knew what Li-Jared had learned! Even Ik was becoming impatient. The time had come for them either to make their escape from this perplexing world, or to steel themselves to meddling in its affairs. They simply could not stay mere observers much longer.

And what about this new arrival, this John Bandicut?

Ik sighed softly through his ears. Light was at last growing in the sky. He rose silently and stretched his limbs. He would allow John Bandicut to rest a little longer. In the meantime Ik would scout the land.

The dawn light, pink and cold, woke Bandicut. He sat up painfully, barely able to coax his aching joints to move. He rubbed the grit from his eyes and stared across the pile of ashes where the fire had been.

His alien friend was gone.

He struggled to his feet, trying not to be alarmed. "Ik?" he called hoarsely. "Are you still here?"

Napoleon whirred. "John Bandicut, are you looking for the other?"

"Did you see him?"

"I believe he is walking in the cluttered area beyond," said Napoleon, swiveling a slender metal arm toward the copse of trees outside their sheltered camp.

"Ah," Bandicut muttered, realizing that he had another need. He glanced around with a slight feeling of embarrassment. He'd never taken a leak on an alien world before. He hiked a little farther into the cleft of rock, then stood facing the wall, sighing, as he emptied his bladder.

He turned to go find Ik.

/// I am still with you, ///

said a quiet voice in his mind, as he walked out among the trees.

He blinked, startled. He had some readjusting to do. /Good! Welcome back! I hope you're making sense of things. Maybe you can help *me* make sense of things./

/// *I will try,* ///

promised the quarx.

Bandicut spotted the tall alien out beyond the far edge of the trees. "Ik! There you are!"

Ik turned and gestured expansively. "Hrrrlll. You note the morning!"

"Yes, indeed," Bandicut said, trying not to limp from soreness as he walked over. "Good morning."

"Good morning," repeated Ik, rolling the words off his tongue. He turned, surveying the land in the early light, and spoke haltingly. "John Bandicut. I must travel far today." He turned to look back at the human.

"Oh."

"I have great need."

Need? Bandicut cleared his throat. "Well, is it anything I could help you with?"

Ik cocked his head. In the daylight, he looked less skeletal and more . . . alien. His eyes, though small by human standard, sparkled piercingly bright in their deepset hollows. His skin appeared leathery but smooth, with a tint that seemed to vary according to the light, from white to a distinct blue. Bandicut wondered what kind of sun Ik had grown up under. Or if he had grown up under a sun at all. Bandicut squinted up into the sky, wondering what that bright light really was, if this wasn't a planet.

Ik watched him think, without answering.

Bandicut returned to his question. "I mean, I'd like to help, if I can." He gestured to his left, toward the cliff from which they had emerged as if by magic yesterday. "To, well, repay you."

"Re-pay?"

"For saving us. Bringing us here." He gestured expansively. "Wherever *here* is. It's better than where we were."

Ik opened his mouth and snapped it shut. "Yes. I have been in this region before. Once. But I don't know it well."

"Ah. You're a stranger here, too." Bandicut nodded, remembering Ik's gesture to the stars last night. "Where is it you come from?"

Ik's eyes seemed to sharpen. "Where? From . . . a world that . . ." He waved vaguely toward the sky. "From another . . . it is called, *rrrr*—" His voice seemed to tighten and rise half an octave. "*Hraachee'a*. Home." His translator-stones flickered in his head, and Bandicut felt the tingle in his own wrists as his stones tried to translate. Or perhaps that *was* a translation—something that he could at least try to get his mouth around.

"Hrack—"

"Hraa*chh*—" said Ik, emphasizing the guttural rasp. "Hraa*chee*'a."

"Hraachee'a?"

"Yes. Urrr, home. It has—had, rather—many names."

Had many names? Bandicut was afraid to ask. "Was it another world, in space? You traveled—" he waved his hand across the sky "—from another, a *different*, sun? Another star?"

Ik clacked his mouth shut, twice. "Another star. Yes." He made a harrumphing sound. "Star of another, a different, a lovely—urrrrr—" *Rasp.* His temple-stones pulsed, as he peered about the copse, looking for something to use as an illustration. Finally he pointed to his own skin. Bandicut's stones tingled, as he heard, "Blue."

"A blue sun?" Bandicut echoed in wonderment. He'd always heard that it was impossible for life to evolve near a blue sun. Too short a life span for the star. Apparently he'd heard wrong.

"Blue-ishhh . . . sun. Yes." Ik's eyes flickered. "Was. But no longer."

Bandicut's heart sank for his new friend. "What do you mean? It's *gone*?"

Ik rubbed the front of his abdomen, eyes darkening. "Gone, yes. So I believe."

The alien's pain was palpable. Ik, too, was an exile—but his world hadn't survived him. "I'm very sorry," Bandicut said softly. "So you were brought here, by someone? Some force?"

Ik swept his arm in an arc. "Six seasons ago."

"Do you know why?"

Ik looked uncertain. He rubbed his fingers along his front.

"I don't know why *I'm* here," Bandicut admitted. "Or even what this place is. Except—" He hesitated.

"Yes?"

"Well, except that someone seems to think I am needed here." At those words, he thought he saw Ik's eyes gleam for a moment. Hadn't Ik said something about "need"? Bandicut frowned and continued, "But I don't know why, or by whom."

"Don't know," Ik agreed. He looked away for a moment, then stared back at Bandicut, eyes glittering. "I have been seeking . . . answers. With a friend. I must set out soon now, to find my friend. We were separated, and he might be in danger. He might have gained information." Ik closed his eyes and opened them again. "Would you—" *rasp* "—wish to come?"

Bandicut opened his mouth. There it was: an invitation. Should he go? If not, what should he do? He had no way to return to his ship. And even if he could return, what then? He'd seen no indication that the owners of this strange world had any intention of coming to greet him.

"I do not know," said Ik, "what we may find."

"Um," Bandicut asked softly, "this friend. Is he of your own kind?"

Ik's breath sighed out. "Not a Hraachee'an, no. But—" his eyes sparked with intensity "—a friend."

Bandicut absorbed that silently. "Is it far? Will you travel very far?"

Ik touched his cheek with two fingers. "Perhaps, yes. He was intending to meet—*hrrrump*—" Ik paused, trying to rephrase. "My friend, Li-Jared, did not join me as planned. He may be, may need, help." Ik became agitated, as though he were intending to stride off that very moment.

Bandicut swallowed. "Well, then, we will try to . . . help."

"You need n-not," said the alien.

/// What are you offering here? ///

/I don't know. But he saved my life, Charlie./ Bandicut reached out with open hands. "I would like to come," he said. "If we can help, I would like to."

Ik's eyes flickered. "I accept—" *rasp* "—welcome your help. But your—" He shifted his gaze back toward Napoleon and Copernicus, perhaps remembering the deadly commotion they had caused yesterday.

"Robots," Bandicut said. "That's Copernicus, on wheels. And Napoleon, on legs." He hesitated. "They must come with me. I would feel—lost, without them. They are very—" he searched for the right word "—loyal."

The alien's stones pulsed for a moment or two. "Hrahh. Loyal."

*/// I'm not sure I know
the word. ///*

/It means you stick by your friends, and people who've helped you./

"That is a good thing, John Bandicut," Ik was saying.

/// Perhaps I should study this, as well. ///

/Take a look under "friends." I don't know what you'll find, but maybe it'll bring back some memories./ To Ik he said, "Shall we eat something and get going?"

Ik clacked his mouth in agreement.

6

STORMS ON THE PLAIN

 BANDICUT SEARCHED IN his backpack and pulled out an emergency ration. "This can keep me going a little while. We could share it—but I don't know if it'd suit your digestion." He glanced around at rocks and grass and trees. "Still, what else is there?"

Ik made throaty clicking noises. "I am uncertain of your food, John Bandicut. But I find much in this world that I can eat." He stroked at the stones in his temples. "This has been done for me."

Bandicut remembered the translator-stones telling him that his own metabolism had been *normalized* for this world. And not just him. The robots had been altered, too.

/// Normalized? ///

/Does that mean anything to you?/

/// Let me ask the daughter-stones. ///

Bandicut was amazed, though he shouldn't have been. /Are they talking to you? They haven't been too chatty with me./

*/// I have been establishing
a certain level of interchange with them. ///*

/Good. You're a useful guy, Charlie./

/// It is my goal to be. ///

Bandicut bobbed his head and spoke to Ik. "I haven't tried the local food yet." But it won't be long, he thought, counting his meager supplies.

*/// According to the stones,
your body chemistry was adjusted
at the time of your entry.
You should be able to eat appropriate
vegetation here. ///*

/*Should* be able? Well, that's better than nothing, I guess./
Bandicut tore open a high-carb nut bar. It tasted . . . a little *off*.
Not rancid or bad, exactly—more like a food whose flavor no
longer quite agreed with him. He took three bites, drank from
his water bottle, and decided that he'd had enough. /I thought I
was hungrier,/ he reflected, aware that he shouldn't be com-
plaining, if this meant that his food supply would last longer.
But his stomach felt unsettled.

*/// Perhaps local food will suit you better,
since your change. ///*

/Let's hope so./ Bandicut leaned toward the robots. "Have
you two run your diagnostics?"

"Affirmative, John Bandicut," said Napoleon. "I find my
expanded protocols intact and functional."

"Expanded protocols? What expanded protocols?"

"My new higher-level programming."

Bandicut squinted at his robot. "Where did this new programming come from, Nappy?"

"I cannot identify the source. However, its time-code appears to coincide with our arrival on the icy hill." Napoleon's
sensors swiveled. "It may take some time for me to fully inte-
grate the new functions."

Bandicut stared at the robot. Is this still *Napoleon?* he
wondered. Or was he dealing with some new creation altogether? For that matter, /Am I still *me*, Charlie?/

*/// According to the stones—
well, to be honest I am not totally certain.
But I believe you are still you.
And your robots are still your robots.
But with . . . enhanced capabilities.
You seemed to feel that they were rather
primitive before. ///*

Bandicut grunted. /Yeah, but I sort of liked them that way./ He looked past Napoleon. "Coppy? You too?"

The wheeled robot tapped in response. "My answer is identical to Napoleon's, Cap'n."

Bandicut blinked. Copernicus's answers were becoming positively nonliteral. "I see. And your power levels?"

Napoleon spoke first. "Ninety-one percent."

"Eighty-six percent, plus twenty-hour reserve after nominal shutdown," said Copernicus.

Napoleon clicked. "Yes, that's right. Make that ninety-one percent, plus reserve. Thank you, Coppy."

The other robot drumtapped.

Bandicut looked up from the robots to Ik. "It seems—" he spread his hands "—that I have smarter assistants than I thought."

"Aha," said Ik, rubbing his chest. "Are they still loyal?"

A band of tension gripped Bandicut for a moment, as he turned from Ik back to the two robots. "You guys still loyal?" /What do you think, Charlie?/

/// *I don't see why they wouldn't be.* ///

"With you for the journey," tapped Copernicus.

"At your service, John Bandicut," said Napoleon.

"I'll take that as a yes." Bandicut began repacking his bag, rolling up his damp clothes and squeezing them into a side pocket. "Shall we break camp, Ik?"

The alien adjusted the rope he had tucked in his leather belt. "Ready, John Bandicut."

They set out through the copse of trees and nearly straight away from the cliff where the portal had brought them through from the icy river. The hiking was easy, over a plain carpeted with ankle-high grass and flanked on either side by distant scarps. The sky overhead turned a chalky blue as the morning wore on, and the air grew pleasantly warm. Copernicus had no trouble rolling through the grass, and after a bit of trial and error, Napoleon found a rhythm of walking in this gravity that enabled him to trot smoothly alongside Bandicut.

Ik stopped several times to pick berries from a species of bush that dotted the land. He ate with apparent relish. Bandicut picked a few berries and rolled them in the palm of his hand. He was going to have to work up the nerve to try one. /Can you save my goose if this is poisonous?/ he asked Charlie.

/// I'm sorry, how would I do that? ///

/Well . . . I guess you'd have to study my memories. Your predecessors were able to able to pull off some pretty impressive healings when I got hurt. I needed it more than once./

/// Sounds like an interesting skill. ///

/It was very handy,/ Bandicut assured him.

/// I will try to study it.
But realistically, I think right now
you're on your own. ///

Bandicut studied the berry; it looked like a small holly berry, but purple. He remembered that holly berries were poisonous. Maybe the translator-stones could protect him, if Charlie couldn't.

"Urrrr, very good," muttered Ik, popping another handful into his mouth.

Bandicut shrugged. "What the hell." He placed the berry between his front teeth and bit tentatively. A taste reminiscent of blueberry and orange exploded in his mouth. It was sweet, tart. Delicious, in fact. He held it in his mouth and waited for an adverse reaction. When none came, he nervously spat it out anyway. He waited a minute, then two, then finally bit another. This time he swallowed. "Mm. That does sort of hit the spot."

"Hrahhh?"

"An expression. It means I liked it." Bandicut picked a small handful, but decided to hold off on eating them. "I'd better wait and make sure I'm not allergic or something."

They started walking again, the robots close behind.

"Ik?"

"Urrr?"

What he had been thinking was, how odd it felt to be

strolling across a pastoral plain, as if on a Sunday outing, with an alien who probably came from the far side of the galaxy—and to think that they were equally far from home.

He shook his head and said, "What is this place, really?"

"Urrr?"

"It seems like—" he groped for words "—a world, or many worlds—"

"Hah."

He frowned at Ik. "But all contained somehow? In one great structure?"

The Hraachee'an kept walking with a tireless stride. "You could describe it that way. It's actually somewhat more complicated."

Bandicut scowled, remembering the apparent size of the thing that had swallowed his spaceship like a whale gulping krill. "Well, are there other people here?"

Ik's eyes sparked for a moment. "Yes. Indeed. Many, many people."

"Then where are they all?" Bandicut cried in frustration. "You're the only one I've met! Except for one sociopathic river, I haven't seen anything that moves. No animals. No birds. Not even any bugs. Much less *people*."

Ik made a burring sound, and glanced sideways. "There are many in other regions. But you are correct. Here, it seems very quiet. Gaaiii. I have wondered why, myself. This is one of the things I wish to learn, John Bandicut." Ik strode on, picking up his speed. The conversation seemed to make him anxious.

Bandicut hurried to keep up. "Just call me John, okay? Or Bandie. That's what my friends on Triton called me."

Ik seemed to realize he needed to slow up, to accommodate his human companion. "John," he said experimentally. "B-Bandie."

"Right. John is my first name. Bandie is my nickname."

Ik made a whiffling sound. "And you come from a world named—" he rolled the word off his tongue with an effort "—Trrrit-t-ton."

"Well, almost." Bandicut explained that he was actually

from a world called Earth but had last been working on Triton, moon of another planet in the same star system.

"Hahh—your people travel among the stars, then," said Ik, rocking slightly as he walked.

"No, just in our own solar system. At least, that was true when I left." Bandicut considered the point. "Actually, I have no idea how much time has passed since then. I suppose it's possible they've achieved star travel by now." A harsh laugh erupted from his throat. "I didn't exactly *plan* to come travelling this way, you know." He blinked, remembering the end of his journey with its heartwrenching view of the galaxy, from the outside. He remembered wondering *why?*—and later hearing the words, *Because you are needed.* His reverie collapsed with a shiver. He looked behind to make sure the robots were following. The four of them were leaving a wake of trampled grass. If anyone wanted to follow them, it wouldn't be hard.

"I understand," Ik said softly. "I did not, either." Then Ik didn't say anything for a while, and just walked in long, rhythmic strides.

Bandicut wanted to ask more, but sensed a deep sadness in the Hraachee'an, which he was reluctant to intrude upon. He nodded to himself, thinking, /I suppose it's better to be part of a band of exiles than one exile lost and alone./

/// I think I would agree.
I hope you find some comfort in that. ///

/Small comfort,/ he answered. But he had to admit, small comfort was better than none at all.

After a time, Ik did begin to explain, haltingly, a bit about his own world and his journey to this place. His last memory of his home was an image of his sun flaring in a dazzling explosion, an explosion that could only have meant the death of everything he knew. He had been diving straight into the sun at the time, and was carried to safety and exile by some technology (he touched his translator-stones) that he did not understand. Before that, he had been busy following the urging of the stones, persuading some of his fellows to flee Hraachee'a in spaceships bearing other daughter-stones. He had watched in shock as those ships plunged into the unstable sun in apparent self-immolation. Then his own ship followed, and sometime later, he found himself here. But what had become of his fellows who had fallen into the sun before him, he didn't know.

"You don't even know if they lived or died?" Bandicut asked.

"I do not," Ik said, before falling silent again.

Bandicut told Ik how *he* had come here, after saving his planet from collision with a comet in a similarly bewildering flight. The resonance of his story with Ik's was profoundly unnerving to him. Ik made no comment, but seemed less surprised than Bandicut. There was, of course, one crucial difference: Bandicut had been able to save his world, while Ik had not. He shuddered a little as he reflected upon that fact.

/// I feel
strong echoes from my own past
as I listen, John Bandicut. ///

/Did your world die?/ he asked silently.

The quarx didn't answer, didn't seem to know the answer.

The sun climbed overhead as they walked, and grew stiflingly warm. Behind them, the little cliff and copse had long since disappeared in a hazy line of hills. On either side, the escarpments were drawing inward, flanking them at a range of perhaps half a kilometer. Ahead, the plain narrowed into something more like a canyon.

Ik picked up the pace again, keeping them equidistant from the scarps. When Bandicut asked why, Ik peered from side to side, rubbing his chest with one hand. "I wish to move without surprises," he answered, striding even faster.

Bandicut glanced right and left, uneasily. /I wonder if he's worried about getting ambushed in that canyon./

/// Ambushed? ///

/Something we used to see in old movies—westerns, especially. Charlie-One was a big fan of them./

/// Should I study those memories, too? ///

/Sure./ Bandicut was breathing hard. He wished he'd stayed in better shape.

/// You used to exercise in a big
circular room. ///

Indeed: the centrifuge room on Triton, where he'd, all too infrequently, worked out under increased gravity. He'd gotten soft in the one-thirteenth gee of Triton. He shifted his back-pack wearily, keeping his legs moving.

Ik spoke. "You must tell me if you need to rest. I am more accustomed to this, perhaps."

Bandicut pressed on for about five minutes more, then panted, "Okay! I need to rest."

Ik came to a halt at once. Bandicut dropped his pack and fell into the grass, gasping. He semaphored to the robots as they caught up, to make sure they didn't run him over.

"This might be a good time to take food," said Ik. He reached into a leathery pocket and placed a small, dark stick in his mouth. It looked like a cigar. He worried it about between his hard lips, then bit off a small piece.

Bandicut found his bottle and gratefully sipped some water. He regretted not looking for a place to refill it prior to setting out. He shrugged and lay back for a few moments, then sat up and asked the robots their power levels. They were down only a couple of percentage points. He grunted. Whatever had been done to them, someone seemed to want them to last. Maybe he should quit worrying about it. "Ik," he asked, "are we going through that canyon ahead?"

"Probably."

"Because you think—what's your friend's name?"

"Li-Jared."

"Because you think Li-Jared came this way?"

"I have seen his tracks in the grass. At least, I believe so."

"Tracks?" Bandicut echoed. He'd seen nothing. "Huh." He lay back, luxuriating in the grass. He heard a tiny rustle and turned his head, squinting. Something was moving, low to the ground. He suppressed a reflex to sit up abruptly. "Ik?"

"Urrr?"

"There's something watching us."

"Urrrrr?"

"In the grass. An animal."

A creature the size of a puppy was just visible now through the blades of grass, sitting up like a prairie dog. It cocked its head one way, then another, while gazing intently at Bandicut. It had a wide face, with tufted ears. Its eyes were bright, as though with intelligence.

Bandicut remained still. He didn't want to scare it away—or worse, provoke an attack. But after a minute, he called softly, "Hello! Can you hear me?" The creature's ears twitched. "I won't hurt you."

The creature's eyes blinked. It gave a short, high-pitched whistle, then vanished.

/// Did you frighten it? ///

/I must have. You know, it sure looked an awful lot like a . . . not a prairie dog, exactly, but something close./

/// Yes.
I caught a memory-flash when you first saw it.
It reminded you of . . . a meerkat. ///

Something flickered in Bandicut's mind, and he suddenly recalled TV pictures he'd seen years ago. Meerkats: tamable African mammals, about the size of prairie dogs, with bodies shaped like bowling pins and gawky but alert faces. Charlie was right.

"Is your observer still there?" Ik asked.

Bandicut sat up with a grunt. "I seem to have scared it away." He peered where the creature had been, but if there was a hole in the ground, he couldn't see it. "I wonder what it was."

Ik clicked his mouth. "I cannot guess. I have been this way only once before. I do not know those who live here." The Hraachee'an rose. "John Bandicut, we must move on."

Bandicut lumbered to his feet. "Whatever you say. We don't want to miss your friend."

"*Rakhh.* No, we do not," Ik said vehemently, and set off at a fast walk.

Bandicut waved the robots into motion.

"Your friend—what sort of danger is he in?" Bandicut asked as they walked.

"I cannot say. He did not appear at our rendezvous. I am quite concerned." Ik strode tirelessly, his eyes focused ahead. "Because of the contamination I spoke of."

"Contamination? It sounds like a disease."

Ik seemed to consider the question. "Perhaps," he allowed. "But more like a—" *rasp* "—enemy."

"Enemy?" Bandicut echoed.

"Yes. Not our personal enemy, so much as the world's."

Bandicut nearly stumbled. "That sounds ominous."

"Hah. Yes. I do not wish to speak much of it, just now. One never knows, in a strange place, whether another might somehow be listening."

Bandicut grunted, hooking his thumbs in his pack straps as he tried to sort that out. "How did you and Li-Jared get separated?"

"Rakh. We entered a portal too many moments apart. It changed destinations between us. I had to work my way back to this place."

"Um." Bandicut had passed through portals twice now, both times blindly. It was sobering to realize that even if you thought you knew where you were going, you could end up somewhere else entirely. He cleared his throat. "Where, if I may ask, were you going?"

"Ah, a place of—" *rasp* "—machines and consoles and communications stones. We had been searching for information." Ik's stride seemed to become heavier, more determined.

"What sort of information?" Bandicut was beginning to breathe hard, but didn't want to break his stride.

"Hah." Ik made a rumbling sound, peering left and right, as though scanning for enemies along the escarpments. "Information about, rrrrmm . . ." Bandicut tried to read Ik's expression, and couldn't. The Hraachee'an's eyes were alight. "About who is responsible for—" and he swept his hand in a bobbing curve, taking in the landscape, then turned his fingers in toward himself and flicked them out toward Bandicut.

"You mean, who built this place? And brought us here?"

"*Haahh!* Yes." Ik shut his mouth decisively, then added, "And, perhaps, if we are very fortunate, information about how to leave it."

Bandicut's heart skipped a beat.

/// You may have more in common with Ik
than you thought. ///

/Yah./ Bandicut strode on with renewed energy. As if in response, Ik picked up his pace.

Bandicut heard a click from the robots, trailing about six meters behind. "John Bandicut," Napoleon called. "I am detecting motion to the left."

"Motion? What kind?" Bandicut glanced back. "Can you guys move up?"

With a whine of acceleration, Napoleon loped alongside. "Coppy is at top speed already."

"Okay, keep an eye on him for me. What are you seeing?"

"Localized movements in the grass. And on the higher formations, small profiles appearing and disappearing. The grouping is moving longitudinally."

"What direction?"

"Parallel to our course, Captain."

"What's this *Captain* bit?" Bandicut asked distractedly. "Coppy calls me Captain, not you." He shaded his eyes, but couldn't see any movement. "Do you still see them?"

"Contact at your nine o'clock, twenty meters distant, in the grass."

"Ik, can you hold up a second?" Bandicut slowed and peered to his left. "Where? I don't—oh, wait—there!" It was a meerkat-creature, bounding through the grass.

"I see it," said Ik. "But I believe we should keep moving."

"Two more, at four o'clock and ten o'clock," said Napoleon.

"I wonder why they're following us. Curiosity?"

Copernicus rolled up alongside. "Cap'n, I have eleven sightings altogether. Shall I provide bearings?"

"I don't think—"

"John—Bandie—I do not know if they will be trouble-some. But I feel a need to move quickly. I have a strong . . . intuition." Ik's face contorted slightly. "If you wish, you may follow behind me."

Bandicut shivered. "No way. We'll keep up."

They began walking again. After a little while, Ik said, "I did not finish explaining. Li-Jared and I have been seeking a place of control."

"Control? Control of what? You mean, this whole re-gion?" Bandicut gestured, without breaking stride, at the hills around them.

"Yes. *No!* Not the region only. For the—" *rasp rasp* "meta . . . world."

Bandicut peered at him. "The what?"

"Metaworld," Ik repeated.

/// I think he means, this entire place.
All of the environments.
The metaworld.
I believe I recall other names, as well.
Metaship . . . Shipworld . . . ///

Bandicut blinked. /You *have* been here before, then./

"John Bandie? You understand?"

Dizzily, he answered, "No, not really. Do you mean the whole—what did you call it? Shipworld? I don't understand it, Ik."

The alien hrrrm'd softly. "Nor I, John. Nor I."

"But—" he struggled to put it all together "—if it's not a planet, it's still *very large,* isn't it?"

"Haww, indeed. Very very large. Much larger than a planet."

Bandicut swallowed. Larger than a planet? What could be self-contained, and larger than a planet? He'd heard of Dyson spheres and ring-shaped constructs; but from what he'd glimpsed on the outside, he didn't think it fit the description of any of those. He remained silent, listening to the robots drone rhythmically behind them.

"We seek greater knowledge of it," Ik continued. "That is why we seek the control area."

Bandicut recalled the chamber just down the corridor from his spaceship. "Ik, when we arrived here, we saw a place with all sorts of consoles and displays—for information, I assume. Or for . . . control." He shook his head. It seemed weeks ago, but was actually just yesterday.

"Yes? What did you learn from them?"

"Nothing. I couldn't get close to them."

"Gaaii—a pity. Do you know how to return there?"

Bandicut sighed. "No. I wish we could have made some contact there." As he said it, he remembered that he had made a kind of contact, during "normalization." But the contact had all been one way, a powerful intelligence studying and evaluating him. He wondered what its conclusions had been.

"Do not despair. Such places differ greatly from region to region. We have learned much, Li-Jared and I, though much less than we would like." Ik peered left and right. "We have learned, at least *rumor*—that there is a—" *rasp.*

Bandicut felt the translator-stones tickling, searching for the words it needed.

"—convergence—" *rasp* "—branching—" *rasp* "—tree of information. A place where information branches and flows, like a powerful stream." Ik's eyes sparkled. "Not a single flow, but a place where one can—" *rasp rasp* "—walk—swim—float—in a sea of knowledge."

Bandicut's stones were buzzing, but the message came through clearly enough. A datanet. *A mokin' datanet.* For the first time in a long while, he felt a sensation he had almost forgotten: his thoughts crowding together in a euphoric glow, then dancing away in drunken pirouettes.

"I have heard it called the *Tree of Ice*—" Ik continued.

His focus was slipping away, into the beginning of silence-fugue. Not again! a part of his mind cried. He was not done with it, after all . . .

/// Is something wrong? ///

The quarx's voice sounded more curious than concerned.

Bandicut muttered distractedly, /I hope you remember how to help me with this, Charlie! Would you look at that./

/// What? ///

/Datanet structures. Holy mokin'—/ Words failed as he peered sideways, at stacked layers of flickering jewellike connections that had appeared, high on the clifftops flanking them. The mere sight of those connections, those pathways, made him dizzy, made him want to reach for the neurolink . . .

/// John, I'm not sure— ///

He could barely speak, except with one small corner of his mind. /Silence . . . fugue. I used to link into something . . . just like this . . ./ He felt faint, as connections winked open around him, rays of light coruscating from distant sapphires and rubies, encrusting the scarps. /And I had an accident—/ Which had put him into a near-coma, and left his neuros dead, except for the intermittent silence-fugue that had haunted him ever since . . . the hallucinations, which the earlier Charlie had found a way to stop.

"John . . . Bandicut?"

/Help me, Charlie!/ he whispered. /Before I go over the edge!/

/// How? ///

/Find the memories!/ He blinked, trying to remain sober and clear enough to maintain his course with Ik. *Don't alarm him . . .*

The Hraachee'an was peering sideways at him, sensing something wrong.

Sparks erupted from the hallucinatory connections, spiraling out like corkscrews. He felt little spikes of pain between his eyes. He staggered, struggled to keep his feet moving in a straight line.

"John, are you—"

"Just having a little . . . flashback," he wheezed. "Ik?"

"Hrrm?"

He fought to keep the clear corner of his mind in focus. "I've had—experience—with the type of place you described. The information exchange. But I had an accident—''

Ik stopped and stared at him.

"And I—" And suddenly his thoughts regathered and clarified, like a chemical reaction abruptly changing color. The datanet gems vanished from the clifftops; the fog evaporated from around his head. "Yes," he murmured. /Thank you, Charlie./

"Hrrm?"

"And sometimes it . . . causes me trouble." He let out a long breath. "I think it's passed now. I feel better."

Ik's eyes flickered. "Good. Perhaps you can tell me later. Right now I believe I sense danger ahead." He began moving quickly again. Toward the danger.

Bandicut was startled to realize that the scarps had closed in on both sides now; they were walking down a grass-carpeted canyon, walled by cliffs. He glimpsed movement in the grass. Meerkats?

He looked back. "Nappy? Ik, wait!" The robots had dropped behind. *"Nappy!"* His yell echoed back from the cliff walls. He could see Napoleon's sensor-array swiveling. The robot sprang forward, and Copernicus kicked up a cloud of dust, speeding to follow. "What the hell are you two—?"

"John Bandicut, we are picking up low frequency sounds, of increasing intensity!" Napoleon called, loping toward him like a mutant silver grasshopper.

"Sounds? What sort of sounds?"

Napoleon halted and stared with black sensor-eyes. *"Droom-da-da-da-droom-da-droom-da-da-da-droom . . ."* The robot sounded like a badly amplified kettle drum.

"It was submodulated and may have been carrying information," said Copernicus, rolling up. "The wavefront began behind us and passed us about one minute ago. We stopped to take readings."

"This is troubling," Ik said, surveying the cliffs. Bandicut noticed for the first time some angry-looking storm clouds overhead. In the silence, he imagined he heard a faint, low rumbling in the ground. "John Bandicut, I must speed ahead quickly. You must catch up."

Bandicut's voice caught. "I hate to get separated."

"I will wait at the end of the canyon. Not much farther."

"But—"

Before Bandicut could finish his protest, Ik bounded away at an amazing speed.

Bandicut swallowed hard. "Let's go, boys. And no stopping!" He set off at the fastest pace he thought he could maintain.

/// What's Ik worried about? ///

Bandicut had no answer, as he glanced up into the darkening sky.

Ik was far ahead. Bandicut tried to pace himself, while still keeping his friend in sight. The cliffs, sharply broken and striated, as if they had been formed by the land jerking itself apart, loomed on either side of him. The grass grew thin and the ground hard under his feet. His steps began to seem like a beating drum, and the motors of the robots like the thrum of alien machinery.

After five or ten minutes, he had to pause, waving the robots on ahead. As he caught his breath, he peered up at the cliffs, torn between fear and awe at their carved beauty, glowing red in a patch of late afternoon sunlight that shone through a break in the dark clouds.

/// Sun's going to set soon, ///

Charlie observed.

/Yah./ He noticed a pounding sound which at first he thought was his heart. It was a rumbling in the ground, coming up through his feet, like an underground train. There was also a distant chittering, like the cries of squirrels. He couldn't see anything moving except the robots, ahead of him. A breeze was picking up, and growing stiff. He forced his legs back into motion.

/// I could experiment,
and see if I can increase your oxygen-use
efficiency. ///

Bandicut determinedly gathered speed. /Okay. But take it in small steps, all right? I don't want to keel over if you make a mistake./

/// Understood.
I'm getting a pretty good idea
of how your metabolic system works.
I think the stones can help. ///

Bandicut pushed himself harder. He soon found that he could indeed pace himself faster. Ik was out of sight now, but Bandicut quickly caught up with the robots. Then he saw Ik standing in the distance, a tiny upright figure almost lost in shadows, but visible against an eerily illuminated cliff-wall that appeared to block the end of the canyon. He heard Ik's voice floating on the wind.

There was a break in the canyon floor ahead. But only when Bandicut staggered to a halt at Ik's side did he realize that the Hraachee'an was standing at the edge of a steep drop-off. He was holding some sort of sighting device up to his eyes.

Bandicut's breath was stolen away by the deep gorge that crossed their path, terminating the canyon-plain like a knife stroke. Not far from where they stood, a smooth groove over the lip suggested a place where water had once cascaded from the canyon down into the gorge. It must have been a spectacular waterfall. He could almost hear its rumble. In fact, he *was* still hearing a rumble, which now seemed to be carried in the air, rather than the ground.

"John—" said Ik. But he interrupted himself, peering through his sighting device. He let out a piercing cry: *"Hiiiieee, Li-Jare-e-ed!"*

"You see him?" Bandicut tried to see where Ik was looking.

Ik pointed, without taking his eyes from the device. "Down in the canyon! *Li-Jare-e-ed!*" His voice echoed back from the canyon wall: "*—ed, —ed, —ed!*" He muttered a dissonant syllable, which sounded like a curse.

"I don't see him," Bandicut muttered. Half the gorge's

bottom was in shadow; the other half was illuminated in a burst of gold and red. A silver thread of water wound down its length. Bandicut half-turned as the robots arrived. "Nappy, do you—?"

"Look there!" Ik interrupted. He handed the sighting device to Bandicut, pointing.

Bandicut held the device to his eyes, and found that it both magnified the distant cliff-wall and centered itself at once on a dark, moving figure. He couldn't see it very clearly, but its scooting movements reminded him of a chimp or a mountain gorilla. "Is that him, Ik? Is that Li-Jared?"

"Yes, but he doesn't hear me!"

Ik shouted again. His words were interrupted by a burst of chittering sounds, and a much deeper rumble. The wind began to moan ominously through the canyon.

Bandicut lowered the optics and looked around worriedly.

"Cap'n, animal forms along the left wall!" shouted Copernicus.

"What kind? Meerkats?"

"There, John Bandicut!" called Napoleon, pointing.

Bandicut started to swing the optics to look, but Ik snatched them out of his hands. "No!" he yelled. "You'll lose Li-Jared!"

"Sorry!"

"John Bandicut—urgent warning!" shouted Napoleon. "Severe atmospheric disturbance!"

Bandicut looked up. The sky over the gorge, far to their right, was bisected by a black tornado funnel. /Damnation! Tell me this is silence-fugue!/

/// I don't think so. ///

A jet-engine crackle filled the air as the funnel approached.

"Aaaiiiieee—*Li-Jarrre-e-e-d-d!*" cried Ik, waving his long arms frantically.

Ik was using the optics now, but Bandicut could just make out the movement of Ik's friend as a small dot low on the far wall of the gorge. It was inconceivable that Li-Jared could have heard Ik's cry. But he must have seen the tornado coming, because he appeared to be scrambling up the cliff wall. *Up?* That made no sense. Unless—

"*Li-Jarrre-e-d-d, wait! NOOOOO!*" cried Ik.

Bandicut blinked, and thought he saw a tiny flash on the cliff wall. He rubbed his eyes; the figure of Li-Jared was gone. "Ik! Where'd he go?"

"Hrahhh!" Ik cried. "Through a port—"

The rest of Ik's words were obliterated by the roar of the tornado.

7

PATHS IN THE DARK

/// To the base of the cliff! ///

Bandicut grabbed Ik and pulled him to the right, waving the robots toward the spot that seemed to offer the greatest protection. All other sounds were drowned out by the roar. They ran in a crouch, beaten down not so much by the wind as by the earth-shattering noise.

The sky overhead had turned sickly green. The funnel cloud, momentarily blocked from sight by the cliff, burst into view with a thunderous blast and screamed down into the gorge. Ik and Bandicut hit the ground, covering their heads with their hands, and shook with terror as shadowy air whirled around them.

The roar seemed to last an eternity. When it finally diminished, Bandicut peered up fearfully and saw the tornado emerging from the far end of the gorge. "My God!" he croaked.

The tornado shot up out of the gorge, spraying rocks and water in a great plume. It thundered back into the sky like a rocket, spiraling up toward the clouds that had spawned it. When its lower tip reached a height of perhaps a thousand feet, it suddenly flipped itself upward like a scorpion's tail and drilled a hole through the cloud layer above it.

The cloud surrounding it coiled and twisted into the funnel; the blackness was drawn in like smoke into a fan, leaving eerie green sky around it. When the last of the murk vanished into the contorted, upside-down tornado, it closed with a tremendous *BOOM!* Bandicut stared up into the sky, open mouthed. The sickly green hue slowly faded, leaving a golden-red sunset glow over the canyon. "Ik?" he whispered. "Did you see that?"

The tall alien rose to a crouch beside him. "Hrrrrrll! John Bandicut—I have never—never witnessed—" Ik lapsed into a mutter that left the translator-stones buzzing.

Bandicut scrambled to his feet and squinted into the sky where the tornado had vanished. "Mokin' foke! Was it just me, or did that thing look *malevolent*? Can a tornado be malevolent, Ik?"

Ik was silent at first. When he looked at Bandicut, his black eyes were lit by two small sparks of fire, one in each pupil. "Hraach! Can a river be malevolent?"

Bandicut shook his head in bewilderment. He did not like this, not at all.

/// It is very strange, is it not? ///

/Strange. Yes, Charlie, indeed. Where the hell are Coppy and Nappy?/ He heard a ticking sound and turned to see Copernicus rolling out from the base of the cliff that he and Ik had not quite made it to. "Coppy, are you okay? Where's Nappy?"

Tap tap. The wheeled robot's scanning array seemed even more battered than before. "Behind you, Cap'n. Some distance."

"Uh?"

"Over there," said Ik, pointing a long finger toward the opposite cliff.

"Good Lord." The other robot was staggering across the canyon floor toward them. "Nappy, are you all right?" he yelled.

Napoleon hobbled a little faster, as they went out to meet it. "I am . . . functional, John Bandicut." Its voice rasped with static. It was covered with scratches and grime on its quantum alloy body.

"What happened?"

"I became airborne, Captain. I have no maneuvering capability in that modality. I reacquired ground contact against a vertical surface. I cannot—''

''The tornado blew you into that cliff?''

''I believe so, John Bandicut. I am no longer able to track the turbulence.'' The robot's sensors spun wildly.

''Well, thank God you're okay. The tornado's gone now.'' Bandicut surveyed the sky over the gorge. The storm clouds had all vanished. But probably no more than half an hour remained before sunset. Bandicut glanced at Ik, who was looking not at the sky, but over the edge into the gorge.

''I must follow Li-Jared,'' Ik announced. ''I must go at once. Do you still wish to continue with me?''

''Continue where?'' Bandicut asked. ''It's going to be dark soon.''

''Here, yes. But through the portal? Who knows?'' Ik raised his sighting device and studied the place where Li-Jared had disappeared.

''Do you know where he went?'' Bandicut was beginning to grow weary of all these changes. Just once, he thought, he'd like to control the direction he was going, and know the reason.

''I cannot say. But the sooner we follow through the portal, the greater the chances of keeping pace with him.'' Ik snapped his sighting device shut and tucked it into his vest. ''I must go. I would be . . . pleased to have you come with me. But if not, we must part here.''

Bandicut stared out over the gorge. ''Can you tell me something first? Was that tornado *meant* for Li-Jared? Or was it just natural coincidence, the way it swooped down into the gorge like that? I'm just wondering. I'd sort of like to know what I'm getting into. For once.''

Ik rubbed his chest. ''Hraach. I think it likely that it was meant for Li-Jared.''

Bandicut swallowed. ''Do you know why?''

''I can only guess that he has somehow disturbed the contamination in the environmental control system.'' Ik was no longer looking at Bandicut. He was peering into the gorge, looking for a path down.

"I just want to understand this. You mean the system that controls this whole place?" Bandicut gestured at the land and sky.

"Yes, the—" *rasp* "—world room—" *rasp* "—continent. Whatever." Ik began walking along the edge. "I must go, John Bandicut."

"World room? Continent?" Bandicut asked stupidly. Following Ik, he was startled to see a meerkat poke its head up over a nearby boulder, then duck back out of sight. "How large a continent?" he demanded.

"Who can say?" Ik found what he was looking for. He sat down on the edge, swung his legs over, and turned to face Bandicut, holding himself up by the strength of his hands and arms alone. "Is this—urrr, good-bye?"

"No, damn it—of course not! What the hell would I do by myself in this godforsaken place?"

Ik made a slight whistling noise. "Then I will assist you in climbing down, if you like." With a lurch, the Hraachee'an dropped out of sight.

Bandicut knelt and peered over. The tall alien was climbing down a nearly sheer wall. There was a ledge about eight meters below. "Mokin' A, you expect me to climb down there?"

> /// Is that a sharp drop?
> Didn't you first meet me after a
> bigger drop than that? ///

/We're in close to one gee here, Charlie. It's not like on Triton./

> /// Oh. ///

"My rope will assist you," Ik called, once he was standing on the ledge. He drew his coiled rope from his belt. Before Bandicut could ask, Ik flung the coil up, holding onto one end. The rope slapped onto the ground beside Bandicut. He reached to pick it up, and was startled to discover that he could not. It was fixed to the stone surface as if nailed down.

"You can climb down. It will not let you fall."

"Uh—" Bandicut stared at it, but could think of only one

way to test the claim. And there was another difficulty. "How do I get the robots down?"

"Urrr." Ik thought a moment, then flung the other end of the rope up. "Fasten it to them, then let them down."

Bandicut picked up the loose end of the rope with a frown. "They're kind of heavy, Ik. I don't know."

"It will hold. Quickly now."

Bandicut tied the rope around Napoleon, the lighter of the two.

/// This is very interesting. ///

/Glad you think so./ He checked the knot, then said to Napoleon, "I'm going to hold the rope and pay it out. You need to hold yourself out from the wall, and try to land on your feet beside Ik. Got that?"

"This is an unexpected procedure, John Bandicut."

"Tell me. Now, did you see how Ik sat down and swung himself around? Do that, if you can." Bandicut braced himself, holding the rope. He hoped he could support the weight. And Coppy was probably twice the mass of Napoleon. "Go, Nappy. Carefully."

The robot swung out and lowered itself by its monkeylike appendages, as Bandicut payed out the rope. Napoleon looked almost like an experienced climber, rappelling down the cliff. He felt lighter than Bandicut had expected—almost as if the rope were somehow supporting some of the load that should have been on his hands. When Napoleon reached the ledge, Ik untied the rope and threw it back up.

"No need to hold it, John! Just attach it, and tell the robot to drive off."

"Uh . . . okay." Bandicut puzzled over the best way to secure the rope around Copernicus.

"Just wrap it! It'll stay!"

Bandicut ran the rope around the robot a couple of times. Then he stood back and said, "Coppy? Just back out over the edge, I guess. *Slowly.*"

As the robot did so, he was stunned to see the rope contract like a rubber band, taking up all the slack. Coppy tipped over the edge, and dropped dangling toward the others. The rope slowly stretched, lowering Copernicus to safety. Ik tossed the rope up one more time. "Just that way. No delay, John!"

Bandicut cinched the rope around his waist and felt it take hold like a boa constrictor. As he turned to climb over, he saw two meerkats peering at him from a boulder. Their eyes gleamed, meeting his. Disconcerted, he lost his grip and slid over the edge. He flailed in the air, dangling from the rope. He floated down until Ik's hands helped him to stand upright.

"You are safe, John Bandicut."

"Mokin' fokin' fr'deekin' hell you say!" he gasped, his heart thundering. "Do you do that all the time?"

"You have been through worse danger, have you not?" Ik asked calmly, coiling up the rope, which had detached itself from both Bandicut's waist and the cliff overhead.

Bandicut grunted. He looked around. They were on an uneven ledge, conceivably the start of a path, but not an easy one. The sun had dropped behind the top of the gorge, and shadows were darkening around them. "Where to now?" he asked, trying to keep his voice even.

Ik pointed across the gorge. "There," he said. "Let us move on."

/// This looks challenging. ///

Bandicut didn't bother answering. Ik was already hiking down the perilously angled ledge, and the robots clicked into motion, following. Bandicut stayed close behind.

There was indeed a path, a difficult one. Daylight was gone by the time they worked their way down the near face of the gorge. Twice again, they used Ik's rope to lower the robots. The third time, they dropped them all the way to the bottom, leaving Ik and Bandicut to make faster progress.

Only starlight illuminated the terrain by the time they reached the stream bed. Ik surveyed the area with his binoculars, then pointed out the route he meant to take, first along the stream bed, then across and up the other side. "In darkness?" Bandicut asked, knowing the answer.

"Quickly," Ik said.

/// Is the darkness a problem? ///
/Well, I don't have lanterns or light augmentation./
/// Maybe I can help. ///

Bandicut felt a tingle in his left wrist, and another tingle behind his eyes. The scene brightened slightly, enough to bring more of the rock features into focus. /That's good, Charlie. That's very good. You're learning this stuff fast./

/// The daughter-stones helped.
And the normalization. ///

"John!" Ik had walked on while he was standing there talking to the quarx.

"Coming!" As he hurried, he saw more meerkats peeking over rocks. They reappeared at intervals as he strode with Ik along the glinting stream.

He wondered if they were trying to tell him something.

They crossed the stream at a narrow point where Ik and Bandicut could jump across without getting their feet wet. The robots simply splashed across. Walking back upstream a short way, Ik paused. "We might wish to sample the water here. And refill our containers."

Bandicut agreed and fished his canteen out of his backpack. Well, here it is, he thought. Time to try the local water. Ik had already knelt and scooped water into his hand. He held it close to his mouth, as though smelling it, then took a taste. After a moment, he drank more deeply. He looked satisfied— which was encouraging, but hardly proof for a human. /How are you doing with those medical studies?/

/// Okay.
I note that the meerkats
are drinking the water, too. ///

Bandicut peered downstream and saw two of the animals crouched at the edge of the stream, lapping at the water. They looked up, their eyes palely luminous, then returned to their drinking.

"It seems fairly pure to me," Ik said. He seemed to understand Bandicut's uncertainty. "I find that I am better able to judge such things since my normalization.'' Ik drew a small, flat pouch out of his vest and immersed it in the stream. After a few moments, he lifted it and sucked experimentally on its corner. He muttered in satisfaction and dunked it back in the water.

Bandicut sighed, knelt, and scooped up some water. He could almost, but not quite, make out his reflection dancing on the stream's moving surface. The water was cold. It looked okay, smelled okay. He tasted it. It tasted okay. Actually it cut his thirst like good beer. He hadn't even realized he was thirsty. He drank a little more, then filled his canteen.

/// Feel okay? ///

/Best water I've tasted in years./

/// Good.
I wasn't sure what I was going to do
if you keeled over. ///

/I thought you said you'd finished your medical training,/ he said, with an edge of alarm.

/// Well, I have a certain
level of familiarity now.
But the normalization already altered
your absorption characteristics,
in much the same way I would have attempted.
It seems to work rather well. ///

/Does that mean I'm immune to poisoning from the water?/

/// Maybe yes, maybe no.
I wouldn't deliberately put it to the test,
if I were you. ///

/Oh./

/// But we'll do the best we can. ///

Ik put away his binoculars and pointed up the steep slope. ''There, John Bandicut. There is the door.''

Bandicut could see nothing but shadows, even with Charlie's light-augment. The cliff was not quite vertical, and looked as though it was crazed with crisscrossing fault lines.

He saw no path, though with the fault marks it was undoubtedly climbable. Preferably in daylight. He took a deep breath. "Whatever you say, Ik."

The Hraachee'an peered at him. "I believe that this may be a—" *rasp* "—changeable door. When we reach it, you must not delay in following me, or we might become separated." Bandicut nodded, and Ik began climbing, hand over hand.

Bandicut watched in amazement as Ik scaled the wall. The Hraachee'an stopped and peered down at him from a perch maybe a quarter of the way up the face. Bandicut felt his breath tighten with a sudden fear that another tornado would come along and sweep them away. Suppose the tornado had been triggered, not by Li-Jared specifically, but by the mere fact of someone approaching the portal.

"John Bandicut—hurry!"

He shook himself. "Shall I start up?"

Ik's rope was already dangling in front of him. He started to wind it around his waist. "John—the robots first!"

"Oh, right," he said dazedly.

/// Your blood sugar seems low.
You should have had something to eat.
I will try to help. ///

Bandicut took a deep breath and bent to wrap the rope around Copernicus. By the time he was done, he felt something like a sugar rush. /Okay, *okay*!/ he murmured dizzily. /Enough!/ He gave the rope a tug. "All right, Ik!"

"Turn the robot, please!"

"Ah." He told Copernicus to face the cliff, as though to drive straight up its face—which, in a sense, was exactly what he wanted it to do. "Go ahead!"

"With you, Cap'—" *Screech*. The rope twanged and tightened, and the robot began a perilous climb up the rocks, grating and bouncing. Bandicut couldn't tell if Ik was doing the pulling, or the rope itself.

Soon the end of the line was dangling in front of him again. "Nappy, you ready?" He turned. "Nappy? Oh, damn!"

Napoleon was crumpled on the ground, his sensors dark. Bandicut knelt and checked the diagnostic panel. It was dead. Either Napoleon had completely run out of power, or something else was very wrong. "Nappy, can you hear me?" Bandicut cursed. The tornado must have broken something internally.

/// Will you leave it? ///

/Like hell I will, Charlie! I might have to carry him on my back, but—/

/// And what then? ///

/How the kr'deekin' hell do I know?/

"John Bandicut—what is the delay?"

"Problem with Napoleon!" he called hoarsely. He passed the rope around the robot, leaving extra on the end, then attached the rest to his own waist. "I'm going to have to come up with him and help him over the rocks. That okay, Ik?"

"Hrrrrrrl. Whenever you're ready."

"Reel us in." Bandicut got the best grip he could on Napoleon and braced his feet against the rocks. He half climbed, half banged against the rocks, rising on the end of the line with the robot just above him. Three-quarters of the way up, his arm got caught between Napoleon and a protruding rock, and he yelped.

Ik peered down. "Are you safe?"

"Yeah!" he gasped, pushing himself from the rock. "Keep going!"

The rope contracted upward. Finally, he heaved Napoleon's crumpled form over the top. It took another effort to get himself up onto solid rock. He gasped, lying in a heap.

"Are you injured?" Ik asked, leaning close.

"My arm hurts. But I don't—"

/// Bruises. Minor laceration.
No breakage of bone. ///

"—think it's broken, though." Bandicut sat up with a grunt and gazed at Napoleon. What the hell was he doing, hauling a dead robot up a cliff?

Ik was probably thinking the same thing. "John Bandicut. Your robot—"

"I know. But I'm not ready to abandon it."

Ik muttered something inaudible and turned to study the cliff face. There was a sizable crevice nearby. Was that the door Li-Jared had gone through? Bandicut squinted, and thought he saw—for an instant—stars shining through the crevice.

"We should not delay." But something in Ik's voice suggested uncertainty.

There was a chittering sound, and three pairs of meerkat eyes glowed in the darkness behind Ik. "Hraah?" Ik sounded startled, but was reluctant to shift his attention from the crevice. The meerkats screeched. Ik looked at them finally, and they fell silent.

Bandicut glanced back and forth. Were the meerkats trying to say something about the crevice? The portal? "Ik, you don't suppose—?" He stared at the meerkats, willing them to speak in words that his translator-stones could understand. The meerkats gazed back at him; then, one after another, they shifted their eyes to the crevice. They *were* trying to communicate. Something had just changed about the crevice, he realized, something in the quality of the light surrounding it. "Try stepping toward it again," he said to Ik.

Ik did so, and the meerkats screeched. "They do not want me to go through."

"Let's wait a moment longer," Bandicut said, eyeing the creatures.

"We are losing time, John."

"I know. But I think they want to help us."

"Why?"

"I can't imagine." Bandicut swallowed and rose to a crouch, hoping that the meerkats would not flee. They didn't. He gently lifted Napoleon, to see how heavy the robot was, as dead weight. Heavy enough. But he could carry it a short distance.

Hiss! Chitter-chitter—SQUEAK!

The meerkats were bobbing their heads excitedly. "Now?" he asked.

Chitter-squeak! SQUEAK!

Bandicut took a breath. "Let's try, Ik."

The Hraachee'an reached into the crevice. His hand seemed to pass through the rock, with a twinkle of starlight. "Urrr, yes. Follow me, John Bandicut." He stepped into the rock and winked out of sight.

Bandicut trembled. "Coppy—*go!*" The wheeled robot spun its wheels on the rock and lurched into the crevice. With a flicker, it winked out of sight. Bandicut took another breath, nodded to the glowing meerkat eyes, and staggered with Napoleon toward the crevice.

Squeak SQUEAK!

"Thanks," he whispered, and fell through. Sparks of light shot in circles around him, and he felt a rush of dizziness. His feet went out from under him on a smooth surface, and he sprawled, losing Napoleon and his balance in one unstoppable movement.

8

THE SHADOW-PEOPLE

/// Are you okay? ///

/I think so. That first step was a bitch./ Bandicut was staring
up at an iridescent ceiling, which flickered with moire patterns that made his eyes pulse. Ceiling? They were indoors?
He pushed himself painfully to a sitting position. Indeed, they
were in a room of some sort, about the size of a typical
human-scale classroom. There was no furniture, but a glassy-
smooth floor and some sloped consoles along one wall. All
the surfaces—ceiling, walls, floor—shone with a pearly iri-
descence.

Ik turned toward him from a silvery window in the far
wall. "Are you all right? I believe we may be near a control
center."

"Good." Bandicut closed his eyes against the shimmering patterns, then opened them to look for a door in the room.
He could see none, nor any sign of the portal that had put them
here.

"The door has closed," Ik remarked, rubbing his chest.
"John Bandicut, your robot looks rather unwell."

"Nappy!" Bandicut scrambled to examine Napoleon,
sprawled on the glassy floor.

Copernicus was there, poking at his partner with a probe.
"Cap'n, Napoleon is not functioning."

"The tornado must have broken something," Bandicut

said. "Shorted out his power supply, maybe. Can you tell anything from the diagnostics?"

The robot clicked. "I am unable to establish a diagnostic link. I can offer no information." Copernicus backed off a short distance.

Grunting, Bandicut opened the only access port he could find that didn't require special tools, a square panel on Napoleon's back. He peered inside, but found nothing. With a sigh, he snapped the panel shut. "I don't know. I hate to say it, Coppy, but we might have to leave him behind. I don't know what else to do. I'm sorry."

Copernicus drumtapped haltingly.

/// I can't help noticing.
"Him"? Napoleon? ///

/Well, he feels like a person to me. I feel as if I'm abandoning him. Killing him, if he's not already dead./

Bandicut left Napoleon and walked over to the window Ik had been looking through. It appeared opaque to him, but he did see his own reflection, and the face he saw shocked him. He had left *Neptune Explorer*—what, less than two days ago, though it seemed much longer. The eyes peering back at him seemed much older. Were they wiser, or just tired and scared? He didn't know. They were the eyes of a poor sap cut off from everything he'd ever known, flung across the galaxy and left for dead, inhabited by an alien mind, altered by alien technologies, with an alien for a friend. What the hell was he supposed to think? Except that it was lonely here. Damned lonely . . .

/// It sounds depressing
when you think of it that way. ///

/It is depressing, Charlie. I don't know who I am anymore. I don't even know who my robots are./ Staring at his reflection, he realized something else. He hadn't grown any stubble since leaving the ship. Had the "normalization" stopped his beard growth?

/// It's possible. If the
system noticed your efforts at trimming,

*it might have judged that you desired your beard
inactivated. ///*

Bandicut grunted in annoyance. /They could have asked
me first./ He sighed and returned to Napoleon. His heart ached
at the thought of leaving the robot behind. But there was really
no point in dragging him any farther. Was there?

"John Bandicut, it is possible we might find places to recharge or—" *rasp* "—rejuvenate your robot."

Bandicut looked up in surprise. "You think so? I don't
know what's wrong with him. It might be more serious than
just needing a recharge." /Charlie, I just thought of something. Could your translator-stones do anything for him?/

*/// Perhaps. Not directly,
I don't think.
But if we could get him to a place
where the stones could intercede . . . ///*

/You mean, like, communicate with a repair service?/

/// Something like that. ///

Ik was speaking, and it took him a second to catch up. "I
cannot . . . brrrik-k-k . . . be certain. But if it is important to
you, can you carry the robot?"

Bandicut pursed his lips. "Not very far. Coppy! Could
you carry Napoleon, if I strapped him onto your back?"

Copernicus drumtapped. "Certainly, Cap'n."

"What's your power status?"

"Seventy-two percent, including reserves."

"Good. Come here." Bandicut lifted Napoleon and
draped him awkwardly over Copernicus's back. Copernicus
clicked and whirred, trying to hold the other robot in place
with two of his gripper arms, but he couldn't quite manage.
Bandicut looked up to see Ik holding out his coiled rope. He
took it gratefully. As he wound the rope around the two robots, he suddenly peered into Coppy's sensor-eyes. "You
gave me your power level differently this time."

"Cap'n?"

"You said, seventy-two percent *including* reserves."

"Yes, Cap'n."

"Mind if I ask why?"

"Well, I—wished to sound optimistic, Cap'n."

Bandicut blinked. "Optimistic?"

"Sixty-seven percent, plus reserves, would not have sounded as encouraging. Cap'n."

Bandicut stared at the machine.

"Is that acceptable?" said Copernicus.

"Yeah," he said slowly. "Just as long as we're clear on what we're telling each other." He rose. /I guess./

"I should tell you," said Ik. "I do not immediately see how we are going to leave this room."

"Ah. Do you know where we are?"

"Not precisely, no. I must take time to examine these consoles. Perhaps you should rest. We may yet have a long way to travel."

Bandicut was, in fact, exhausted. He shuffled around for a moment, circling like a dog preparing to lie down, and finally stretched out on the hard, glassy floor. He was surprised to feel it give a little, under his weight. Before he could think about it much, he was asleep.

Ik did not rest immediately. He studied the consoles for a while, before concluding that he could do nothing without the correct access protocols. But he recognized the consoles' type, and thought he knew in very general terms where they were now, which was something, at least. He believed they had traveled a considerable distance from the tornado plain; but he did not think they had left the continent.

Was Li-Jared still ahead of them? That was the question. Ik had discovered no sign of his presence here. But Ik imagined that after watching that tornado dive upon him, Li-Jared would have been reluctant to linger in any one place without some assurance of safety. So even if he *had* been here, he probably had moved on at once.

Which meant that he must have found the way out of this room. Ik, for the moment, was stymied on that count; but he wasn't unduly worried. Either the portal would reappear and take them to another location, or they would find a way to the other side of this window. He couldn't see much through it—

the pane seemed to pass only a narrow wavelength band—but it did look like a corridor of some kind beyond. Where there was a corridor, there should be civilized activity not too far off. Ik made a slow circuit of the room, lightly touching the walls with his fingertips. He felt no response, no tickle, from his voice-stones. If there was anything here for them to connect to, it was apparently inactive. Very well, then—if he could not pursue Li-Jared, he would use the time to collect his thoughts.

There was much that he did not understand here, but he did have a kind of faith about things, based on his experience. He and Li-Jared had been separated and reunited several times in the two turns of seasons they had been friends. It was as if they were caught up by eddies curling around a great invisible whirlpool, and drawn back, time and again, to help each other in times of need. Was it random chance, or intentional manipulation? Ik couldn't say for sure, though he had his suspicions. But one thing he was sure of was that someone wanted something from Li-Jared and him. And now apparently from John Bandicut, as well. What that something was, he didn't know.

Several times he and Li-Jared, who in the beginning had had nothing visibly in common except their stones and their status as exiles, had found themselves plunged together into circumstances of dire need—not their own but someone else's. They had never been able to say no to the need—and their presence had always made a difference, to someone. But quite apart from the sense that his life was no longer entirely his own, Ik had often felt that something else was missing from the picture; something was incomplete in the way he and Li-Jared struggled to find their way here. He felt, certainly, an infuriating sense of ignorance about their role in this world, and the identity of those who determined it. But now he wondered: was John Bandicut a missing piece of their destiny on Shipworld, someone they had not known they needed until he arrived?

Ik sat crosslegged on the floor, and studied Bandicut. The human was stretched out flat, in a deep meditative trance. It was apparent that Bandicut and Ik had knowledge and skills to offer one another, though the role of those metal creatures was less clear. Ik rather liked his excitable human companion, but he could not help wondering: did Bandicut have even the slightest inkling of what he had gotten himself into, by joining with Ik? The complexity and uncertainty, the frustration, the risk?

Probably not. And perhaps that was just as well. It was not as if Bandicut would be better off alone. Ik rubbed his fingertips on his chest and murmured softly to himself. These questions could not be resolved now. And it was time he, too, took some meditative rest.

Something startled Bandicut awake: a dream about walking . . . through duststorms and whirlwinds, with voices chittering at him to walk faster, faster . . .

He blinked awake and sat up, wincing. He had a painful stiffness in his back. Ik was sitting nearby, eyes closed. It took Bandicut a moment to remember where he was; and when it all came back to him, he didn't feel a lot better. They were in a room, somewhere. Trapped. And he needed a bathroom. Badly. He wondered what people used for bathrooms around here.

/// Let me pose the question to the stones.
In the meantime, I believe you've been given
greater endurance in that area. ///

/Swell./ He got up and walked the perimeter of the room, running his hand along the wall. At the beginning of the third wall, he was startled when a large oval dematerialized, revealing a cubicle beyond. /What's this?/

/// Um, I think it's a bathroom. ///

He stared suspiciously into the enclosure. Finally he stepped cautiously inside, and glanced back at once. The opening was obscured by a shimmering translucency. /So where's the—you know, plumbing?/

/// Turn around. ///

He did, and saw a haze of light dancing around him, with sparkles and swirls. After a moment, he felt a certain kind of *relief.* Then the lights faded. Was it measuring him for a custom-made commode?

/// *Uh, John?* ///

/Yeah?/

/// *Do you still have to go?* ///

He blinked. /Oh. I get it, you mean we're done?/

/// *Pretty good system, huh?*
I mean, when you have who knows how many
different species to service. ///

He gaped around in amazement. /Uh, yeah, I guess. As long as they don't take the wrong thing out. If you know what I mean./ He stepped out of the cubicle, and found Ik waiting. "Your turn," he said wryly.

"Hraah."

While he waited for Ik, Bandicut took a bite from his carbonut bar and swallowed some water from his bottle. Then he stood at the window and cupped his eyes to the silvery surface. He could make out vague geometric forms of light, but not much more. As he pressed his hands to the pane, his wrists touched the glass. It suddenly turned opaque. But beside it stood an open rectangular doorway. Surprised, he leaned through the door. A wide corridor of shimmering light stretched away as far as the eye could see. The doorway was located at the elbow of a sharp bend in the corridor. "Whoa!"

"You have found the way out!" Ik exclaimed, emerging from the bathroom.

"I guess so." Bandicut pulled his head back in. "But the way out to where?"

Ik stepped into the doorway to look. "I do not know. But if Li-Jared was here, then he most likely went out this way. And we must follow."

"Yeah. But Ik? What if he *didn't* come this way?"

Ik clacked his mouth. "Because of the changes in the portal? That is possible. But in that case, I know no other way to follow him, except to press onward. But recall your own belief that the meerkats were guiding us."

Bandicut remembered, and felt a sudden weight of responsibility. They didn't really *know* what the meerkats had in mind. He had trusted them, but purely by instinct.

Ik was gazing at him, eyes gleaming, perhaps guessing his thoughts. "John Bandicut, you should know—there is something about this world that—" *Rasp. Rasp.* He seemed to struggle with his thoughts. "Something that brings people together in unexpected ways. Eddies, or—" *rasp* "—turbulence. I cannot explain it. But—"

Bandicut stared at him, remembering the chaos calculators of the translator back on Triton, which had worked their way through seemingly infinitely complex calculations to find the cometary danger to Earth—and in consequence, had brought him here. Had all that happened by coincidence?

"Li-Jared and I have been separated before. But we have always found our way back together. Despite the very great magnitude of this world." Ik's eyes closed, and opened again, like some great lizard's.

"Then I guess we should go this way," Bandicut agreed. He decided not to mention the coincidence that had brought Ik along to Bandicut and his robots just when he was needed.

/// Mm. Indeed. ///

"Very well. Are you ready?"

Bandicut hoisted his backpack onto Copernicus, and secured it along with the other robot. "Can you carry all this?"

Copernicus drumtapped and rolled forward to join Ik in the open doorway.

"Have you learned anything at all about this place?" he asked Ik.

"Only that I think I know the *type* of place that it is." Stepping out into the corridor, Ik peered both ways.

Bandicut felt a rush of amazement as a bright, streaming light washed over him. It was like stepping into a holo special effect, and much brighter than it had seemed from the doorway. Liquid streamers of light rippled along both walls, conveying an impression of endless, high-speed movement around the bend in the corridor. The corridor was oval in cross-section, the walls curving up to an apex, where a darker strip with lighted cross-hatchings ran its length. Bandicut started to feel dizzy. It looked like a *long* corridor; the ribbons of light seemed to converge toward infinity.

Ik was studying the view in both directions, using his sighting glasses. Bandicut could see little to distinguish the two directions, but Ik murmured, "We can only go—hrrm, one way, if we wish to make any speed."

"Why's that?"

Ik swept his hand to the right. "It's a one-way transport field. There is probably another, somewhere, going the other way."

It was not just an optical illusion, then. Bandicut wondered if they ought to be on the lookout for speeding vehicles. Were they at risk, as pedestrians?

"I do not believe Li-Jared would have set out against the direction of flow, unless he had a specific reason."

"You think he was here, then?"

"I cannot be sure." Ik rubbed his chest. "But this looks like the sort of transport that might take us to . . . a control unit. He would expect me to look for him in such a place." Ik handed the binoculars to Bandicut.

He peered through the lenses, and found them perfectly focused down the streaming, psychedelic sightline of the corridor. He felt the magnification click up, and up, and up—each time revealing a dimmer and more distant stretch of the corridor—until, at last, it centered on a cluster of tiny, flickering, sparks of light *very* far down the corridor. Despite the distance, he imagined an intensity in the pulsations and color changes in the sparks.

/// That view!
It reminds me of something! ///

The quarx sounded breathless. With fear? Or excitement?

/Is it something that I ought to know about?/
/// I don't know.
I feel a great . . . pull toward it.
I want to go that way. ///

/Um./ He asked Ik, "What is that, way down there?"

"I cannot say for sure. But there is activity, at least. I think it wise to proceed that way."

Bandicut handed the binoculars back. "We're with you."

Ik snapped the binocs shut and tucked them away in his belt. Then he stood at the righthand edge of the corridor. He *hrrm*'d for a moment, brushing his fingers along the wall. His fingertips disappeared into the ripples of light, scattering silvery sparks into the light-slipstream. "Put your hand here."

Bandicut hesitated, his hand half extended.

/// Are you afraid of it? ///

/Mokin' foke. I don't want to be electrocuted./

/// It's safe, I think. ///

/You think./ Bandicut followed Ik's example, and felt a tingle.

"And—touch the robot."

"Coppy?" When the robot rolled closer, he put his other hand on top of its metal shell. A moment later, Copernicus extended a manipulator arm into the lightstream.

"Now . . . *think* about . . . traveling down the corridor." Ik turned and faced downstream.

"What do you—?" Bandicut began, but didn't finish, because the floor beneath him began flowing like a pool of molten mercury, and he was gliding silently forward, as if on skates. "Uh—" He looked up from his feet and was stunned to see Ik a considerable distance ahead of him, accelerating down the corridor. "Coppy?" he called, glancing over his shoulder. The robot was gliding right behind him. "Ohkaaay." With the flicker of a wish, he felt himself speeding up, with no sensation of friction, to keep pace with Ik.

The cross-hatchings in the ceiling flickered, then blurred with acceleration.

The corridor was a lot longer than he had guessed, even peering through the binocs. Judging by their apparent speed, it must have been hundreds of kilometers long. Periodically the streamers of light split apart like vertically-separated rail spurs, bracketing long stretches of window between them. The windows were darkened, but he caught glimpses through them of arcs of light and shadow. It gave him a sense of great, machinelike shapes and blazing discharges of energy, as though he were speeding along the overlook of a vast, mysterious factory.

Perhaps they were. Ik, alongside him, remarked, "There are many such sectors in this continent. It is a very large place, and there is much to be constructed and maintained."

"Do you have any idea what that is over there?"

"Who knows? A power system? A continent-bridge? A star-spanner? Who can say?" A moment later, Ik leaned back against an invisible support and closed his eyes.

Bandicut stared in disbelief at his friend, snoozing as they flew headlong down the corridor of light. He was hoping for another glimpse of a window; but when none came after a minute or so, he hesitantly leaned back himself, and found that he could float quite comfortably as though in a reclining chair. After a moment, he closed his own eyes. No harm in resting a little, he thought. God knew he was in no danger of falling asleep.

He blinked his eyes open with a start. He didn't know what had awakened him, but he felt a tingle in his wrists. Both daughter-stones were flickering visibly.

*/// They're recharging themselves
from the transport field. ///*

/Oh,/ he thought dazedly. He thought he could see something sparkling ahead.

"Slowing," Ik said.

The cross-hatch blur overhead began to flicker again as they decelerated. The sparkles far ahead were visible to the naked eye now, but hard to gaze at for long. They reminded Bandicut of the tortured view he had once had of the translator back on Triton, and the feeling that the translator had seemed to exist on a different plane of space-time from his own. He recalled thinking that it looked like an atom's eye view of a nuclear reaction. This thing ahead was like that, too.

/// Yes . . . ///

the quarx whispered, transfixed.

As they drew closer, he began to imagine that he saw

shapes moving in the display: shadowy upright forms walking in otherworldly, flickering flames. /Shadrach in the fire,/ he muttered suddenly.

/// Say again? ///

/Shadrach in the fire. And—what were their names? I forget. Old Testament story./

/// What's an Old Testament? ///

/The Bible, you know? There's this story about these God-fearing guys who were thrown into a furnace by an evil king, because they wouldn't worship him./

/// Ah. And did they burn up? ///

/No. That was the good part. They walked around without getting a whisker singed. Those shadows up there remind me of the story. I wonder what they are./

/// People, I think. Shadow-people.
John, this is really . . . ///

The quarx sounded lightheaded, faint.

/What, Charlie?/

/// . . . resonating. ///

/Yeah?/ Bandicut squinted. The shadowy figures were becoming starker, and really were starting to look like people. Not human, necessarily, but people. "Ik?" he started to ask.

"Hrrrm," said the Hraachee'an. "I think we are about to meet the local—" *rasp* "—maintenance crew."

They glided in like a train into a station. Before he knew it, they were surrounded by pulsing lights, and his skin tingled as though he were too close to lightning. Then they were surrounded by the shadow-figures, twitching like jerky animation characters as they floated to a stop. The shadow-people were dark and angular; up close they looked scarcely humanoid at all—more like clusters of fluttering black triangles stuck together like leaves. They looked like a surrealistic holo ad.

"Ik?" Bandicut murmured. "Do you know how to talk to them?"

"I will try." Ik turned to two of the shadow-people, his hands opened but held close to his chest.

The shadow-people rustled and made vaguely musical sounds. One of them turned toward the other, and as it turned, showed an almost two-dimensional aspect. They nearly vanished when they turned sideways, and Bandicut had the unsettling feeling that something had *twisted* dimensionally in his plane of sight. Almost as if they were . . .

/// Fractionally dimensional.

Yes, ///

Charlie whispered.

/Ah./

Ik said something that Bandicut didn't catch. The rasp of his stones indicated that they hadn't quite caught it, either.

The two shadow-people turned and twisted, and said something that sounded like a violin being tuned. *Wheeewhooo.* They seemed to quiver and almost contract out of existence, then expand again.

Ik said something else. *Rasp.*

The stones were trying, but getting nowhere.

It was unclear whether the shadow-people were understanding his words. After a moment, they swiveled and nearly vanished, then reappeared and sort of *slid* down the corridor a short distance toward a cluster of more shadow-people. Ik gestured to Bandicut with a sweep of his hand. They followed the shadow-people, Copernicus whirring behind.

/You said this was—resonating, Charlie?/

/// Yes, ///

the quarx said dreamily.

/What's it remind you of?/

He felt the quarx struggling to gather memories, powerful memories. They were too blurred for him to understand.

/// It's the kind of people they are.

John, they're fractal-beings.

Like me. ///

Charlie spoke with a startling wistfulness.

Bandicut blinked and shivered, despite himself. */They*

spook the hell out of me. I wonder if we affect them the same way./

/// They seem spooked by something.
But I wonder if it's us. ///

Ik was approaching the cluster of shadow-people, with Bandicut about four steps behind. Ik started to say something, but was interrupted by a sound of violins being struck in sharp ascending notes. *Whreeek! Whreeek! Whreeek!* Black triangles twisted and waved in agitation.

"Ik—what is it?" Bandicut realized he was hanging back a little, and wasn't sure if it was out of deference or fear.

Rasp. R-rasp. "Not . . . trouble . . . meaning." He caught a halting rendition of Ik's voice, apparently directed not at Bandicut but at the shadow-people. Bandicut suddenly understood something: his comprehension of Ik's speech was aided not just by his own stones, but by a link with Ik's stones. And right now, Ik's stones were busy trying to talk to the shadow-people.

Whatever Ik had said, it didn't seem to make the shadow-people happy. They came back with more violin shrieks, and one of them fluttered toward Ik. The Hraachee'an backpedaled hastily.

Bandicut ducked out of the way, wondering what the hell was going on.

Rasp. Rasp.

Whreeek! Whreeek! Whreeek!

Ik raised his arms, waving them across each other. "No—no—didn't—" He was trying to dissuade them of something, but wasn't succeeding. The shadow-people fluttered their triangles, and one of them, who seemed taller and more sharply angular than the others, floated toward Ik. It swept an arm of triangles at Ik, and the Hraachee'an tumbled backward to the floor.

That was enough for Bandicut. "WHAT THE HELL ARE YOU DOING?" he yelled, ducking away from the shadow-person's reach. The being paused, and drew back a meter or so. Furious, Bandicut crouched beside his friend. Ik looked stunned, but unharmed.

/// *They seem angry about something.*
But I can't tell what. ///

Before he could say a word, his thoughts were obliterated by a thundering, crackling, rocket-exhaust sound—followed by a bone-shaking *BOOOOOM-M-M!*

9

FACTORY FLOOR

BANDICUT DUCKED INSTINCTIVELY, half shielding Ik with his body. When there was no further concussion, he looked up, trying to see what was going on. *"Coppy! Can you tell what—?"*

He was interrupted by a chorus of violin cries, and the sight of the shadow-people fleeing down the corridor like leaves on a whirlwind. They vanished through a curtain of pulsing light.

"Cap'n!" Copernicus called, his voice tinny against the din. "It came from ahead of us!"

Ik struggled to his feet. "That may have had something to do with Li-Jared! They seemed angry about him. We must follow!" With that, Ik set off at a run after the shadow-people.

"Let's go!" Bandicut cried hoarsely to Copernicus.

He half expected to be electrocuted when they passed through the pulsing barrier of light, and he did feel a momentary wave of dizziness. Then he felt himself shunted away from the corridor into a wide, gloomy, kidney-shaped space full of shadow-people and incomprehensible objects that looked like sculptures on pedestals. Shadow-people were fluttering from pedestal to pedestal, their cries changing timbre and rising and falling through the musical scales.

"—control station!" Ik was exclaiming.

Bandicut turned around in bewilderment. Were those pedestals consoles? For controlling what? He turned the other way, and his breath went out with a rush. A broad window had appeared on his left, carving a swath through the undulating shape of the wall. Through the window, arcs of lightning were jumping among vast, dark shapes of machinery. The factory. Did these consoles control the factory?

*/// I believe the shadow-people may be
in charge of the factory floor. ///*

Through the window, he thought he glimpsed billows of smoke, and a flicker of flame.

"They are very angry!" Ik cried, stepping to his side. "They believe Li-Jared caused that!"

"What do you mean? *How?* Ik, what's happening out there?"

"He may have tried—urrrm, who can say? I need to find out—or connect with—"

Ik was interrupted by a loud screech of tearing metal. A heartbeat later, Bandicut realized that it was the shadow-people, or perhaps the consoles speaking *to* the shadow-people. They were growing more agitated than ever, and about half of them began crowding into an angled recess near the window. With a rippling flash, something seemed to open in the wall, and the group of shadow-people was gone.

Ik strode toward the tallest of the remaining shadow-people. It looked like the same one who had knocked him flat a minute ago. *Rasp* "—try to help!"

Whruueeeek! The shadow-person shook the fluttering shadow-leaves of one arm—it seemed to have three or four arms—and danced away from Ik toward a nearby pedestal. It, or he, seemed to be the leader—the foreman, maybe—of the factory crew. And he didn't look too happy about Ik's and Bandicut's presence.

*/// I'm beginning to get a sense about this.
They're scared, really scared,
of whatever's gone wrong.
They clearly suspect that
we had something to do with
the malfunction. ///*

/Well, Ik thinks Li-Jared did!/

/// I don't think that's what he— ///

The quarx's words were drowned out by another crackling roar, like the one that had preceded the explosion. Bandicut braced himself for another explosion, but the roar tapered off. The foreman-shadow spun away from the control pedestal. *Heeeeuu! Heeee-r-r-ruu!* It waved a cluster of leaves at Ik, who had stepped up to another pedestal.

Bandicut felt a twinge in his right wrist. ". . . infection . . . control . . . (bad bad) . . ." He blinked. What was that?

Rasp "—trying to help!" Ik barked.

Hriike! Hriike! ". . . other said . . . (bad bad) . . ."

/I'm not following./

/// The stones are starting to get a handle
on the violin-talk. ///

"John, there's a control malfunction out in the factory!" Ik shouted. "If Li-Jared ran afoul of something—"

Hriike! Hriike! Hreeeee! ". . . (bad bad) . . . danger . . . deaths . . ." The foreman-shadow danced threateningly toward Ik.

Ik made urgent sweeping gestures with his hands. *Rasp.* "—trying to find out—would not purposely do such a thing— never!"

"*What* wouldn't he do?" Bandicut cried, turning between the Hraachee'an and the foreman-shadow. "What's gone wrong?"

The floor shook, and there was a deep *KER-CHUNNNNK!* that sounded like an enormous brace collapsing. The foreman-shadow cried out like violin strings breaking, and with a frantic wave swept most of the other shadow-people toward the recess where the first group had vanished. There was another flash, then they too were gone. The remaining three shadow-people hugged close to the consoles near the window.

"My God, Ik—*what's happening?*"

Ik touched the control pedestal, and for a few seconds, an atomic fire danced in his face. He looked dazed as he turned to Bandicut. "I believe the malfunction is spreading. I cannot decipher enough to be certain, but I think it was caused by the contamination that I told you of."

Bandicut stared at Ik, open-mouthed. "The thing that caused the tornado, and the ice attack? Then what are we—oh, Ik, no." This was way out of Bandicut's league. Ik was going to intervene, to try to undo whatever it was that his friend Li-Jared might have done that had set off a new round of destruction. "Ik, you aren't proposing we go up against that thing, are you?"

"The shadow-people call it the—" *rasp* "—demon— bogey—" *rasp rasp*.

Bandicut could feel his translator-stones spinning through his thoughts, trying to find the right word.

"—the—" *rasp* "—boojum." Ik snapped his mouth shut and turned to look out the window.

Boojum.

/// ??? ///

Bandicut's mind was reeling. /Look under "fairy tales," Charlie. The boojum was the deadliest kind of snark. This can't be real./

Ik turned back. "It may be aware of us, as well."

"Aware of *us?*" Bandicut stared out the window at irregularly erupting flames.

"It seems that the boojum has seized control from the shadow-people. They are terrified of what it is doing, but they can't seem to stop it." Ik peered back out the window.

/ Hell's bells./ Bandicut turned, hesitantly, toward the consoles.

/// What are you going to do? ///

/ I don't know. This has to be some sort of—I just thought maybe I should have a look at the console. It's probably just a big datanet, right?/

With a strange mixture of confidence and desperation, he stepped to the nearest pedestal. The object mounted on top of it was neither a sculpture nor a console screen; however, within certain of its concave surfaces he found himself peering into places of deep and somehow distorted darkness—as though they were not quite part of this physical continuum. He felt a cold breeze ripple up his spine as he brushed his fingers over the surface. He couldn't quite discern the surface; his fingers slid off without any sensation of touch. But his gaze was caught. And now there were sparkling points of light down in the twisted darkness, and whispering voices that he could not quite understand. But he could not turn away from them.

His wrists burned.

/// The stones are trying . . . ///

He shuddered, echoes reverberating of his melding with the translator back on Triton. But these voices were different; they chittered and shrieked coldly. He felt unwelcome here. But they were far from being in complete harmony; he was aware of many voices, controlling myriad systems and subsystems, and they were not all in agreement, not at all. They were screeching, crying, pattering, whispering, drumming.

Nothing was clear, except certain unmistakable currents of *power* that ran through this thing he had touched. And he slowly became aware that he was dangerously close to getting in the way of that power . . .

"Hraaachhh! John Bandicut!"

Something was pulling on his arm. Ik. Bandicut struggled to wrench his eyes from the console. He felt one of those voices reaching up, catching, and tugging at his thoughts. It held him for an instant of glaring scrutiny, then let go—but not before he felt the thing identify and *recognize* him. As it released him, shivering, he broke the contact and backed away from the console, reeling dizzily. That thing he had just touched was overriding all of the safety controls out in the factory.

He didn't know what it was. But he knew this: he had just revealed himself to something within the system, something that hadn't quite known him before, something . . . malevolent.

"John! Come!" Ik pulled him over to the window. The remaining three shadow-people were fluttering like unhappy bats at their presence, but Ik rasped something sharp at them, and they kept their distance.

Bandicut tried to see what was happening beyond the window, but it was like trying to pick out a landscape at night by flickering lightning. Smoke. Shadows. Strobelike flashes.

When they were gone, he did not know what he had seen.

"We must go through," Ik said.

"Why? What can we do?"

"We must try to correct the malfunction. Li-Jared went that way, and something went wrong as he passed. He may have been trying to prevent it! But this is stronger than he was!"

The boojum. Bandicut shivered, remembering the presence he had just revealed himself to. He stared through the window, trembling with fear. *What am I doing mixed up in this?* he thought. "Ik, I don't even know what that is out there."

"I understand. You need not come. But I must go." Ik strode to the place where the shadow-people had disappeared. The remaining shadow-people quivered, but did not interfere. Ik peered about, looking for a way to actuate the doorway. "I could certainly use your help, though."

Groaning, Bandicut waved Copernicus over. He studied the wall. /Any ideas?/

/// *Try pressing your right-wrist stone there.* ///

Bandicut felt a twinge as he touched the wall. A flash of light made him blink, and he was aware of something opening, and closing, and then he was standing in near-darkness.

They were on an immense platform that jutted out from a wall into a space of gargantuan proportions—a cavern of darkness broken by eye-searing flashes of light, and resonating with ominous booms. Bandicut shaded his eyes. It was the same view they had seen from the window, but enormously magnified in intensity. The flashes fleetingly illuminated an astoundingly long, convoluted structure that stretched from right to left as far as the eye could see. He could not begin to guess what it was.

On his left, he saw fluttering black shapes, almost invisible except when a strobelike flash lit the place. Ik strode toward them.

Whreeeek! Whreeeek! Whreeeek!

Bandicut could barely hear the shadow-people over the

general din, and he couldn't hear Ik talking to them at all. /Mokin' A, Charlie, what *is* this place?/

"*John Bandicut!*" Ik shouted. "There are explosions on the factory floor! It's got to be shut down!"

As he followed Ik across the platform, his eyes seemed to adjust to the contrast of light and dark. The shadow-people were clustered on the extreme left, with more of them fluttering down a series of ramps beyond the edge of the platform. Out in the mammoth cavern, Bandicut was beginning to make out more clearly the outlines of immense machinery, though it was still etched in shadow and strobe. Tremendous electrical discharges repeatedly shattered the darkness, but the effect was dimmed now, as if he were wearing dark glasses. /Are you doing that?/ he murmured, trying to comprehend the scene.

/// Does it help? ///

/Yeah, but I still can't make sense of it. For all I know, they could be building a starship in here./ The sense of enormity nearly overwhelmed his senses.

//// Bigger than that, I think.
I'll bet Ik was right.
It might be a star-spanner. ///

Before he could ask the quarx to elaborate, he saw a gout of fire below the edge of the platform, jumping and spreading, and billowing clouds of smoke. Only a little of the smoke reached the platform, but it had the biting, acrid smell of a chemical blaze. "Ik!" he coughed, backing away from the edge. "What are you going to do?"

Ik scanned the scene with his binoculars, not answering.

A group of the shadow-people fluttered off the platform and down a spindly walkway that seemed suspended from nothing. *Whreeek! Whreeek!* The foreman-shadow glided toward Ik, shaking his triangle hands.

Ik lowered his binocs and gestured. Whatever he said was lost in the din.

Bandicut suddenly noticed Copernicus moving dangerously close to the edge of the platform. He stepped forward to call the robot back. As he peered over the edge, he glimpsed an immense, bottomless well, a tremendously wide shaft dropping away into infinity. His knees almost buckled at the sight. The shaft was half-obscured by flame and smoke, but far below, it was luminous with ghostly plasmas, glowing gases writhing upward in spirals. A great flame billowed out, closer to Bandicut, obscuring the view. But he'd seen enough to give him a sudden intuition that whatever that great shaft was, there was something wrong inside it—something in the way the plasma was surging upward. The nearer flames were bad enough; but if all that plasma energy far below were loosed upward in a single, great conflagration . . . The prospect terrified him.

Much closer below, but lit by the glow of the plasma, he glimpsed shadow-people streaking along an access path. They seemed to be running toward the fire.

/// They must be trying to reach
a local control substation
to shut things down. ///

/But if they couldn't stop it from that control room—/
/// Something must have been blocking them. ///

Bandicut's thoughts were interrupted by Ik backing into him. The Hraachee'an was pointing down, shouting something to the foreman-shadow. "Control there, near the—" *rasp* "—tube!"

Hreeek! ". . . Yes! . . ." *Hreeek! Hreeek!*

So there were, indeed, control substations down there. Bandicut squinted down into the dizzying emptiness, and caught a faceful of smoke. Flames erupted below, rising not quite to the height of the platform, but high enough to send him reeling backward, coughing violently. He had glimpsed shadow-people on a catwalk down there, dangerously close to the flames. He blinked smoke from his tearing eyes. "What are they trying to do?" he yelled, coughing.

The foreman-shadow fluttered around him, like a family of bats wheeling about his head. *Skeeeuuuuuuuu!* the foreman-shadow wailed, close to his ear.

Charlie did something to interpret, and a visual image unfolded in his mind: three streaks of light like pointers, marking separate locations below the position of that team of shadow-people. Was that where the control units were? He got just enough of a look to make his head swim.

A moment later, somewhere in the middle of the dark well below, he saw a great circle of plasma shiver free of the cylinder wall and begin rippling upward. The sight made him freeze like a deer in a spotlight. The glowing gases moved *fast*, and when they erupted from the top of the plasma tube, a powerful burst of flame shot out from somewhere beneath the platform, fanned upward by the plasma stream. Bandicut crouched for cover, but not before he saw the accessway below—and the shadow-people on it—curl and shrivel in the flame. Then it flashed up past the platform with a roar that sent all of them reeling back to the wall.

When the blast subsided, the air was filled with a keening *Skrreeeeee! Skrreeeeee!* Bandicut and Ik staggered to their feet and returned cautiously to the edge. The foreman-shadow was wailing and swinging his triangle-hands in grief, or fury. The accessway below was gone, and the shadow-people with it. The foreman-shadow screeched, then darted off the left side of the platform, leading the remaining group of his people down another pathway.

Bandicut stared after them, stunned. He felt as if it had been humans who had died moments ago. He felt Charlie struggling to say something, but the quarx was shaking in the shelter of his mind, even more affected than he was by the deaths of the shadow-people. /Charlie, I—/ He couldn't speak either.

With an urgent cry, Ik herded them to the right, opposite the way the foreman-shadow and the others had gone. The flames cast enough light for Bandicut to make out a spiderweb of catwalks. Below, something seemed to be drawing the fire down into the huge plasma tube, which was flashing ominously.

Ik pointed. "We must go that way! As Li-Jared did!"

Bandicut stared at him, dumbfounded.

"They chased him away, but he must have been trying to

help. There must be a way to a control unit around all this." Ik paced along the right-hand edge of the platform, studying the layout.

"Ik, if the shadow-people can't—"

His words were drowned out by a series of ear-numbing *thuds,* like artillery bursts. Bandicut heard Ik's next words through an after-rumble. "They think we and Li-Jared—" There were more bursts. Ik urged him toward a narrow ramp against the wall. It slanted down toward a maze of walkways that appeared suspended from air and darkness. Bandicut tried to yell a question to Ik. But Ik kept pointing. "Hurry!"

Bandicut trotted down the ramp. Copernicus was behind him, his left wheels barely on the walkway, Napoleon and Bandicut's bag swaying precariously on his back. Ik followed Coppy. "I told them we would try here!"

Bandicut nodded and kept going. He was terrified of losing his balance. The ramp intersected a wider walkway, which extended out from the wall. They were now suspended in the air, well off to the side of the platform. At the next intersection, Ik pointed down, and they descended, switching back and forth, until Bandicut was completely disoriented. Flames billowed some distance away. He glanced up, and was stunned to see a black mass above them. They were well below the platform, in the abyss of darkness. He had no idea where the shadow-people had gotten to. "Ik, if you know where we're going," he gasped, "why don't you take the lead?"

"Hraahh! I fear you may stumble, or pause, and I won't see you."

Bandicut drew a shuddering breath. "Yeah," he said, and plunged on downward. Thunderbolts flashed in the distance, but from here at least, he could no longer see the plasma tube.

His relief was short-lived. He turned out onto a spindly, swaying catwalk, and after about ten meters, glanced down and saw billowing tongues of fire, clouds of smoke, and luminous plasma ghosts shimmering below him. He sucked a breath, every muscle in his body clenching.

"*Hrrrrrlll!* Come back!"

Twisting fearfully, he saw Ik and Copernicus back at the last intersection. The catwalk was too narrow for the robot. He choked as smoke wafted into his face. He tried to turn around, but the catwalk shook too much. There was nothing but a thin guide wire for safety, and it felt as if it would shred his hands if he gripped it too tightly. He would have to trust to his balance. He took a step backward, and another . . .

By the time he was back with Ik and Copernicus, his legs were buckling. He gasped and waved Ik onward, then followed Copernicus. He practically kept his eyes shut for the next few minutes. He tried to emulate Coppy's fearlessness, but that was beyond him. The only thing that kept him going was terror of being left behind.

At last Ik pointed to their goal, still below them: a large vertical structure like a pillar, rising from darkness below to darkness above. Encircling it was a small platform. And on the platform was something on a pedestal. A control unit.

He still couldn't see how to get there from here, so he wasn't ready to count it in their grasp. They were completely unprotected from the plasma tube and the flames, just like the shadow-people who had been destroyed. He glanced around through the murky darkness, trying to locate the foreman-shadow and his workers. Against the massive bulk of dark machinery, the strobing arcs, and the ghostly fire of the plasma, he had no hope. But Ik was peering through his binocs, to the left. ''There!'' Ik shouted, pointing toward a nest of spindly walkways on the far side of the plasma tube. Bandicut was amazed to see several moving black spots against an eruption of flames. The flames seemed to be blocking the shadow-people's path. The spots retreated in another direction, and he lost sight of them.

/// *They're trying to do the same thing we are.* ///

Bandicut grunted—and lunged forward in terror as a flame blossomed behind him, enveloping the walkway he had just crossed. He followed Ik and Copernicus over a long catwalk, all the way across to the massive pillar that Ik had pointed to. Looking down, he could see, against the glow of the plasma, a jumbled landscape of struts and braces and incomprehensible hardware. If he fell from here, he wouldn't fall into the plasma fires. He'd break his neck on alien machinery, instead.

"I cannot see which way to the controls!" Ik cried. The control platform was almost directly below them now. An incomprehensible spiderweb of walkways twisted around it. "I think we must—"

Ik was drowned out by a rumble as a tremendous cloud of acrid smoke boiled up past them.

"—go different ways!" he finished, pointing out two possible routes down. Bandicut swallowed grit and tried to follow the traceries of metal. Neither of them looked like paths that Copernicus could follow.

Ik motioned to him to try a zigzag walkway that hugged the pillar. Ik would try a narrow catwalk that veered away from the pillar, but connected with others angling back at a lower level. Bandicut shouted to Copernicus, "You stay here!" Without waiting for a reply, he raced down a rippling flight of something like stairs, while Ik darted out across seemingly empty space.

The stairs led to a ramp, then more steps. Flames erupted closer and closer to him as he hurried downward. The heat came in blasts, and he caught himself once on a stanchion, to keep from plunging over the edge. But his gaze went down, and he saw something happening far down in the plasma tube that made him breathless with fear: a whirling chain reaction of discharges that blossomed and multiplied in the space of a second, creating an intense and accelerating swirl of blazing plasma. It appeared to be building out of control.

He heard a crash and looked up. Above him, a walkway had broken under Ik's weight. The Hraachee'an was dangling from a section of catwalk, swinging helplessly over empty space. *"IK!"* Bandicut shouted. He started to run back to help his friend.

"NO NO NO—*HRAAHHH!"* Ik bellowed. "GO ON! GO ON! GO ON!"

He knew Ik was right. It would do no good to save his friend from falling, only to have them all die in a massive plasma explosion. *"Hang on!"* he screamed, and continued his descent. He could see the control pedestal below him now. It was on a small platform set at the end of a short walkway sticking out from the huge pillar. Bandicut staggered to a halt next to a ladder that provided access down the pillar to the walkway. His heart nearly pounded out of his chest. He swung himself around and kicked with his feet to find the rungs. They were awkwardly shaped—more like smooth, rounded protrusions than rungs, and set too far apart. Nevertheless, he began working his way down.

It took an eternity to get a third of the way down the ladder. He paused, clinging dizzily to the protrusions. It took all his strength just to hang on. He had about ten meters yet to go. He heard another rumble below. He kept moving, trying not to look.

/// I think you'd better look. ///

/Uh?/ He peered down into the bottomless plasma tube—and hugged the rungs in terror. The spiral of plasma energy was blazing even brighter, and spitting off thunderbolts into the walls of the tube. And *way* down in the shaft, far below the spiraling gas, a bright ball of fire was roiling upward. As Bandicut watched, the ball reached the plasma spiral, and with an eruption of energy, they billowed up the shaft together like magma up a volcano.

"Mokin' foke!" he whispered. He had maybe ten seconds before that plasma fire would blaze out of the shaft and envelop them all. He drew an acrid breath. /Charlie, can you help me jump straight?/

/// ??? ///

/I've got to hit that platform. *Now.*/ Without waiting for an answer, he leaped out from the ladder, turning in midair. For a second that seemed like an hour, he fell toward the control platform, toward the fire . . .

He hit the platform with a bone-shuddering impact, collapsing at the knees. He grabbed the control pedestal for support. It seemed to squirm and writhe in his grip, but it kept him from falling. It burned where his wrists touched it, but he couldn't let go, because something bloomed into his mind with showering drops of light, and a gridwork of lines filled with floating icons, and underlying that, a fireball of plasma billowing up like a piece of a living sun.

And something in him translated his cry, /STOP IT! STOP IT! SHUT IT OFF!/

And he felt an echoing wave roll out through the control grid:

∗∗ Override emergency! Quench and seal! ∗∗

And the writhing piece of sun below him flickered and darkened, and something slammed with near-earthquake violence, and he gasped against the control pedestal, shutting his eyes; and when he opened them again and looked down, there was only a wall of darkness below.

10

HROOM

 /GOD DAMN,/ HE whispered, his heart pounding. /Are we safe now?/ He felt the quarx trying to answer, but there was interference. He was still linked to the control unit. He tried to disengage . . . and could not.

He felt a shiver of fresh fear. /Let go of me, damn it!/ he whispered, trying to jerk free. He felt a tug from *something*, which he could not quite identify. But it was aware of him, and aware of what he had just done. He felt a brief flicker of anger—*rage*, almost—but it winked out an instant later, and he felt an entirely different sensation: coldly unemotional control modulation. Then the system's hold on him was gone, and he was free. He straightened up from the pedestal, bewildered.

/// *Don't engage it again!* ///

/I'm not about to,/ he whispered, as the adrenaline began to drain away. /What just happened?/

Charlie answered as though he had witnessed a miracle.

/// *I think we were all*
very, very lucky. ///

Bandicut stepped back from the control pedestal, trying to get his breath back. /Yeah. But did you feel what I just felt, in the controls? I thought this thing was supposed to be an isolated unit./

/// Not entirely, I guess.
But it did seem to have
emergency interrupt priority. ///

/Uh-huh./ Bandicut drew a deep breath and looked around. His knees throbbed from the jump, and his jaw ached where it had slammed against the control pedestal. But he was alive. Below the platform, he could see flames and smoke, but also clouds of vapor that looked like flames being extinguished.

Whrrreeeek-whooooo!

He turned and spied, across the emptiness where the shaft had been, a cluster of shadow-people streaming along a walkway toward another control unit. He thought he recognized the foreman-shadow, waving frantically, whooping. Bandicut waved back, wondering what the creature was saying. /I guess *they're* okay. I guess we're all—/ and he suddenly remembered /—Ik!/ He searched the darkness overhead. He couldn't find his friend in the jumble of shadows. *"IIIKK!"* he shouted.

After a moment he heard a faint cry: "Hraaahh!" He finally spotted Ik dangling from the broken catwalk.

/Christ, Charlie, we've got to get back up there!/ He took a step, and staggered as a blaze of pain went up his right leg. He must have torn something in his knee.

/// I'll do what I can to inhibit the pain.
Later, we'll work on healing. ///

Charlie was already damping nerve impulses. He felt numbness spread up his thighs.

/Okay, enough. I've got to be able to feel them move./ Taking hold of a rung-protrusion, he began the laborious climb back up the ladder. He was terrified that Ik would fall before he could get there. He was about halfway up when he heard, faintly, "Thank you, Copernicus."

Copernicus? Bandicut squinted up, but couldn't locate his friend. *"IK! Are you—?"*

His last words were drowned out by a distant grinding and arcing, and what sounded like a blast of steam. Then he heard, "I am safe now, thank you. *John Bandicut, are you all right?"*

He flushed with dizziness as he clung to the ladder. "Uh—yeah! I'm okay!" he gasped. It was doubtful that Ik could have heard him. He resumed his painful climb.

As he neared the top of the ladder, he saw Ik standing above him, rope in hand. He climbed the last few rungs, finally accepting Ik's help as he struggled over the difficult threshold from the ladder to the walkway. He rose to face his friend. "You got back!"

"With the help of your robot. I would have fallen if it had not pulled me back in. We must return to free it!" Ik swept his arm in a joyful arc. "John Bandicut—you did this?" he cried in seeming disbelief. "You saved our lives! And you saved all this—" he swept his arm over the factory floor "—from destruction!"

Bandicut gulped a tremulous sigh. "I guess so, yeah. But it was the stones, really." He rubbed his wrists, which were still stinging from the contact with the controls.

"Hrrrrm." Ik's eyes glinted with inner light.
/// *The stones translated.*
But you had the capacity to make the contact.
It was your command that stopped it. ///

/Okay, whatever./ Bandicut shrugged and gestured to Ik. "I guess we'd better get going back." He almost added, *to safety,* but somehow that would have seemed preposterous. They still had a long, perilous walk ahead of them.

"Copernicus is waiting for us," Ik agreed, and they began the climb back up the spindly ramps.

First they heard a whirring, like fans starting up. Then lights started coming on: position markers, like tiny colored stars in the firmament; then bright spotlights scattered widely; and finally great overhead floodlights filling the cavernous space. Bandicut paused, squinting, trying in vain to take in the breadth of the factory space. Even illuminated, it was an impossible sight. He peered along the length of the great central structure, the "star-spanner," Charlie had called it. It looked like . . . he couldn't say what, exactly. Maybe some sort of monstrous particle accelerator. It seemed to stretch into—not quite infinity, surely—but it didn't seem to end, either. It extended almost to the limit of sight, before dwindling sharply in a way that defied normal perspective. It hurt his eyes a little to look at it.

/// *It's a star-spanner, all right,* ///

Charlie said, with some satisfaction.

"A remarkable structure," Ik said, behind him. "It is only partially finished, I believe."

"Star-spanner," Bandicut muttered. "What does it do?"

"It spans the stars, I believe."

Bandicut squinted back at him, but Ik urged him onward with a gesture.

They found Copernicus stuck near the place where he'd rescued Ik. His bent sensor-array rotated toward them as they approached. He was wedged into an opening between two support beams, where he had apparently braced himself while extending a long, telescoping manipulator-arm to the section of walkway which hung like a broken appendage. Copernicus had pulled the broken segment in, and was holding it secure against the support structure. Napoleon and Bandicut's back-pack were lying nearby.

"Coppy! Are you all right?"

Copernicus drumtapped. "Cap'n, I am pleased to see you safe and well. I'm afraid I am immobile, however."

"We'll get you out, don't worry. Ik tells me you saved his neck! Well done, old buddy!"

"I merely secured the structure so that he could climb free. It seemed the best course of action."

"Indeed," said Ik, behind Bandicut. "I am in your debt, Copernicus."

Tap tap.

"Can you let go of that thing now, Coppy?"

The robot released the walkway section and it swung free with a clang, and a rhythmic squeak. Copernicus turned his wheels in an effort to move, but they merely skidded on the metal surface.

"Wait." Ik positioned himself against a support strut, then applied leverage against the robot's body. Copernicus rocked, his motors whining. Bandicut edged around to the other side. Together they finally pried the robot free, with an ear-piercing metallic scrape.

Copernicus backed to a place of relative safety. "Thank you, Cap'ns. May I ask—has the emergency passed?"

"We think so." Bandicut peered down. The plasma tube remained sealed off, and he saw no flames or electrical arcs. He wondered if the plasma tube had been the energy source for the star-spanner; then he shrugged, glad it wasn't his job to worry about such things.

"Let us return to the platform, shall we?" Ik said, placing Napoleon onto Copernicus's back.

They had not gone more than a dozen meters along the catwalk before they were stopped by a *WHOOOP! WHOOOP! WHOOOP!* reverberating around them. A swath of sparkling light swept down from the ceiling toward them. Dancing in the light were half a dozen shadow-people. "What in the world?" Bandicut asked wonderingly.

The light enveloped them in its shimmering glow. *Hohuueeeeee!* cried a shadow overhead. ". . . come . . ."

Before he could reply, Bandicut felt a curious lightness and realized that he was already airborne, floating up the shaft of light, the shadow-people fluttering before him. Moments later, the light faded, and they were standing on the platform from which they had begun their mad rescue effort—how long ago? Less than an hour, surely.

Ik said something he didn't catch. A large number of the shadow-people were gathered, and the foreman-shadow was at their front, fluttering and bowing. At least, that was how Bandicut interpreted the waving movements of the foreman-shadow's upper body and head—like a slender tree whipping back and forth in a gusting wind.

Hreee-kuuu . . . hreeee-kuuuuuu . . . whooeeeee . . .

Bandicut stood in baffled silence as the shadow-people played a mournful string concert before them, his thoughts reverberating with fragments of translation. ". . . tragedy . . . boojum . . . (bad bad) . . . factory safe . . . your help . . . boojum gone for now . . ." Bandicut exchanged silent glances with Ik, wondering if this was a thank-you or a lecture. He could see the star-spanner better from here. It looked a little like a stupendously long series of generators and coils in an endless train, or possibly the longest crankshaft in the universe. He suddenly felt very tired, and realized that he was teetering on the edge of helpless laughter, or maybe silence-fugue.

/// Hang on, I'll do what I can. ///

/Please,/ he whispered, stifling a snort of laughter. Mercifully, he felt the urge subside as his thoughts began to clear.

/// I believe, ///

the quarx remarked,

> */// they seem to understand now*
> *—the shadow-people—*
> *that we were opposing the boojum.*
> *I believe you have earned*
> *their honor. ///*

Bandicut blinked, not sure what to say.

"Hraahhh!" said Ik. He turned to Bandicut. "It seems that they wish to take us to a place of safety and rest. By chasing the boojum away, you appear to have freed certain transport systems, as well."

Bandicut glanced to make sure that Copernicus was still with them, glanced to make sure that *he* was really here. He was starting to feel like a hallucination. "Well," he said. "Okay, I guess. I'm ready for some rest."

Ik said something to the shadow-people, and the sparkling light appeared around them again. Something like a blazing ring-shaped halo passed over them from front to back, dazzling Bandicut. When he could see again, they were standing in another place altogether, hazy orange and pink. He couldn't quite focus on it. "Ik—"

"Holding—" *rasp* "—transition area."

"Oh—"

After a long breath, and another flashing halo, a large, low-ceilinged room materialized around him. He looked around in amazement. It looked like a lounge, with soft lighting and irregularly shaped tables scattered throughout a space that was broken up by waist-high partitions. He felt a sudden cascade of associations, and his knees almost buckled under him. The place reminded him of the rec room back on Triton—and he suddenly, breathlessly, imagined Julie Stone walking into the room, her blue eyes shining and her smile inviting him to a game of EineySteiney pool. And then they would retire to . . . *oh, Julie* . . .

He shuddered with a rush of grief and loneliness.

/// This is a difficult memory for you? ///

Difficult? He wanted to laugh and cry both. Difficult?

/// Would you like me to
block it? ///

/No!/ he almost shouted aloud.

/// I'm sorry, I— ///

He closed his eyes for three heartbeats. /Never mind. It's all right. Yes, it's difficult—and no, I don't want it blocked. I loved her, Charlie—as much as you can love someone you've only known for a few days. It felt like much more./

The quarx's tone was almost wistful.

/// Love?
Is this, perhaps, something I could
ask you about later? ///

He sighed. /Later. Yes./ He blinked his eyes open. They were all here: Ik, the two robots, the shadow-people. And now he saw other figures farther away in the room. Not shadow-people, not humans, not Hraachee'ans. They were too far away to see very well; but some were tall and some short, some were splayed out like starfish, and some appeared to twitter in the air like the shadow-people, except that they were more light than shadow. "Ik?" he whispered. "What is this place? Who are all those people?"

Ik rubbed his chest. "I believe this may be where the shadow-people—" *rasp* "—reenergize and sustain their presence here." Ik pointed to their left, and Bandicut saw shadow-people swarming like bees around a place where the wall seemed to dissolve into an area of darkness a few meters across. It wasn't a static darkness; it seemed to swirl and fluctuate, with little flickering shots of light, and as he stared at it he thought it actually seemed a kind of tunnel. He thought he saw a couple of the shadow-people flit into it and vanish.

/// That's it.
They're translating from one fractional dimension
to another. ///

/Mm?/

/// They don't live in this continuum
without interruption.
They shift away, to rest. ///

Bandicut found the sight hard on his eyes. /I hope they don't want us to shift away with them./

/// We'll find out. Look. ///

Bandicut saw the foreman-shadow fluttering toward them. *Whreep-a-whrreeep!* He felt a vague rustling in his mind as the translator attempted to sort that out. What emerged seemed to be an invitation: "... rest ... restore ... speak to us ... help to understand ..." But he had a feeling that the foreman-shadow had said considerably more than that.

"Uh, thanks," he murmured, glancing to see what Ik was making of this. The Hraachee'an had his head cocked, and was studying the foreman-shadow, who now seemed to be waving a triangular hand in the direction of the dimensional-tunnel-thing. /Oh, great./

/// Hold on.
I'm not sure it's what you think.
I believe he's offering to
update your translator. ///

/Huh?/

/// Linguistically.
It might make conversation easier if you
gave it a try. ///

Bandicut frowned, as he felt Charlie nudging him toward the cluster of shadow-people. Ik was moving that way, and he supposed if Ik could do it ... The foreman-shadow continued making *wheep*ing sounds, and he felt a sense of "... a little closer ..." and, following Ik's example, he stood just outside the edge of the twisting, shadowy disturbance, and he nervously stretched out his fingers toward it. And he felt—

practically nothing, just a light buzz in his wrists.

Whreeep-whreeep! ". . . understand us better . . . our words clearer? . . ."

/// Ahh. ///

Peering at the foreman-shadow, Bandicut thought he could see something new, a tiny spark of light, within it.

/// Answer him, ///

Charlie suggested.

"Oh, um—*yes,*" Bandicut croaked. "I think so."

"Yes, indeed," echoed Ik.

The foreman-shadow fluttered and whooped. ". . . we are pleased . . . pleased . . ." *Wheeek!* ". . . regret the recent confusion . . . grateful for your help . . . would you like refreshment and restoration? . . ."

"Um—yes, please," Bandicut whispered, and Ik rumbled assent.

The foreman-shadow gestured, fluttering, and led them away from the dimensional device and over to a set of . . . lounge chairs, which Bandicut was fairly sure had not been there a few minutes ago. *Wheeee.* ". . . fill your thoughts with your needs and wishes . . ."

Dizzily, Bandicut sank into a wonderfully padded chair. With almost dreamlike urgency, he found himself imagining a cool beer, and some fried potatoes, and fish and vegetables . . . and it didn't take long before he started imagining someone to share it with, and then his mind filled with thoughts of Julie Stone. Only this time it wasn't the heartache of the loss that he felt, but warmth and desire . . .

He started, and realized that he had passed into a very deep reverie, and was quite . . . stimulated. He blushed and sat up a little straighter and hoped no one had noticed.

/// That was very interesting.
Were those thoughts related to the
"love" you were speaking of earlier? ///

Bandicut grunted. He noted that Ik was sitting crosslegged on a low pad, lost in his own reverie—or perhaps sound asleep. There was a platter in front of the Hraachee'an, with several large objects that looked like roots. Bandicut glanced down and realized that he had a tray, too, and on it there was a plate of fish and chips and steamed baby carrots, and a frosty mug of beer. /Whoa. Am I dreaming this, Charlie?/

/// Nope.
You've earned your reward, I guess. ///

/Can I actually eat this stuff, do you suppose?/ He looked around for the foreman-shadow. Copernicus, parked beside him, was enveloped in a golden nimbus of light. Recharging, perhaps? He turned around and saw the foreman-shadow floating just behind him, like a waiter hovering over his shoulder. Bandicut gestured toward the table. "You can, uh, join us if you want."

The being fluttered, edging forward almost imperceptibly.

Bandicut sighed with impatience. /I don't want the damn thing in awe of me./

Wheeep. The foreman-shadow fluttered close enough, and held still enough, for him finally to get a better look. It still had that shifting-in-and-out-of-reality look to it, its angular hands and body twisting ceaselessly, going from black to smoky near-invisibility to black again, as though it were made, not of dark matter, but of constantly opening and closing slits in the local fabric of space.

/// *That's not too far wrong.* ///

But up close now, Bandicut could again see little sparks of light around and through its body—more of them than before—and he had a sudden intuition that maybe those were its eyes. He cleared his throat, wondering if he could make eye contact.

Something must have happened, because the foreman-shadow moved even closer and spoke in a more subdued voice than usual. ". . . thank you . . . we understand now . . . you are working against the—" *tingle* "—boojum . . ." *Wheeooore.* ". . . welcome help . . . this struggle of many—" *tingle* "—seasons/cycles/years . . ."

/Working against the boojum? Me?/

/// *Well, you did, didn't you?* ///

/Yes, but—/ Bandicut glanced to see if Ik was listening. The Hraachee'an was asleep. He blinked back at the foreman-shadow. "Do you have a name?"

The foreman-shadow made a low *wh'rooom'm'm*ing sound, just at the lower edge of Bandicut's hearing range.

"Um," he asked, "was that your name?"

Wh'rooom'm'm. ". . . affirmative tone . . ."

Bandicut nodded to the being as his thoughts wheeled. /Hell, I can't call him that. I can't even pronounce it./

/// Maybe you could approximate it,
as you do mine. ///

Bandicut cleared his throat. "Listen, would it be all right if I called you *Hroom?*"

Wh'rooom'm'm. ". . . affirmative tone . . ."

"Well, then, nice to meet you, Hroom. I suppose you wonder who the hell I am."

Whrrooop. ". . . your partner . . . has told us much . . ."

"My partner?" He glanced in Ik's direction.

/// He means me.
I've found that I can communicate with them,
somewhat. ///

/???/

/// When you received your update,
I perceived the slight dimensional shift
that I needed. ///

/Ah./

/// And I conveyed that you are a human,
that you are a stranger here,
and lost,
and that you desire only to help. ///

Bandicut thought about that. On a sudden impulse, he reached for the beer in front of him. Lifting the glass, he peered approvingly through its amber clarity, then carefully took a sip. It foamed in his mouth. He choked a little on the excessive carbon dioxide as he swallowed. He was stunned to realize that it actually tasted like beer, more or less. He took another swallow, and set the mug down. "Thank you," he murmured, trying not to burp. "For the beer, I mean."

Whrrrrp. ". . . is there anything we can do . . . to help in return . . ."

He glanced sideways. Though Ik was asleep, he felt certain that the Hraachee'an would want him to ask. "Well, there is that other fellow, Li-Jared. He's a friend of Ik's." He gestured toward the sleeping Hraachee'an. "We believe he was also trying to work with you, against the—"

Whreek?

"—boojum."

Who-o-o-uuu. Hroom fluttered his hands. ". . . the one we—" *tingle* "—blamed for the . . . calamity . . ."

"Yes."

". . . your friend said this . . . that the one called . . ." *Whred-d-d-d.* The shadow seemed to stutter, trying to produce the sound.

"Li-Jared."

Whrrrrep. ". . . has been attacked by the boojum . . ."

Bandicut nodded.

". . . we would help . . . do you wish to see where he is now? . . ."

"You *know?* You know where he is?"

Whreeee. ". . . we will try to . . . locate him for you . . ."

"We would appreciate that very much," Bandicut whispered.

". . . require time . . . rest and sustain . . . will return with news . . ." And with a tiny squeak, Hroom fluttered away.

Bandicut stared, open-mouthed. Finally he shrugged and began to consume his beer and his fish and chips.

11

MEMORY LANES

/// Shall I tell you what I've learned
about the shadow-people? ///

/Sure./ Bandicut pushed his tray back and settled into the deep pads of the chair with a greater feeling of comfort than he had felt in a long time. Except, he realized suddenly, for his throbbing knees. Charlie had been deadening the pain, but it hadn't done him any good to walk around as if he hadn't injured himself. /Damn. Didn't you say something about doing some healing?/ He thought of the way he had crashed down onto that control platform, and winced at the memory.

/// I'm working on that.
But you don't come with diagrams, you know. ///

/Sorry./

/// However, I think I've checked out the damage.
It appears to be some torn cartilage,
and maybe some strained ligaments.
I can work on it while we talk. ///

/Fine./ He would probably be just as happy not thinking about it, he realized. /So. The shadow-people. An interesting bunch. I'm starting to feel almost fond of Hroom./

/// Indeed.
I would like to learn more about them.
But I did get a bit of a glimpse
while you were near their translational field.
Let me tell you. ///

/Okay./ Bandicut closed his eyes, willing himself to relax. His body couldn't quite seem to decide whether to let the beer act on him or not.

/// Let's do this the easy way. ///

And with that, Bandicut passed into a sleepless dream.

The shadow-people (he perceived) had come to this place a very long time ago, from a world—well, perhaps *world* wasn't the correct term, but from a *place* that was most unlike this one. The shadow-people retained a memory of their origins; they still thought of it as "home," and gave it no other name. What the quarx had glimpsed of their memories seemed to reflect a place of astounding physical stresses, full of space-time-altering gravitational shear zones. He could not identify it precisely; possibly it was the surface of a cosmic string, or something violently changing, like the gravity well of two neutron stars orbiting and threatening to collide, twisting space-time and thundering with radiation. It was, in any case, a perfect place for translations in and out of greater-than-three fractal dimensions.

But (Bandicut thought, imagining the cataclysmic energies) places like that wouldn't last long, would they? How could the shadow-people have had time to evolve?

If they did evolve there (noted the quarx).

Meaning?

Who knows? They might have been seeded, or *created*—but whatever, they lived in a very different timescape, where moments could be eons. Any time-comparison was practically meaningless, even in quarxian terms. Ultimately, they were forced out of their home by catastrophe—possibly colliding neutron stars, though the quarx's comprehension remained uncertain on that score—and they came to Shipworld. It was a strange and marvelous story: an entire population of shadow-people, rescued to the safety of the metaship, where their particular skills were tremendously useful to the maintenance of an enormous, and highly complex, ecology.

Images flickered in Bandicut's mind, confusingly: Charlie

catching glimpses, in the moment of their connection with the translation-field, of the shadow-people's history; shadow-people crafting and repairing strange, fractionally dimensional machines, without which significant parts of the metaship could not function; shadow-people ranging, not everywhere in Shipworld, by any means, but widely enough that he should not be surprised if he met brethren of Hroom, elsewhere.

But how were they brought here?

Possibly through a star-spanner.

An image shivered into place: a tremendous machine, like strange generators in a long line, or the most enormous crankshaft in the universe. It dwindled into infinity—not quite through four-dimensional space-time, but through something called "n-space," weaving through the light-years as a thread through a seam, joining distant worlds and stars in a twinkling web.

I'll be damned (he breathed).

Shipworld was full of n-space connectors; in fact, much of its own structure was joined together by n-space connectors of various sorts. And the much longer links of the star-spanners reached to more worlds than he could count.

And from that point, the next question came bursting: Was there a connector to Earth? To the solar system? Was that how he had gotten here? Could he use that method to return? (His heart pounded at the thought of seeing Julie again. His pulse raced, his face flushed. Time seemed suspended, as he waited for the quarx to answer.)

/// I don't think so, ///

said the quarx with a sigh, breaking the spell that had linked them in the dreamlike reverie.

*/// At least, I have no knowledge
or memory of one.
I assume that's why you were brought here
by ship and by translator. ///*

Bandicut let out a slow, angry hiss, as the buoyant glow faded. /Is there *going* to be one? Ever?/ He had a sudden vision of alien planning committees, debating for millions of years whether or not to build an extension to Earth's solar system.

/// I don't know.
My knowledge is quite fragmentary.
I'm sorry. ///

/Damn. *Damn*, Charlie. I wish you'd never told me! Bad enough I'm stranded here, do I have to listen to how other people can go home any time they want?/

/// I—well, that's not really
how it is, I don't think.
Not like a rapid transit system,
hop on, hop off.
It's no trivial matter,
operating star-spanners.
My memory is that they
open only when someone has a very strong
reason for wanting them to open. ///

/My reasons aren't strong?/ Bandicut asked angrily, reeling in pain. That momentary glimpse of a future that would never be—of Julie, love, home—had been enough to rake open all of his wounds when it was torn away.

/// I didn't realize
it would bother you this much. ///

/You live inside my goddamn brain. How could you not know?/

There was a long moment of silence.

/// I'm still learning, John.
About you, about me, about Shipworld.
Don't forget,
I'm cut off from my home, and my origins,
too. ///

/I haven't forgotten,/ he snapped. But in fact, he thought guiltily, he had. The quarx had just as much right to feel resentful as he did. So shouldn't he be a mensch like the quarx, and somehow rise above it? He cursed silently and opened his eyes.

Something black fluttered in front of him. *"Huh!"* he

grunted, startled. "Who's there?" But the flutter was gone. With an effort, he focused his eyes and looked around. Ik was now surrounded by a privacy veil of some sort, and appeared to be still asleep. On Bandicut's left, there was nothing except—a flutter of black again.

It solidified enough to be recognizable as a shadow-person. *Whwrreeeek?*

Bandicut cleared his throat. "Um, hi. Hroom?" He cocked his head and thought, It doesn't look like Hroom.

/// It's not. ///

/Who is it, then?/

/// I'm not sure. ///

The shadow-person drifted sideways, then back. *Heeeuuuuu.* ". . . message from . . . leader . . . has found the one you sought . . ."

Bandicut sat up straight. "Li-Jared?"

The shadow fluttered again. *Whriiick.* ". . . (affirmative) . . . cannot reach him at this moment . . . but friend safe . . . resting . . ." The shadow-person bobbed up and down, punctuating the message.

Bandicut frowned, wondering if he should wake Ik. They had had a very difficult day, and while he had no idea how much sleep Ik needed, he knew *he* needed more. *Safe*, the shadow-person had said.

*/// If you can remain still for a few hours,
I think we can take care of those knees. ///*

Bandicut nodded, and said to the shadow-people, "We don't want to risk losing him. Can you let us know immediately if he starts moving?"

Whreeeooo. ". . . yes yes preparing a way to take you there . . . rest now . . ."

Bandicut sighed in relief. Soon enough, he could learn what Li-Jared had found that was so interesting; and Ik could be reunited with his friend.

He glanced far across the wide room, where he could barely distinguish the shapes of beings moving about, beings whose presence probably ought to have ignited his curiosity. But their concerns right now were probably as distant from his as his were from . . . well, a bartender's in L5 City. He felt as if he were ensconced in a quiet corner of one of the galaxy's biggest cocktail lounges, and was too blindingly tired to appreciate it. He felt a sudden, acute desire to be alone. "Can you get me one of those?" he asked, pointing to the screen around Ik.

Whreek. The shadow fluttered away, and a gauzy curtain formed around him.

Bandicut sat back, and found that his chair reclined comfortably. /How 'bout that?/ he murmured. And before he knew it, he was fast asleep.

He drifted in and out of sleep, half aware of his dreams, dimly aware of occasional movement outside his private area, the elements of his inner and outer consciousnesses blending in a foggy haze of wistful desire. Julie was in his dreams, and his brother and sister-in-law; and he kept asking them, *Where's Dakota? Is she all right? Is Dakota safe? Does she know I'm here?* And his brother looked at him in puzzlement, shaking his head, until Julie came and lifted his arm up over her shoulder, and pointed. Of course—Dakota was right here in the lobby; she'd come to visit him in space, just as she'd promised.

Of course. In the dream. But here, now, there *was* someone who might have been Dakota—an adult Dakota—or at least a human woman. *Human woman?* That in itself was pretty interesting, he thought in a cottony half sleep.

At that, he started almost-awake, blinking. He imagined someone or something nearby, moving past his privacy screen—shadowy and yet real, someone very like a woman, with dignity and poise in her movements, with dark streaming hair floating airily as she walked by, and out of sight. He nearly woke completely then, but a quarxian voice soothed him, saying,

/// Not human, not human, ///

and he felt consciousness slipping away again, with the urgent thought that perhaps that wasn't Dakota, but *Julie.* And then he had no further dreams that he knew of.

∞

Whreeek! Whreeek! ". . . wake wake wake . . ."

He groaned. It took a moment for the urgent cries to penetrate the haze of sleep; then his eyes flew open. "What?" he muttered.

A smoky window had opened in his privacy screen, and through it he could see the flutter of several shadow-people. One might have looked familiar, but who could tell. "Okay!" he grunted. "You can get rid of that curtain!"

The screen vanished.

Whreeek! Whreeek! ". . . (urgent urgent) . . ." The shadow-people stormed around him.

He tried, dizzily, to get his bearings. They had awakened Ik, too. The Hraachee'an was unfolding himself to stand up from his pad.

A shadow-person darted forward, whirling back and forth as if to talk to both Bandicut and Ik at once. *Whraaeeeeee!* ". . . must come at once . . . he is fleeing . . . in danger . . . fleeing . . ."

"Hrrraah!" croaked Ik, his voice gravelly almost beyond recognition.

"*Who* is in danger? Li-Jared?" Bandicut felt an immediate flash of panic at not awakening Ik with the news that Li-Jared had been found.

Ik's eyes burned. "Urrrr, L'Jar'd?" He made a long rasping sound, and his voice finally became clear. "Li-Jared is in danger? Where?"

Whraaeeeeee! ". . . come . . . come with us . . . (bad bad) danger . . . must help . . ."

Bandicut staggered to his feet—too quickly. His right knee burned as he put his weight on it.

/// Try to go easy there. ///

/Oww. I thought you were healing it./

/// I was. I did.
The structural damage has been repaired.
But there'll still be soreness
and inflammation. ///

/You sound like Doctor Switzer,/ Bandicut muttered, though not without a flush of gratitude.

/// Who? ///

/Someone you never met. Can I use it?/

/// Yes. But try to be gentle. ///

Whraaaaeee! "... (urgent) no delay ..." The shadow-people were swarming as if gathering themselves to flee.

"John Bandicut, your robots!"

The robots! As he turned, a golden nimbus was just disappearing from around Copernicus and Napoleon. "Coppy?"

There was a ticking as of hot metal cooling. Copernicus rolled forward and backward, as if in self-appraisal. "Power level one hundred percent, Cap'n," he announced. "That's based on my new capacity."

"Say again?"

"I am somewhat disoriented, Cap'n. Total capacity is increased six-and-one-half-fold over previous value. Explain, please?" Copernicus rotated his sensor array, focusing on Bandicut, who was wondering just what had gone on inside that golden halo.

The shadow-people were stirring into a near frenzy of urgency, and Ik was gesturing frantically. "We'll figure it out later!" Bandicut said. "We've got to go. Lead on!"

Wheeeoreeeoreee!

A shaft of light coalesced around them all, transporting them away through a shimmering haze.

They came to rest in a place of electrical fire. Bandicut saw nothing like walls; they were surrounded by glowing gases, swirling and convecting as though in some fabulous chemist's retort.

He saw a flutter of shadow, and recognized the foreman-shadow approaching in haste. *"Hroom!"* he called, and his voice resonated as if through a tunnel. "What's going on?"

Whruuuruuuruuuruuu! "... has escaped through a—" *tingle* "—connector, pursued by boojum ... (bad bad) danger ... disruption of—" *tingle* "—vast power systems ... beyond our reach ..."

"Hraaah!" Ik barked. "Li-Jared? Why didn't you help him?" His blue-skinned hands waved in the air, and he looked as if he would have run off brandishing a sword, if there'd been anywhere to run. But they were still trapped in this strange cell of plasma fire, and Bandicut wondered if they were in fact in one of the shadow-people's fractally displaced dimensions.

/// A fair guess. ///

Hroom seemed to expand and contract like a balloon being jerkily inflated and deflated. *Whraaauuuu!* ". . . saw him sleeping safe . . . (wrong wrong) . . . thought to take you there . . . boojum may have intercepted the image . . ." As he spoke, a dark window opened in one of the swirling clouds of gas, and Bandicut saw a being curled up on a floor, sleeping.

"Li-Jared!" groaned Ik.

At that moment, the being sprang up, startled by something—and darted away down a long, dim corridor. He looked amazingly chimplike as he streaked away, a small satchel swinging behind him.

"We must follow!" Ik cried.

Whraaaruuu! ". . . out of reach of our transport . . . can only take you to where he was . . ."

The image explained where words failed, as another view come into focus: Li-Jared crouched in a room, peering out a window into space. He had a dark face with a pair of eyes that shone electric blue and gold. Through the window, a long structure was visible, stretching away into space like a bridge to nowhere. He kept glancing at a panel on the wall. Suddenly a portal irised open before him, he sprang through, and it closed behind him. Moments later, a silvery version of Li-Jared was visible beyond the window, jetting out toward that long, bridgelike structure.

As he approached it, there was a sudden flash. Li-Jared sped away, darting behind the bridge-structure. Two explosions puffed out from the structure, crumpling portions of it like paper.

"Dear God," Bandicut breathed.

". . . can take you there . . . no further . . . (regret regret) . . ."

"Aleika!" Ik cried. "Hurry!"

Hroom waved his triangle-hands, *whreeek*ing up the frequency scale into inaudibility. ". . . at once! . . . put you at the farthest point we can reach . . . help if we can . . ." A pattern began forming in the surrounding clouds, revealing a threadlike tangle of lines which Charlie recognized as a map.

/// It shows the limits of
the shadow-people's reach, ///

said the quarx as he tried to probe the logic of the twisting lines. The pattern was completely incomprehensible to Bandicut.

". . . come to you again if we can . . ." And with a final, earsplitting *shwreeeeek* ". . . Godspeed! . . ." Hroom suddenly spun end over end like tumbleweed caught up in a gust of wind, and Bandicut had a bizarre sense of the room flattening and twisting. Then the glowing clouds of gas closed in around him.

12

FIGHT OR FLIGHT

 BANDICUT BLINKED, CATCHING his breath, and realized that the gases were streaming away into nothingness, and he was standing in a small chamber, shivering from a sudden draft. He was directly under an air vent. As he stepped away, he felt a thudding boom.

/// Explosions? The boojum? ///

Bandicut grunted and said to Ik. "I hope we haven't just been moved into the line of fire."

Ik grumbled wordlessly, looking around.

Tap tap. "Cap'n, I don't know where we are, but I sense seismic disturbances," Copernicus reported. "And could you please untie Napoleon? His kicking is beginning to interfere with my sensor-array."

Kicking? On Copernicus's back, Napoleon was twitching energetically, restrained by Ik's rope. "Nappy!" Bandicut cried. "Can you hear me? Nappy? Can you stop kicking? *Stop kicking!*"

With a metallic groan, the robot ceased its movements. Ik quickly removed his rope, and Napoleon lurched and slid off Copernicus's back with a crash, along with Bandicut's backpack. "Napoleon, are you all right?" Bandicut cried, catching the robot too late. He felt a brief tingle as Charlie tried to probe through the finger-on-metal contact. He felt a momentary rush of *confusion.*

Napoleon sat up and swiveled, focusing his sensors.

"John Bandicut!" he rasped. "Danger! Tornado!"

"Nappy, the tornado's gone! You've been out of commission, buddy. I'm glad you're back." /But what a time to wake up!/ Bandicut looked up at Ik, who had turned away from the reunion to examine the chamber they had landed in. It was clear he was frantically worried about Li-Jared.

/// I believe that Napoleon
is still engaged in internal programming repair.
If I had time, I might try to help. ///

"I am—" *click* "—disoriented," Napoleon said, turning with a jerk to look at Copernicus. "We are all still here?"

"Yes, we're all here," said Bandicut, his voice shaking with conflicting emotions. Ik had just touched a control panel, and a huge door slid open to reveal a chamber that looked awfully like an airlock. Its walls were lined with puzzling-looking pieces of hardware. "But I have a feeling we might be going somewhere else real soon." Bandicut grabbed his backpack off the floor and replaced it on Copernicus's back. Copernicus closed a gripper to secure it.

"Indeed, John Bandicut." Ik strode back to join them, wrinkling his bony, blue-skinned brow. His eyes flashed. "I believe Hroom sent us here so that we could make use of this equipment. We must pursue Li-Jared."

"Pursue him where?" Bandicut asked. His breath went out as a huge window blinked open in the wall, revealing distant star clusters—and the half-demolished structure that they had seen in Hroom's vision, stretching diagonally across the view. Clouds of debris were still billowing outward from the explosions.

Ik's gaze was intense. "We must follow him out there. I see no other way."

Bandicut opened his mouth. *What am I doing here?* he wanted to say. *Why me? Am I going to get killed following Li-Jared?* But no words came out. He wasn't about to leave Ik, and he knew it. Besides, he thought, Li-Jared might have important information, information that could help *him,* too.

/// Interesting rationalization.
But there's no question, this looks risky.

> *Why don't we review Hroom's map*
> *and see if there's another way around. ///*

/Hroom's map was incomprehensible./

> */// Let's take another look, anyway. ///*

A small window opened in Bandicut's mind, displaying a memory-reproduction of the map. It was even less decipherable to him than before, a dense spiderweb of lines filling a space that was itself highly irregular in shape.

> */// I'll need to study it. ///*

/Can you do it fast?/ Bandicut cleared his throat. "Ik! My friend Charlie—" he tapped his temple "—thinks we might be able to find a safer way around. To meet Li-Jared."

"Didn't you see the map?" Ik strode into the airlock and began inspecting the equipment.

"Huh?"

"Hroom doesn't know where the connector ends! There is a great *bend* in the layout of the metaworld. It is not exactly . . . well. It is hard to explain. If we had more time, perhaps we could learn another way. But what's the good of transporting through many—" *rasp* "—worlds/continents/environments to meet Li-Jared, if he is destroyed by the boojum in between?"

Bandicut stared at him. "You got all that from that map?"

> */// I think he might be right, John. ///*

Ik gestured toward the bridge extending out into space. "This is an uninhabited power-connector. It is out of the shadow-people's range, and there is no one else who can intervene." Bandicut swallowed, remembering the plasma tube that had nearly shortened their lives, back at the factory. Ik peered at him, clearly understanding what he was thinking. "There may be danger. But I do not believe that this is of the same order as the factory plasma tube. It may even be inactive. And remember—the boojum, too, may be distracted. It is dangerous, but not all-powerful." Ik's face drew taut in a fashion that Bandicut interpreted as determination, as he turned back to the hardware. "In any case, we will be suited, and that will give us some protection."

Bandicut drew a ragged breath. /Charlie, is this crazy? I need help here./

         /// Do we want to try to save Li-Jared? ///

/Yes, but—/

         /// You made out okay saving the shadow-people,
                           didn't you? ///

/Well, yeah, but—/

         /// There are no guarantees, of course. ///

"Cap'n, my power levels are sufficient," said Copernicus, rolling close to him. "Napoleon is less certain. It appears his repair was interrupted by the emergency. We believe he is recharged, but his programming appears to be suffering from disequilibrium. It may take time for him to regain full function. But I can carry him again, if need be." Which sounded to Bandicut like an offer to volunteer.

Bandicut stared at Napoleon, who was teetering toward them. His walk improved visibly even as he crossed the airlock floor. "John Bandicut, I can convey myself," Napoleon rasped. His head jerked to one side, and he slowly rotated it back to peer at Bandicut. "If you give me instructions."

/What do you think?/

         /// Well, I just hope— ///

Charlie seemed to measure his words.

         /// —that this disequilibrium doesn't
                  cause . . . problems. ///

"I remember that one," Napoleon said, staring at the Hraachee'an.

"Ik," Bandicut said.

"Ik. We are following . . . assisting him."

"Yes."

Ik, paying no apparent attention, lifted a silver unit that looked rather like an enormous metal crab. "I believe this may fit you, John Bandicut. If you wish to continue with me."

Bandicut sighed. He took the unit gingerly, startled by its light weight. It was clearly made of some exotic metal. "Okay," he said at last. "What do I do?"

"Open it. Climb inside." Ik was already inspecting the other units.

Bandicut searched in vain for a latch. On an impulse, he pressed his left wrist to the suit. The front popped open. He peered inside. It had a featureless, velvety interior, dull black.

"For your robots." Ik handed over two similar suits, one longer, one fatter.

"I don't know about the robots," Bandicut said doubtfully. "I don't know what they'll be capable of, out there. But I don't think they'll need suits."

"Not even for communication? For propulsion?" Ik opened the suit he had picked for himself.

Good point, Bandicut thought. He supposed there was no harm in checking it out. He used his wrist stone, and the fatter carapace snicked open. He lifted it over Copernicus. It closed with a quicksilver ripple, then changed shape to a crablike version of Copernicus—really, more like a crab crossed with a submarine. From somewhere inside the shell, Bandicut imagined he heard a *tap tap*. "Coppy?" No answer. But then, he wasn't in the commlink yet himself.

He turned to Napoleon. "Can you back into this thing?" Napoleon staggered a little, but complied. Bandicut closed the suit, and it underwent a similar transformation. He slapped its shoulder, and the encased robot raised a hand in salute. Bandicut turned and saw Ik flashing like a chrome man inside *his* suit, making a gesture that undoubtedly meant, *Hurry up!* Bandicut backed into his own.

The blackness of the velvet deepened to midnight, and for an instant, he felt that he was stepping into a bottomless hole. The front closed on him, blinding him. His breath caught: he was sealed in a coffin, no way out, couldn't see, couldn't breathe, couldn't move—

/// Hold on! ///

The front of the suit blinked into transparency, and he felt the entire structure of the suit mold itself around him. He peered down the inside lining, and all that he could see was a smooth gray surface where the velvet had been. He saw no controls, but he could breathe okay.

"HRAAAHH—HURRY!!!"

The blast in his ear nearly deafened him. /How do you turn down—?/

Ik's voice continued, more softly, "I am going to—" *rasp* "—depressurize. Are you ready?"

"Wait! Napoleon, you there? You okay?"

"Affirmative, John Bandicut. Controls functional."

Bandicut blinked. "Coppy?"

"Roger."

The shimmering Ik strode to the end of the airlock. A moment later, Bandicut imagined that he heard a faint hiss of air leaving the airlock. Then the airlock irised open to black space. *Uh*—he thought, and realized that he was floating. He turned his head, and wondered how to rotate his body. At the thought, his wrist tingled, and he turned. The robots floated into view. "With you, Cap'n." "Ready for flight, John Bandicut."

"I'll be damned," he muttered, as the robots jetted alongside him out the portal to where Ik was floating in space. Bandicut's heart nearly stopped as he saw a darkness full of dim, tiny galaxies, and then as he turned, the spiral ocean of the Milky Way glowing palely but majestically, like the light of some mystical eternal city. He held back a cry of pain. As long as he'd been sealed inside the shipworld, it had been possible to forget, at least for a little while, how unimaginably far from home he was. But out here, floating in the void beyond . . . he felt as if the light of the galaxy would sear a permanent scar, an imprint upon his soul.

He forced himself to turn from the ghostly light, and he joined Ik and the robots, moving toward the power-connector that arrowed out into the darkness beyond, its tiny marker lights dwindling as though into an undersea gloom. That was where Li-Jared had fled, into that emptiness. Puffs of dust were still drifting outward like tenuous smoke rings from the structure.

"The boojum must have caused great damage when it pursued him," Ik said. "It must have caused power nodes to overload."

And will it do the same thing, chasing us? Bandicut wondered. He tried to focus on the structure of the connector itself. In width, it was almost human in scale, probably no more than a kilometer or two across. It looked rather like an enormous truss bridge, a half-open tube that might have provided a pathway for vehicles as well as power. It was constructed of geodesic segments and arcs and straight lengths of various materials, some of which looked like metal and others like glass. The direction of Li-Jared's flight was marked by blasted-out sections, leading away into the darkness.

Bandicut saw one marker light moving against the night, and for an instant, he thought he had spotted the fleeing Li-Jared. /Charlie, do you see that?/

/// Yes, but— ///

Bandicut suddenly realized that the light was on a moving vessel, a spaceship—not on or even near the bridge, but at a considerable distance beyond it. He shivered, as the momentary flurry of hope evaporated, leaving him with a feeling of lonely solitude.

/// I'm sorry.
Chances are, that ship has nothing to do with us.
This world appears to have many cultures,
many peoples
passing in the night without notice. ///

Bandicut wanted to say something like, *Why can't we call for help?* But he couldn't find the words, and the vessel's light soon passed out of sight.

He shook his head, and flanked by the robots, followed Ik through a gaping hole into the long structure itself. On the inside, it was an open shaft of impressive proportions—much larger-seeming than from the outside. He had a sudden feeling of vertigo. If they flew down the inside of that shaft, it would be like falling out of control down an incredible mineshaft of winking lights, and glass, and twisted girders.

"I see no other way for him to have gone," Ik murmured. And with that, the propulsion unit on Ik's back flickered, and he shot away down the power-connector.

Bandicut nearly choked as Ik dwindled in the distance. *Wait!* he wanted to cry. And then: *I'm coming!* He felt a slight pressure against the back of his suit, and was aware of incredible acceleration, mostly in the form of the sudden blurring of the shaft around him. The silvery glint of Ik stopped dwindling, and began to grow again as Bandicut closed the gap. He glanced nervously to both sides. The two robots were still flanking him.

There was plenty of clearance all around, but he still felt the threat of impending vertigo and loss of control. He tried not to look straight ahead, but angled his gaze sideways along the shaft's inner walls. There was some illumination from maintenance lights, and in that intermittent glow, the occasional blown-out sections gave an extrasurreal quality to the place. In one glance to the right, he saw a cloud of twinkling particles. Bits of demolished glass? Despite the damage, long stretches of the shaft glimmered and glowed; it was by no means dead.

As if to demonstrate the point, a pulse of dazzling actinic light blossomed out of the distance ahead, flared around him, and vanished behind him. It was followed by another—and another—leaving him breathless.

/Have we just become targets here?/ he wondered, when he was able to think again.

/// *I'm not sure,*
but I think that was normal activity.
If the boojum were trying to target us,
it probably could. ///

/Mm,/ he muttered. He drew alongside Ik and said, "Who built this thing, anyway? And what's it supposed to do? It's incredible."

"When I have the answers to that, I will have satisfied one of my goals, John Bandicut."

/Do you know, Charlie?/

/// *Count me with Ik.* ///

He grunted, dissatisfied. "Then, do you know why the boojum is doing this? Why it's trying to kill Li-Jared? And destroying all this property?"

"I cannot say for sure. But I suspect that Li-Jared has

gained knowledge that the boojum does not wish him to have. Knowledge, after all, was his goal. Our goal.''

Bandicut swallowed, thinking about all of their talk about seeking knowledge of this world. He peered to his left, at the silvery carapace that hid Ik's face, and imagined that Ik was peering back at him.

"John Bandicut, I wish I knew more. But I know this: that the boojum *seeks control*—and seeks to destroy those who oppose it. And I know also, that there are many who oppose it.''

"Many? You mean, like, the builders? Or the people who *run* the place?''

"Well, yes—the masters of Shipworld oppose it, I believe. But also others.''

Bandicut squinted. They zoomed through an enormous arch, where a massive junction of some kind had been blown apart. The effect was so silent that it almost felt like a scene of ancient destruction, undisturbed for eons. And yet, this had probably happened within the hour. /It's like a war,/ he thought, torn between fear and wonder.

>*/// I think I'm starting to understand*
>*something that Hroom tried to convey to me. ///*

/What's that?/

>*/// I believe it is a war.*
>*A struggle for domination, anyway.*
>*And most of those who live in Shipworld*
>*are innocent of the struggle.*
>*They don't know the sides,*
>*or even that there is a conflict.*
>*And yet, many of them may suffer for it. ///*

Bandicut shifted his head right and left, trying to make sense of a long series of strange geometric shapes. They flashed past an arcing electrical discharge. /Except for the shadow-people, I've hardly even seen anyone living here. Where are they all?/

>*/// Ik noted that, too, remember.*
>*I think it's a question of where we were.*
>*My impression, from Hroom,*

> *is that there are peoples who have either died*
> *because of massive systems failures,*
> *or been forced to move*
> *to new living areas. ///*

/War refugees?/ He looked left, then right, and suddenly realized that the robots were no longer in formation with him. /Oh, mokin' hell. Charlie, have you seen—?/ He broke off the question, turning as far as he could without spinning the suit. "Ik, is there some way to look behind in these suits?" He tried to keep panic out of his voice. "I've lost sight of the robots!"

"It should give you a mirror view if you ask for it. I do not see the robots, either."

"Damn! I've got to slow down. I may have to go back."

"Wait—testing long-range scanners. Gaiii! Why didn't I think of them before?"

Bandicut's heart was pounding. "How do you turn it on? Do you see—?"

"I could have been searching for Li-Jared."

Damn it, forget Li-Jared for a moment! Bandicut swallowed and croaked silently, /Translators, can you get me long-range scanning, to the rear? I'm looking for the two robots./

The view ahead shrank to a dot. A new view exploded, the rear view. He shuddered, his stomach lurching as he experienced a sudden sensation of flying backward, as fast as he'd been flying forward. He strained to focus on the receding landscape. /Can you scan for a target?/

Specify modality.

/How would I know? Radar, infrared—whatever the hell you've got! Can you isolate the two robots?/

The image blinked and shifted, changing color, then cycling rapidly through a dozen different false-color views and changes in magnification. Suddenly it froze. The image was dark red, and grainy with magnification. In its center was a grotesque-looking crab shape. Copernicus, in his suit. And he was zigzagging back and forth across the image, back and forth across the shaft. Where the hell was Napoleon?

"Coppy!" Bandicut shouted. "Can you read me,

Coppy?'' /Translator, how far back is that? Can you slow me, turn me around to go back?/

/// *Can I help, John?* ///

/Yes! Talk to it!/

/// *Okay, Copernicus is about*
eighty kilometers behind us.
We are modifying your flight path.
Slowing. ///

/Don't lose Ik!/

/// *Maintaining fix on Ik.*
He is slowing, too, but not as fast. ///

"Ik!" he called. "Coppy's fallen way back! I don't see Napoleon. I've got to go look for them."

"Quickly, then! I have a fix on distant activity. Explosions, I believe! It could be Li-Jared. I dare not delay!"

Bandicut chafed, desperately wanting not to be separated from either the robots or the Hraachee'an. "Okay, Ik! *Coppy! Can you read me?*"

In the image, he saw the silvery crab of a robot swerve sharply one way, then another—left, right, up, down. A narrow scale on the right of the image, which he realized was a range indicator, jumped; then he felt a surge, and the indicator began to close again. Coppy had decelerated suddenly, and Bandicut's suit had responded by slowing in kind. "*Coppy-y-y-y!*" he yelled.

In answer he heard a rasp of static, and finally a voice, through the static. "Cap'n, have lost contact with Napoleon. Search pattern no good . . . may need assistance . . ." His words after that were lost in static.

Bandicut cursed. /Charlie, can we turn around? And keep the lock on Ik?/

/// *Turning.*
I'll try to keep that lock,
but I can't promise. ///

Bandicut felt a slight but dizzying surge, and saw a flicker in the image. He was rotating to face the other way. "Ik! I'll try to rejoin you as soon as I can!" He felt a knot in his stomach, and realized just how badly he did *not* want to leave one friend for another. /All right, Charlie—pour it on!/

The image blurred with speed, then slowed again. For a moment, the suit seemed to lose the fix on Copernicus. Then it focused again, and the image was much clearer, and the range indicator had narrowed drastically.

/// Here's zero magnification. ///

Copernicus was a small but growing silver spot in the distance. /Can you scan for Napoleon?/

/// Trying. ///

"Coppy, what was your last contact with Napoleon?"

The voice was clearer this time. "Cap'n, he veered to map the structure on the left while I mapped the structure on the right. We lost contact two minutes and thirty-seven seconds ago."

Bandicut thought of the speed they were travelling, and Napoleon's difficulties in movement after reawakening. He never should have let Napoleon fly solo! "Did he—he didn't *crash*, did he?"

"I saw no such indication."

"Then do you think he's—?" Bandicut's voice suddenly caught, as he realized he didn't know *what* he was thinking. Lost control? Gone amok?

"Cap'n, he appeared to be flying without difficulty. Until I said something that seemed to disturb him."

Bandicut blinked as the robot came alongside. "What do you mean?"

"I expressed concern that we could be acting on misleading information."

"*What?*"

"Supposition, Cap'n. I thought it a logical possibility that we could be pursuing a phantom—or flying into a trap. How do we know that the shadow-people's information was accurate? Or our own scanner images? What do we know of these systems, after all?"

Bandicut felt his pulse race. "Coppy, if you had some basis for thinking that, why didn't you say it before?" He felt a trickle of sweat run down his back. He peered around at this empty, but living, power shaft—knowing that he had no idea where he was, or what his options might be if Coppy was right. Ik was out of sight now. "Ik!" he cried out. "Can you still hear me?"

"Hrrrm . . ." came a distant, staticky response.

"We began mapping to gather data," Copernicus continued. "I did not see Napoleon depart from formation. But following one of my turns, he was gone."

Damn! Bandicut thought. He swiveled hard left, then right, scanning the mystifying structure of metal and glass and God knew what else, searching for any sign at all of Napoleon. He could be hundreds of kilometers from here by now. "Coppy, I don't even know *how* to search for him. We can't search the whole damn structure!"

/// Try calling to him. ///

/What? Hasn't Copernicus been trying?/

/// Can it hurt to try? ///

Bandicut shrugged. "Napoleon!" he shouted. *"Nappy, can you hear me? Nappy-y-y-y!"* He rotated through a full three hundred sixty degrees, searching.

To his astonishment, he was answered by a sharp rasp of static. He glimpsed movement, and jerked himself in a quick turn. A second silver crab, this one elongated, flew out from the jumbled landscape of the shaft wall, and darted toward him. "Nappy!"

Copernicus shot out to meet the other robot, but Napoleon flew in quick, evasive maneuvers around Copernicus and darted close to Bandicut.

Rasp. "John Bandicut, danger—*danger!*" screeched the metal voice of Napoleon. "Protect me from that machine!"

"What machine?" Bandicut searched frantically for an enemy, perhaps some berserk machine controlled by the boojum.

"That one!" Napoleon cried. "It's trying to harm me, *trying to contaminate my programming!* Protect me from Copernicus!"

Bandicut stared, dumbfounded, then whirled to see Copernicus fleeing into the cover from which Napoleon had just emerged.

₿

FRIEND OR FOE

 "COPERNICUS!" BANDICUT CRIED.

Ik joined him, dropping into formation with a silver flash. Copernicus shot past Ik and rocketed ahead of them all down the shaft, hugging the wall. "What is the meaning of this?"

"I wish I knew!" Bandicut watched in helpless despair as Copernicus dwindled in the distance. He spun to look at Napoleon. "Nappy, are you out of your mind? What's all this about? Why did Coppy just run away?"

"John Bandicut, we must be vigilant!" screeched Napoleon.

"Yes! But for *what*?"

"Betrayal!" cried the robot. "It's all around us!"

Bandicut stared at Napoleon in disbelief. "What are you talking about?" He peered fretfully down the endless power-connector. /Charlie, can we keep a lock on Copernicus?/

/// Trying.

He's moving awfully fast. ///

Ik interrupted his efforts at comprehension with a staccato bark: "We must!—move!—on!"

"I know," Bandicut said hoarsely.

"I am picking up further explosions ahead of us. We must investigate. Is Napoleon functional?"

Bandicut assumed that Ik meant, was Napoleon *trust-*

worthy, and he didn't know the answer. "Nappy, can you follow us without veering off?"

Napoleon's voice was slow but clear. "I am able to follow, John Bandicut."

"We don't have time to screw around. If you're going to have problems, tell me now."

"I will remain vigilant."

Bandicut grunted. "All right, let's go! Let's see if we can catch Li-Jared *and* Coppy."

"Rakh!" said Ik, and shot away.

Keeping formation with Ik was easy enough, but Copernicus was well out of visual sight now, moving at reckless speed. The tiny marker in the tracking window that was Copernicus disappeared periodically into the wall of the power-connector, then reappeared further on. He seemed to be flying evasively. Because of the explosions the scanners were picking up even further on? Or because he was afraid of Napoleon?

"Nappy," Bandicut asked, profoundly disturbed not just by Copernicus's flight, but by Napoleon's behavior. "Why did you say that about Copernicus? What has he done to you? And why did he run?"

"I felt great disruption!" Napoleon rasped. "Great disruption all around, and fear!"

"You said he was trying to contaminate your programming!"

"Fear!" echoed the robot. "Fear for our mission! And for your safety!"

"But Nappy." Bandicut could find no words to convey his bewilderment, and his fury at the turn of events.

> /// *This might not be a good time*
> *to press the question.* ///

/Why not?/

> /// *He's flying stably, holding formation.*
> *But he may be having personality problems,*
> *trying to integrate changes in his*
> *programming.* ///

Bandicut frowned, not answering.

/// *And we must at least consider—* ///

/What?/ Bandicut asked, though he knew exactly what Charlie was going to say.

/// *Just—the possibility of*
interference with his programming. ///

/"Contamination," you mean?/

/// *Well, the boojum does seem to function*
quickly and unexpectedly,
causing mischief but not exposing itself long.
We should consider that
Napoleon might have been meddled with,
when he was repaired. ///

/Charlie, do you really think that's what's happened?/

/// *I think it's possible.*
That doesn't necessarily mean probable.
He was, after all, under the care of
the shadow-people. ///

/Yeah, and so was Copernicus. So why do you think Copernicus ran away?/

To that, Charlie offered no comment. Bandicut dizzily imagined reporting this dialogue, and all of the possibilities it was fraught with, to Ik. And he could imagine Ik's answer. *Get rid of the robots.*

Which was not at all an unreasonable suggestion, objectively speaking. It was also a suggestion he would not dream of taking.

He watched the endlessly streaming landscape of the shaft as they arrowed down its middle. It was dangerously hypnotic. He began to wish that he had something to eat or drink. A moment later a tube appeared at the corner of his mouth. He took a sip of a clear, sweet liquid, which revived him somewhat.

Still, he nearly jumped out of his skin when Ik yelled, "*Hraahh!*" and decelerated sharply.

"Uh!" he grunted, feeling a modest shift of his weight, as his suit decelerated at what had to have been about a hundred gees.

/// We just passed something. ///

/Coppy?/

/// I don't think so. ///

The suit gave him a series of rapid-fire scans to the rear, and he saw Ik practically colliding with a shiny bipedal figure that had emerged from the side of the shaft. They had flashed by so fast, Bandicut had completely missed it. Now they were spinning around each other in quick circuits. As he slowed, Ik and the other accelerated to rejoin him. He became aware of Ik jabbering on the comm. "Are you safe? We feared for your life!"

The answering voice—*Li-Jared's?*—was oddly metallic, perhaps because of his suit comm, perhaps because Bandicut's translator-stones didn't know what to do with it. *Bwang bwang.* Bandicut's wrists tingled for a moment, before he heard, "Terrible . . . terrible attacks! Destructive overloads . . . great wave! Nodes ahead already destroyed . . . may have passed . . . can't be sure."

Ik's voice overlaid Bandicut's strained efforts to understand Li-Jared's words. "Very near thing, indeed! The shadow-people warned us of your danger and sent us after you."

Bwang! "They are no longer angry, then? Good." The chromed being suddenly pointed at Bandicut and Napoleon, as they matched speeds and began to accelerate again. "Who?"

"My new friend John Bandicut—and his robot, Napoleon. John Bandicut, Li-Jared! We have found him at last!"

Bandicut cleared his throat, as they flew down the shaft at blinding speed. "Nice to, uh, meet you," he said to the mirror-silvered figure, which in its suit looked like a chrome gorilla. Li-Jared's suit appeared less bulky than theirs.

Bwong. "Friend of Ik's, I should be willing to meet."

Bandicut blinked, uncertain whether to consider that a friendly greeting or an expression of reticence.

Ik continued, "Another of our party—a robot, Copernicus—has fled ahead of us. It has been accused by this one of possible contamination."

Li-Jared made a sweeping gesture. "Then let us—"
bwang-ang! "—stay as far from it as possible."

Bandicut grunted. No way, he thought.

"Hraah, Li-Jared, that robot saved my life not long ago," said Ik.

Bwuhh.

Bandicut waited for a translation, but none came. When Ik spoke again, it was in a firm voice. "We must pursue it. We do not *know* that it is contaminated, and something else altogether may be going on. Can you fly faster?"

In answer, Li-Jared rotated slightly. The back of his suit sparkled with red fire, and he accelerated smoothly into the lead. "John Bandicut," said Ik. "Let us see if we can catch Copernicus."

As quickly as he could form the thought, Bandicut accelerated to keep up with Li-Jared. Ik kept pace on one side, and Napoleon on the other.

The landscape of the shaft gradually changed, almost like mountains giving way to river valleys and plains. Bandicut watched the ribs and crenelations of the shaft open up to form basins with huge, mysterious structures etched into their sides. Like sprawling river-confluences, the basins seemed to branch off to the sides, but where they led was impossible to tell. They sometimes passed those basins for minutes at a time, at whatever dizzying speed they were making, which gave Bandicut some sense of the size of the things. He envisioned a vast web of these power-connectors, joining wings of the metaworld from all directions.

/// *A reasonable image, I think.*
It is a very large world,
no question. ///

/How large is it really, Charlie?/ He was feeling a little faint from the sheer sense of magnitude.

/// *As large as your solar system,*
I would guess.
Or larger.

> *With all of the n-space connectors,*
> *it's hard to say. ///*

/Oh,/ Bandicut whispered.

The tiny point in his scanner that was Copernicus continued to draw away, with occasional zigzags. Napoleon remained quiet. Bandicut wondered if he dared trust either robot now. He called out to Copernicus repeatedly, but there was no answer. Whatever had frightened him, had frightened him to the core.

The quarx seemed to become lost in his own thoughts, perhaps occupied with his gradually emerging memories. The flight down the shaft began to seem endless.

Bandicut woke from a doze to the sound of Ik and Li-Jared talking.

"If your information is correct—"

"—may be able to seek help from the Maksu—"

"If it is *correct*. But it is from a connection that the boojum might have—" *rasp* "—infiltrated."

"Only after I found the reference," Li-Jared was saying. "That is why—" *brrr-k-dang* "—it is so angry. I am certain that it wants that information kept hidden."

"But why?"

"—does not wish us, or anyone else, to learn—"

"Or to escape?"

"—or to interfere."

"Then," Ik said slowly, "we should try very hard not to interfere. It is not the boojum we want, but freedom."

"Amen," Bandicut murmured aloud. He hadn't understood much of what he'd just heard, but he understood that last part, and he was all in favor of it.

Ik and Li-Jared fell silent for a moment, perhaps startled to find him a part of the conversation. Li-Jared broke the silence by saying, "But do not forget . . . many innocents stand to be harmed by the boojum, as well."

"I do not think that we have forgotten," Ik said dryly. To Bandicut, he added, "Li-Jared found a connection point such as you and I discussed. The kind that—'' he paused a moment, perhaps to convey emphasis indirectly to Li-Jared ''—you yourself are quite familiar with.''

Bandicut blinked, as Li-Jared made a sound of apparent puzzlement. A datanet. Li-Jared had linked with a datanet?

''And he learned much about the place where the sort of knowledge we seek flows in streams and waves—''

''But *not* its precise location,'' Li-Jared broke in. ''Ik, we should not be discussing—'' Li-Jared was interrupted by a bright flash of light ahead, followed by another.

''What was that?'' Bandicut asked nervously.

/// Electrical activity? ///

Charlie's speculation was punctuated by a spectacular arc of lightning across the shaft in front of them. Bandicut held his breath, as the arc was followed by another ahead, and several behind. A heartbeat later, they were speeding through a raging electrical storm. /What is this? Has it found us?/

/// I'm not sure, but— ///

WHAAAMM!

A blast knocked him into a head-over-heels tumble. As he struggled for breath, his suit righted itself and steadied its course. It took him a lot longer to stop shaking. Lightning continued to flash around him. ''Ik—what—?'' he panted.

Through a hiss of static, he heard Ik's voice, but he couldn't make out words. Another arc blazed directly in front of him, and as his eyes swam and watered, he was almost certain that for a moment he saw a small ball of lightning *inside* his suit.

''—through it soon—''

/// John, hang on.
I think your suit can protect you.
That was a direct hit we took a minute ago. ///

Bandicut stared ahead in terror as they flew through the dazzling eruptions. After a few seconds, the lightning subsided, but a bluish light continued to ripple and squirm along the walls of the shaft, all around them.

''John Bandicut, are you still there?'' Ik called.

''Yeah—I'm okay!'' Bandicut wheezed. He peered and

saw Napoleon still in formation. "What the hell was that?"

"Energy flux. It did not seem directed. Perhaps caused by the boojum's random destruction."

Bandicut muttered as the rippling light faded along the walls. They were now zooming through a glass tube, and he thought he could see dim stars or galaxies through the walls. Ahead, he could just make out a vague, but enormous, dark shape. The next section of Shipworld? He hardly dared hope. He glanced back over his shoulder and saw the blurred patch of the Milky Way.

He shivered and looked ahead again. He'd lost the tracking lock on Copernicus. "Ik—do you have Copernicus on your scanner?"

"No longer."

Damn. Bandicut watched several glittering arches sail over his head. His suit began to decelerate.

"John Bandicut, look!" Ik was pointing with a silvery crab's claw out the left side of the shaft.

There was a definite structure out there now, far too vast for a single glance. Tiny spots resolved into marker lights along the thing's edges and lines. They dwindled out of view in all directions, except down. Below was the emptiness of intergalactic space.

Bandicut glimpsed a flicker of light ahead. "Energy flux approaching," Ik cautioned.

"Follow me," Li-Jared said suddenly. "Silently, if possible." He decelerated sharply and veered left toward the shaft wall. Bandicut did not manage even a silent *ulp!* before his suit followed. Ik and Napoleon kept pace perfectly. The shaft wall blurred past them at dizzying speed, very close now.

He wanted to cry, *What are we doing?* but his voice caught as they executed a sharp pitch-up, another deceleration, and a left sweep, straight toward an outward bulge in a section of the wall that looked like cut crystal. *Unh!* he started to say—and then the glass wall revealed an opening right in the middle of the bulge, and they shot through it into space.

Bandicut found himself breathless at the sudden clear view. Not that he could make out the overall shape of the

Shipworld structure; it was much too large. But its surface seemed stark and bright compared to the section they'd left behind. As he scanned across the expanse, he saw several moving lights. Spacecraft in flight? They were all quite distant, and widely separated from each other. Nonetheless, his heart raced. Images of L5 City bubbled up. Was that *commerce* he was seeing? Normal life? For someone, anyway? His mind filled with visions of civilization—people working and living and traveling in space, people who could tell him where he was and how things worked. *People,* yes!

But humans? As quickly as his heart had inflated with hope, he felt a draining despair. He would be a fool to expect humans. But his spirits began to rise again when he spotted a series of converging strobe lights that looked for all the world like the approach lights to a spaceport on Earth. "Ik," he muttered, "where are we going?"

"We may be in danger. Silence, please."

Bandicut realized suddenly why they had taken this evasive course out of the power tube. The boojum might have used up its firepower in the connector, blowing up all those power nodes, but that didn't mean it wasn't waiting for them at the endpoint.

Did Shipworld have outer defenses? Could the boojum fool the defenses into thinking that the four of them were orbiting debris—or even an enemy to be destroyed?

And where was Copernicus?

They flew straight away from the power-shaft, then veered inward again, toward the outer edge of Shipworld. Every few seconds, they made new, abrupt course changes, but always drawing closer to Shipworld. Bandicut endured the jolts in silence, wishing they could just fly over to that landing port etched in strobes.

And then he understood, as a thread of green fire rippled out toward them from somewhere on the perimeter of that landing zone—and Ik and Li-Jared plunged them into further violent maneuvers. For a moment, his forward view was filled with bright green flashes, and he felt something like a body blow, insulated by his suit. His suspicions were right, then; the boojum had subverted the defensive systems. And he had just felt—

"Near miss!" Ik cried, and veered again.

/// John! ///

He blinked and realized that the suit had just put up new tracking information. He tried to focus on it: a point of light weaving against a station-shaped grid.

/// It's Copernicus, yes? ///

He stifled an outcry, while he tried to eyeball outside what the scanner view was showing him on the grid. Was that a silver flicker, close to the station wall?

/// He is flying evasively, too. ///

/Yes, but evading us? Or the boojum?/

Charlie's answer, if he had one, was interrupted by another jarring maneuver, and an emerald blaze—

—and a rocket-crackle in his ears—

His vision turned to a sheet of fire, and he began tumbling. He heard Ik's voice, full of static, and Li-Jared's. And he was suddenly very hot and prickly inside the suit, and he wondered if this was where he was going to die.

/// That was—really—bad— ///

THUD. THUD. Two much smaller impacts, and he felt the tumbling stop, and then a course change. The fire in his eyes slowly faded, and his vision began to clear. Ik was holding him on one side, and Napoleon on the other. They had stopped his tumbling and were physically carrying him through their evasive maneuvers.

"—John Bandicut?"

He began to croak an answer, but the words were taken from his throat by the view. The surface of the station was much closer now, and he could see a series of small, reflective domes on its surface, like soap bubbles. /What—?/ He saw Copernicus flicker across the surface, darting one way, then the other. Before he could draw a breath to speak, the robot zipped into one of the soap bubbles and winked out of sight. "Coppy!" he shouted.

"Stay tight!" Ik snapped, and they veered twice more, and then were flying dizzyingly close to the outer hull. A crackle of green fire thumped another near miss. Ik veered left, left again, then right, and down—wrenching Bandicut by the arm. One more twist—an emerald haze—and a huge silver bubble loomed before them. He caught a reflection in the bubble of a fiery bolt behind them, then they flashed through the bubble and it was gone.

"HRAAH!" Ik boomed. "Is everyone here?"

Bandicut was still trying to get his breath. "Yah—" he gasped "—but I saw Copernicus go into a different—"

"I know," Ik said. "We must find out where we are now." His silver-crab suit held fast to Bandicut's as they jetted inward toward a great, solid surface.

They were inside a huge, palely lit dome—probably a force field of some kind. Ahead, in the watery light, Bandicut expected an airlock entrance. Instead, he was stunned to see that they were dropping headlong into a wooded park.

He felt a pull of deceleration and an attitude rotation. For a moment, he lost all vision in front of him. Then, abruptly, they were standing together in a small clearing, surrounded by trees.

14

AT THE WATERING HOLE

 BEFORE BANDICUT COULD gather his wits to ask questions, Ik's suit split open and the Hraachee'an stepped out. Bandicut silently asked his own suit to do the same.

His visor went dark, there was a soft hiss, and the front of his suit popped open. He stepped out, amazed. The air smelled like moss and cedar, with an additional tang he could not identify. He turned around in wonder, thinking that he could almost have been in a domed-in park on Earth—though at second glance, none of the trees looked quite like any terrestrial tree. For one thing, they were all translucent, with a silvery-green glow shining through them. Overhead, the "sky" was the pale, silver glow of the forcefield bubble, which apparently was designed to allow objects like spacesuits to pass through while keeping air in. Perhaps it could distinguish living drop-ins from hazards such as meteoroids.

"John Bandicut, are you injured?" Ik asked, waving his arms in a wide arc. It was impossible to tell whether he was attempting to convey meaning, or just stretching.

"No," Bandicut grunted. "I'm okay. But where are we?"

"Uncertain." Ik turned to watch Li-Jared's silver suit open at the top and contract like a shrinking, elastic liquid into a basketball-sized globe at Li-Jared's feet. Li-Jared slouched forward to greet them. He was about five feet tall, and wore a blue, silken-looking body suit. His skin was covered with short, brown hair, and he appeared more simian than humanoid.

Except for the two eyes. They were shaped like a cat's pupils, vertical and narrow, but vivid gold, except for a blaze of electric blue across the middle, which appeared to be horizontal pupil slits. He stepped toward Bandicut with an almost fluid movement. "Bwang," he said.

Bandicut felt a tickle in his right wrist.

/// Hold up your stone, ///

Charlie suggested.

/// Maybe he's got them, too. ///

/I'll show you mine if you show me yours?/ Bandicut thought dryly. He raised his right wrist to display his translator-stone. The embedded gem pulsed like a charged diamond.

"Ah!" Li-Jared cried. With both hands, he tugged open the front of his body suit enough to reveal the thick hair covering his chest—and two twinkling jewels about where his breastbone ought to have been, white gem on top and emerald two inches below. Bandicut kept his wrist up for a moment, feeling a soft buzz. Then his stone went dark.

/// Try talking now. ///

Bandicut cleared his throat. "Hi. Can you understand me now? My name is John Bandicut."

"Yes." The other's blazing eyes drilled into his. "I am pleased to meet a friend of Ik's. I see you too are an immigrant to Shipworld. What do you call your . . . species?"

"Human. Man. And yours?"

Li-Jared shifted his gaze to Ik, then back to Bandicut. "Man? *I* am called man."

"Uh—"

"Where do you come from, John Bandicut?" The electric-blue bands in Li-Jared's eyes narrowed to thin lines.

"Earth. It's a planet—" Bandicut gestured helplessly up toward the dome-sky "—out there in the Milky Way galaxy somewhere."

"We are all from that galaxy somewhere," Ik observed.

Bandicut frowned. "I hadn't realized that. What is your planet called, Li-Jared?"

Li-Jared scratched what might have been an ear on the side of his head. "Home. My world was called *home*."

///*I think perhaps we have a*
small translation problem.///

Bandicut cleared his throat. "Um—we called our world 'home,' too, but its proper name was Earth. Do you have another word for your world?"

Li-Jared blinked. It was a startling effect; the electric-blue pupils winked out for a moment, then shone again. "We called it—*good* home—"

"Yes, of course. But don't you—"

"Or—" *bwang'ng* "—Home with Green, Beautiful, Perilous Sky."

Bandicut wondered if he could shorten that without insult.

Li-Jared said something else, which sounded like "Karellia."

Ik broke in, "We should not be standing here. We were only just under attack by the boojum. John Bandicut, do you wish to free your robot from its suit?"

Napoleon was still encased in the tall silver suit, its arms twitching up and down as though waving for attention. Bandicut touched his right wrist to the front of the silver suit. It opened like a clamshell.

Napoleon clicked and stepped out of the suit. "John Bandicut, I am ready and at your service."

"Great, Nappy. I'm afraid we've lost Copernicus for now. I may be counting on you even more than usual." It occurred to him at that moment that Copernicus was still carrying his backpack. So he had no tools, no food, no clothes. He gave a dark sigh. "Napoleon, this is Li-Jared. A friend of Ik's. Do you remember Ik telling us about him?"

"Of course," rasped the robot. "I am on the lookout for treachery at all times."

Li-Jared blinked, twice.

"That's *not* what I—"

"As for Copernicus, I am uncertain. I fear he may have been touched somehow by the . . . boojum. I will endeavor to protect you from any such influence." Napoleon swiveled his scanners. "Cap'n, where are we?"

"I don't know, and don't call me 'Captain.' That's what Copernicus calls me, not you." Bandicut shivered, and looked around the park. "Ik, where are we? And where do we go from here?"

"We must find a map. Li-Jared, is there not a significant civilization on this side of the continent?"

"Indeed, I believe this is—" *Buh'wang.*

"Hiii? I had not realized—"

"Yes, I saw a marking at the other end of the power-connector. It is one reason I fled the way I did. There will be Maksu here. I believe they can help us find the ice caverns."

Ice caverns? Bandicut thought.

"The nexus. The connection to the Tree of Ice," Ik explained.

"Oh."

"And we must move quickly, before the boojum locates us here," Li-Jared said.

"Why hasn't it found us already?" Bandicut asked, with a flash of annoyance that everyone seemed to understand about the boojum except him.

"It's not all-powerful, you know," Li-Jared said, peering through the trees. He suddenly pointed. "This way, I think." He picked up the ball that was his spacesuit and set off. The others followed, carrying their empty spacesuits awkwardly under their arms.

Bandicut hurried to keep up. He refused to let go of his question. "If it's not all-powerful—"

"It lives within a system where it is not wanted," Ik said. "It works great mischief and destruction, but most of the time it stays in hiding, protecting itself from the system's defenses."

They followed Li-Jared through a stand of glimmering, translucent trees, and up over a small knoll. On the far side of the knoll, a wooden footbridge arched over a stream. Li-Jared headed that way, but stopped at a loud wheezing sound. A tall, whiplike being with an array of tiny eyes rose up from the bank of the stream and waved numerous arms at them. "We are closed now! You cannot stay!" Bandicut heard, through the translator-stones. "How did you get in?"

"We had to make an emergency landing," Li-Jared answered. "We had no choice."

"We are closed for maintenance," said the being.

"In addition, we wish to return these suits to the custody of maintenance," Ik said.

The vaguely treelike creature made a whistling sound. "This is most, most irregular. Yes, I suppose that could be done. But I must register your arrival. This is a park, not an immigration station. Really, this is not at all conventional."

Ik rubbed his chest. "We were wondering if you might tell us our actual location. And perhaps direct us to a—" *rasp rasp*.

There was no translation.

The being shivered. "You must consult a map, sir! It is not my job to locate such places!"

"I meant no offense. I will consult a map," Ik said hastily. "Perhaps you could direct us to one."

The tree-creature made a hissing sound. "Please follow me. And bring your refuse with you."

It led them across the bridge and through a long bower of living trees. At the end of the bower was a heavy wooden door, which swung open at the tree-being's touch. Ik held the door while the others sidled through with their bulky space-suit-shells. They entered a wood-paneled room, and the creature went behind a counter and bent out of sight for a moment.

/Does the translator already know these people?/ Bandicut wondered, surprised by the ease of communication.

/// *Apparently so.* ///

Ik propped his spacesuit shell against the counter and waved a bony hand in the air. "Where might we register?"

The whiplike creature straightened up, holding a small object which it pointed at the four companions. A fan of necrotic blue light erupted from the object and swept over them, then winked out. "You are registered," the creature said, with apparent distaste. "And here are your tokens." With a slender hand, it held out four dull, coinlike disks.

Bandicut peered suspiciously, but Ik reached out without hesitation. A wink of light greeted his fingertips, and seemed to illuminate him from within for an instant. The whip-creature tossed the other disks into the air, and three twinkles of light flickered into Li-Jared, Napoleon, and Bandicut. He felt no discomfort, but had a curious, momentary sense of *connection,* as though to a datanet. Then it was gone.

The whip-creature said, "That is your preliminary allowance. You may go now. Leave the spacesuits here. But I assure you maintenance will not be happy."

"Please convey our appreciation to maintenance," said Ik. "Can you tell us where we might gain access to a map?"

The creature waved to a door on the far side of the room. "Outside, to your left. And now, I really must ask you—"

"We're *going!*" Li-Jared interrupted, as he led the way to the door.

They found the map-console easily enough, but that was dull compared to the rest of the view. They had stepped out of the office onto a high overlook—a towering atrium balcony, at least a hundred stories high, judging by the myriad levels visible on the opposite side. While Ik hunched over the console, trying to make sense of their location, Bandicut wandered over to take a dizzying look. He leaned cautiously over a too-low railing and gazed down upon an astounding promenade, which could have been the largest shopping mall in the galaxy. It appeared full of living beings of one sort or another, most of them the size of fleas from where he stood. *People!* Not human, no—but for the first time since he'd arrived on Shipworld, he felt a real breath of hope. He might actually be in a place where he could meet citizens in ordinary life and discover what this place was all about—not in flight or conflict, but just in daily existence. Was it possible that there could be humans here, or at least a place for him, after all that had gone before?

/// Perhaps, perhaps, ///

whispered Charlie, responding it seemed not so much to Bandicut's thoughts as to some deep wistfulness within himself.

Li-Jared peered over the railing, beside him. "Does your 'home' have anything like this?"

Bandicut blinked, feeling a moment of vertigo. He drew a slow breath. "Sort of. But a lot smaller." He was thinking, not of Earth proper, but of an extended mall that ringed L5 City—or used to, a thousand or a million years ago, before he left.

/// Don't draw conclusions without facts. ///

Bandicut frowned.

"A bit ostentatious, I think," Li-Jared said. "I find these—" *b'wang* "—carbuncles of civilization to be rather overdone. Still, that's no reason to see it destroyed." The chimplike being craned his neck to peer up toward the ceiling. There was something like a sun up there, but refracted or reflected through some very odd geometric effects.

"Destroyed?" Bandicut said puzzled. "Why should it be destroyed?"

Li-Jared lowered his gaze. "I do not say that it should be. But why should a star-spanner factory be destroyed? Why does the boojum do what it does?"

"I don't know," Bandicut answered.

Li-Jared flicked his fingers—a shrug?—and turned away to rejoin Ik.

Bandicut sighed and craned his neck up and down, and judged that—even at this dizzying height—they were less than halfway up from floor to ceiling. The atrium balconies were interconnected here and there by graceful, asymmetric arches—single spans connecting opposite sides, though not necessarily joining floors of equal height. Sargasso-like plants drifted through the open air like balloons riding air currents.

Bandicut caught himself swaying, and backed hastily away from the railing. He nearly stumbled into a being that was walking behind him, a slouching quadruped built like a tiger, but with an anteater's face. Napoleon whirred and caught him with an extended arm. "Sorry," Bandicut grunted. The alien grumbled something that the translator ignored, and continued on its way. Bandicut shrugged, watching it disappear around a corner. A moment later, he felt something like a sharp mosquito bite on the back of his neck, and smacked himself with his open hand. He felt a momentary full-body tingle like a mild electric shock. He looked at his hand in alarm. But if he had killed an insect, there was no trace of it on his palm.

Li-Jared was watching him, his pupils narrowed to thin slits. "It may have been nothing," he said.

Bandicut felt his own eyes narrow. "What do you mean?"

Li-Jared flicked his fingers absently. "There are small pests to be found most anywhere in this world. Some are living, some not. Some are n-spatial, and merely seek to drain a tiny bit of . . . quantum stability." Li-Jared blinked in that jarring way, then added, "That may have been all it was." He turned back to Ik, leaving Bandicut feeling most unsettled.

/// May have been all it was.
I thought I felt something go out of you
with that bite. ///

Bandicut focused inward. /Something like . . . "quantum stability"?/

Charlie hesitated a moment.

/// Something like . . . information, ///

he said at last.

Bandicut stared into space, only half aware of his mouth slightly open in an expression of stupidity. He closed it. /Mokin' foke,/ he thought.

Li-Jared bwanged as Ik left the map-console.

"I believe I have found what we need."

"Lead on," said Li-Jared.

Bandicut set his jaw. "Lead on *where?* To find food, or a place to stay? I have to tell you, I'm getting tired of all this running around." He waved his hands. "And what about Coppy? Are we going to look for him, and try to find out what's wrong?" Bandicut's breath caught. He was surprised by his own outburst.

Ik's small black eyes sparkled with inner light. "Coppy, no. Not directly. I would not know where to look, I fear. But, John Bandicut, it may cheer you to know that Li-Jared and I have been in this atrium city before, and we do know our way around it somewhat. I have requested a tracking call on Copernicus. We should be notified if he makes contact with the system. It is the best I know how to do just now."

Bandicut flushed with frustration. "Then might I ask, what *have* you found?"

"A—" *rasp* "—watering hole," said Ik.

They located a transport mechanism, recessed in an alcove. It could easily have been mistaken for an elevator. For several seconds, they stood among oddly angled mirrors, with Bandicut trying to look around to get his bearings. The next moment, they were standing in a place of gloomy darkness.

He coughed involuntarily. The air was full of incense. As his eyes adapted, he saw lights in the darkness—shaded, like Chinese lanterns. "What this?" he croaked, trying to breathe the incense without choking. He saw tables, arranged in a large, seemingly random pattern, not just on the floor, but in the air in a three dimensional array. It was too dark to see what was holding the tables in the air. Each table held a small, luminous globe, and that appeared to be the sole source of illumination in the room. "What are we going to—?" As he began the question, he realized that he was *floating,* and his words came out as a squawk.

"Can you see well enough?" Ik asked, close by. "The light here is mostly ultraviolet."

Wonderful, Bandicut thought. And me with no sunblock. He looked down and realized that some of the fibers in his jumpsuit were glowing brightly in the black light. He squinted instinctively, which did little to improve his vision.

/// I believe your "normalization"
will protect you from the ultraviolet. ///
/That's a relief. Can it let me see, while it's at it?/
/// Hm. Let me work on that. ///

"This way," said Ik, pointing to an unoccupied table. Bandicut squinted harder, startled to realize that most of the tables were in fact occupied, by shadowy shapes of light and darkness. He couldn't make out what any of the occupants looked like.

/// It's not your vision.
It's supposed to work that way. ///

Bandicut felt himself gliding into a seat, around a small circular table from Ik and Li-Jared, and Napoleon. /Charlie, is this a fr'deekin' *bar*?/ He shook his head, thinking, *watering hole.* Of course.

He drew a deep breath and looked around. He was suddenly conscious of a very low-frequency thrumming sound, pulsing in and out of his hearing range. Music?

/// John, I have not heard that song in . . .
well, I cannot imagine how long! ///

Charlie sounded amazed, and delighted.

/Ah,/ Bandicut said, disconcerted. Their table, he realized, was not stationary, but was floating slowly through the darkness. So were all the rest of the tables in the room, drifting in a peculiar minuet, rising as if on air currents, and falling and gliding in slow, curving paths that had no apparent pattern. No wonder he hadn't been able to see what was supporting the tables; nothing was.

Shaking off a wave of dizziness, he peered at Ik, who had leaned forward over their table lamp and was gazing into it with fierce concentration. Another system interface? Bandicut glanced at Li-Jared and was startled to see him engaged in a handwaving conversation with a shimmering, ghostlike being hovering beside him. A moment later, a fist-sized bubble of a fuming green liquid appeared in front of Li-Jared. A similar bubble appeared before Bandicut.

"May this . . . be to your liking," said Li-Jared, in a halting translation of what Bandicut decided was probably a toast. He bowed in acknowledgment, and lifted the vaporous green bubble to the light. Li-Jared brought his own drink to his mouth and appeared to sip directly through the clear bubble.

Bandicut hesitated. The stuff looked corrosive as hell. But

maybe the normalization would take care of this, too. /Should I?/ he asked. /It looks radioactive./

/// Sure, what the hell. ///

/Watch it, you're starting to sound like Charlie-One./ He took a deep breath. /I hope you know what you're talking about./ He brought the bubble to his puckered lips. A cool flame passed between his lips, down his throat, into his stomach. The sensation was bracing, but not unpleasant. He felt a glow in his fingertips, and relaxed a little. It would probably do him good to relax. Quit worrying. He'd had too many worries.

Ik looked up from the lamp. "I have made contact. A representative of the Maksu will meet with us shortly. Let us hope we can supply suitable information in exchange."

Maksu? Information? Bandicut wondered, rather lazily, what Ik was talking about. He also wondered, vaguely, if his mental edge was beginning to slip away.

/// John, before you drink any more of that— ///

/Eh?/ He turned the bubble in his hand.

/// You are definitely losing your edge.

Before you do, shall we check out Napoleon? ///

/Mm./ Bandicut stared off into the darkness. He thought he saw something like fish moving through the deepsea gloom. /Sure. Is there a robot repair shop around here somewhere?/ He wasn't imagining things; there *were* fish moving out there, ripples of blue and silver moving through a haze of smoke, like murky water. He looked away, blinking. He felt as if he were on a raft at sea. He felt a flurry of seasickness.

/// John, that drink is affecting you. ///

/How? You mean there are no fish?/ He glanced out of the corner of his eye where the fish had been.

/// No, I mean the seasickness. ///

He felt a powerful rush of dizziness.

/// I'm trying to stabilize it.

Is that better? ///

/Awk. Other way./ The dizziness faded abruptly, and he gasped with relief.

/// Good. Let's do this while we can.
Could you reach out and
put your hand on Napoleon's head? ///

/Yah./ Bandicut gulped. He felt his mind clear a little, and he frowned and did as Charlie had requested. Napoleon peered at him, but remained silent. Bandicut's hand tingled with the familiar sensation of Charlie reaching out; and what he felt was the presence of something *not quarx*, something reminiscent of the quickness and complexity of the datanet, and yet not quite like that, either. It was something almost living. Almost.

/Nappy?/ he thought in wonderment.

The answer was a twitchy hash of confusing input, and he sensed that Charlie was busy trying to interpret it; but if it made any sense to the quarx, it didn't to him. /Charlie—?/

He sensed a reaction of *not now,* and a concerted effort on Charlie's part to penetrate some particular haze of confusing patterns. It was like watching a probe in murky water, trying to map an obscured terrain. He felt at once helpless and intimately connected, as tendrils of awareness and uncertainty flickered back and forth. Was Charlie trying to reprogram the robot, or just to understand what had happened to it?

The boojum? Had the boojum touched Napoleon?

Would it touch *him*?

Bandicut shivered with sudden fear, felt sweat trickling down his neck. He felt a contact with something deeper. Something he couldn't name. There was a sudden electric rush, and a feeling of control slipping away.

He shuddered with a wave of fear . . . *no no no no no* . . . and not just fear but revulsion, and *bewilderment* . . . and he reeled inwardly, tensing and struggling to guard himself, to protect that which was *him*.

He had no idea how long he sat that way, rocking slightly forward and backward until the wave passed; but when he unclenched his fists, his palms ached from the bite of his fingernails. He drew short breaths, trying to focus on the others around him. Napoleon was crouched motionless; Li-Jared was sipping from his pink bubble, apparently unaware of anything wrong; Ik was staring into the yellow globe.

/// John, are you all right? ///

Charlie called huskily, and he realized that it was not the first time, but the fourth or fifth time that the quarx had asked.

/I'm not sure,/ he whispered. /What was that? The boojum?/

The quarx's voice was a soothing presence.

/// Not the boojum, no.
It was Napoleon. ///

/Napoleon?/ he asked dully.

/// He was scared. Is scared. ///

Bandicut swallowed. /But of what? The boojum? Copernicus?/

Charlie didn't answer at once. Then he spoke slowly, with uncertainty.

/// Maybe, John. Maybe.
But mostly, I think he's scared
of being alive. ///

Bandicut absorbed that in silence. /Alive?/ he said finally. /Do you really mean—?/

/// I think he's hovering on the brink, John.
He's changed. ///

/Yes, I know, but—/

"Hraaah," said Ik, leaning across the table, his bony face sculpted into a skull-like countenance by the globelight. "I believe the Maksu are approaching." His eyes flickered at Bandicut. "Are you and your robot well?"

Am I well? Bandicut thought. What a question.

/// John, I think Napoleon is scared.
But I have no sense that he is
wrong, if you understand my meaning.
I sense no malice or concealed motives. ///

/Good./ Bandicut nodded slightly. "Yeah, Ik. I'm just a little . . . disoriented."

"And Napoleon?"

"He's still recovering from his repairs, I think. But he seems okay, as nearly as I can tell."

"Then would you mind remaining here, while I go introduce myself to the Maksu?" Ik inclined his head to Bandicut's left. Bandicut was startled to see another table floating close to theirs, without privacy barriers. He could see the table and its lightglobe clearly, and the patrons floating at the table. Was it one, or many? It looked almost exactly like a swarm of fireflies, with the same greenish yellow light—except that the light was not blinking, but pulsing with nervous intensity, as the . . . beings . . . swarmed in slow orbits around one another.

"Um, is that—?"

"Indeed," Ik said, rising. "They seemed rather . . . reserved, when I made contact. I believe it might be better if I spoke with them alone, to start with. Li-Jared, will you stay with John Bandicut?"

Li-Jared's eyes blinked dazzlingly.

Ik rose and floated across the gap between the tables. As he settled across the table from the swarm of fireflies, a sparkling shroud rippled into existence, concealing them. Bandicut looked uncertainly at Li-Jared. With a twanging sound that Bandicut guessed was a laugh, Li-Jared took another sip from his bubble. "John Bandicut, human man from Earth, do you have a shorter name?" Li-Jared asked at last.

Bandicut chuckled with relief. "Call me Bandie. Or John. And do they serve anything here that won't take the top of my head off?" He held up his green-glowing drink with a grimace. He recalled how the shadow-people's lounge had read his mind as to his tastes. "Like beer, maybe?"

Li-Jared twanged another laugh and spoke to the glimmering ghost which at that instant appeared over his shoulder.

"So would it be all right if I called you a *Karellian*?" Bandicut asked, holding his half-meter-high pilsner glass up to the light. He studied the amber bubbles in the beer while watching Li-Jared out of the corner of his eye. "And you could call me *human* or *Earthman*? For the sake of simplicity?"

"For simplicity," Li-Jared agreed. His eyes seemed to be glowing more diffusely as he drank, though possibly it was Bandicut's vision getting foggy. He had found himself with a remarkable thirst for the beer, even though he knew he would be wise to limit his intake. Li-Jared was becoming more voluble as *he* drank. He seemed to be growing more comfortable with Bandicut's presence, though he still cast an occasional pointed glance at Napoleon, who thus far had not moved, except for a periodic sensor sweep. The robot had spoken only once, and then to say, "None for me," in apparent reference to the drinks order, though the waiter-ghost had at that point already disappeared.

"Bandie, then," Li-Jared said, hunching over the table. In that moment, he looked more simian than ever; an instant later, the effect was shattered as he turned his face up, gold and sapphire eyes blazing at Bandicut. "I have traveled far with Ik. We have experienced many hazards together, in search of information that we hope may, at the very least, *tell us who is meddling in our lives!*"

"Yes!" Bandicut whispered, startled by the Karellian's vehemence.

"And—" Li-Jared's voice softened a little "—may also, if we are successful, give me a way to return home." He closed his eyes and turned away for a moment.

Bandicut's voice trembled with sympathy, and echoes of his own acute loneliness. "You miss your home a lot, don't you?"

"*Aaaannnngggg,*" Li-Jared cried. "I miss the forests and plains, and most of all the sky, the emerald sky, the beautiful, perilous sky. The stars that flare and swirl dangerously, and make life itself a fragile treasure." Li-Jared's voice shook as he spoke, as if into the emptiness of the surrounding gloom.

Bandicut was almost afraid to answer. But when the Karellian's eyes shifted back in his general direction, he found his voice and said, "Are there other . . . Karellians . . . whom you miss, particularly?"

Li-Jared's eyes flared, then dimmed. "Some. Some."

"Do you believe they're still—"

"Alive? Who can say?" said Li-Jared, reading his thoughts. "Who can say?"

Bandicut nodded. He took a long draw from his pilsner glass. The beer was rich and hoppy, with a good head. Whoever or whatever had made it had read his memories well. "Perhaps," he said at last, "we can all search together. I, too, would like to find a way home. Though I can't help thinking that everyone I cared about is probably long gone." He felt a rush of dizziness as he thought of Julie. Why? he thought. Why did it have to happen? The Earth and the comet—and even Charlie—getting between me and the first woman I ever really thought I had the slightest chance of . . . loving.

"Perhaps we can," said Li-Jared, mercifully interrupting his thoughts. "But Ik's home, you know—Hraachee'a—is no more. It is destroyed." Li-Jared's voice was cold, flat, metallic. "Ik has nowhere else to go." He bobbed his chimplike head and seemed to peer appraisingly at Bandicut. "Ik feels that you are a trustworthy companion. That you might be able to help us."

Bandicut flushed. "And you're not sure."

The Karellian's head bobbed again, side to side. "I mean no offense. But I do not—how can I explain?—make friendships lightly."

Bandicut nodded. "No reason why you should, I guess." He gazed off into the darkness, studying this strange place where the tables orbited in a three-dimensional waltz. Ik and the Maksu were out there somewhere; the tables had moved apart and he'd lost track. And he was definitely not hallucinating the fish; there was an area, slightly above him now, where glowing undersea creatures drifted and flitted, flashing a neon glow. They, and others like them, had been moving slowly in and out of view. He wondered if they were patrons in the bar, or ornamentation.

His eyes shifted to his right, and his heart pounded suddenly faster. Across the room, he saw someone floating into the halo of light surrounding a table. He rose involuntarily, thinking that the person looked almost human, female; he caught a glimpse of a crimson gown, just a momentary swirl, and dark hair, and then a hazy curtain took whoever it was into darkness.

/// John, I don't think— ///

He was still blinking, trying to get his eyes to focus better. It was too late for a better look, but the glimpse had left him breathless, frustrated, and startlingly aroused.

He suddenly remembered: something like this had happened once before, in a dreamy half-vision. He had nearly forgotten; it had happened in the lounge of the shadow-people. /Charlie, are you sure? Do you have any idea who, or what—?/

/// No, but I would tell you
if I thought it were human. ///

"There is, of course—" *buh-hnnng* "—the matter of the boojum," said Li-Jared.

"Uhh?" Bandicut shivered, disconcerted by the sudden change in the stream of thought. He struggled to focus on Li-Jared. "Yes. Of course. The boojum. I don't even know who, or what, the boojum is. Much less why it was trying to kill you."

"But you want to know, are you a target sitting here with me. Yes?"

"Yes," he whispered.

"Let me tell you a tale," said Li-Jared.

15

STRANGE TURBULENCE

 "THINK," LI-JARED SAID, "of a vast, dark sea—a place of great interlacing currents, warm and cold layers, unexplored chasms, and swarming life— more kinds than you could count in a million years."

Bandicut stared at him, unsettled by the seeming change of subject. Out of the corner of his eye, he glimpsed a tailfin disappearing into a fold of darkness.

"Think," Li-Jared said, "of just one species of life within that sea—an intelligent species, perhaps, striving to control an almost uncontrollable environment. Think of the complex social groupings, and all the complexities that might have grown within that one species."

"Yes," Bandicut murmured, wondering what this had to do with the boojum.

"Think now of a single current carrying a family, or a clan, or a thread, of that species."

"Yes."

Li-Jared's eyes narrowed. "Think of one individual within that clan. And think of an infection, a . . . virus . . . within that individual."

Bandicut frowned, saying nothing. But Li-Jared's eyes blazed at him, demanding a reaction. He cleared his throat. "Is this all a—what would you call it—*metaphor?* Or are we talking about a real ocean, a real species, a real individual?"

He took a long pull from the oversized pilsner glass.

Something in his tone appeared to offend Li-Jared. The Karellian stiffened. "I am telling you a tale," he said, his voice turning to tempered steel, "as we tell tales on my world."

"Uh, sorry—I didn't mean—"

"And yes, it is a metaphor."

"Ah. Then is it a metaphor for . . . Shipworld?"

Li-Jared's eyes dimmed, then flared blue at the pupils. "I am not yet finished," he said, his voice still metallic. "You could, I suppose, apply it as a metaphor for Shipworld. But that is not what I meant."

"Oh," Bandicut said contritely.

"It is a metaphor," Li-Jared said, his voice softening, "for the Tree of Ice."

"Uh?"

"The Tree of Ice. The synthesis of all the intricately intertwined systems that maintain Shipworld. What we, personally, can reach from here is merely the iceline. The iceline is one small thread of a great—" *bwang* "—tapestry."

"Oh," Bandicut croaked.

"Now," said Li-Jared, returning to his story, "think of that virus attacking the control system—the mind, if you will—of that individual member of the species we were discussing."

Bandicut nodded, trying to wrap his thoughts around Li-Jared's story. "Okay. Can we name this individual something? That might help me follow a little better."

Li-Jared appeared to struggle with the idea. "If it will help. I suppose."

"How about if we call it an eel," Bandicut said. "An eel named Joe. Is that all right?"

Li-Jared blinked. "An eel named . . . Joe."

"And Joe has a virus."

The simian-alien's voice twanged. "Very well. The individual, Joe, is influenced by that virus in unexpected ways. He gains certain *abilities*. Such as sharing his neighboring eels' thoughts. And influencing his neighbors—without their quite realizing it—as he himself is influenced, without his quite realizing it, by the virus. And eventually he finds that he can rub, physically, against his neighbors, and so pass the virus to them. And Joe slowly becomes—"

"A troublemaker?"

Li-Jared paused. "Well, yes. He, or perhaps his virus— the two can no longer be distinguished, you see—does not approve of the way his clan has been schooling, or perhaps the currents they have been following. He realizes that if he can influence enough of his fellows, they may be able to attack and kill a living barrier that channels the ocean currents."

"A reef. They want to kill a reef?"

"Yes. If they kill the reef they will open a new channel, and the old pattern of currents will be altered, and swept away."

Bandicut thought about that. "And what happens to the clan?"

Li-Jared's eyes flickered. "The clan will join with Joe, or be swept away."

Bandicut grunted. "And which is the boojum? Joe, or the virus?"

"I'm not certain," the Karellian admitted. "I have heard it told both ways. What matters, aside from the immediate peril, is this: the virus came into Joe's sphere through the turbulent movements of the sea. Now, the sea is full of viruses, and most of them will never find a host or create such distress. But the sea is—" *bra-hang* "—chaotic, and such systems will continuously produce unexpected changes."

Bandicut shivered. This was beginning to sound altogether too much like Charlie-One's talk of dynamical chaos in solar systems. And look where listening to that had put him.

"Over and over—maybe only one time in a million, but that is enough—the turbulence carries a virus to infect a host, and it acts, and sometimes it hides for a time, and then acts again, and spreads—" Li-Jared traced random movements through the air with his shiny black fingers.

"And that is what the boojum does?" Bandicut said softly.

A black fingertip stabbed into the light. Yes.

"Is it *alive*? The boojum?" He glanced at Napoleon, who had been sitting motionless all this time. Touched by the boojum? Maybe not. Alive? Maybe. And what about Copernicus?

Fingertips flicked upward. "I don't know."

Bandicut expelled a breath of frustration. "I don't get it. Why don't the people who *control* the control system—"

"Tree of Ice," Li-Jared corrected.

"All right, Tree of Ice. Why don't they step in and *remove* the damn boojum? It's just a contamination, right? Isn't that what everyone calls it?"

Black fingertips flicked upward.

"Do they know? Do they care? They must!" Bandicut waved his hands. "Someone cares enough to keep this place running. What about that big atrium? What about the shadow-people, and maintenance? There's civilization here! Someone must be in charge of it!"

Li-Jared scratched the side of his head. "It is a difficult question. There are organizational structures, yes, which keep both the environments and the societies functioning. But there are so very many—and each so different from the others!" His voice twanged like a plucked banjo string. "Atrium City, where we are now, is a complexly structured society. I have been here before. I do not care for it much, but it is a useful mingling zone, a melting pot—and a good place for seeking information."

I certainly seek information, Bandicut thought wearily. He rubbed his eyelids with his thumbs. "Isn't there someone who's just in charge of *Shipworld*? Who controls this Tree of Ice, anyway?"

The Karellian's eyes blinked completely shut, then blazed open again. "That, my fellow traveler, is just one of the things that Ik and I have been trying to discover."

Bandicut stared at him for a moment longer, before taking a deep draft of his beer.

They sat in silence for a while. Bandicut found himself gazing into the darkness, wondering where the "woman" he had seen was now. It was all too easy to fantasize about

Julie—or any other human woman—in a place like this, where a mysterious individual could appear in a flash and swirl of color, then vanish before the eye could focus.

Li-Jared seemed to guess at his thoughts. "Did you see something? Or someone?"

"Oh, just—" his voice caught, as embarrassment and loneliness bubbled up together "—just someone for a second reminded me of a woman back . . . home. Someone I left behind. It didn't really look *like* her, but—"

"You saw someone of your own species?" Li-Jared said sharply.

"No—at least I don't think so. But she did look *almost* human." He scowled, drumming his fingers on the table. "Still—suppose I wanted to find someone in this place— someone I knew was here, but I didn't know where? How would I do it?"

The Karellian stretched casually. "I suppose I'd ask the iceline for a tracing." He gestured toward the light globe on the table. "That's how Ik contacted the Maksu."

Bandicut stared at the lamp. Iceline. Connection with the datanet, the comm, the . . . Tree of Ice? The thought gave him a little shiver. Sooner or later, he would have to interact with it. He felt a powerful urge—and a deep reluctance. He remembered the fleeting touch of the boojum, when he'd linked with the system back at the factory. But surely people linked with the iceline all the time, and they didn't all come into contact with the boojum. Ik had said that the boojum spent most of its time in hiding.

"Do you suppose maybe they're dead?" he said suddenly. "The ones who are in charge, I mean. What if *nobody* is controlling the Tree of Ice?"

The Karellian muttered to himself for a moment, his eyes dimming with thought. "I have wondered that, on occasion. But no, I do not think so. I have felt myself subject to the influence, the *manipulation,* of someone sentient, someone alive."

Someone alive? Bandicut stared into the darkness of the lounge where tables orbited and danced, and thought of the translator, back on Triton, whose daughter-stones lived in his wrists now. The translator, whose actions and instructions had saved Earth from a comet, and also brought him to this place of exile. Why? Was *he* the price of saving Earth? His sacrifice, in exchange for the life of his homeworld? A more than fair price, he supposed—but for what conceivable purpose?

"Why," he asked finally, "are they manipulating you? What do they want from you?"

Li-Jared's gaze narrowed. "If I could discover that—"

Bandicut felt a sudden fury at the incomprehensibility of it all. "Well, bloody hell, if the boojum is opposed to the people who are controlling us, then maybe it's not all that bad!"

Li-Jared's eyes welled with light. "No," he said softly. "The boojum wants only to destroy—I don't know why. I don't want that. I want freedom. I want to know why I am here. And I want to leave."

Bandicut imagined that he could read a lifetime of sadness in the Karellian's eyes. But before he could respond, Li-Jared stirred and said, "Ik."

"Hraah. Li-Jared, I must ask your assistance." Ik had reappeared silently and was floating beside the table. "The Maksu wish to speak to you of your knowledge concerning the boojum. This might provide a satisfactory exchange, knowledge for knowledge, for them to direct us to the ice cavern. John Bandicut, may I leave you here for a short time? The Maksu are most . . . reserved."

Bandicut shrugged. "I'll be fine. As long as they don't mind me lingering over my beer." He indicated his half-empty glass.

"You may stay as long as you like. If you need to reach us, address your need to the globelink. It will contact us." Ik nodded to the light globe on the table, and gestured to Li-Jared.

Bandicut watched them float across empty air and disappear into the privacy zone of the Maksu's table. The other table gradually drifted away again. /Why do I have this feeling?/

/// What feeling? ///

/About the Maksu, and the ice caverns, and all—that I'm in danger of being dragged into something I may regret. I'd sort of like to look around a little, and see if there are any humans in this place—or even anybody almost human. But it's not as if I want to leave Ik and Li-Jared, either./

*/// It does seem that
what they're looking for
may also be what you're looking for.
Yes? ///*

/Yes, but—well, I don't *know,* really. I get the feeling that danger has a way of following those two around. And now—ice caverns! Intelligent fireflies! It just makes me very nervous./ He drummed moodily on the table.

*/// Well, you've got one robot missing,
and another going through a difficult period of
adjustment.
It might not be the best time to leave
your partners. ///*

Bandicut grunted. /Maybe not. But damn it, you know—just once in a while, I'd like to be able to think of my own future. Find out if I still *have* a future. Instead of always chasing after someone else's. You know what I mean?/

The quarx made a soft, sad, chuckling sound.

*/// Do I?
Does a bear drink in the woods? ///*

Bandicut fingered his glass, nodding. The quarx had it no easier than he did.

It occurred to him, suddenly, to wonder if he could order a bowl of popcorn in this place.

It seemed like a very long time after Ik and Li-Jared had left, though perhaps it wasn't really, when he lowered his glass to reach for a handful of too-salty popcorn, and saw a privacy zone sparkle open, maybe twenty meters away in the darkness, just above eye level. The swirl of crimson fabric caught his eye. /Charlie—/ He blinked, and wished, and with a sparkle his own privacy screen dropped away, giving him a more open view.

*/// She really does look almost human,
doesn't she? ///*

murmured the quarx.

Indeed she did. His eyes drank in her features: auburn hair that flowed like a mane, down the back of her neck and between her shoulder blades. A body shape that appeared nearly human, though the loose fabric of her robe or gown concealed her features somewhat. Whatever she was, she walked on two legs, with two arms that swept out at the right places. The one hand that was visible looked long and slender. The eyes were at once alien and human—almost Asian-looking, but with a gold shimmer around a jet-black center.

The woman (he couldn't help thinking the word) turned in his direction as she stepped away from her table, gown swirling to reveal slippered feet. Her face was oval, with striking cheekbones, and a nose that quivered as she breathed. Her gaze flickered and met his, and his heart almost stopped. Her eyes seemed to widen, as though she were wondering: *Are you my species?* Her robe pressed momentarily against her body with her motion, giving him a fleeting impression of a muscular torso, and two pairs of bumps on her chest that might have been breasts. Four breasts?

Bandicut frowned. /Should I say something?/ He was suddenly aware that he had drunk quite a lot of beer, and he was holding a handful of popcorn halfway to his mouth.

*/// I don't know.
This is really your department. ///*

/Well, I can't just let her walk away./

In the time required for those words, she had broken off her gaze, continued her movement, and stepped off into the darkness. She began floating to Bandicut's right, and down. He dropped his handful of popcorn, lurched up, and took an uncertain step away from his table. Wait! Let's talk! he cried silently, his voice caught in his throat. He glanced down, saw his feet hanging in midair, and gulped back a momentary vertigo. He blinked hard, shifted his gaze, and looked for the alien woman again.

She had vanished into the gloom.

He searched the darkness frantically, but in that moment of dizziness, he had lost her. "Damn!" he whispered to the emptiness. "Damn!" /Can you enhance my vision any more?/

/// *I'm trying—but I think she's gone.* ///

Cursing his clumsiness, he reached out for his table to steady himself, and floated back into his seat, trembling. Napoleon swiveled his sensors and began to say something, but Bandicut cut off his words with an angry gesture.

He pressed his palms together, resting his chin between his fingers, and stared into the darkness. /There has to be some way—/

/// *Maybe the iceline can help you.* ///

/Iceline?/ He thought about it for a moment, then leaned forward and placed both hands around the globe in the center of the table. /How do you suppose this works?/

/// *My guess is it's a simple interface.*
Just ask it for what you want.
But I'd be ready for anything. ///

Bandicut felt the quarx gathering his concentration, preparing to help him interpret, if necessary.

He cleared his throat. "Hello," he said in a gravelly voice. "If you can understand me, please reply." There was no answer. He focused his thoughts. /Can you understand this?/

The globelight flickered.

/Does that mean yes?/

<<<AFFIRMATIVE. DO YOU HAVE A REQUEST?>>>

He closed his eyes. The voice had sounded more like a bank machine than a datanet. /Yes. Can you track an individual for me?/

<<<SPECIFY.>>>

He felt himself growing lightheaded. /The woman, or individual resembling a woman, who just left here./

<<<CLARIFY REFERENCE.>>>

Bandicut twitched his gaze away from the flickering yellow globe, to indicate the direction of the vanished creature. /She just went that way. And her physical, um, morphology resembled mine, somewhat./

<<<DO YOU REFER TO THE . . .>>> There was a transla-

tional buzz for a moment. <<<. . . THESPI ADULT FEMALE, CLOTHED IN A LOOSE-HANGING RED GARMENT? TWO LEGS, TWO ARMS, ONE HEAD—>>>

/Yes!/

<<<ONE MOMENT. CHECKING CONFIDENTIALITY STATUS ON THAT REGISTRATION.>>>

/Uh?/

/// *Perhaps it cannot tell you about her,*
without clearing it with the individual herself. ///

/Oh./ Bandicut kept his eyes glued to the globe.

<<<THANK YOU FOR WAITING. THAT INDIVIDUAL IS REGISTERED FOR CONFIDENTIALITY. FOR A SMALL SURCHARGE, YOU MAY REQUEST MEDIATED CONTACT, VIA THE ICELINE MEDIATOR. YOUR OWN CONFIDENTIALITY WILL BE WAIVED TO THE FIRST DEGREE IN THE EVENT CONTACT IS MADE. DO YOU WISH THIS SERVICE?>>>

/Uh?/ Bandicut wondered how he would pay a surcharge. /Yes,/ he answered, figuring there was no point in worrying about it.

<<<ONE MOMENT, PLEASE . . . .>>>

He tapped the table with his fingers.

<<<CONTACT HAS BEEN MADE. YOU HAVE BEEN IDENTIFIED TO THE INDIVIDUAL AS JOHN BANDICUT, HUMAN OF EARTH. YOU ARE PERMITTED THE FOLLOWING INFORMATION: SHE IS AN ADULT THESPI THIRD FEMALE . . .>>>

/Third female?/

<<<. . . AND HER SYSTEM SIGNATURE IS A BRIGHT RED SUN. ONE MOMENT FOR TRANSLATION DIFFICULTY . . .>>>

He waited impatiently.

<<<JOHN BANDICUT, CAN YOU PROVIDE THE NAME OF A BRIGHT RED SUN, FROM YOUR VOCABULARY?>>>

/Um—"Antares" would be one./

<<<HER ICELINE SIGNATURE FOR YOU, THEN, IS "ANTARES," A BRIGHT RED STAR. THAT IS ALL THE INFORMATION THAT CAN BE—>>>

The voice cut off.

Bandicut waited. That seemed odd, the way the globe had just stopped in midsentence. But then, the whole system was odd. *Antares?* /Is that how I could reach her, if I wanted to? Through the sys—the iceline?/ There was a deadening silence, and he thought with alarm that perhaps he should look up from the globe, break the connection. Something was wrong.

He tried, and could not. He did not know how it had happened, but he could not look up from the globe; could not move a muscle, not even to blink an eye. He was completely locked into the iceline, and though he could now feel a distant change rippling through the connection, he could no more react to it or remove himself from it than he could walk out of this bar and back into the smelly, noisy rec room on Triton . . .

Neptune . . .

Sol system . . .

Orion spiral spur . . .

Sagittarius arm . . .

A shudder passed through him as he felt that knowledge pass out of him as if through silently moving lips.

Something had hold of him, and it wasn't the iceline itself.

/Charlie?/ he whispered, and even that thought took a terrible effort.

From the quarx there was no answer. Charlie had fallen silent—or been silenced—and he hadn't noticed it happening. His skin prickled.

Boojum.

Bandicut felt a rush of fear, and tried to stop it, but couldn't. He tried to identify the force that was gripping him, to locate it and push it into the open; but he couldn't touch it, or see it, or feel exactly where it was in his mind. As he struggled, in silent desperation, to free himself, he was aware of a new physical sensation, not quite a spasm but a *tightening* of certain muscles. It seemed to be creeping through his body, searching for a particular point of control. And then it found what it wanted. He felt a sudden sharp pressure on his windpipe.

What? he thought, finding himself suddenly struggling to breathe. It was becoming an almost overwhelmingly difficult effort to draw air into his lungs, to expel air. He fought for breath; his lungs began to burn.

He could scarcely comprehend what was happening. So quick, so deadly. There were no hands choking him, but his own muscles turned against him . . . his breath had become a strangled rasp. Where was Charlie? Gone?

How could this have happened? So suddenly.

He could die. Was about to die. Strangled by the boojum.

You bastard, he managed to think, barely able to form the thought before another sharp tightening made words impossible to form in his mind.

A gray darkness began to enshroud him. His ears were ringing in the silence. He managed to think a wistful good-bye to Charlie.

And then . . . something slipped and jarred in his mind. He felt what was left of his thoughts veering abruptly, wildly, out of control. Not just out of *his* control, but any control. Voices clamored around him. In his last moments of consciousness, he was careening off into the madness of silence-fugue. He was free, *free*—but only for a moment, only to drown at the bottom of a deep, dark sea.

16

MISSING PARTIES

 THE MEMORIES AND impressions folded and unfolded with blinding speed, sorting and resorting and never quite coming into focus. What was it that had led him to flee? Fear? Danger? Real? Imagined? Surely real: his last sight of his companions had been of them fleeing from the same whippets of energy that Copernicus himself had evaded. But they had not followed him into the metaship, at least not at the same location. He had watched as long as he'd dared, and then set out to reconnoiter.

Copernicus sat, paralyzed with thought, atop a low rise overlooking a small settlement of unfamiliar beings. They were not humans, nor Hraachee'ans; he did not know what they were. They were four-legged, and appeared to spend significant portions of their time—when not engaged in heated verbal communications—working at or around the soil, paying particular attention to low-growing foliage. They did not appear to be mining; he did not know what they were doing. He had already decided that he would not risk approaching them, if he could avoid it.

But he had seen something in their settlement that interested him. Terminals. Data-connect points. Access of the sort that he badly needed. Perhaps, if he kept looking, he would find other terminals, away from unpredictable aliens. He needed to make contact: not just with the datanet, but with his companions.

And he had to make sense of the voices he'd begun hearing in his head. >> . . . *can you hear us . . . vital that you answer . . . Napoleon not responding . . . must respond . . .* >>

They were not human voices, and not Napoleon's. Was it the voice of the boojum? Should he obey? No way to tell; couldn't be sure.

He searched his memory for clues. What was he supposed to do now, cut off from his partners? What was he to make of Napoleon? He was to assist and protect John Bandicut, wasn't he? Or were these voices his new masters? He remembered being afraid, and Bandicut reaching out to protect *Napoleon,* who was behaving irrationally. But why? Had they all fallen prey to the boojum?

Copernicus needed time to think, but more than that, he needed information. Wherever he was, it was time to move on.

Turning, Copernicus drove down the hill away from the village. He had seen a long, flat path that seemed to resemble a road. If he followed the road, perhaps he would find more terminals.

And perhaps then he would also find the answers he needed.

Ik sighed through his ears, as the Maksu fireflies buzzed and flickered about the table. They reminded him of the sparkles he often saw before his eyes when he came out of certain sleep-meditations. Ik was due for some sleep-meditation right now. He had been in a state of alertness for too long. He glanced at Li-Jared, who was stirring restlessly, and Li-Jared's eyes flashed, conveying his thoughts: *These creatures make me nervous.*

Ik was not about to disagree.

The Maksu-swarm flew together in close, orbiting whirls, making a sound like a low, structural metallic groan. *"Your information is valuable, though alarming,"* Ik heard through the voice-stones in his head. *"We would seek any further information you may acquire about the boojum."*

Ik rubbed his chest with his fingertips. "Of course. And your exchange?"

The Maksu moaned, *"A group will conduct you to the Tree of Ice nexus, 'ice caverns,' and there will attempt to assist you in making contact with the metavoices. We cannot guarantee contact, nor can we guarantee any information you might receive in the caverns."*

"We understand that," Ik said, catching Li-Jared's eye. The Karellian flicked his fingers casually.

The Maksu continued, *"We do not expect physical difficulties. However, interference from the boojum or other influences may occur at any time. In such cases, we cannot be responsible for your personal safety, or for the completion of your journey."*

Li-Jared bwanged indecipherably. He undoubtedly found the disclaimer irritating, even while expecting no more nor less.

Ik touched his stones thoughtfully. During the entire discussion of the boojum and their own recent experiences, the Maksu had buzzed with fear. They seemed terrified of the boojum, though whether out of concern for the integrity of the iceline, or concern for its danger to them personally, he couldn't tell. The iceline network provided considerable information exchange through this sector of Shipworld—not just Atrium City, but a wide region spanning several continents. As nearly as he could gather, the Maksu did not use the iceline as a medium for their distributed colony consciousness. But as dealers in information, they were keenly aware of its role in keeping data flowing.

"We always take responsibility for our own safety," Ik said. "However, in the interests of taking the longer view on the question, we would prefer a certain readiness to provide mutual assistance, if necessary."

The Maksu buzzed for a few moments, but in the end simply left the question hanging. What he heard in translation was: *"We are agreed, then?"*

Ik and Li-Jared exchanged glances, and agreed.

The Maksu swarmed higher above the table, to depart.

"Inform us when you have rested, and we will complete the arrangements. If you have further business to conduct, do not hesitate to contact us."

Ik bowed, and as the privacy curtain dissolved from around them, the Maksu streamed away into the gloom. Ik looked at Li-Jared with relief; his friend's eyes were dim with fatigue. "I am glad to be done with that. I too find the Maksu tiring. And now I am sure that John Bandicut anxiously awaits our return."

Li-Jared muttered his assent. Ik led the way, letting his thoughts touch the local control system for help in finding their table. He felt a nudge that sent them floating through the air toward a partially shrouded table.

"John Bandicut!"

There was no answer. Ik hurried, and passed through the hazy screen around the table.

It was empty.

Ik called to Li-Jared in alarm. "John Bandicut is gone!" Neither man nor robot sat at the table. But there was a puddle of liquid spilled from a glass that was now lying on its side, and a quantity of large, puffed grain kernels strewn across the tabletop. For a moment, Ik thought he had come to the wrong table. But no, John Bandicut had been drinking from that tall glass. Had he gone for a walk—perhaps to find a relief area? It seemed unlikely that he would have left the table in such a state.

"I fear something is wrong," Ik said as Li-Jared joined him. He touched the table globe, rolling his tongue in dismay. The globe was still lit, but there was no response from it when he reached out with his thought.

Click Click.

Ik looked up. Behind Li-Jared's hunched form, an inorganic maintenance unit floated into the privacy zone. Li-Jared's eyes flared, but he dipped a shoulder to let it pass. It floated forward and hovered over the table like a game ball, bristling with probes and attachments.

"Is there difficulty with the unit?" the inorg buzzed.

"It would seem so. Our companion disappeared while we

were away," Ik rumbled. "I want to track him, but the globe does not respond."

Click click. "Malfunction was detected at the local iceline control node. I was dispatched to investigate."

Ik felt the muscles behind his ears twinge. He watched as the inorg drifted, humming, close to the globe light. He glanced at Li-Jared. "Do you think it could be the boojum?" he murmured.

"The robot, you mean? Perhaps it was contaminated, after all, and overpowered him?" Li-Jared circled the table warily, peering for clues.

Ik considered the suggestion, as the inorg did something that caused the globe light to wink out. "It is possible. But if there was a malfunction in the globe light or the iceline, what I fear is . . ." He hesitated. "I do not truly know what to fear."

Li-Jared circled back to him, eyes blazing. "I fear the robot." His gaze swept the darkened room outside the privacy zone. "It is a pity. I was almost starting to like your new friend."

"That is remarkable in itself," Ik murmured. "I wish John Bandicut were here to appreciate it."

"He does, after all, have stones," Li-Jared said.

Ik hrrm'd. "I think more than that, my friend, that John Bandicut has skills and perspectives that you and I lack. We are a good team, Li-Jared, but I have often felt that we are incomplete. John Bandicut may be the missing component."

The globe light blinked back on. *Click click.* "System contact is reestablished. Do you wish to try again?"

Ik felt a steely chill. Did he wish to try? Of course. How else could he hope to find John Bandicut? But what if the iceline malfunction was connected to the boojum? "Do you know what caused the problem?"

"System disruption, cause unknown."

"Gaah," Ik muttered, and leaned forward over the globe. This time the light sparkled and danced at the edge of his thoughts. /Request tracking tag on companion John Bandicut, human of Earth,/ he thought silently.

The iceline's response was immediate: <<<THAT REGISTRATION IS CLOSED.>>>

Ik's eyebrows hardened. /Please elaborate./

<<<NO ELABORATION AVAILABLE.>>>

He hesitated. /Can you provide tracking tag on companion Napoleon, robot of Earth?/

<<<ONE MOMENT. PRESENT LOCATION OF THAT INDIVIDUAL IS ATRIUM, LEVEL ONE-ZERO-FOUR NORTH, VICINITY OF ADDRESS NUMBER ONE-SIX-SEVEN-SIX.>>>

Ik rumbled softly to himself. What could the robot possibly be doing? And why would it have left—unless it was under the boojum's control, or out of control? He and Li-Jared would have to proceed with great caution. /Is there,/ he asked the globe, /anyone organic or inorganic with the robot?/

<<<THERE IS ONE UNIDENTIFIED, ORGANIC LIVING BEING IN CLOSE PROXIMITY. NO FURTHER INFORMATION AVAILABLE.>>>

Hraah. /Thank you./ Ik straightened from the globe. The inorg was still hovering over the table, and he informed it that the globelink appeared to be working.

Click click. "Very good. We apologize for any inconvenience caused by the malfunction." The unit buzzed again, then floated away into the darkness.

Ik told Li-Jared what he had learned, and they did likewise.

As she sat in silent repose in her hotel suite, Autumn Aurora (Red Sun) Alexandrovens, iceline signature Antares, wrestled with newfound confusion. It was a disconcerting state for the Thespi third female. But lately she had been feeling this way far too often.

Twice tonight she'd been taken by surprise. First the glimpse of that being in the lounge, whose racial features so strikingly resembled her own. He was not a Thespi male, but he was astoundingly close in appearance, compared to anyone else she'd encountered on Shipworld. She'd sensed his interest at once, his startlement, his hesitation. And his . . . alienness, even in his similarity. She'd been so unsettled, when he'd just stared at her without making any greeting, that she'd practically fled in her confusion. And then in the midst of her transport back to her hotel had come the iceline contact: a query from that very same one, through the iceline mediator.

John Bandicut was his name. Human was his race. Earth was his homeworld.

She'd given him a signature for making contact, but he'd made no attempt to do so.

She was torn by conflicting desires. She found it excruciating to simply wait for his call. How long had she been seeking others of her kind? A year, at least. And now: not her wish, exactly—but something tantalizing, and yet alarming. The iceline gave her a name trace, and the answer was a shock. A John Bandicut had been present in the southern continent, where a star-spanner factory and much of the surrounding population had nearly been destroyed by a control system demon. That information set her pacing, until she forced herself to sit and focus.

She knew the incident all too well. She'd been there herself—in the vicinity, that is, though she'd had nothing to do with it. It came during a tour of the area, part of her ongoing, futile search for leads to any possible fellow Thespi exiles. Her search was interrupted by evacuation alarms sending hundreds or thousands of citizens into shelters. When she learned how close she'd come to disaster, she abandoned her fruitless search there and took the first transport north, to Atrium City, the closest thing she had to a home. And tried to put the whole thing out of her mind. Control demons scared her. She'd heard too many reports of their mischief lately.

But now, it seemed, that event was following her, in the person of John Bandicut, almost-Thespi.

Keep a safe distance.

Good advice, she thought. But the truth was, she wanted to know more about this, this *human*. She rose again and began walking through the grottolike spaces of her quarters, in and out through the curved formations, past the small pool, pacing more like a first female in the height of courtship than a coolly reserved third female whose role was facilitation, not passion. It wasn't that she felt an *attraction*, but she certainly felt an intense curiosity.

And that, she knew, was dangerous. It was curiosity, of course, that had begun the chain of events that had almost cost her life, back on the Thespi homeworld. Curiosity about passions, about relationships forbidden to those of her caste. And yet . . . now, as then, her curiosity could not be denied.

She touched the knowing-stones in her throat, wondering what the risks might be. She closed her eyes, reaching out to brush the cool stone walls with her fingertips as she paced; and she thought, if this human John Bandicut tried to contact her, she ought to have made up her mind how to answer.

There was an annoying buzz in his ears as he ran, gasping for breath, lost. It was persistent, that buzz, but erratic in tone and volume. Bandicut finally realized what it sounded like: a mosquito-thing that had bitten him, a long time ago. It had taken something from him—information, or quantum stability, someone had said. It scared him to remember it.

He didn't remember much else. A fog shrouded his mind, one layer of obscurity folding into another, a maze with intangible walls, dissolving and reforming in incomprehensible patterns. He knew there had been an attack.

Someone trying to kill him.

And that was why he was running. There were aliens in pursuit—terrible, screeching beings brandishing long, thin, sparkling blades. Panting, he sprinted down one last stretch, then gasped, slowing to peer over his shoulder through blurred eyes. They were gone now; he'd outrun them.

It didn't mean he was safe, though. His comrades had all abandoned him, Charlie had abandoned him, his robots had abandoned him. All alone, he'd been making his way through a forest, dodging ogres and braving treacherous crossings over a bottomless valley. He didn't know where he was, but perhaps he could find shelter in a cave somewhere.

He felt a low barrier before him, smooth against his hands. He was standing near the edge of the precipice again. Dangerous; but better to know where the precipice was than to risk stumbling into it! He leaned over, peering into the shadowy depths of the canyon. He heard a distant cry, felt a rush of vertigo, and tottered back again to regain his balance.

Careful, careful. There could yet be aliens about, and some of them could control your mind, make you go over the edge without even knowing what you're doing.

Careful.

He took a deep breath and turned away from the canyon's edge. He limped into a gloomy opening and returned to the foreboding woods.

After some prowling, he came to a series of smaller openings in the dense growth, a sort of maze of shelters. Perhaps he could rest awhile in one of those. He squinted, trying to peer into the gloom. Yes, it was secluded in here, and empty. He went three steps further, then collapsed in a heap. Alive, but exhausted. And alone.

Or maybe not. He raised his head abruptly; he thought he saw a beast now, shambling about among the shadows. He swallowed back a rush of fear. But the beast, too, was settling down to rest, rasping to itself. He didn't know what kind of creature it was. It seemed interested in him, but appeared to intend him no harm. He decided to let it stay.

Yes, he'd let it stay . . . for a while . . .

And then his consciousness slipped away.

As he hurried with Li-Jared, Ik found his fears for their friend warring with his anxieties about the plans they had made with the Maksu. He worried that the boojum might attempt to interfere with their quest for the ice caverns. Why it would care, he wasn't sure; but he suspected it didn't want anyone acquiring knowledge about the metasystem, knowledge that might threaten its own plans. And if the boojum interfered, they could forget about help from the Maksu. Already terrified of the boojum, the Maksu seemed paralyzed by the thought of what it might do if aroused.

Not that Ik was eager to take it on himself. But if it came

to that, how could he not do his part in the struggle, in the interests of the long view? And now, this—Bandicut's disappearance. What a pity if he were taken by the boojum, or dead! Bandicut not only seemed like the partner they had not known they were missing; he seemed someone who at least had the potential for taking the long view.

"This is a quicker way," Li-Jared said, grabbing Ik's arm and pointing toward a cluster of fastlifts.

Ik exhaled through his ears, bringing his thoughts back to the task at hand. "Should we? If the boojum is tracking us, it might not be wise to take a lift that is under iceline control."

"And if it is doing something to your friend, then every delay counts," the Karellian pointed out.

"Hrahh." Ik gestured and followed Li-Jared into the fastlift. Standing together in a bubble of light in a shaft, they streaked upward.

Ik blinked in the changing light, remembering the light of the hot blue sun of Hraachee'a. He missed it terribly. Blue stars, while achingly beautiful, did not live nearly as long as the slower-burning yellow stars that the majority of inhabited worlds circled. Ik's people had grown to maturity knowing that life, even on a planetary scale, was frightfully short. They had, of course, died when their sun blew—an experience that drove home to Ik the ephemerality of life, and reinforced in him a lifelong habit of taking the long view.

He wished he had more company in that respect.

The great open space of the atrium sprang into view as they rocketed out of the shaft. When the bubble let them out on level 104, Ik grunted in satisfaction.

"No boojum yet," Li-Jared noted.

"If we are fortunate, it has gone back into hiding. This way to one-six-seven-six." Ik pointed along the atrium balcony. They had to pass a crowd of serpentine beings coming the other way along the balcony. The serpents sprawled across most of the walkway, and they hissed and muttered, giving way with ill grace to the Hraachee'an and the Karellian. Ik was fuming by the time they were past the crowd.

"Easy, my friend," said Li-Jared. "I may have been hasty before. The Bandie has survived a great deal already. Let us trust him to survive this, too."

"The boojum becomes bolder, ever bolder," muttered Ik, lengthening his stride. "I wonder if there is anything in the iceline that can stop it anymore."

"Perhaps, perhaps not," said Li-Jared. "But let's not count our companion out just yet."

Ik glanced at Li-Jared, startled. Our companion? Perhaps being left alone to share a drink with Bandicut had done the moody Li-Jared some good. Until this, of course.

Ik glanced at the numbers on the passing openings and doorways. Their destination was a long way down.

The buzzing was what brought him back, not to full consciousness, but to a dreamy, eyes-closed half-awareness. After a moment, Bandicut realized that he was, after all, only remembering the buzz rather than hearing it; but the memory was powerful enough to make his mind reel. Buzzing. Silence-fugue. Boojum.

It had attacked him, tried to kill him. Only the eruption of silence-fugue had saved his life, by jamming the boojum's deadly inputs in his brain.

He shivered, as the memory replayed in his mind.

Whatever else, he knew the touch of the boojum now. He didn't think he'd ever forget it, or fail to recognize it, no matter how it might try to disguise itself. He still didn't understand its nature, but he understood more than he had before.

But still, his mind was filled with questions, with thoughts of chaos.

Turbulence.

Nonlinearity.

He remembered Charlie-One and Charlie-Two deluging him with incomprehensible images of chaos calculations. Phase-space, attractors, strange attractors, meta-attractors: the medium in which chaos and order were drawn, one out of the other, like handkerchiefs from a magician's hat. The quarx's translator had treated such things as the stuff of ordinary life. Bandicut hadn't understood much of the imagery, just enough to know that the translator's knowledge of it had saved the lives of billions on Earth.

And then had caromed him like a pinball out of the galaxy—and landed him in Shipworld, a place that seemed awash in turbulence and chaos. And it seemed to want him to do something here. *You are needed.* But for what?

Chaos.

The boojum.

Li-Jared had implied that the boojum might have emerged from chaotic processes. Perhaps it had ridden in on the winds of space, an unwanted byproduct of the sifting of living beings into this world from elsewhere. Or perhaps it had arisen right here, spawned by turbulence in the very place where it lived now: the control system, the datanet, the iceline, perhaps even the Tree of Ice. Perhaps it was a once-benign entity that had mutated, turned destructive and cunning.

Whatever its origins, he knew it now to be a living contamination in the system, like a computer virus, maybe, but far more dangerous and pernicious. It was alive in every sense he could imagine. It thought. (He had *felt* it think.) It feared. It hated. It lusted. (For what? Chaos?) Did it reproduce?

Bandicut shuddered at the thought. He heard a clicking nearby, but it was receding into the distance. He tried to focus on it, but couldn't quite, though it was familiar.

He'd lost the thread of his thought. He groaned softly, and did not resist drifting back into the murk of unconsciousness.

The address turned out to be a dusty, disused-looking doorway. Ik peered in, found a wooden door ajar. He pushed it open cautiously. There was no sign of life inside.

Dust stirred and floated into view.

"Ik, use care." Li-Jared's voice was soft, penetrating, behind him.

"Hrrrm." Ik stepped through the doorway, keeping close to the wall, and willed his eyes to adjust quickly to the low light level. It was an empty room, apparently the front room of a cluster, perhaps an apartment space. There was nothing here but dustballs.

"This does not look promising," Li-Jared murmured.

Ik silently approached the next doorway. It appeared to lead to a back room or to a hallway. Ik was accustomed to exploring new places in Shipworld—it was practically a way of life now—but he wasn't used to sneaking. His hearing sharpened in the silence.

He found himself in a dim hallway, with four rooms on the left side. The electronic doors were turned off. He peered carefully into the first two rooms. Empty. The only light in each was the soft glow of a safety light. He heard a faint clicking. He turned quickly, saw Li-Jared's eyes narrow to bright slits. The clicking sound was familiar. "Who is there?" Ik rumbled.

He was answered by a faster clicking. It was coming from down the hall.

"*Hwahh!*" said Li-Jared, pointing.

A metal probe stuck out of the last doorway. A tiny camera eye glowed. Whirring, a metal robot stepped into the hallway. "Ik, sir! I am overjoyed to see you! Please hurry!"

"Napoleon! What has happened? *Where is John Bandicut?*"

"In here! In here!" the robot cried. "I am unable to help him, and there is no response to my emergency signal! I believe we are out of range of Triton control. Can you assist?"

"Rakh!" Ik cried, and hurried past the robot into the dusty room.

John Bandicut was crumpled motionless on the floor.

17

POSTFUGUE

VOICES INTRUDED ON his barely wakeful consciousness.

"John Bandicut! John Bandicut—do you have any awareness? Are you—" *rasp* "—injured? John Bandicut?"

Bwang bwang . . .

Click, rasp. "I register breath and pulse. John Bandicut, please respond. I am certain you are alive, Captain! Please respond!" A metal hand poked at him urgently.

The poking hurt.

Bandicut jerked and blinked his eyes open. He was in a dim place, staring up at a ceiling; at least, he thought it was a ceiling. A small light was shining in his eyes, and it seemed connected to the metal probe that was plucking at him. "Would you for Chrissake *stop* that?" he barked.

"Captain?" A strained metal voice.

He squinted. Several shapes were moving over him, and he couldn't quite make out any of them. But he knew one of them was Napoleon. He remembered a beast following him into the forest, and lying down nearby.

"What the hell?" he grunted. He waved Napoleon's light away irritably, and pushed himself up to a sitting position. His head throbbed.

"We hoped you would tell us what happened," said another voice. Li-Jared. He felt something else—Ik's hand on his shoulder, steadying him. He looked up at Ik and managed a wan smile.

He hadn't been abandoned, then. Of course not; that was the silence-fugue talking. And the fugue was gone, thank God. He still had a ringing in his ears, but he no longer feared pursuit by tall aliens.

He also no longer felt the presence of a quarx in his head. /Charlie? Are you there? *Charlie?*/ An icy chill ran up his spine. Had the boojum killed the quarx, then? He remembered at the end, when the boojum's grip had been throttling him, and the quarx had fallen abruptly silent. /Charlie!/

"John Bandicut, what happened? Were you . . . attacked?"

He nodded with difficulty. "Yes," he whispered. "It tried to strangle me."

"Hraah! Napoleon?"

"*No!* It was—" He swallowed, remembering the sensation of that angry and violent force within his own mind. "The boojum. In here," he croaked, tapping the side of his head. "Took control of my muscles." He put a hand to his throat.

Napoleon clicked in distress. "We were fearful for your safety, John Bandicut. Can you move?"

Bandicut grunted and staggered to his feet, with all three of the others trying to help him. He peered around the dismal place. "Dear God, how did I get here? Never mind. It was the damn silence-fugue."

"The what?" asked Li-Jared.

"Silence-fugue. I'll explain later." His mouth was dry, as he swallowed. "It kept the boojum from killing me. But it got Charlie." He pointed to his temple again.

Li-Jared was staring at him with those blazing, electric-blue eyes. Ik muttered softly; it was impossible to tell what he was thinking.

Bandicut sighed. "Can we go someplace else?" he asked hoarsely.

"Hraah, good idea."

∞

Where Ik took them was to a hotel. He seemed to know what he was doing, and soon they were following a small, floating robot—an *inorg,* Ik had called it—down a corridor to the suite that the Hraachee'an had rented.

"It is satisfactory," Ik said to the inorg, dismissing it. "Well, my friends?" He gestured around the spacious sitting room. Though decorated in livid reds and oranges, it looked fairly comfortable, with the assortment of rigid and padded seating surfaces that Bandicut was coming to expect. Ik had declined to pay extra from their limited credit for a custom-decorated suite.

Bandicut sank into something like a sofa, with a sigh of relief. He looked around. There were three doorways leading to private rooms. Li-Jared was peering into the rooms, and made a bonging sound that seemed to indicate approval.

"I must say that I am looking forward to some rest," Ik said. "But perhaps we should first talk."

Bandicut realized that his head was far from clear. Nonetheless, he agreed and sat forward to explain what had happened between him and the boojum. Ik and Li-Jared were deeply troubled by his story, though Ik pointed out one possible silver lining. If the iceline had cancelled Bandicut's registration, the boojum might think that it had succeeded in killing him—and would now leave him alone. Bandicut shrugged, thinking that he would rather have the quarx back and take his chances with the boojum. He turned the conversation to what Ik and Li-Jared had been doing. "What did you find out from the—" he searched his memory "—Maksu? And have you learned anything at all about Copernicus?" He glanced at Napoleon, who was hunkered down almost mournfully beside him.

"To the last, sadly no," Ik said. "But as for the Maksu . . ." He explained to Bandicut what had happened in the meeting—the exchange of Ik's and Li-Jared's knowledge of the boojum for the promise of a conducted trip to the ice caverns. "We hope," Ik concluded, "that you will wish to accompany us. But I would be dishonest if I did not admit that there could be risk."

Bandicut stared at him, momentarily at a loss for words.

Li-Jared cocked his head, saying nothing.

"You need not decide now," Ik reassured him. "We are going to rest awhile before we contact the Maksu again." He snapped his rigid mouth shut in what looked like a frown. "But I must say that I would miss you if you did not join us."

Bandicut nodded. He certainly had no desire to give up the only friends he had in Shipworld. But neither did he want to rush off headlong into some new adventure that he didn't understand. He'd done enough of that for a lifetime.

He desperately missed the voice and counsel of the quarx.

Finally he said, "Thanks, Ik. I would . . . certainly miss you guys, too, if I didn't go with you." He glanced at Li-Jared; the Karellian's eyes pulsed. Bandicut cleared his throat, suddenly remembering Antares: Thespi third female, and closest thing to a human he'd seen on this crazy world. "Uh, look, though. I'd still like to try to make contact with that . . . person . . . before I think about leaving. At least find out who or what she is. And hell, I don't even know anything *about* this place. The hotel, the city. The continent, the whole damn world. Would you mind explaining some things to me?"

"Ask away," said Ik. "Now is the time."

Bandicut drew a deep breath, and began asking. And Ik answered, and Li-Jared, and they talked about Atrium City and Shipworld until Bandicut could not hold his eyes open any longer, and finally they each chose a room and went straight to sleep.

Bandicut rolled over, yawning, and sat up on the bed. *Bed!* He rubbed his eyes, as it all seeped back into his consciousness. It was the first comfortable night's sleep he'd had in a long time. But not a quiet night. His dreams had been full of words and images of Shipworld . . .

(How large *was* the place? Billions of kilometers? Or larger?)

(Hard to say; it was discontinuous, not all of its parts connected in normal space, but joined by "n-space connectors," with intermittent but near-instantaneous movement among them.)

(But all of it outside the galaxy?)

(More or less. Except that there were those "star-spanners," linking thousands of worlds in the galaxy to this one. Not continuously, of course; they opened unpredictably, and only for brief periods, no doubt at a staggering expenditure of energy.)

(To transport people here?)

(Or there.)

(Or whole cultures.)

(But who ran it? Who maintained it? Who worked at city hall?)

(Different in every sector. Some places the shadow-people. Some places others. Different economies, societies, redundancies in infrastructure—as though someone had wanted to ensure that the failure of one would not mean the failure of all. And yet, there was a common thread . . .)

(The Tree of Ice?)

(Yes.)

(And that was what appeared to be threatened by the growing contamination in the control system . . .)

Bandicut grunted, shrugging off the swirl of memory-voices. He stood up, rubbing his eyes. It would take a long time to assimilate the whole picture, with its myriad details. He'd probably forgotten half of it already, while he slept. He turned his thoughts inward. /What do you suppose they use for a shower around here?/

And then he remembered that, too.

Damn.

It was likely, he knew, that the quarx would reappear eventually—in a new incarnation, which might or might not remember him, and would certainly not remember much of what had gone before. Hell of a note to start the day on, with the death of a friend. He felt a sudden upwelling of grief, and the pangs of loneliness that came with it, and he thought, I can't go through this again. I can't. Charlie, why did you have to die again?

He felt a disconcerting shiver, as though a dog were waking up and shaking itself inside his skin.

  /// Die? Who died? ///

Bandicut stiffened.

  /// Don't mourn me till I'm gone. Please. ///

"Charlie!" he cried, and squeezed his eyes shut. /Where have you been? Where were you? You didn't answer!/

  /// I think I just . . . woke up.

  I don't know where I was, John.

  I remember your being hooked into the iceline.

  And something came at us— ///

/Yeah, it came at us, all right./ Bandicut involuntarily touched his throat.

  /// It was the boojum? ///

He didn't answer, didn't have to. He felt the quarx shuddering in his mind, and realized that the boojum's attack had been as traumatic to the quarx as to him. /Charlie, the only reason I survived was silence-fugue. Were you knocked out by the attack?/

He could sense the quarx's thoughts rolling and turning, trying to reconstruct what had happened.

  /// Knocked out.

  Yes, I think that describes it exactly.

  John, are you laughing or crying? ///

Bandicut tried to control the silent eruptions in his chest. He wiped away a tear. /I dunno. Jesus, Charlie, I'm so glad you're alive, I feel like doing backflips!/

  /// I'm glad I'm alive, too. ///

Bandicut hopped a little and walked around the small bedroom, decorated in shades of charcoal-grey and purple. He wondered for whom, or what species, it was designed. He shook his head, not caring. However, he did need to shower and use a bathroom, and his clothing stank—and all of his spare clothes were in his backpack. With Copernicus. Hell. Copernicus.

  /// We'll find him, John.

  You've got to trust. ///

/Okay. I'll trust./ He paced, suddenly full of agitation. /Do you know where I can find a shower around here?/

/// How would I . . . oh, wait a minute.
Put your wrist up to the mirror there. ///

/Ah, right. Of course./ He raised his forearm.

The mirror shimmered and vanished, and a cubicle opened in front of him. He peered inside, then walked in. There were no visible fixtures. But a moment later, a warm, sparkling mist began to surround him. He felt his bladder go empty. He sighed with relief and began peeling off his clothes.

He stayed in the shower for a *long* time.

When he finally stepped out of the mist, he found his clothes hanging on the cubicle wall, cleaned and pressed and restored to new-looking condition. He fingered the light blue cloth in amazement, trying to decide if his jumpsuit had been destroyed and replaced with a brand-new one. But the stitching looked the same, and it felt just like his own jumpsuit, minus the threadbaring effects of age.

/// Nice.
As long as we stay in the hotel,
you won't need your bag. ///

/Mmph,/ Bandicut muttered. /*If* I stay, you mean. I wonder how much credit I have, anyway./ Ik had described the monetary credit system used in Atrium City. As new arrivals, they were given starter-accounts to see them through the settling-in period. But eventually they would have to perform some sort of service to maintain their balances.

/// Perhaps you could check on a terminal. ///

/Right. With the iceline./ Bandicut zipped up his jumpsuit and ran his fingers through his hair. /What if it tries to suck out my brains again?/

Charlie twinged.

/Well, never mind. I'm stuck here, so I guess I'd better get back up on the horse./

/// ??? ///

/I mean, I can't go around avoiding contact with their datanet forever. I'll just have to be careful, and watch out for the damn boojum, that's all./ Peering into the mirror, he parted his hair roughly with his fingers, and strode out into the sitting room.

Napoleon rose to greet him, from beside the terminal.

"Nappy! Have you been logging onto the system, while I was sleeping?" he asked, meaning it as a joke.

"Yes, Captain," Napoleon said, without a trace of irony. "I've just received a message from Copernicus."

"You *what?*"

"It came in on the terminal." Napoleon pointed to the translucent-topped pedestal. "It was idented for me. I took it, believing that at level-one connection, text only, I would be able to screen out any dangerous soft-attributes. I thought it better not to wake you unless it was absolutely necessary."

Bandicut stared at the robot, astounded.

/// *Extraordinary.*
Napoleon seems to be growing in initiative
by the hour. ///

Bandicut blinked, and sank slowly into a chair. "What was the message, Nappy?"

The robot's red-lighted eyes seemed to shift focus. "The text was as follows: *I am safe, I have vital information, and I urgently need your help. Are you with John Bandicut? Are you uncontaminated? Can you prove it?* End of message." Napoleon's eyes focused again, on Bandicut. "How do you think I should answer?"

Bandicut stared at him, with a tight knot in his chest. He felt as if he had just heard from a missing child. *Urgently need your help . . .* "What do you make of it?" he whispered.

Napoleon clicked. "Since he did not identify the information, I speculate that it might be in reference to the boojum. That is the last subject we discussed."

Discussed? Bandicut wouldn't have called the confrontation between the two robots, just before Copernicus hightailed it away from them, a discussion.

"I have been trying to devise a way to prove to Copernicus that I am uncontaminated. So far, I am at a loss."

"Well, considering that when we last saw him, you accused *him* of being contaminated—"

"Yes," said Napoleon. "That is true. I was frightened at the time."

"Frightened?"

"And disoriented, yes." The robot hesitated. "I was frightened by the boojum attacks. I felt vulnerable. I had only just been repaired by the shadow-net—"

"Shadow-net?"

"Iceline subset used by the shadow-people. They were very thorough, but unfamiliar with my structures. There was concern about possible boojum contamination, and I may have picked up some of their concerns. Fears, really."

Bandicut squinted at the robot, his neck hairs prickling at the notion of the robot feeling fear.

Napoleon continued, as though in confession. "When we were fleeing through the power tube, I became alarmed about the possibility of more subtle attack—and the possibility that the contamination might have reached me, or Copernicus, through the shadow-net. Soon I observed Copernicus flying erratically, or so I believed. I did not know why. I may have . . . panicked." With a rasp, Napoleon fell silent.

"I see," Bandicut said slowly. "And do you still think, now, that Copernicus was contaminated by the boojum?"

Napoleon was silent for a few moments. "Probably not," he said at last. "But I cannot be certain."

Bandicut got up and paced. "And what about you?" he said, turning to squint at the robot. "Are you certain that *you* are not infected?"

Napoleon whirred, but did not move. "How can I be certain? I *believe* I have not been infected. But how can I be certain, John Bandicut? How?"

To that, Bandicut had no answer. Instead he asked, "Did Copernicus say where he was?"

"I have given you the complete text of the message."

"But what about the system? Didn't the iceline give you any clues?"

"John Bandicut, I made only level-one contact with the iceline. I felt, in view of your recent experience, that deeper involvement might be unwise. Was I wrong?"

"Hell." He didn't know what he thought. He wanted more information, but not at the cost of Napoleon being hit by the boojum.

/// Permission to speak freely? ///

/Sure./

/// It's a difficult problem.
But which is worse—
to risk Napoleon in an iceline contact,
or yourself? ///

Bandicut blinked, staring at Napoleon. /I'm not sure,/ he said softly. /He's practically alive./

/// True. But not quite.
Not yet. ///

Not yet. Charlie was probably right. And Copernicus had said he needed help—urgently. "Nappy, can you send Coppy a reply?"

"Of course, Captain."

"All right." Bandicut pinched his lower lip. "Tell him this: 'YOUR MESSAGE RECEIVED. WE ARE UNCONTAMINATED. PLEASE CONTACT US AT ONCE FOR FACE-TO-FACE COMMUNICATION! SIGNED, JOHN BANDICUT.' That ought to do it."

"At once, Captain." Napoleon strode to the terminal. He pressed a probe to it, it flickered for a moment, and he turned to face Bandicut. "Message away. Shall we wait for a reply?"

"Yeah," Bandicut said. "Let's wait for a reply." He sat back, massaging his forehead.

Five minutes later, Napoleon whirred into motion again, returning to the terminal. His contact lasted only a moment. "Text only," he reported.

"Damn. Let's hear it."

"Quote: *Unable to risk direct contact via iceline. MUST have confirmation of your free state. If you are willing, please show yourself in public shopping area, Level 146, block 1012-*

1070, within one hour. Hroom and rest of shadow-people need your help! Shipworld needs your help! Copernicus.'' Napoleon paused. "What do you think, Captain?"

"Hell's bells," was all he could think to say.

18

IN THE ATRIUM

 /// *John, are you certain that this is wise?* ///

/Of course I'm not certain./ Bandicut shrugged and turned away from the closed doors to Ik's and Li-Jared's rooms. Knocking had produced no results. Maybe they were just sleeping; maybe they couldn't hear him knock. But he was reluctant to barge in on either of them.

He couldn't *not* go to Copernicus, not after that urgent plea. And he didn't think it was the boojum impersonating Copernicus; he didn't think the boojum would have invoked the shadow-foreman's name. *Hroom needs your help.* That did not sound like the boojum's voice to him. Anyway, with luck, the boojum thought he was dead.

"Napoleon, you're sure we can find our way around out there?" he asked the robot.

"Captain, as long as the maps I downloaded are accurate, there should be no problem."

Bandicut was not wholly reassured, but he could not avoid taking some risk. For Copernicus's sake. And Hroom's.

/// *I've no quarrel with your intentions.*
But shouldn't you at least leave a message
for Ik and Li-Jared? ///

/I would, but there's nothing here to write on. And anyway, could their translators make any sense of my handwriting?/

/// Why not use the terminal? ///

/Wouldn't that tell the boojum where I'm going?/

*/// If it's reading your mail, it already knows.
But as you say, it probably thinks you're dead. ///*

/Mm./ Bandicut cleared his throat. "Nappy, can we leave a local message for Ik and Li-Jared on this terminal?"

Click click. The robot stepped to the terminal and placed a sensor probe against a shiny plate on its side. "I believe so, yes. You can leave voice if you like. Simply speak what you want to say."

Bandicut thought a moment. "Begin message. 'Ik and Li-Jared, we have received a message from Copernicus and have gone to answer it. I was unable to wake you. We will be at—' " He glanced at Napoleon. "What was the address?" Napoleon repeated the block numbers. " 'Right. Nappy says he can find it. Coppy's message sounded urgent; we'll leave it so you can read it for yourselves. We should be back soon— with Copernicus, we hope.' " He let out a long breath. "End message." He turned to Napoleon. "Can you leave Coppy's message for them?"

Napoleon retracted his probe. "Done. Are we ready?"

Bandicut waved him toward the door. "Let's go. And remember your origins."

"Captain?"

"You're a recon robot. So remember everything you see out there. And don't call me Captain."

"Aye aye, John Bandicut." The robot hummed with seeming excitement, and led the way out.

The sitting room, which he vaguely remembered as being on a little spur off a long hallway, let him out into a twisting corridor that gave a feeling of being in an ant's nest. It looked not at all familiar. As they walked, he realized that they had not passed a single other door, or even a corridor intersection. Perhaps the hotel allowed one to go *only* to one's own room. Did it reroute the hallway each time someone came and went?

Whatever the explanation, the hallway let them out into a lobby ornamented with shallow pools and streams, and plants that were rooted in rock, in water, in air, and even a few in soil. Sunlight streamed in through angled skylights. He glanced, in passing, at the other hotel patrons—a wide assortment of bipeds, quadrupeds, crawlers, and rotiforms. The sight stirred an odd mixture of feelings: wonder at the alienness and variety, a deep longing for some sense of connection with them, and a terrible loneliness for Earth. He wondered what Julie was doing, or would have been doing right now, if their lives were not separated by an impossible gulf of time and distance.

/// Coppy. Focus on Coppy. ///

"Yeah. Lead on, Napoleon." He followed the robot outside to a fastlift that whisked them up some unknown number of floors. They emerged on a balcony and walked to the edge of the vast atrium. Bandicut fingered the handrail and peered over, shivering at a sudden memory of standing at one of these railings while half out of his mind with silence-fugue. The people on the bottom floor looked like microbes now. He swallowed and stepped back. Overhead, the sun—or whatever it was—cast a dazzling blanket of light, not from a point source, but more like an unfocused band in the sky. He could not tell whether it came from miles up, or just a few stories above the top floor.

"John Bandicut," Napoleon urged, "we need to go this way."

Bandicut gestured him onward. "You know where we came out, right? And the hotel?"

"Yes, Captain," Napoleon said patiently.

They walked until they reached one of those terrifying, spindly arches spanning the atrium. Several tall, green bipeds were crossing the arch toward them, half-walking, half-floating. They stepped off close to Bandicut, seeming untroubled by the height. The opposite side of the atrium, where the arch ended, looked colorful and full of activity. "You're about to tell me we have to cross this thing, aren't you?" he asked.

"Yes, Captain. That's our destination, over there. That's where we hope to find Copernicus."

Bandicut peered across, and remembered to breathe. What was over there? Stores, maybe? He studied the arch. The thought had scared him before; now they were, if anything, even higher in the air.

/// I seem to see a memory of
your crossing several of those,
while fleeing from the boojum. ///

He shivered as Charlie flashed the memory to him. /Yeah, but I was insane at the time./ Running from aliens with swords. He pressed his lips together, thinking, I can't just give in to the fear, though, can I? And we do have to find Copernicus. /Theoretically I should be able to cross this, right?/

/// You mean without plunging to your death? ///

/Yes. And thank you for the word choice./

/// Sorry.
Let me ask the translator-stones. ///

"It is a narrow passageway," Napoleon observed, springing up and down a little on his metal legs. "But we have crossed these before."

Bandicut said nothing.

/// The stones say you won't fall. ///

/Good./ He moved toward the beginning of the arch. "Let's go find Coppy."

/// Unless, of course,
the safety systems are compromised. ///

/You just had to say it, didn't you?/ Bandicut took a deep breath and stepped out over the abyss.

It was at once exhilarating and terrifying. He tried not to look down. His heart was pounding; he felt as if he were walking a tightrope. The robot whirred behind him, distracting him for an instant. He stubbed his right toe, and stumbled, and felt a sickening lurch as his weight shifted. *You're dead.* But he wasn't; the transport-field caught him and floated him up, a few millimeters above the slender arch. *Dear God!* He was shaking now, but he stared resolutely straight across, taking deep breaths, and tried not to think about what the boojum could do to the transport-field.

The boojum was apparently occupied elsewhere. The arch landed him gently on the far side. He gasped, staggering for the first few steps—and suddenly felt himself reliving, vividly, the first time he had stepped off a moving slidestair as a child. The terror this time was not much different.

Napoleon landed right behind him. "Interesting, isn't it, Captain. Exciting."

"Is that what you thought? I'm glad one of us liked it," he answered. "Now, do you know where we are? Where we're supposed to go?"

"I believe we are there," Napoleon replied, striding toward what looked like an open maze of gardens and shops and terminals and fast-food establishments. It was a well-populated little mall which wouldn't have seemed too far out of place back in L5 City. The population mix was as varied as in the hotel lobby. Bandicut saw a number of low, squat beings who looked like stumps with pincers, and he was not disappointed when Napoleon suggested they move away toward another group of shops. There he saw two apparent brethren of the officious treelike being who had met them upon their landing in the park. They kept walking.

"Do you know what we're looking for?" he asked.

"We presume Copernicus will be waiting, or perhaps observing us first," Napoleon answered unconcernedly.

"We presume."

They continued through a glittering shop full of holo images and rumbling music. It was a dizzying experience; every time Bandicut turned, there were images of faces and places and abstract patterns erupting in the air before him, then imploding back in startling cascades. It seemed to be a form of entertainment, though for all he knew it was a classroom. He blinked away from the holos and realized that he'd been unconsciously swaying to a thrum of dissonant music. "Captain," said Napoleon, "can you explain the purpose of this place?"

Bandicut squinted at several slender tree-beings and something that looked like a young alligator standing at large, metallic boards with flickering lights. The alligator touched a lighted bar, and the music changed to something Bandicut imagined a shadow-person might like—high-pitched shrieks with no discernible rhythm or melody. The alligator switched a fernlike tail back and forth, and appeared to dance back from the board. "Actually, I think I can," he said.

The robot clicked. "Yes?"

"It's a damn recording shop."

/// Recording shop? ///

/A music store. I'll be b'joogered./ Bandicut laughed, despite his nervousness, as the alligator-alien danced back to the board and touched another lighted bar. The music changed to something with a recurring bass thrum. /Charlie, they've got teenagers on Shipworld. I'll be damned./

/// John—am I missing something? ///

/If you don't know, I couldn't possibly explain it to you. If you ever start remembering those TV shows that Charlie-One loved so much, maybe you'll understand./

Charlie was silent for a moment.

/// I guess I'll try to remember those things, ///
he said at last.

Oddly lifted, Bandicut walked on, out of the recording shop. He surveyed a semi-open area that looked rather like a fast-food palace—gaudily decorated, with colored lights and potted plants and small design panels inset into ceramic walls. Various patrons were gathered near a chrome counter, where they took turns pressing fingers or limbtips into small, lighted recesses. Bandicut watched in puzzlement. He saw no trays or food emerging. Come to think of it, no one appeared to be eating, although more than a few beings were gathered around tables in little alcoves. He moved for a closer look, and suddenly the air was filled with chiming sounds. He stepped back, and the chiming faded. /What do you suppose this is?/

The quarx was silent, apparently idealess. Napoleon stood beside him, scanning. Bandicut grunted and focused on a serpent-being with turquoise skin, hunched over a table. He had assumed, before, that the creature was eating; but now he realized that it was staring into a flickering display in the tabletop. As he watched, the serpent suddenly reared up, eyes bright, and roared, *"HH'ZAAAAAHHHHH!"* It reached out with two big webbed hands and made excited clenching motions in Bandicut's direction.

Bandicut edged backward, and bumped into one of the stump-creatures he'd seen earlier. "Excuse me," he muttered, in response to a twittered protest. He moved away from both beings, but the serpent was now waving its hands in another direction anyway.

"Captain John, are you in danger? I see no sign of Copernicus." Napoleon had his sensors spinning, in an undoubtedly futile attempt to comprehend what he was seeing, or perhaps to locate his fellow robot.

"No, it's all right, Nappy. Keep looking. Maybe Coppy isn't here yet. Let's see what we can learn." Bandicut watched the stump-creature waddle up to the counter and stroke a series of lights with its brown pincers. It was impossible to tell what it was doing. There was a willowy biped moving about the area who seemed to be working there. "Excuse me," Bandicut called.

The creature approached. *"Squeeee?"*

"Ahh, can you help me?"

"Varooooo!" It pointed with a delicate tentacle toward a glowing panel on one of the partitions. It placed its tentacle on the panel, and seemed to want Bandicut to do likewise.

"Uh—"

/// Why not? ///

Bandicut shrugged and reached out to touch the warm surface. He felt an immediate tingle in his wrist.

/// Ah. The stones are responding. ///

Bandicut spoke again. "Can you help me?"

"Certainly," said the creature, drawing its limb away with a graceful bow. "What may we offer you?"

"Well, I was wondering—what are those people doing? Do you serve food here?"

The being chuckled melodically and pointed over Bandicut's shoulder, toward the back of the marketplace. "Eat—over there," it warbled. "Not here, sir."

"Ah."

"But we would be most pleased to serve you here, sir."

"Aha. And—what is it that you do here? If I may ask. I'm afraid I'm new here."

"Of course you are new. We offer you something special, a welcome for our newly arrived guests." The creature fluttered several of its limbs. "Would you prefer table or counter? We have some very fine positions open."

Bandicut turned his hands up. "Table for *what*—if I may ask."

"Very fine tables," the creature continued. "For—" *spleee* "—long-term betting, lottery investment, and various—" *spleee* "—forms of life insurance. And at the counters—games of chance, with instant winnings day and night."

Bandicut opened his mouth. "You mean this is a *casino*?"

"The finest in the atrium," said the being, with a flourish of a tentacle.

"Good lord."

"May I seat you and your inorg?"

Bandicut took a deep breath. "No, I'm . . . sure it is very fine . . . as you say," he stammered. The creature placed a tentacle gently upon his forearm, and he felt ever so slight a tug toward the games. "I'm afraid, though—" he jerked his arm back "—that I prefer to dine first."

"Of course," said the being, and with another bow, turned away.

At the nearby table, the serpent was bent back over its game, in what appeared to be ferocious concentration. Bandicut had the feeling that its win had been short lived.

"Let's go, Nappy. I don't think we're going to find Copernicus in here," Bandicut muttered under his breath.

"Indeed, where do you think we should look next?" asked the robot, whirring alongside.

"I don't know. But I'm hungry. Maybe he'll expect *me* to be looking for someplace to eat."

The eating establishment in the back turned out to be a colorless place, decorated in oxidized-aluminum grey, with a few bits of trim in a darker charcoal. Perhaps neutrality was the intent. There was no serving counter, but a series of small, cramped tables—half of which were occupied by customers seemingly ingesting food. The tables had centerpieces that looked like terminals. /Iceline connection?/ he asked Charlie, sliding cautiously into a corner table.

//// I'm not sure. Wait.
The daughter-stones say, based on past experience,
that these are probably local terminals,
not connected to the main iceline. ///

Bandicut nodded, relieved not to have to worry about meeting the boojum in the course of ordering a grilled-cheese sandwich. He touched the terminal and silently ordered. There was a pause while the terminal tried to sort out, through the translator, his inner impressions of what, exactly, a grilled-cheese sandwich and coffee might be. Then, after another pause, it informed him that he had no registration, and therefore no credit. Hell, he thought—and asked the terminal if Napoleon could pay for him. After a bit of negotiation, Napoleon extended a probe and the order was completed.

"Thanks, buddy," he told Napoleon, with sincerity.

A minute later, a small napkin appeared, bearing a flat, grey, three-inch-square object, and beside it a small cup of steaming black liquid. From the amount of steam rising from the cup, he guessed that it must be near the boiling point. The aroma was familiar. Used motor oil, he thought. He frowned and nudged the cup away, and picked up the sandwich. It was firm, not hard, and looked as though it could at least physically be chewed. He hesitated, and nibbled off a bite. It was slightly greasy, slightly salty, and otherwise tasteless.

//// I guess not all establishments
in this city are of the same quality. ///

He remembered wistfully how good the popcorn and beer had tasted in the bar last night. He had no idea how one earned spendable credit around here, but had a sudden intuition that if he were to remain in this city, he would likely wind up eating this kind of food more often than the other. He was still debating whether to swallow.

/// *I'd say, judging by your physiologic signs,
that it's safe.* ///

/Safe. But not necessarily pleasant, right?/ He finally swallowed, gagging just a little. He decided that it wasn't actually *bad,* it was just flavorless, colorless, and textureless. He put the sandwich down.

"John Bandicut," Napoleon said suddenly, rising. "I believe we have a call."

"Copernicus?"

"Can't say, but I felt a tingle. I must find an iceline terminal. There, I believe." He crossed to a nearby partition and halted before a mirror-surfaced panel. He placed a probe on it and turned his primary eyes toward Bandicut. "It is not active."

Bandicut looked around. There were a dozen similar patches around the eatery. "I think it's a decoration, Nappy."

Clicking, Napoleon rose to maximum height. "Do you see—"

"Let's look outside."

As they left the eatery, Bandicut reminded Napoleon that if it was Copernicus calling, he wanted to talk. "I understand," said Napoleon. He located a terminal and made the connection. After a moment, he said, "Captain, it *was* Copernicus—but another text message."

Bandicut swore. "What did it say?"

"It begins, *Thank you for allowing me to observe you. I am not physically present in your area, but am reassured by the sight of you both. Do not, repeat, DO NOT speak the rest of this message aloud in public.* It then continues with additional, and I must say, alarming, information."

Bandicut stared at Napoleon. "What do you mean?"

"If the message is correct, I understand why Copernicus did not wish others to hear it. Is there someplace private where we can talk?"

Bandicut took a deep breath. "Let's get back to the hotel. Fast."

19

DECISIONS

"CAPTAIN." THE ROBOT paused in the front lobby. "Before we return to the room, you may wish to review this message privately."

"Why's that?"

"It contains a suggested course of action which may be contrary to what your companions want to do."

Bandicut blinked, suppressing a momentary dizziness. Mokin' foke, he thought. He looked around the lobby. "Over there," he said, pointing to a secluded corner. They walked over and sat on a long, low cushion. They were flanked by two pools populated with fat eels and bulbous fish; otherwise, they were alone. "Okay, let's have it."

Napoleon clicked. "Could you sit closer, please?"

Bandicut stared at him, then nodded. He leaned forward and put his ear against the robot's external speaker. "How's this?"

"Better. I am concerned that we not be overheard." The robot's metallic voice was nearly inaudible. "Copernicus reports that the boojum may be intending an attack against a critical Shipworld structure. Soon."

Every muscle in Bandicut's body coiled involuntarily. He had trouble breathing.

"Shall I repeat?" asked Napoleon, raising his voice slightly.

"Negative." Bandicut finally drew a deep breath. "Tell me what he said."

"Following the warning not to speak in public, quote: *Shadow-people believe boojum is planning attack on critical life-support infrastructure. Defense inadequate. Many lives, including yours, are at risk. Request meeting in secure location; coordinates attached. Must have further confirmation you are uncontaminated. Your help urgently needed! Pan pan. Bring all those with translator-stones! Come at once, please! The address—*"

Bandicut sat up abruptly. "Jesus, Nappy!"

Napoleon paused, then raised his voice to a normal soft volume. "Well, the address appears to be outside Atrium City."

Bandicut closed his eyes, nodding. *Attack on critical life-support infrastructure . . . Jesus.*

/// Sounds as if we should go, I'd say. ///

/Yeah, but—Charlie, why us? Aren't there *systems* to take care of these things?/

/// Maybe the systems are corrupted.
He asked for "all those with translator-stones."
That's you. Ik and Li-Jared, too. ///

Bandicut's head was spinning. He stood up. "Nappy, we've got to get back to the room."

"Agreed, John Bandicut. But please—how can I prove to Copernicus I am uncontaminated, without direct contact? I do not believe he will allow that. If I *were* contaminated, such contact could endanger him."

"Maybe he has some idea," Bandicut said helplessly. He suddenly cocked his head, squinting past Napoleon. In the pool just beyond them, two thumbnail-sized fish eyes were sticking up out of the water. Looking at him. Or listening? He shivered with sudden, unreasoning fury. Were even the damn ornamental *fish* spies around here? He stepped quickly to the stone-lined edge of the pool. The eyes—or ears—vanished as he grabbed a large stone and smacked it down into the water. He grabbed for another, but through the disturbed surface of the water, he saw the fish dart into a hole, out of sight.

"Captain? Shall we go?" said the robot.

He looked around, not sure whether to be angry or sheepish. "Yeah," he grunted. "Let's go."

"Hraah, John Bandicut!" Ik cried as they entered the sitting room. "You are safe! We were afraid for you!"

"Why did you take such a risk, going out alone?" Li-Jared chided. "Why did you not speak to us?"

Bandicut's head hurt; his heart was still hammering. "I knocked, but you were both asleep. Look, I'm *okay*. But we have to talk. Now. We've gotten several messages from Copernicus."

"Yes, we saw the messages you left," Ik said. "What else have you learned? Did you see him?"

"No." Bandicut scowled, pacing in front of the orange wall. "He was just watching us on a monitor or something. I don't know how—through the iceline, I suppose."

Ik's deepset eyes flickered in his blue skull. "You were not suffering another—what did you call it—silence-fugue?"

"No, afraid not. But Coppy says he needs our help, right away. Nappy, would you repeat the message?"

He watched the others' reaction as Napoleon recited Copernicus's words.

The electric-blue slits of Li-Jared's eyes narrowed; then expanded with intensity. "What installation is it going to attack? Did he say nothing more?"

"No. And I haven't been able to talk to him directly."

"Did you learn anything else?"

"Yeah, I learned the mall food stinks."

Li-Jared waggled a black-fingered hand. "We could have told you that, without your risking a trip out alone."

Bandicut shrugged defensively. "I wasn't alone. I had Napoleon and Charlie."

"Charlie?" Li-Jared queried.

Bandicut touched a fingertip to his forehead. "He's back."

Li-Jared's face wrinkled. He seemed to want to ask about

the quarx, but before he could do so, Ik interjected, "This message from Copernicus—it would seem he is asking for Li-Jared and me, as well. 'All those with translator-stones.' Indeed."

Bandicut nodded soberly. "Yes. And I know you're planning to go with the Maksu to—"

"Yes, but *this*—we must consider. A threat to life-support infrastructure? Most disturbing. It could imperil all of us, everyone on the continent."

Bandicut nodded.

Li-Jared looked at Ik. "You believe we should go, then? You and I? This is—"

"Distressing, yes! But if we find the ice caverns, only to have our lives threatened from another direction—"

Bwong-ng. Li-Jared's eye flashed angrily. "But what do we know of this, really? No doubt this robot of Bandie's is very loyal, assuming it still has free volition. But should we not investigate, before making rash judgments?"

"Indeed," Ik said. "John Bandicut, can you contact Copernicus and ask for further information?"

"We can try, sure. But isn't there someone else we ought to call, too? Some authority?"

"And say what? We know no details. And it might only increase the danger, if the boojum senses an alert. It might attack sooner."

"Well, but—"

"In any case, if the shadow-people know of this, it is unlikely we could find anyone better to notify."

Bandicut frowned, and waved Napoleon to the terminal. "Okay, Nappy. Let's send a reply."

"Yes, Captain."

He closed his eyes. "And quit calling me Captain, dammit. Copernicus calls me Captain."

"I withdraw the form of address. What shall I say, John Bandicut?"

He blinked, pulse racing. "Quote: *Your message received. We must—emphasize must—have more information. Do you not trust us? Please make direct contact at this terminal.*

And—'' Bandicut thought frantically. They were testing Copernicus as much as Copernicus was them, after all. "Tell him this: *Do you remember who saved your metal ass in the laser boring tunnel? Do you? Say that to him.*"

"Aye," said Napoleon, and reached out to the terminal.

"It is sent. And now, Captain, I must think on this matter of proof. In case he does not have a test already in mind." Napoleon settled into a parking configuration, his manipulators folded in front of him. He looked unnervingly like a large silver praying mantis lost in contemplation. Bandicut could not help envying the robot's ability to park and shut down at a moment's notice. He felt a burning tension between his shoulder blades, and knew that it would only get worse before he heard from Copernicus.

"Had you considered the question of going with us to the ice caverns?" Ik asked.

Bandicut started. The ice caverns had been far from his thoughts. "Well, some. But I hadn't really decided." He turned his hands up, vaguely embarrassed. "It's not that I'm ungrateful, or don't want—"

"Haaiii." Ik waggled a hand in the air. "It is reasonable to consider the question carefully. Don't you agree, Li-Jared?"

"That depends, I suppose."

"Let me clarify. You and I, Li-Jared my friend, might well be considered hazardous company, so long as the boojum is around. Should he not weigh carefully the risk of venturing out with us?" Ik placed a long, bluish finger upright against his chest and studied Bandicut for a moment. "We value your company, John Bandicut. But you are wise to be cautious."

"I'm beginning to think," Bandicut said drily, "that *I'm* the one who attracts danger, not you."

"Forgive me for interrupting," Napoleon said. "I believe we have a reply." He rose to face the terminal.

Bandicut waited, not breathing.

Napoleon turned. "Text-only. Quote: *I indeed remember, Cap'n, your foolish and heroic effort on my behalf. Sorry, un-*

able to risk higher-level contact. Afraid of contamination.
Please bring Napoleon to attached location coordinates, for
further details. Mayday Mayday. No delay, please! End of
text. I have checked the map and confirmed that the coordinates are well outside the urban portion of this city-state. It
appears accessible by local transport known as streaktrain.''

Bandicut closed his eyes and took a deep breath before
turning to the others.

Ik's eyes were flickering with intensity.

"Well—" *bwang* "—are you going to take us to see him
or not?" asked Li-Jared.

Bandicut stared at Li-Jared, and almost smiled. "Any idea
where we go to catch this streaktrain?"

A check of schedules showed an hour remaining before the
next train going in the right direction. Ik and Li-Jared wanted
to order a meal before they left. But Bandicut had something
else in mind. "Could you order something for me? There's a
personal call I want to make before we go."

Ik and Li-Jared peered at him. "Are you sure?" Ik said.
"After what happened last time—"

"I'll be careful," Bandicut promised. "The boojum stays
in hiding most of the time—you said that yourself. Anyway, it
thinks I'm dead now. Right?"

"Hrrm."

He could tell, without a word from Charlie, that the quarx
didn't like the idea. But even Charlie had to agree that it was
necessary to take risks sometimes.

/// Smart risks, John. ///

/Yeah, well—okay. But watch my flank anyway, huh?/

There was no answer, not in words anyway. But he sensed
Charlie taking up a watchful attitude, not that either of them
had a clear idea of what they could do to defend themselves if
the need arose. Still, he had a gut feeling that the boojum
wouldn't try the same thing twice in a row.

The terminal glowed faintly as he leaned over and peered
into it. /Please establish contact with Thespi third female, iceline signature Antares./

There was a momentary delay. Then:

<<<WE DO NOT READ YOUR REGISTRATION CODE. PLEASE IDENTIFY YOURSELF.>>>

He realized he had not thought this through completely.

<<<PLEASE IDENTIFY YOURSELF.>>> The iceline sounded as cold as its name.

Nothing for it but to plunge ahead. /John Bandicut, human of Earth./

<<<WE ARE SORRY, BUT THAT REGISTRATION HAS BEEN CLOSED.>>>

/Well, *I* am sorry,/ he answered, /but that cancellation is in error. I am alive and well, thank you./

<<<ONE MOMENT. MOVE CLOSER TO THE TERMINAL, PLEASE.>>>

Bandicut hesitated, then leaned forward. He saw a sparkle, then the connection with the iceline blossomed like an electrical spike, dancing at the ends of his synapses. He felt the iceline taking a reading, a comparison of his inner topographies with some baseline measurement held far away in a storage branch, the mortuary perhaps. For the barest instant, he glimpsed a flickering vision of the iceline connection with the Tree of Ice, and it made him breathless; he felt as though he had just peered into the heart of a galaxy, full of light and motion and bewildering complexity. His senses tingled like a warrior's, scanning for any sign of his enemy. He would smell it if it came near; he felt sure of that.

Something was coming his way. What?

An answer.

<<<THE MATCH IS CONFIRMED. WE ACKNOWLEDGE YOU ARE ALIVE. REGISTRATION WILL BE RESTO—>>>

/WAIT!/ he shouted.

<<<ARE YOU ADDRESSING THE SYSTEM? REGISTRATION IS PREPARED FOR REENCODING.>>>

/Do *not* renew registration./

The system paused.

<<<DO YOU PLAN TO DEPART THIS CITY-STATE? IT COULD BE TO YOUR ADVANTAGE TO RETAIN YOUR REGISTRATION.

REASONS AVAILABLE UPON REQUEST. YOU MAY REQUEST AB-
SENTEE STATUS, IF DESIRED.>>>

/No. I wish *new* registration. I have reason to believe my
confidentiality has been breached./

<<<RECORDS INDICATE YOU RELINQUISHED CONFIDEN-
TIALITY VOLUNTARILY.>>>

/To the one called Antares, yes. That's not what I mean./
Bandicut's heart was pounding. This might be his chance to
avoid attracting the boojum's attention again. It clearly did
not monitor all iceline activities, but emerged from hiding to
work its mischief. Possibly its presence was triggered by key
words—names, for instance. /My registration was cancelled
without my authorization. This was a malfunction. I believe
my previous registration to be vulnerable to a contamination
in the system. I request a new registration. Please transfer
credit and data regarding iceline signature Antares from old
registration. Do not provide any other forwarding./

The iceline was quiet, while his unusual request was
bumped to a higher level of command.

/// Interesting idea. I hope it works. ///

Bandicut didn't answer.

<<<REQUEST APPROVED. PLEASE PROVIDE NEW IDENTIFI-
CATION.>>>

He thought quickly. /Bandie. Most recently of . . . Triton./

<<<IDENTIFICATION ACCEPTED. DATA TRANSFER COM-
PLETE. YOU WISH CONNECTION WITH INDIVIDUAL CODE-
NAMED ANTARES?>>>

/Yes./ He sensed the quarx holding its breath—and its
tongue.

A moment later, the iceline spoke in a more melodic tone.

<<<ICELINE SIGNATURE ''ANTARES'' WISHES TO KNOW IF
YOU ARE THE SAME INDIVIDUAL AS THAT PREVIOUSLY SIGNED,
''JOHN BANDICUT.''>>>

/Answer in the affirmative./

<<<SHE WISHES TO KNOW WHY YOU CHANGED YOUR SIG-
NATURE.>>>

/You may tell her I was affected by an iceline system mal-function./

<<<VERY WELL.>>>

/Are you going to—/

<<<CONTACT ESTABLISHED.>>>

Bandicut felt himself suddenly falling, as though down into a great emptiness . . .

The sensation lasted only a moment. And then he was float-ing—bodiless, it seemed—in a strange labyrinth of mirrors and floating images. He turned slowly, peering into the mir-rors and seeing not his own face but images of stars and plan-ets and landscapes . . . and somehow knew that he was viewing an assortment of worlds from which denizens of Shipworld had come, a rogue's gallery of forsaken, or lost, worlds. He wondered if Earth was somewhere in this gallery. He felt a piercing ache at the thought.

(I have not yet found my own world here,) said a mind-voice, at once velvety and hard-edged.

(Do you miss it?) he asked without thinking, and in that instant he *felt* the other's powerful longing, and realized that he had made contact.

One of the mirrors faded to transparency, revealing a face that seemed strong more than delicate, and yet to his eyes strangely beautiful. Antares was clearly not human, and yet was very humanlike. Her face was framed by auburn hair, flowing back from her brow. Her small nose quivered with each breath. The eyes were as he remembered them—slightly slanted, with a fold in the corner, her gaze a golden halo sur-rounding jet-black pupils. The intensity of her gaze held his like magnets. He could scarcely breathe.

(Antares?) he thought, and the thought floated into the labyrinth like a breath of wind.

Her reply was just as clear. (Greetings—Bandie? Or shall I address you as John Bandicut?)

(Either. Both. I am—pleased—)

And he was suddenly aware of the degree of openness of this connection. His words were floating up not so much from his thoughts as from his feelings. If he'd intended to be guarded with his emotions, the opportunity was already lost.

(Yes, as you see. It is dangerous—but good. How else to know the dangers without trying, *quaaa?*)

The connection surged with a potent array of emotions, and not all his, not at all; but they were too many and too bewildering, and some too alien, for him to sort out. A shiver rippled through him, reminding him of the power of the boojum. But this was different.

(You were, *uuuhhll,* attacked?) Her query sang with overtones of empathy—and apprehension. (By demons in the iceline?)

(Boojum,) he whispered, and with the word came a deep, rolling sensation of mythical power and fear.

(Boojum . . . ?)

(You know of it?)

(Who does not know of it? And yet who knows very much?)

With those words, he sensed fear seeping out of her toward him, an alien and unnerving fear. He could not discern details, but he knew that she too had been through great trials—and great fear. The sensation was altogether too confusing; he tried to draw his thoughts back, to study the face of the Thespi woman. But his words emerged with a dreamy quality, and a wistfulness. (You accepted this contact. Why, if you are so afraid?)

He felt his own confusion reflected back to him, from her. (Do you not search for those of your kind—or those who resemble you?)

His heart nearly stopped, and there was a kind of frightened laughter reverberating through the halls of his mind. He felt a longing that was not his own, that arose out of a place of mist, and mountain peaks, and dancing bands of light in the sky . . .

(Your world?)

(A glimpse only . . . a memory . . .)

(And did you leave it—) he felt a sharp pain as his words raked past his own memories (—by choice?)

Her lips turned up into something like a smile. But the reverberations of her laughter turned to flint, and he knew whatever that look was, it was no human smile. (Did *you* choose to be exiled among strangers?)

(No. No. I am sorry.)

As he spoke, her golden eyes seemed to cloud. Three slender fingers touched her cheekbones. (You are new here. There is much you do not understand.)

Feelings of shame, regret, anger rushed to the surface.

(You fear danger in this contact,) he whispered, feeling an upwelling of anxiety: fear of the boojum and of the unknown, and excitement in the possibility—the risk—of their tracing one another from this contact.

Her response was both puzzling and reassuring. (Danger, yes—but not in the way you fear. You cannot trace me, nor I you. Not unless we both agree. That is not the danger. The danger is in the *knowing*.)

(???)

(The knowing, each of the other. And the need. And the risk that we *might* so choose.)

(And is this a great risk?) he thought, struggling to understand, and to contain the great fount of need and loneliness that would have swept away his words if he allowed it.

On her auburn-framed face was an expression he couldn't read, but her eyes were wide and probing. (You are in danger; even now you fear the boojum.)

Waves of concern. He thought of Copernicus and his inexplicable messages. (Don't you fear it?) he whispered.

(Deeply, deeply; and yet it is not trying to kill me, you see. You have shown me much. And of the star-spanner factory, I already knew.)

(???)

(I was there. A bystander.)

A crest of dizziness rolled over him, with fleeting memories of warning gongs and transporters carrying thousands of beings to places of shelter. He was suddenly aware of the gulf between Antares and him, in their relative danger from the boojum. If she were prudent, she would end this connection now.

(There is much I must consider, Bandie John Bandicut. And perhaps you as well.)

(Please—Bandie. Or John.)

(Bandie, then. We have made contact, and perhaps we will do so again. We both have much to search for, yes?)

(Yes,) he whispered, sensing that she was preparing to end the conversation, and not wanting it to end; the thought of breaking it was like telling a man dying of thirst not to drink from a running spring.

/// Ask what you most want to know, ///

Charlie whispered.

Stunned, he looked inward and realized what the quarx meant. (Antares?) he asked. (Have you ever seen, or heard of . . . another like me, in Shipworld? Another human?)

Antares' eyes narrowed slightly. (I have not,) she said softly.

He'd expected it; nevertheless, his answering sigh was like a moan of wind through old rafters: (Nor have I seen any like you.) And it seemed that her disappointment came whistling in concert with his.

For a moment, there was a difficult silence. Then her voice, like a taut wire: (I feel a certain . . . potential for kinship, Bandie John . . . Bandie. But I am most uncertain of the risks, which I scarcely understand.)

(I can't blame you for that. But perhaps—)

(And now I must go. I have much to consider.) Antares' eyes were black orbs now, the golden rings around her pupils so thin as to be nearly invisible. (Perhaps we will speak again. Good-bye, Bandie John Bandicut.)

(But—)

Her face faded back into a shimmering mirror, and then the silent labyrinth of mirrors faded to nothingness, and he was staring into the sparkling face of the iceline terminal. /Damn,/ he whispered, stung by the abruptness of her departure.

<<<CONTACT TERMINATED. DO YOU HAVE FURTHER NEEDS AT THIS TIME?>>>

It took him a moment to regain a sense of ordinary speech patterns. /No, I don't have no fokin' mokin' further needs,/ he rasped.

<<<SAY AGAIN?>>>

/Break. End contact./ He straightened from the terminal. "Son of a bitch," he sighed in frustration. He turned and saw Ik and Li-Jared at the other end of the room, calmly eating from small food containers.

Ik held a container out to him. He clearly had been keeping an eye on Bandicut. "Is everything satisfactory?"

Bandicut walked over to take the container, then shook his head. "I'll explain later." He ate three bites without tasting them, then set the food down. "I'm ready to go when you are," he said abruptly.

20

COPERNICUS RENDEZVOUS

 THE STREAKTRAIN RIDE was almost like being back on Earth, a fact that caused him pangs of homesickness even as it reassured him with a sense of familiarity. Soon after departure, they zoomed out of a tunnel into open countryside, riding in something that was recognizably a train, speeding along a fine silver thread that wound through a stunningly pastoral terrain. The train's interior offered a variety of seating arrangements, and they settled into a partially secluded little alcove with facing seats. Bandicut rested, gazing out the bubble-window, and did his best to put Antares out of his mind. At one point he glimpsed, before the train's speed carried them away, several groups of stocky bipeds walking through cultivated fields.

It had come as something of a surprise that Atrium City was little more than an extended shopping mall in one corner of that sector of the continent known locally as the Fourth Civilization, a name that he assumed was less prosaic-sounding in the original language. Atrium City was a melting pot and a place of commerce but, for most of the population, not a permanent place to live. Most of the peoples of the Fourth Civilization lived scattered through the wide hinterlands. It was largely an agrarian society, but it supported a handful of cities, which served as trade and touring centers and points of immigration.

Atrium City was soon far behind them, and they were

passing through rolling farmlands, the streaktrain zipping along at perhaps a few hundred kilometers per hour. Bandicut kept thinking about Copernicus and the boojum, and Copernicus's reply to his final question. *I indeed remember your foolish and heroic effort.* And he kept wondering, could the boojum have produced an answer like that, if it were impersonating Copernicus? He didn't think so. It might have been able to extract the information, but he doubted that it could have produced such a humanly robotic reply.

He was convinced that he would recognize the boojum's touch now, if he encountered it again. But he still didn't understand its intentions. Or understand why they, of all the people on this world, had been asked to oppose it. He became aware that Ik was watching him from the opposite seat, and he shifted his gaze inside. "So."

"Hrahh."

"Do you understand what's going on?"

Ik tilted his head.

Bandicut pressed his lips together. "With the boojum. With us. What's so special about *us,* that we're being put in the line of fire? We're not even natives here."

"Who is?" Ik remarked. His eyes dropped to Bandicut's hands, and wrists. The translator-stones? Ik glanced at Li-Jared, who was staring in the other direction, but fingering his own top stone on his breastbone.

"Is that it?" Bandicut asked incredulously. "The translator-stones?" He hadn't really noticed whether any of the aliens he had seen in Atrium City were equipped with stones; but maybe if stones had been in evidence, he would have noticed them.

"Of course it's the stones. And what the stones imply." Li-Jared turned and leaned forward, but paused in thought before speaking again. "The boojum is attempting to take control of Shipworld, and it views organic life as a threat to its progress. It may already have penetrated the inner defenses of the Tree of Ice."

"Hrrm, well, that could be true—"

"And *only* someone on the outside can defeat it now. That is my belief," said Li-Jared.

Ik's eyes sparkled with uncertainty, but he did not contradict the Karellian.

"What you're saying," Bandicut said slowly, "is that we, because we have stones, are supposed to do what the Tree of Ice cannot?" He felt a chill as he stared at his friends.

It was, perhaps, an unanswerable question. Li-Jared's fingers flicked upward in a shrug, and Ik merely cocked his head.

Bandicut exhaled, closing his eyes, searching his memories of contact with the boojum, wondering what he was missing that could make sense of this. What had he felt in the boojum? Intelligence, will to dominate, malice. But why malice toward him? A grudge, because he had defeated the boojum once? Or was it simply that the translator-stones marked him as an enemy?

Strange attractors.

The phrase slipped into his thoughts, but he wasn't sure where it had come from. It seemed an appropriate literal description of the forces that had brought him together with this company; with the boojum. But he sensed that there was more to it.

/// Chaos theory? ///

He stared out the window, not answering. Chaos theory, yes: the images of phase-space, those weird transmogrifications of data that mapped turbulent systems, displaying patterns of stability and instability in unexpected ways. Those curious scribbled pictures that emerged in phase-space from common chaotic systems—butterflies and vortices and God knew what else—almost like bizarre gravitational orbits. Strange attractors in graphical form: loci of activity that represented "convergence" of forces here, and "bifurcation" of forces there.

Charlie's voice brushed at the edges of his thoughts.

/// There is something about the boojum
that fits into those images. ///

Undoubtedly the quarx was right. As he watched the farmlands spin by, he thought of the complex infrastructures that had to be maintained here, in this gargantuan spaceship orbiting the galaxy far from any sun. Air, water, nutrients, and energy to be endlessly recycled. Weather to be controlled in vast environments like these farmlands. Food supplies to be grown, synthesized, distributed. Transportation systems. Information and communication systems. Social structures. And virtually all of it subject to potential chaotic fluctuations, any one of which could be deadly. And somehow in that complexity, the boojum had arisen. Was it created by someone? Or did it owe its very existence to the turbulent forces of chaos?

/Whoever gave us the translator-stones knew something like this might happen, didn't they?/ he thought suddenly, as the train snaked through a dense, purplish forest, and then in an eyeblink shot across a breathtaking river canyon.

/// *I must admit, I share your suspicions.* ///

Bandicut nodded to himself. /And I think maybe they knew that we'd all wind up together in this./ He thought of how he and his robots had been transported from wherever their spaceship was, practically into Ik's path. It had been inevitable that they would meet.

Charlie didn't answer. But he seemed troubled.

/Why, Charlie? Why?/

It was late afternoon by the local shifting of light, as Copernicus prepared for a final foray. It would be another half hour before the next streaktrain was scheduled to arrive down below, which was the earliest that he expected to see his friends. Nevertheless, he felt a need for vigilance against whomever else might be watching. It was vital that the drop be made in secrecy. Copernicus rolled out from under the low, bushy shrub and down a slope covered with dried conifer needles. Then he set out over hard flat ground toward the place where he would be making the drop.

The instructions blazed in his memory-cache as a constant reminder: >> . . . *timing and security essential . . . clear and present danger . . .* >>

>> Acknowledged. >>

Acknowledged. What more could he have said? But even as he acted to carry out the instructions, he had so many more questions.

Since passing by the small farming village, Copernicus had been making his way along the edge of an agricultural and wilderness district. He had found datanet terminals to be ubiquitous, even here in the wilderness; and with great care, he'd connected to the datanet and tracked the whereabouts of his comrades. He had decided that, until he knew more, he should remain alone and unobserved—avoiding population centers—while learning as much as he could about the nature of the boojum and those who were trying to stop it. He still had to learn which of those two categories Napoleon fell into.

The whole process, of course, had been complicated by these mysterious voices in his mind. It had taken a while to ascertain that they were not the boojum's, but the shadow-people's. Apparently, while giving him a recharge and general upgrade, they had also given him a capacity for receiving their signals directly, by some mechanism unconnected to the iceline. If the presence of the voices was startling, the information they conveyed was positively unnerving. It was a steady flow of details on the probable intentions of the boojum, and its efforts to destabilize the iceline and the physical life-support systems that kept Shipworld functioning. Though Copernicus was no longer in the shadow-people's geographical territory, they clearly regarded him as an ally.

Not that everything they told him, or asked of him, made sense. But from the beginning, he did his best to clarify . . .

>> Please define request. Define context of information. >>

At first he was uncertain whether they could hear him. But by and by an answer came.

>> . . . *request you convey information by secure means to John Bandicut and company . . .* >>

>> For what purpose? >>

>> . . . *we may require their help, most urgently . . . condition of Napoleon unknown, not responding to transmissions*

. . . do not approach them directly . . . do not entrust data to iceline . . . under no circumstance entrust the following data to iceline . . . >>

And with that, he had been forced to reconsider his priorities. **Foremost imperative: protect the safety and well-being of John Bandicut.** But properly defined, did that mean he should subordinate the *immediate* welfare of the captain to that of Shipworld, the captain's home?

Such thinking was not in his original programming. But extrapolation suggested that a danger to the environment was a danger to the captain himself. This was not just a logical proposition. Copernicus knew it on a deeper level. Further indication of turbulence: changes in *awareness*. Copernicus was growing. It was both a frightening and an exciting prospect.

There were many things that Copernicus wanted to know, and for which he needed to talk to John Bandicut. But first he had to know that Napoleon was free of the boojum's control. Their last interaction had been terrifying—and he'd hardly displayed coolness under fire himself. He'd panicked— fearing contamination through Napoleon, fearing that if contaminated, he might himself turn on his friends. And what had he accomplished, except to isolate himself from everyone who mattered to him? Still . . . Napoleon was not now responding to the shadow-people, and they didn't know why. Before he could rejoin his friends, he needed to know that it was safe.

And in the meantime, the shadow-people's requests grew more urgent.

>> . . . imperative, imperative . . . attack may be imminent . . . details follow . . . urgently request assistance of John Bandicut and all who bear stones-of-voice-and-power . . . >>

>> Contact made. Urgency conveyed. Proof of Napoleon pending . . . >>

The details regarding the boojum were stored and organized. John Bandicut would make of them what he could. And by watching both Bandicut's reaction and Napoleon's, Copernicus would attempt to determine whether Napoleon was genuinely free.

There would be no black-and-white, digitally clear answers. The initial observations gave him hope. He would have to judge his friends by their behavior, by their personalities. It might be all he would have to go on. Intuition, John Bandicut might have called it. He didn't know if he had much intuition; it wasn't something that robots were normally programmed to wield. But he had to try.

He involuntarily tightened his grip on the captain's backpack, as he drove steadily across the field toward the rendezvous point.

"But they tried to save your world," Bandicut was saying, "and they failed?"

Ik placed his fingertips together before answering. "Indeed. And I was brought here out of the fires of the cataclysm."

"But why do they do these things? What's in it for them?" Bandicut was not ungrateful that Earth had suffered a kinder fate than Hraachee'a. But he didn't understand it.

> /// *I have this memory*
> *of Charlie-One telling you of such things.*
> *Didn't he speak of many worlds being saved,*
> *some with his personal assistance?* ///

There was a tremor in the quarx's voice, as if he too were beginning to understand, for the first time in this life, what was in store for him and his future quarxly descendants.

Bandicut hesitated, thinking that whatever happened to the quarx was likely to happen to him, too. /Yes. But I didn't understand it back then, either./ And back then, he had been in a state of shock at the very notion of having an alien intelligence in his mind. He hadn't always focused that well on the big picture.

Li-Jared spoke. "I guess that there must be thousands of intelligent species on this world. Do you suppose all those races began their lives here?"

Bandicut blinked. "Were they *all* brought here by . . . whoever controls the translators?"

"I cannot say for certain," Li-Jared admitted. "I have

personally encountered only a small fraction of them. And some cultures, at least, seem to have lost all memory of their origins. But I've spoken with a number who clearly recall in a historical, if not personal, sense, their peoples being transported here from other worlds."

"You mean dying worlds?"

Li-Jared hesitated. "Perhaps. In some cases, I believe so. In others, I am unsure. There is a problem, you understand, when one probes into these questions, of distinguishing legend and mythology from factual history." The Karellian's fingers drummed in little outward flicks against the window-bubble of the train.

"In any case," Ik said, "it is my suspicion that *we* are here, in some sense, in payment for services rendered to our homeworlds. And for this we carry voice-stones to assist and guide us. I received mine shortly before my journey here. And Li-Jared likewise."

/// I suspect he may be right. ///

"You mean we've been sold as slaves?" Bandicut shivered. How much payment was a world worth?

/// Not slaves, exactly, no.
But we do seem to be expected to serve,
in various ways.
Or perhaps invited is a better word . . . ///

/Invited?/ Bandicut stared blankly out the window for a moment, not believing it, thinking of endless servitude with his translator-stones as masters. It was not a happy thought.

/// John, I don't think so.
I believe that the stones are here
on your sufferance. ///

/My sufferance?/ He wondered if that really was true. If so, then he ought to be able to order them out, if he wanted to.

/// Well, I suppose, but— ///

/Stones,/ he thought, /let me see you prove that I'm free if I want to be./ Before he could reconsider, and lose his nerve, he held out his hands, palms up. /Leave my wrists./

Charlie yelped in alarm.

/// John, wait! ///

He felt a sharp burning sensation in both wrists, and a moment of dizziness. When the dizziness passed, his eyes focused again as two baseball-sized globes of light shrank suddenly to lifeless pebbles in the palms of his hands. His hands shook, as he held them. "I'll be damned," he whispered.

Ik and Li-Jared gaped at him in astonishment.

"Haaii, hrrrakh-how-kodientakhh-rakhh—"

"Braangg-b-dang-g'hung—"

"I was just—just trying—I wanted to see—" he stammered, suddenly terrified that he had done something irreversible. He couldn't understand a word that Ik and Li-Jared were saying, and they probably couldn't understand him, either.

/// John, this is scaring me.

I think you've made your point.

I also think we'd be lost without those stones. ///

Bandicut swallowed. /Yeah. But I had to know, Charlie. I had to know./ He drew a deep breath, rolling the stones in his hands. /Okay, stones—if you can hear me—thank you, and you can go back now./ And then he held his breath.

For a moment, nothing happened. Then the stones twinkled, first the white diamond in his right hand, then the black bit of coal in his left. Then his breath went out with a gasp as he felt something like a wave of electricity pass through him. The stones flared, and when the wave of dizziness passed, his wrists were stinging; but the stones were flickering again, beneath his skin.

"Hraahh! John Bandicut, what was the meaning of that?"

Bandicut took a moment to regain his equilibrium, then finally managed a half-smile. "Ah—sorry, I didn't mean to scare you guys. But I was testing something."

Bwuh-hong. "Testing what?" Li-Jared's eyes had narrowed to fierce slits.

"I wanted to see if the stones were my masters, or my servants."

"Ahh, hrrrm," said Ik. "And were you satisfied with what you learned?"

Bandicut shrugged. "Yeah, I guess so."

Ik cocked his head. "We do have freedom to move and make our own choices, John Bandicut. Though I confess that we seem, Li-Jared and I, to find our way into the path of trouble more often than we would like."

"Trouble, like the boojum?"

"Yes." Ik glanced at Li-Jared, who was now staring moodily out the window, as if to avoid the conversation. "Like the boojum."

Bandicut nodded slowly, as he felt the train begin to slow. *And I have joined you, haven't I?*

Copernicus rotated his arm joints to lift Bandicut's backpack. He placed it on top of a small outcropping of rock, flanked by trees, but not far from the streaktrain platform where his friends would be arriving. He hoped he had given Napoleon clear enough directions. The train was not yet in sight, but Copernicus was beginning to sense electromagnetic and acoustic pulses in the metal guide-band that snaked across the land below. The train would be here soon. He needed to leave his message and get out of sight.

He could only hope that the boojum was not observing his actions. There was no reason to believe that it was. But the boojum seemed to have many unusual abilities.

Copernicus's mechanical arms swiveled back and opened his top maintenance access port. He had just enough dexterity to locate and grasp a datachip in his memory section. Not just any datachip, but the one that he had erased and loaded with the contents of his message. He tugged the chip free, then held it up for inspection. It was a small, black sphere with shiny connector-bumps. It felt a little strange to be examining his own datachip, as though it were just some component off a shelf.

It appeared undamaged. Copernicus cradled it with one manipulator, and used another hand to open John Bandicut's bag. He extracted the captain's pocket notepad and placed it carefully on top of the bag, and the datachip on top of the notepad. Then he backed away. He heard a low, distant hum. The streaktrain was just coming into view below, through the trees, gliding along its silver ribbon. Copernicus rolled away quickly, aiming his cooling fan down over the dusty rock, to blow away his treadprints.

Then he climbed the slope back to his spying place.

Disembarking, Bandicut felt as if they were stepping from civilization into a holo of the American Wild West. Beside the train track stood a station consisting of a boarding platform and a small shelter. There was nothing else to see but scrub, rocky slopes, and thin clusters of trees. The sky overhead was clear blue and seemingly infinite. As the streaktrain pulled away and vanished around a bend, the silence and emptiness seemed complete. Charlie-One would have loved it.

Li-Jared peered around skeptically. "You say your robot knows where to go from here?"

"That's what he said. Napoleon?"

"Follow me," the robot chirped, and strolled across the train's guide-band, toward a wooded hill.

Bandicut and the others exchanged surprised glances, then followed, stepping carefully over the gleaming ribbon of metal.

/// I don't think it can electrocute you. ///

/Can't you ever sound more certain about these things?/ He felt a tingle as his legs straddled the rail, and he practically hopped away. /Feels electrified to me!/

/// Naturally.
But the power's too weak to hurt you, unless you
apply some sort of power-field gizmo to it. ///

/Are you thinking this stuff up on the spot, or are you really remembering it?/

/// It's not so much that I'm remembering
the stuff
as that I'm remembering how to summon it up
from the stones. ///

Bandicut grunted and strode up the slope after Napoleon. The robot appeared quite clear about where he was going, though there was no evidence of a trail up the hillside. Muttering something about a "coordinate grid," Napoleon chose a zigzag path, occasionally springing up onto rocks with his metal legs, but never tackling a steeper ascent than the others could handle. Bandicut was beginning to breathe hard when Napoleon called out, "Familiar object in sight!"

He quickened his pace. "Coppy?"

Napoleon reached the top of an outcropping. "Negative. Your personal bag."

"My bag?" Bandicut crested the hill. Sure enough, Napoleon was crouched over his missing backpack, examining something on top of it. "What the hell? Is that my scribblie pad?" Bandicut picked up the two objects the robot had found. One was indeed his notepad, which he had been carrying in his backpack; the other was a computer datachip. From Copernicus? He turned it over in his hand. Black, spherical, with nublike silver connectors—and markings in English.

His friends caught up. "What have you found?" asked Ik.

Li-Jared looked around. "I see no robot."

"Cap'n, I judge that Copernicus has been here," Napoleon said.

Bandicut peered at the notepad. "There's a note from him here. It says, 'Face-to-face meeting impossible at present. I have encoded on the accompanying datachip all the information I have gathered on the boojum's plans. An attack may be imminent on a critical ecologic reserve for this continent. Please review this information at once!' " Bandicut paused, thinking: *And how do we know this chip isn't infected?* He shook his head and continued, " 'The notepad has insufficient capacity to convey the full information. Regarding the safety of attaching this chip to Napoleon's memory bus, I append here guidelines for the safe attachment of the unit. Napoleon, please use the following protocols before accessing the contents of the datachip—' " Bandicut looked at Napoleon. "There's a bunch of code here. Can you understand it?" He held up the notepad for Napoleon to scan.

Napoleon grasped it, tilting the screen. "I'll have to download it, Cap'n." The robot opened a small access port on his right side, turned the notepad until he had it oriented correctly, then held it up to the access port. "I have the optical link."

"Do you need any help?"

"Negative. Finished." Napoleon handed the notepad back to Bandicut.

"And?"

"I am evaluating the protocols."

"Well, take all the time you need to be sure." Bandicut glanced worriedly at Ik and Li-Jared.

Napoleon stirred. "Cap'n. It is a so-called *condom protocol,* designed to insulate my bus from dangerously active elements of code. I estimate its protection level as ninety-eight percent reliable. Do you consider that sufficient?"

Bandicut frowned.

/// *May I?* ///

Charlie inquired, nudging his hand slightly toward the robot.

/Huh? Sure./ Bandicut touched his fingers to Nappy's upper casing. "Hold still for a second, Nappy. We want to check something."

"Affirmative. Permission granted for Charlie to come aboard."

Bandicut blinked.

/// *Thank you, Nappy.*
Okay, I see the layout pretty well.
I'd agree with Nappy's assessment.
The condom protocol looks like
a genuine effort.
It's very good—but it's impossible
for it to be foolproof. ///

Bandicut considered. /But probably Coppy's not infected, because if he were, he wouldn't have made a genuine effort. Right? Did it look like Coppy's work, and not the boojum's?/

/// *I'd say so.* ///

/Well, then—I guess you gotta take chances in life./ He breathed a silent prayer and said to Napoleon, "Let's give it a try."

The robot snapped shut the small access port and opened a

larger one. "If you would hand me the chip . . ." He took the black marble from Bandicut and deftly maneuvered it into an empty port. "Checking. Establishing protocols. I have a working connection."

Bandicut rubbed his jawbone anxiously.

/// I could monitor for you. ///

/That might put *us* at risk. Let's wait a little longer./

"Captain," said Napoleon, his voice suddenly altered, deeper. "Information coming in. I am developing a picture . . ."

"Picture of what?" Bandicut's hands were clenched in front of him, as if to wrestle the information from the robot.

"He sounds different. What's happened?" Li-Jared dropped to a defensive crouch.

Change of voice? Change of personality? "Nappy—?"

"Whreeeek! Whreeeek!"

Bandicut jumped back, startled. The sound had come from Napoleon, but the robot was frozen, unmoving. "Napoleon?"

For a moment, he thought he heard Copernicus's voice coming from Napoleon's speaker. "—unclear, say again—" The voice sped up to a chirp, then a squeal, interrupted twice by blasts of staccato noise that might have been static, or harsh, compressed voices. Abruptly, the sound cut off. Napoleon remained frozen.

/// Is he—? Should we—? ///

/I don't know. Wait—/

Napoleon suddenly began swiveling his head, scanning the landscape, up and down in all directions. A small indicator light was flickering at the base of his sensor array; he was transmitting signals.

"Napoleon!" Bandicut barked. "Answer me! What's happened?"

Napoleon's sensors swung to peer at him. "John Bandicut, the danger is imminent! We must act quickly. I am searching for Copernicus, but he is not answering!"

"The message, Nappy! The message!" Bandicut reached out to the robot, then drew his hands back. /Wait, Charlie! Not yet. He's acting too weird. It could leak over./

/// But you can deal with it!
It's just like your datanet back home. ///
/My datanet back home didn't have fucking boojums in it trying to *kill* people./

/// No, but what is the boojum
but a complex operation in a fancy datanet? ///
/It damn near killed us!/

/// But you gotta take chances.
You said that, right? ///

Napoleon was rasping and clicking, and having trouble speaking. "Must go—now—shadow-people—"

"*Damn* it, Nappy, are you hit with the boojum? Talk to me!"

"Negative, negative, negative—the shadow-people—" Napoleon clicked helplessly, his upper sensors still swinging.

"Kr'deekin' hell." /Okay, Charlie—do it!/ Bandicut slapped his hands onto the robot's body and shut his eyes, willing himself to see what the quarx was seeing. He reeled with a rush of dizziness; he saw a racing expanse of black and white dots.

/// This is bewildering . . . ///

He gulped back nausea.

/// Wait, there's the message. ///
/Did it get him?/ Bandicut whispered in fear.

/// No . . . ///
/Then what—?/

/// Mokin' foke— ///
/What?/

/// He's just confused, that's all.
Too much input; he needs help . . .
Ah. ///

/Explain!/

/// He's not infected.
He's struggling with ambiguity—
torn between concern for Copernicus
and concern about the danger.
If I can get his mind off Copernicus—
okay, I think he can talk now. ///

"Nappy?" Bandicut said hoarsely, lifting his hands away.

"Hrahh!" cried Ik. "Is he—?"

"I am unharmed," said the robot suddenly, in a normal voice. "I was having . . . difficulty absorbing the data. It included not just communications from the shadow-people—"

"The shadow-people!"

"—but also Copernicus's own perceptions and thoughts. It was as if I could almost *touch* Copernicus. But he was not there, and he would not respond. I found it most disconcerting. I apologize."

"The danger!" Bandicut shouted. "What is the danger?"

"Captain, if these communications are genuine—and I believe they are—this entire continent is in peril. The boojum's interest has focused on a massive storage-tank farm, containing roughly a planet's worth of atmospheric reserves."

"Atmospheric reserves? Explain."

"It is a supply of oxygen, nitrogen, and other reserves in solid, liquid, and gaseous form needed for maintaining atmospheric equilibrium throughout the continent. The shadow-people believe that the boojum intends to destroy that depot." Napoleon's sensor-eyes seemed to probe them each in turn, as he swiveled. "They say they cannot protect it without our help."

"This is extraordinary!" growled Ik. "Is there no defensive guard for this tank farm?"

"There is," said Napoleon. "But the boojum may have discovered a way to neutralize it."

Li-Jared's eyes were pulsing with fire. "What can we do that the shadow-people cannot?"

Bandicut squinted. "That's a good point, Nappy. Do the shadow-people maintain the tank farm?"

"Negative," said the robot. "It is outside their territory. The shadow-people can work only within critical range of the n-space activators that join the shipworld continents. They cannot exist far from the open space-time interstices created by the activators. They can guide us toward the endangered area, but they cannot get to it themselves."

"Just like the factory floor," Ik muttered darkly.

"Christ, Nappy! You mean we're supposed to fly off on some wild posse-chase with no more evidence than that?" /This is weird, even for the shadow-people./

/// *But you did something like it once before.* ///

Bandicut thought of a spacecraft rocketing toward collision with a comet. The memory made him shudder.

"I believe we must go," insisted the robot.

Bandicut swallowed. "You *believe* we must go?"

"The evidence is in the datachip: Copernicus's memories of the shadow-people's messages. And their messages are highly persuasive."

"So you're convinced it's real?"

"I am convinced," said the robot.

Copernicus watched from above as his companions discussed the message. His evaluation of Napoleon was positive. His friend showed no sign of contamination by the boojum. He seemed stronger, more self-confident, more complex; but he still seemed to be Napoleon.

This was good news. Copernicus had been alone now for what seemed a very long time, in a very strange world. At last he felt he could answer Napoleon's call, and reveal himself. And be reunited, finally, with all of his friends.

A soft *blatt* of static interrupted his thoughts.

>> . . . *require your assistance elsewhere once more . . . request that you go, at once, to another place where we cannot* . . . >> It was the shadow-people. But he seemed to have caught only a fragment of their message.

>> **This is Copernicus of Triton Station. Was preceding transmission addressed to me?** >>

The reply was faint but audible: >> . . . *Copernicus of Triton Station . . . urgently request your assistance . . . request you delay contacting your companions . . .* >>

For a few moments, Copernicus considered the request in dismay. Delay contacting his companions? Back on Triton, such a request would not have troubled him in the slightest.

But now? He had been waiting so long. And there was the question of John Bandicut's safety, his first priority.

With a flush of uncertainty, he spoke to the distant shadow-people. **>> Please clarify, what is the nature of your urgent request . . . ? >>**

21

INTO THE BELLY OF THE WHALE

ANTARES STUDIED THE message she had just received. It was from a Stendart she knew, an associate of the Maksu. It reported that a group of the Maksu had contracted to guide a small company of outlanders to a place known colloquially as the "ice caverns." The apparent purpose: to attempt direct contact with a primary knowledge-node of the Tree of Ice, in hopes of discovering a way to leave Shipworld and return to their homeworlds.

Antares had, from time to time, heard of the ice caverns—always in casual conversation, and never very informatively—and she had never been able to learn whether they were anything more than legend. So a report of an expedition to find them would have been interesting in and of itself. But what really caught her notice was the identification of the company involved. A "Hraachee'an" named Ik. A "Karellian" named Li-Jared. And a "Human" named John Bandicut.

John Bandicut. How extraordinary.

This man, this Human, certainly kept himself busy. New to Shipworld, he had already come out of two deadly battles with the iceline demon. (Or boojum—his name for it. According to her knowing-stones, the name had mythical overtones in his language that matched its reputation for stealth and treachery in the iceline.) But one thing about this John Bandicut: although he seemed to have a knack for bringing the boojum down upon himself, he also seemed to have a knack for surviving it.

During their brief contact, Antares had found herself hesitant about being drawn too near to Bandicut's sphere of activity, without first knowing more about him. She was not exactly regretting that choice now, but she was wondering if she had been too cautious. *It was reasonable prudence. You felt his need, his longing. You were right to be wary—you've given in to longings before, and paid for it. But remember your need, too. Don't be a slave to it, but don't be afraid of it, either.* She still knew next to nothing about his species; but the empathic sense had been strong, the sense that they were alike in striking ways, if different in others. And, he had knowing-stones. And now here he was, off on a quest for the ice caverns.

The ice caverns! The talk of them had always made her think of Thespi legends of long-lost "wisdoms," mythical grails of power. She'd long ago put out feelers to see if anything might be learned about the ice caverns—thus the message from the Stendart. She'd done so in the faint hope that somewhere in the legend there might be clues to who the masters of this Shipworld were, and how she might contact them, and perhaps learn why they had brought her here, from almost certain death at home. Why did *they* care that she was sentenced to die? She had never spoken directly to the Maksu, those reclusive dealers in information—partly because she had little knowledge of them, but also because she had nothing to trade. But now, to learn that the Human and his friends would soon be en route to the ice caverns, with the Maksu!

Antares touched her throat, where her knowing-stones pulsed, as she pondered the matter. Did she want, one more time, to risk friendship with someone who so clearly signified danger? She thought of Ensendor—companion, teacher, lover, and witness against her in trial—and her lips turned up in pain and fury. But this Human was not Ensendor; and anyway, did she really want to continue her exile in solitude? And suppose these aliens really found a way to leave Shipworld; would she want to go? She wasn't sure. But she knew she'd rather have the chance to make that decision.

With a soft murmur of resolution, she crossed the grotto-like room to the iceline terminal, and began composing a message to the one known as Bandie.

After consulting with Ik and Li-Jared, Bandicut touched Napoleon again. He wanted the quarx to take a closer look at the memory-recordings from Copernicus.

/// They seem genuine to me, ///

Charlie opined, as he opened a window for Bandicut to glimpse the transmissions from the shadow-people.

It was a bewildering swirl of input: some of it auditory, some of it transformed to a visual landscape. The visual part was incomprehensible; it looked like mountain peaks rushing past a spinning airplane, the mountains alight with blotches of incandescent danger. He caught enough in verbal form to recognize the voices of the shadow-people. The words came too fast to follow, but they were filled with shrieks of urgency and need. /Charlie?/ he asked dizzily.

/// There's a lot here, and it is confusing.
But I believe the shadow-people. ///

/But how can they possibly know what the boojum is planning? Do they say?/

/// They observe patterns.
They say they listen to the iceline,
and talk to the Maksu and to other data-merchants;
and they know people who can hear
the Tree of Ice. ///

A roar rose in Bandicut's mind as he saw a dozen streamers dancing, a dozen rivers converging at a waterfall. As he watched, the waterfall froze; and he heard a low, secondary thrumming, which he sensed was a growing composite of many views of the boojum's activities.

/// They're good at putting things together.
Like the translator. ///

The waterfall erupted into motion again. The roar became unbearable. /Enough!/ he cried, and the window closed to silence.

Staggering back from the robot, it took him a moment to recover. "It's real—" he gasped "—as nearly as I can tell. The shadow-people are *scared* of this thing. If they're right, then this whole continent really is in danger. Maybe the whole Shipworld. They say there's no one else in a position to help. I can't believe I'm saying this, but I think we should do what they ask."

"Hrrrrl," Ik growled. "We will have to contact the Maksu, and hope they will accept a delay."

"Charlie says the shadow-people talk to the Maksu. They can probably get a message to them."

Li-Jared was still in a crouch, swinging his head from side to side as if studying a large map on the ground. "All right." *Bwonng-ng.* "Krikey damn shit. Let's go, then." He rose. "Where do we meet the krikey damn shadow-people?"

"Granite-Three-Down on the streakline," said Napoleon.

Bandicut gave him a startled glance. "Is that a station? You know where it is?"

"Yes," said Napoleon. "Are we agreed, then?"

Bandicut put away his notepad and hefted his backpack over his shoulders. "Yeah. Let's move." And together they started down the hillside.

Copernicus watched his friends' departure with regret. He had accomplished the most urgent part of his mission here. But it pained him to let his friends leave without contact. Was he making the right choice? Would this other mission help to assure John Bandicut's safety, in the end? The shadow-people had argued that it would. He had no evidence of this; and yet, it was a logical extension of his decision to collaborate with the shadow-people, with Hroom and his friends.

The shadow-people had promised to send representatives to his companions, to guide them to whatever awaited. But Copernicus was aware of—no, he *felt*—a sense of loss, almost a wistfulness, in their departure. He decided finally to do one last thing here.

He waited until the westbound train arrived. Then he transmitted: **>> Napoleon: I am sure now. Thank you for trusting me. Urgent business calls me away; but if you prevail in your mission and I in mine, we may yet meet again. Godspeed. Copernicus. >>**

He broadcast the message twice, then switched off his receiver while he settled down to wait for the opposite-bound train. If Napoleon protested his departure, he didn't want to hear it. He turned his thoughts instead to how he was going to accomplish his next job, of which he had only the sketchiest understanding.

He had not the slightest idea how his companions were to accomplish their mission, either. But that was out of his hands now. He trusted that they would find a way.

Napoleon spoke as they waited on the platform for the next streaktrain. "The shadow-people affirm that they have contacted the Maksu and informed them of the delay."

"How do you know that?" Bandicut asked. "Are they talking to you now, too?"

"Affirmative. I should have been hearing them before. They gave me that ability when they repaired me, but their procedures were interrupted by the call to pursue Li-Jared. The data from Copernicus included some error-correcting code, which I have inspected and implemented."

Bandicut could only stare at him.

The streaktrain arrived like softly gonging windchimes, and they stepped aboard. But Napoleon hesitated, halfway in the door. Bandicut glanced back. "What is it?"

The robot whirred back into motion, crowding in behind him. "Nothing, John Bandicut. It's all right."

"*Nappy.* What just happened?"

The entryway sealed, and the train rocked almost imperceptibly as it accelerated from a standstill. The robot's eyes seemed to darken. "Copernicus just called to say good-bye."

Bandicut opened his mouth. "He—"

"Yes." Napoleon recited the message he had just received. "I replied, but received no response. What do you think he's doing, Cap'n? The shadow-people won't say."

Bandicut shook his head. "I wish I knew, Nappy. I really wish I knew." He found a seat beside Ik and watched as Napoleon plugged himself into a power source for recharging. He thought of all the questions he still wanted answered; but instead of asking them, he closed his eyes and went to sleep, as the streaktrain sped across the unwinding countryside.

He awoke to the sensation of the train slowing. "Our station?" he murmured.

"Apparently," said Ik, stretching.

Bandicut closed his eyes again, savoring the last moments of sleepiness. He didn't want to give it up. Especially not to go into battle with an invisible foe.

"Perhaps no one will be here to meet us, and we can all go home," Li-Jared said in a droll tone that Bandicut was beginning to recognize as Karellian humor.

"Perhaps," Ik said, leaning to peer out the window as they glided alongside a platform. "But I thought I just saw some shadow-people out there."

"Pity," Bandicut said with a yawn. He hoisted his backpack. "If we're going, let's go."

On the platform, however, there was no sign of shadow-people. Bandicut gazed around, wondering what sort of settlement they had landed in this time. It wasn't the emptiness of the Wild West anymore. Rising above a sculpted wall were humped buildings that appeared carved out of living stone. A dozen or so other passengers had gotten off the train with them, mostly a group of giraffe-headed centaurs, who disappeared straight into the waiting room. When Bandicut peered after them, he saw the last one vanishing down a ramp. Toward a subway?

Napoleon headed that way, also. "We are to proceed to the underlevel transport, then northward," he said. Bandicut followed, with a shiver of déjà vu. As they stepped off the ramp onto what looked like an Earthly subway platform, Bandicut glanced around for the giraffe-people. They had already disappeared. He peered up at an overhead dome and remarked to Charlie, /Just like the subway in Nuevo L.A., but without the graffiti. Wait a minute, where are the tunnels?/ He looked up and down the length of the platform. At each end were huge silver disks, like plugs. He stepped close to the silver ribbon-track, and found himself pushing against a sudden resistance. /Well, you can't jump off onto the track here, I guess./

*/// John, I find it difficult sometimes
to picture what your homeworld was like. ///*

/You and me both./ Despite this reminiscence, he was aware of an increasing difficulty in summoning memories of the past. It was not that he had forgotten, exactly, but more as if his memories were being silted over with slowly hardening sediments of newer cares.

"This is the way to the—" *rasp* "—underbelly," Ik said, pointing to an engraved sign on the wall.

"Huh? Underbelly?"

*/// I think he means,
into the substrata of the continent,
toward the underside of the metaship. ///*

/Ah./ Bandicut studied the sign. It was covered with incomprehensible glyphs. "Aren't there any maps of the place?"

"Well, just this." Ik pointed to a smooth panel flush with the wall.

Bandicut moved sideways a little, and a spidery line drawing became visible. It was a complex, three-dimensional puzzle; the only thing he could decipher was a flat domed section at the top, spanning the map. That must be the open land above, where the streaktrains ran. Below "ground" level was a bewildering maze of subsections, which seemed to scroll endlessly, like a computer display, as his eyes moved downward. He would have to study this a long time, he thought, for it to make any sense.

"Is this for us?" called Li-Jared.

Bandicut turned to see a burnished, snakelike vessel glide into place beside them. He glanced to the right, where it had come from, and saw only the silver plug. A door appeared in the vehicle, and Napoleon stepped toward it. "Nappy, are you sure this is it?"

Ik was squinting at some symbols on the side of the train. "It says 'Maintenance Only.' Weren't we supposed to take the northbound train?"

"I believe this is the correct train," said Napoleon, and stepped aboard. Bandicut glanced helplessly at his friends, and shivered at the thought of the door closing and the train whisking Napoleon away, while the rest of them stood here debating the question.

The robot peered back out. "It is empty. It appears to be waiting for us."

Bandicut shrugged, and they boarded. The doorway disappeared, and through the forward window they could see the silver plug in the platform wall glimmering. The train did not seem so much to accelerate as to dim like a light, then brighten again, flashing down a smooth-walled tunnel.

The streaming movement of lights in the tunnel walls turned into a mesmerizing flicker. Bandicut was scarcely aware of any other movement around him.

Whreeeeeek!

He nearly jumped out of his skin—and whirled like a drunken ballet dancer.

"Hraachh!" Ik cried.

Apparently the shadow-people had been hiding in the back of the train, or perhaps in some pocket dimension that had disgorged them into the others' presence. Whatever the case, three whiplike figures of shadow were now fluttering among them like frantic dervishes. It took Bandicut a moment to get his breath back. "What are you doing—trying to scare us to death?"

Whreek whreeek! ". . . urgent, urgent, grateful . . . come with us . . ."

"Yes, yes! Who sent you here? Was it Hroom?" Bandicut blinked from one to another, trying to decide who was talking.

". . . message from Hroom'm'm . . . great trust in you . . . great victory . . ."

Bandicut's thoughts darkened. Great victory. The factory floor? It was practically an accident. He hated to think of the false confidence *that* could engender. "So," he said cautiously, "you are friends of Hroom? Is he involved in this?"

The shadow-people jangled back at him. It was like listening to a roomful of first-year violin students. His translator-stones were buzzing. ". . . unable to be here . . . Hroom'm'm sent us . . . is elsewhere now . . ."

Ik interrupted their choir. "Can you explain what this is about, tell us what we're supposed to do?"

Whreek-reek-reek. ". . . will take you to a maintenance node . . . show you the danger . . . the way to it . . . the others who may help . . ."

Others? Bandicut thought.

The shadow-people fiddled almost harmoniously. ". . . we have arrived . . ."

Bandicut hadn't even noticed that the train was slowing. But in fact it had come to a stop. Not at a station platform, however. They were still in the tunnel.

At that moment the left-hand tunnel wall glowed and vanished, and a sparsely lit cavern yawned, looking more like an industrial space than a subway platform. ". . . subway maintenance stop . . ." the shadow-people twanged. ". . . unscheduled stop . . . will proceed downward from here . . . make our movements inconspicuous . . ."

Smart, Bandicut thought. As long as the boojum isn't watching on some maintenance camera, it should be just fine.

/// *The shadow-people do seem to know what they're doing.* ///

/Yeah./

". . . follow? . . ."

"Yeah," Bandicut murmured and led the others off the train.

"One could easily become lost in these corridors," Ik observed, as they descended the fourth or fifth winding ramp, through a shadow-world of girders and walls and heavy, incomprehensible equipment.

"Feels like we're in the belly of a whale," Bandicut murmured. "Now I know how Jonah must have felt."

Ik glanced his way.

He shook his head. "Sorry. Human reference. An old story."

Ik hrrrm'd and moved on.

They were definitely in the belly of the shipworld now. Bandicut doubted he could find his way back to the subway if his life depended on it. They had made at least a dozen turns, and each level and corridor looked different from the one before—usually darker and gloomier. And yet there was a dreary sameness to it all. The lighting was never quite right, as if centuries of grime covered the light fixtures, whether they were long tubes and crevices along the walls, or globes erupting from the ceiling. It felt much like the bowels of any immense urban or industrial facility on Earth, except that they hadn't seen anyone even marginally resembling a human. Perhaps that was part of the resemblance, though; places like this on Earth had always seemed designed to squeeze the humanity from anyone unlucky enough to be stuck in them.

Such inhabitants as they did see were mostly squat, multilimbed beings who looked as if they had been born to drive forklift modules. No one spoke to the passing company; the workers all seemed occupied by custodial or maintenance tasks, none of which looked pleasant. Was it just in the nature of the surroundings that no one talked, or did these creatures somehow sense that they should ignore the interlopers? Bandicut wondered if those squat beings were bred to enjoy—or tolerate, anyway—work that no one else wanted to do.

He also wondered how much farther down they could go before they hit the bottom of Shipworld. He began to imagine that they were descending through the underdecks of a sunken, sea-going vessel, miles below the surface of a midnight-dark ocean; he imagined them drawing ever closer to the bottom of the hull, where mud and pressure squeezed against frigid steel, against plates that at any moment could buckle and cave inward. A wave of lightheadedness passed over him, spinning dizziness, as he saw a wall of seawater thundering in to crush him and everything else in its path.

/// Whoa, John!
This is no time for a fugue! ///

The quarx did something, and he started, as if waking abruptly from a nightmare. He took a sharp breath, and carefully looked around and counted his companions: Napoleon, Ik, Li-Jared, the shadow-guides . . . yes, they were still here; and yes, they were safe, and not under an ocean. No one seemed to have noticed anything wrong. /Thanks,/ he whispered.

/// You gave me a hell of a scare. ///

He let his breath out. /Me, too./

They descended one more time, to a level lit only by small, phosphorescent markers. Even with Charlie augmenting his vision, Bandicut could scarcely see, and he instinctively crowded closer to his friends. He realized suddenly that he was seeing new shadow-people around him instead of forklift drivers. They were passing pockets of even deeper gloom on either side, pockets of seemingly bottomless darkness— doorways of spatial transformation, perhaps. He shivered, crowding closer still to his friends.

Their shadow-guides surrounded them. *Whringingg* ". . . will pass through . . . n-space channel . . . take you closer to what you must face . . ."

The shadow-people brought them to a rectangle that looked almost like the door to a freight elevator . . . until it became transparent, and beyond it there was blackness streaked with soft, slowly shifting brushstrokes of magenta light. One shadow-person flitted in; the others *wheek*ed and urged their guests to follow.

Ik strode ahead, and vanished as a streak of light. Li-Jared followed. Bandicut glanced back at the desolation behind, not sorry to be leaving it. With a murmured, "Thanks for the tour," he stepped through with Napoleon.

There was a brief flicker and he felt himself falling, then floating, in near darkness. He had become enveloped in a thin, silvery forcefield or spacesuit. His friends were nearby, similarly clad. He glimpsed the movement of shadow-people, nearly invisible in the dark. But there was something else here, too. Or some*one*. He rotated slowly, and saw them: three vast, luminous creatures that looked like something from the bottom of a very deep, alien sea. It was impossible to judge their size; they stretched out in undulating waves like enormous, luminescent bead-curtains in the night. They were a kind of jellyfish, perhaps, hanging in space—or ocean—he couldn't quite tell which; there were no stars here, but neither did he feel any sense of watery movement.

*/// I believe we are in a transitional continuum,
not of your space. ///*

/Ah./ Bandicut cleared his throat, wanting to break the silence, but not knowing what to say. "Hello?" he croaked at last.

The shadow-people fluttered, trying to respond. *Wheeeek wheek!*

There was no translation.

Whreeeuuuu. ". . . are the . . ." *Whrreeeeee.*

Bandicut's translator-stone jangled, trying to find words to fit the sounds. /What—?/

Charlie seemed to catch some meaning.

/// Far-flung travellers? ///

The stones found something in his memory that suited and completed the translation: ". . . magellan-fish . . ."

He blinked, confused.

Whreeeek. ". . . n-dimensional travellers . . . explorers . . . returned to this safe harbor . . ."

"What does that—" Ik began.

". . . here, the boojum cannot listen . . . or interfere . . ."

"Are you saying," Bandicut said dizzily, trying to absorb the implications, "that these *magellan-fish* are going to help us against the boojum?"

". . . guard you . . . take you where we cannot . . ."

As they spoke, one of the magellan-fish turned in a ponderously graceful movement, revealing a row of huge eyes like darkened glass. For a moment it simply stared; then the nearest eye grew like an enormous pupil dilating. It expanded silently until it engulfed Bandicut and his friends; and everything changed in an eyeblink. Bandicut felt himself suddenly enfolded in the being's sensory sphere, looking outward through its eye.

It took him a dozen heartbeats to comprehend what he was seeing: an etched surface bewildering in complexity, a tremendous maze illuminated by . . .

The perspective shifted, and he saw a vast whirlpool of light.

Whirlpool of light?

The perspective shifted again, and at last he understood what it was: the outside of Shipworld, illuminated by the distant light of a vast galaxy stretched across the sky. The individual features on the surface were indecipherable, but the viewpoint shifted in three more quick jumps, until in the center of his view was an image that was unmistakable: a tremendous assembly of spheroidal storage tanks, nestled into a sheltered crook of the vast expanse of the metaship.

He could not begin to gauge the dimensions of the tank farm. It looked almost like a cluster of fish eggs. But something told him that Earth's orbiting L5 City might easily be swallowed up in a single one of those tanks. And there were a *lot* of tanks.

He felt something new, from within. A presence, expanding in his mind, almost like the quarx when he was imitating the neurolink. But it wasn't the quarx. It was something less quick, something deeper, more ponderous . . .

It spoke, and its voice reverberated like the thrum of a blue whale.

\# IS THIS THE PLACE IN DANGER? \#

Stunned, Bandicut whispered, /I think so. Yes./

\# AND IF THIS IS DESTROYED, THE DESTROYER WILL CONTROL ALL THAT WE SEE? \#

Bandicut struggled to respond. He didn't know enough to answer. But he had not been alone in hearing the question. A metal voice resonated in his ears. *"This is the target. The boojum moves as we speak. If the tanks are destroyed, all life on the continent must migrate or die. Five hundred million sentient beings. And the boojum will control all the power systems that remain.''*

As he listened to Napoleon's voice, Bandicut could only think, *Five hundred million people may die! Why isn't the bloody thing defended?*

But before he could do more than reel at the question, something began happening out in the tank-farm. It started with a ripple of blue light at one edge, a not-quite-focused shimmer, momentarily obscuring the tanks. The line of light brightened, then began to move, to creep across the field of tanks, in a slow procession that spanned the width of the field. As it passed over the tanks, it generated white sparkles of light.

And behind those sparkles, the first tanks exploded.

22

TESTS OF WILL

COPERNICUS WAS IN the city and he was lost. He swung his sensors, looking for a map-terminal. Getting to Atrium City by streaktrain had been simple enough, but finding the one he sought here was not so easy. Atrium City was a large and confusing place, and the visual identifiers he'd been given did not always correspond to the electronic position markers that the shadow-people had passed on to him. Perhaps by consulting a map he could reconcile the differences.

He finally located a terminal, and connected briefly to download the map information. A brief analysis suggested where he had gone wrong, several levels below. He turned to begin backtracking.

It made him feel uneasy to be venturing into the same city that not long ago had given refuge to his friends. Now, they were off to a new danger, while he prowled their recent locale. There was nothing *wrong* about it; it just felt odd. He wondered what John Bandicut would have thought about these latest instructions. Copernicus could not himself decipher the purpose of the shadow-people's request; he had agreed to it, trusting that in time he would understand the reason.

Once he'd located the misplaced identifier—an empty storefront where he'd been looking for a crafts market—he began to find his way. There was the hotel ahead—one of hundreds in Atrium City. He rolled into the lobby, located a terminal, and called the room of the one he had come to see.

A voice answered, indecipherably. He sent a text message, using an interlanguage which the shadow-people had provided: *"My name is Copernicus. I am an inorganic servant and friend of the human, John Bandicut. Have I reached the one named Antares?"*

She listened to the robot in disbelief. "Please repeat. You want what?" Antares leaned forward, staring at the wheeled norg, and wondered if she had been foolish to let it into her room. But she hadn't wanted to speak in a public place, so she'd taken the precaution of renting a pair of security-norgs from the hotel to guard her while it was here. Still. It unnerved her to hear this thing *invite her to do exactly what she herself wished to do.*

"You are asked to go with the Maksu, to meet John Bandicut in the ice caverns," said the robot.

It was altogether too strange. Who, in Shipworld, knew that she might be interested in meeting with John Bandicut? Her last message to the human had come back as undeliverable. "Who sent you?" she demanded, pushing her hair back from her eyes. "Bandie?"

"Negative. I was sent by the shadow-people."

She stared at it in puzzlement. "The shadow-people? Why do they want me to do this thing?"

"It was stated that your empathic powers might be valuable. Beyond that, I do not know," said the norg, sensors glimmering. "I was merely asked to convey the message—and to accompany and assist you, if that is agreeable."

"I see," said Antares.

"There will be no charge for the services of the Maksu. That has been arranged by the shadow-people."

Antares's knowing-stones buzzed, working hard to process the robot's words. They worked better in concert with another pair of stones; but in her conversation with Bandicut, her stones had been imprinted with enough of the human's language to serve. Still, she wished she could extract some empathic feeling from this conversation. ''I must consider this request,'' she said finally, rising to take her leave of the norg. ''May I give you an answer in a few minutes?''

''Of course,'' said Copernicus. ''But I emphasize—time may be growing short.''

Antares squinted at the robot. She gestured to the security-norgs to keep an eye on it while she retired to the next room. To think. And to pack a bag.

''It has begun,'' Napoleon said softly.

''Mokin' foke,'' Bandicut whispered, watching through the magellan-fish's eye the advancing line of light and behind it the explosions, like distant fireworks, of atmospheric storage tanks.

Ik was visible as a ghostly outline against the strange, watery space that was the inner world of the magellan-fish. When he spoke, his voice reverberated oddly. ''Why does this structure's defensive system not work?''

''And where are the shadow-people?'' Bandicut tried to look around; the effort resulted in a strange twisting sensation, like some sort of mental gyroscopic effect.

/// They've left us, I think. ///

A ripple of affirmation passed through Bandicut's mind, and he knew that the magellan-fish was listening to them, and to their thoughts.

''We are beyond their reach now,'' said Napoleon. ''But according to their data, the tank farm is protected by an array of forcefield bubbles, intended to shield it from meteroid damage or external attack. However—''

''Is it failing?'' Li-Jared's gaze flared like blue fireflies in the darkness of the magellan-fish's eye.

''The boojum has infected it, and disrupted the harmonic tuning. It is generating an altered resonance pattern through the forcefields. The waveforms of cohesion are beginning to combine destructively,'' the robot said.

''I don't follow,'' Bandicut said.

/// I think I do. ///

said the quarx, riffling through his memories at blinding speed.

/// Remember this picture? ///

In his mind, Bandicut glimpsed an old, grainy flat-holo of a disaster recorded two centuries before he was born, but still shown in classrooms: a narrow road-bridge arching across a river chasm—not in stable tension, but heaving up and down like a gyrating strand of rope. The vehicles on it were bouncing and sliding like pitiful toys. Moments later, the bridge collapsed into the river below. /I remember that. Tacoma Narrows, right? The bridge hit a harmonic resonant frequency, then became chaotic and shook itself apart./

/// Same principle here, I think. ///

"You mean—"

"It has subverted the defensive shield," Napoleon said. "Remember, it is a *force*field. Focused wrongly, its waveforms compress and stretch the tanks themselves—heating them, distorting their molecular structure. And finally destroying—"

"—the very tanks it is supposed to protect!" Ik exclaimed.

As they spoke, several more explosions flared at the edge of the tank farm.

"We must intervene at once," said Napoleon.

 # IT IS TIME? #

"Yes," answered the robot.

/What the hell—?/ Bandicut felt a lurch in the pit of his stomach—not so much a feeling of movement, as of distortion. When he could focus again, he saw that he was now floating in the *midst* of the enormous tank farm. The magellan-fish? he thought dizzily. He howled in sudden pain as his left wrist vanished in a blaze of white light. An attack? He blinked, stunned to realize that it was the black translator-stone, the energy-transformer. The same stone, at Triton, had once turned him into a vision of a terrifying alien. "What's happening?" he cried.

"Hraaaaaahhh!" he heard thinly. Ik was some distance away, floating just above the atmosphere tanks. From Ik's head came another blaze of light—Ik's translator-stone.

Bwr'ang, he heard distantly. Beyond Ik, a third point of light marked Li-Jared's position.

Napoleon's voice echoed in his ear. "You must use the stones. The magellan-fish will guide and coordinate."

Bandicut felt a sudden pressure in his mind. It was the translator-stone, speaking.

Release control.

/What—?/

You must release control, if we are to help.

/But I don't know how—/

                /// Let it work, John.
                It knows what to do. ///

Charlie's voice seemed strained, as though the stones were pushing the quarx aside to wield their power directly through Bandicut's mind and body.

Let go. Please.

/Okay—/ He concentrated . . . and wasn't quite sure how . . . but felt something within himself letting go, releasing a measure of control to the power in his wrists. The fire in the stone blazed forth into a miniature sun—only for an instant—then went dark.

Gasping, he tried to peer through the spikes of afterimage in his eyes. He felt himself floating higher above the tanks; he could at last see what was happening.

On the horizon a line of rippling blue fire was marching forward, swelling as it approached. Silent explosions filled the sky behind it, eruptions of much brighter light. Each explosion represented more atmospheric gas than he could imagine. Clouds were billowing behind the line of explosions, vital reserves blasting into space, turning to particles of snow as they dissipated.

In the almost surreal silence, time seemed to hang suspended. How much of that gas could Shipworld lose before people started to die? How soon would the continent die? And how many explosions could the remaining tanks absorb before they all went up in a chain reaction? The stones were trying to stop it. But the wavefront was advancing fast.

YOU WILL MOVE WITH THE WAVES, AS THEY COME.

"How?" Bandicut whispered. The magellan-fish had translated them here, directly into the line of the approaching attack.

Napoleon rasped, "We must interrupt the destructive wavefront—"

"—or we'll be popcorn in about thirty seconds," Bandicut muttered, watching the brightening glow of the wave.

"The stones will generate cancelling waveforms. If the timing is precise, they should interrupt the chaotic progression, smooth the flow—"

Bandicut stared at the advancing wave of destruction. "We don't have that kind of energy! Do we?"

"The idea is not to pit strength against strength, but to turn the boojum's strength against itself. Timing is crucial. Prepare to move."

NOW.

Bandicut's questions were lost in a dizzying shift. When his vision cleared, he was hanging much closer to the oncoming deathwave, directly in front of it. He could just make out Ik and Li-Jared strung out in a line with him. /What are we doing? Charlie? *Someone?*/

The boojum-wave looked like an approaching tsunami, swollen with fire instead of water. In moments it would overwhelm them. How long would bodies of flesh and blood last under that?

They had maybe five seconds . . . four . . .

His wrist blazed, and the flash of white light intersected with the boojum-wave, flaring outward as it struck. The boojum-wave dimmed almost imperceptibly, but kept coming.

. . . two . . . one . . .

With a lurching shift, Bandicut was elsewhere. Gasping, he struggled to focus. He was still among the tanks, the wavefront marching upon him, but it was a little farther away. His wrist blazed out again.

/// John, it's working! ///

/It is?/ he cried in disbelief.

And that was when he felt it touch his mind.

It.

The boojum. A ripple of dark intelligence, a shudder of dread . . .

He recognized it at once. How it had found him he didn't know. But it was in his thoughts, and it knew him. And it knew what he was doing. He felt its surprise—and its anger, not just that he was here opposing it, but that he was alive. The boojum had thought that it had gotten rid of him. It had thought that when organic life was dead, it *stayed* dead.

/Charlie!/ he whispered—he could still move thoughts and words, but for how much longer?—he could feel its grip tightening. /It's *here.* Can you help me?/ He felt himself beginning to quake.

There was no reply, but the quarx was scrambling to react. Something else was reacting, too—not Charlie and not the boojum. It was stirring in his mind, *struggling.* He cried out—then understood what it was, and why the boojum had not yet struck him down. It was the magellan-fish in his mind, and its strange power was contesting the boojum's. In touching the forcefield waveforms, the magellan-fish might have unwittingly provided entry for the boojum. But it had also risen to his defense.

He felt the two forces locked in struggle like ancient warriors, with his mind the arena. He could not cry out. He could do nothing except . . . try not to die. He could only fight to keep his mind and his thoughts intact, to remember who he was, *what* he was . . . *human.*

Where was Charlie? He couldn't call out to Charlie.

The wave of destruction was sweeping toward him. His stone flared—it had its own mind, at least—and its flare hit the wave again, bleeding it of a little more of its power. But not nearly enough to save him when that wavefront hit.

They had to move. But they couldn't, unless the magellan-fish moved them. And the magellan-fish was caught, locked in battle with the boojum.

/// *You . . . must . . . intervene.* ///

whispered a faraway voice.

/Inter—/

HELP . . .

/—vene?/ It was becoming harder and harder to keep his own thoughts in motion. It was as though two enormous hands were locked together in his mind, gripping his own thoughts between them. How could he possibly . . . ?

The wave was growing, coming closer.

SEE . . . CREATE . . .

He blinked, and something opened, a window or framing view that instantly changed his perception of the struggle. With a ripple of inner vision, he saw the two combatants in a new image. One of them was a silver, flashing shark speeding in tightening circles around its prey. The other was not one fish but a school of fish, all iridescent and neon colors, swarming in fantastic rippling waves through this very strange sea, this realm inside his mind, inside the magellan-fish's mind. Were these images real—or symbolic, like a neurolink sim? He sensed that they had the power to move and spin and strike out, to kill . . .

/Charlie, how can I—?/

/// Be . . . ready . . . ///

The shark and the school were not two hands grappling in motionless paralysis, but two forces in swirling movement. The hunter was all deadly force, fast and powerful. The school had strength, too, in fluid movement—but it was being hemmed in by the ferocious speed of the shark. The school weaved and twisted, turning in upon itself—protecting Bandicut, but prevented from moving as it intended, *prevented from transporting Bandicut and the others,* and making the next move to halt the destruction of the tank farm.

Bandicut blinked slowly, dazed thoughts caught in a circle.

The shark's eyes shone, gloating, as it thwarted each effort of the school to escape its orbit. Its teeth flashed as it spun by the school, startling individual fish, snapping. It wasn't catching the fish, but it didn't have to; it only had to contain them until its violent work was done.

CREATE . . .
Yes; but how?
/// Neuro . . . sim . . . ///

He felt a charge of understanding. Create a new image?
The images were symbolic, but if they were the focal point of
power, he might be able to deflect or distract the boojum-
shark. There was no time for elegance or thought; he strained
to imagine this as a neurosim VR game, and he created his
own image as a hard, bluntnosed fish, bristling with spines.
Yes. Gathering strength and speed, he hurled himself at the
shark.

The boojum didn't see him coming. He rammed it from
the side—and felt the impact as a physical slam. He spun
away, gasping, but turned to come at the shark again. It had
swung about hard, startled, recognizing the presence of a new
foe. Now it recognized *him*—and charged in a sudden fury. Its
teeth gaped wide, and he had an instant to remember how the
boojum had almost killed him once before.

He shuddered and twisted left and down, then up, right,
and hooking into a dive. The shark swerved, following. It was
faster but less maneuverable. He climbed sharply, presenting
his spiny back to it—and it shot by him, snapping and just
missing.

He turned, as it circled. Behind the shark, the school
flashed in a rapid curling arch, then passed overhead in a glo-
rious wave of color—and the sea quivered, then changed. The
water became bluer, and glowed with an intense blaze of sunlight. Bandicut was startled to realize that the light was coming from his left wrist, and from two other, more distant
sources.

At that moment the boojum-shark recognized its mistake.
While it was distracted by the image of the virtual-Bandicut,
the magellan-fish had moved them in real space. The stones
were flaring now with their clearest shot yet against the destructive waveforms of the subverted forcefield.

The boojum-shark shot toward the surface, Bandicut forgotten. Bandicut gazed up at the dancing overhead waves as
the flash from the translator-stones hit the surface. A tremen-

dous burst of wave-cancelling energy radiated outward. There
was a perceptible *darkening* as the waveforms weakened. The
water changed again, abruptly, as the magellan-fish moved
them once more. The stones flared, hit the now-smoother surface, and the remaining waves collapsed to darkness. The
shark hit the surface, too late to stop it, and vanished like a
raindrop into water. *KK-THOOOM!* A shudder of helpless
anger reverberated through the sea, then faded.

Bandicut held his breath. The waves in the sim-sea were
gone. The vision quivered; the sea turned a deeper blue, then
black—and he found himself gazing at the tank farm, from
overhead. The boojum's rippling surf of destruction had vanished completely—cancelled out by the bursts from the translator-stones, just like the waves in the sim-sea. The wake of
damage it had left was bad enough: a wide swath of demolished tanks, and enormous clouds of cryogenic snow drifting
into space. A lot of atmosphere had been lost. But far more
had been saved. Probably three-fourths of the tank farm was
intact. A blue glow began to reappear around it—the defensive forcefield reenergizing. This time it looked stable.

Was the boojum gone?

/// I think so, ///

the quarx said, emerging from wherever he'd been crouching.
He sounded shaken.

"The interference has ceased," called Napoleon, from
somewhere.

Ik called, "How was that—"

"Bandie, did you do that?" Li-Jared interrupted. "I do
not know quite why we are alive." Li-Jared was a tiny figure
jetting across space toward him. "I saw something very
strange a few moments ago."

"I guess I did some of it," Bandicut gasped. "But mostly
it was the stones—and the magellan-fish. But where's the
boojum now?" He felt something jangling in his mind, something nasty and dark, like the fading memory of a nightmare.

 # FLED. GOOD CREATING. WELL DONE. #

The magellan-fish's voice boomed in Bandicut's
thoughts. It was at first a welcome sound. But Bandicut felt an

inner rumble—not a fading aftershock, but something else growing, as if the thundering voice had triggered an avalanche.

Then the silent bomb went off.

A black hole billowed open in him, and blackness came pouring out of it, into his mind, like a withering fire. It was unmistakably the boojum—or the boojum's work. A mine left to kill him? Out of the jaws of victory—?

He clenched his eyes shut, unable to cry out.

/// Let me take this one! ///

Charlie cried, rising.

/No—wait—/

There was no stopping the quarx from leaping to his defense—and no stopping the ribbons of darkness that lashed up within his mind, springing in a tangle to catch the lifeforce of the quarx in a killing chokehold. The trap wrapped itself around Charlie and tightened—

There was a shriek of agony, a piercing wail.

—and shrank down to a pinpoint—and vanished.

Bandicut screamed. */Charlie!/*

His thoughts rang in echoes.

He gasped in shock and pain. It had happened so fast. The attack. The quarx had saved his life. But Charlie's own lifeforce had been uprooted, choked, and destroyed.

/Charlie!/

There was no answer. There was only emptiness.

Charlie was gone. And this time, he feared, it was for good.

13

THE ICE CAVERNS

"IF IT IS your intention to guide me, then let's be on our way." Antares gestured to the exit and began walking down the corridor with long strides, her satchel swinging on her hip. The norg named Copernicus rolled ahead of her. The hotel security-norgs left them in the lobby, and they continued out into the Atrium. "I hope you know where we're going."

"Affirmative, Lady Antares," said Copernicus, whirring as it chose its course without hesitation. It had offered to carry her bag, but she wasn't going to let someone else be her porter, even if it was a norg. Once, as an empathic facilitator of rank and standing among her own people, she might have been happy to do that. But things were different now. Practice was turning self-sufficiency into a habit.

They passed over the atrium, then descended in a fastlift to an intercity train station. The norg led her to a streaktrain that was standing open for passengers, and settled in silence beside her after she chose a seat. Antares accepted the silence willingly; she was absorbed enough in her own thoughts. Soon they were underway, slipping at quiet speed across a wild and varied countryside.

"How far away are these ice caverns?" she asked.

Copernicus tapped softly. "They are in the interior of the continent. An hour on the train to meet the Maksu, a transporter jaunt with them to the far side of a mountain range, through several other environments, then down into a subterranean cavern system. Then we will be there.''

"Oh," she said.

"It shouldn't take long at all," said the norg.

"John Bandicut, we must think of moving on." Ik hovered near him, his eyes gleaming through the half-mirror surface of the forcefield spacesuit.

"Right," Bandicut answered with difficulty. The loss of Charlie had hit him hard. By now, he thought dully, he ought to be used to Charlie dying. But this time, he had felt the very essence of the quarx's spirit being crushed out of existence by the boojum's trap.

ONE OF YOU IS NO LONGER AMONG US.

The magellan-fish's statement was a cell door clanging shut.

"What do you mean?" Li-Jared asked, turning to watch as Napoleon floated toward them. He suddenly turned again, toward Bandicut. "Is it—?"

"Charlie. Yes."

"Urrrr—"

"I thought I felt something at the end," Li-Jared said. "Was it—did the boojum attack you personally again?"

"Attack, yes. But this was not the boojum itself, I don't think. More like a trap it left behind."

"A—" *rasp* "—virus offshoot?" Ik asked.

"Possibly. It felt more like a bomb."

Ik peered at him for a long moment. "Are you harmed? Has it left you?" Ik's concern seemed to resonate in the open darkness of space.

How should I know? Bandicut thought, peering across the expanse of the tank farm, and the station beyond. There were already small maintenance units flying over the tank farm like bees, surveying the damage and starting repairs.

"Bandie?"

"I think so," he said. "I felt it leave, or disappear anyway, after it killed Charlie." And he suddenly realized that he had felt something else, too: the boojum had seen more in his mind than just the presence of the quarx. Something important. But what?

Napoleon drew close, sensors blinking. "Did the boojum kill Charlie?" His voice sounded strained, almost sorrowful.

"Yes," Bandicut said.

The robot's eyes flickered. "I regret that. I . . . *knew* Charlie."

"At least we succeeded in what we came here for," Ik murmured. "There seems nothing else for us to do here. I suggest we consider how best to move on."

"To the ice caverns?" Li-Jared asked.

Bandicut started to reply, and felt the words freeze in his throat. He suddenly knew what the boojum had seen. "Oh damn," he muttered. "*Damn.* I think—" His voice caught. "I think the boojum may know what we're intending to do next. And this might seem crazy, but—I think it's angry. Really angry. If it finds the ice caverns before we do, there might not be any ice caverns for us to go to."

"Rakhh!" Ik cried. "After all this? We must find a way to return! We must contact the Maksu!"

"I believe," said Napoleon, "that the shadow-people have already asked, on our behalf, for assistance in the next stage of our journey."

"Assistance? From whom?"

The tank farm shimmered and vanished, and Bandicut felt once more that quivering sensation of movement that was not quite movement. Blackness closed in around them, not of space, but of the n-dimensional transition zone, lit with swirls of magenta, where they had first met the magellan-fish.

The creature's thoughts rumbled in his.

 # MAKE CLEAR YOUR NEED. CREATE. #

Bandicut blinked in confusion. Create? "Do you mean the way we did with the boojum? The shark?"

Ik seemed to loom closer, though they were still in that curious confinement within the magellan-fish's eye. "Is it saying it can take us to the ice caverns?"

Li-Jared's eyes gleamed. "If it could bring us *here*—"

 # MAKE CLEAR. HELP US SEE. #

Bandicut thought furiously. "I don't know what the caverns look like. Does either of you?"

"They look like—" Li-Jared's eyes pulsed, but he didn't finish his sentence. He seemed to be concentrating, perhaps trying to focus on a mental image.

 # UNCLEAR ... HOLLOW ... #

Bandicut blinked.

 # SHOW WHAT IS THE HEART. #

Charlie would have understood this, Bandicut thought, struck suddenly by an absurd danger: Where might they end up if the magellan-fish misunderstood their intentions? How far could it take them? To the wrong end of Shipworld? The wrong end of the galaxy? *Home?*

 # NOT AS YOU THINK. PLACES WE GO, YOU CANNOT. #

Oh.

 # WHAT IS THE *HEART*? #

And Bandicut suddenly understood. It didn't want to know the outward physical appearance; it wanted to know ... "What is it *like*?" he blurted.

"Hraah?"

"The connection with the Tree of Ice. What will the magellan-fish *feel* when it makes contact with that? How will it know when it's found it?"

"Ah—" said Ik.

Bandicut recalled the recent battle with the boojum, and thought with horror: Could it have gotten a clear image of the caverns? Could it be destroying them even now? "Ik, if the boojum can find it before we do—" He interrupted his own words to try to form a mental image of ... something like the datanet, or the iceline, but with far denser activity.

 # WE BEGIN TO SEE. BUT THERE ARE MANY SUCH. #

Of course: the iceline, and other control systems. Too many threads of information.

Li-Jared seemed to pick up on his thought. "It would be a place of great convergence, of intersection, of cross-connection. It is a ... microcosm ... of the Tree of Ice."

"Tree of Ice?" Bandicut stared, struck by a sudden thought. "Why don't we ask it to take us right to the Tree and be done with it? Go to the *real* heart!"

Li-Jared seemed to shift and squirm inside his spacesuit, as if trying to absorb the thought. "Actually," he said, "I am not sure that the Tree exists as a discrete physical place. It may consist of many, many nodes—each one as complex and powerful as the ice caverns. And if it did exist in one place, I am not certain that we could—" He hesitated.

"Survive an encounter with it?" Ik said.

Bwong-ng. "Yes."

"You make it sound almost like a god," Bandicut said.

"A what?"

Bandicut shook his head. "I was thinking of Earth myths. There were gods that . . . well, if you met them face to face, you—never mind, you can't possibly know what I'm talking about. Look, we've got to show the magellan-fish, somehow!"

"But we don't *know* where it is," Ik cried in exasperation. "The Maksu were to have led us."

Napoleon rotated in space. "Transmissions from the shadow-people have been erratic in this location—but the last message indicated they asked the Maksu to meet you at the caverns."

SOON. WE MUST LEAVE SOON.

"All right, maybe the magellan-fish can recognize the Maksu. Can you show it what they're like?" Bandicut had never met the Maksu. But he felt his own thoughts well up with images of the neurolink, a lifetime ago. He was sure it was a poor cousin to the ice caverns; nevertheless, he felt the magellan-fish's thoughts moving in his, observing his images, and perhaps understanding his reservations about them. And in another corner of the fish's mind, it was viewing Ik's and Li-Jared's memories of the Maksu.

THESE ARE SEEN. AND KNOWN.

"Yes?" said Ik.

AND THE OTHER.

The other? What other? Bandicut had felt the fish recalling Charlie, and puzzling over Charlie's absence; and he wondered if it was looking for Charlie, and he wanted to say, no no, Charlie's dead—he's gone.

But the magellan-fish wasn't responding directly. Something flickered from its thoughts through his. Something about the boojum. Was it looking for the boojum?

No! he began to cry out. He didn't want to find the boojum again.

With a soft shudder, everything changed again. The darkness began to shimmer with flashes of heat lightning, and for a moment, all he could see was the intrusion of light and its afterimages in his eyes. He heard Ik and Li-Jared crying out. He became faint from a dizzying *shift* that sent blood rushing from his head. He blinked, and the darkness was gone, but a mistlike veil surrounded him. He was standing on solid ground now, and all around him were surfaces of water-carved rock. *Caverns.* They were illumined by a glimmer of light from a source he could not see.

And not too far off through the caverns, he glimpsed something that shone with a diamondlike glitter. *Ice?*

He was startled to realize that his spacesuit was gone. He felt naked without it. His voice trembled. "Ik? Li-Jared? Nappy?"

"With you," rumbled Ik, from somewhere nearby.

The magellan-fish's voice echoed:

IS THIS THE PLACE YOU SEEK?

For a long moment, Bandicut felt an electric uncertainty. Was it? It looked like it could be. But . . .

Brrr-kkdangg. "I feel it. The activity. It's like a soft buzzing. This is it!" Li-Jared murmured in astonishment.

THEN HERE WE WILL LEAVE YOU.

"Wait! Not yet!" Bandicut tried frantically to confirm Li-Jared's statement, to detect any sense of neurolike activity. If they were left in the wrong place . . .

The veil of mist began to dissolve. The magellan-fish's thoughts seemed to be growing distant.

WE ARE PLEASED TO HAVE KNOWN YOU. WE CARRY YOUR THOUGHTS. FAREWELL.

"Wait!" Bandicut cried.

But the veil, and the magellan-fish, were gone.

The norg was true to its word. After leaving the streaktrain, Antares found herself peering up into a striking mountain range, its towering, fluted cliffs dark in the early twilight, but with edges and tips aglow from the sunset. Copernicus led her up into a cleft in the nearest mountain, perhaps a fifteen-minute walk. About the time they were deep enough in the shadows to feel lost, Antares began to hear a soft buzzing sound. She looked around in puzzlement. A cloud of flicker-bugs emerged from the shadows, swirling and dancing in the air. They looked like flickerbugs, anyway; they were winged creatures about the size of Antares's smallest fingertips, and in their luminosity they resembled a kind of gossamer-winged insect from Thespi Prime.

The Maksu? she thought. She hadn't known what to expect, except that they were colony creatures, one consciousness in many. Was this contingent part of a much larger Maksu consciousness?

She stood erect, arms at her sides, studying them. From the cloud of bugs came a groan like that of a large metal structure under stress. *"Friend of the company—greetings,"* came their words, through her stones.

"Greetings," she answered. "My name is—" she hesitated "—you may call me 'Antares.' However, I am unsure of your reference to 'the company.' "

"Lady Antares," said the norg, with a sharp tapping sound. "I believe they refer to the company comprising Ik, Li-Jared, and John Bandicut. You have been invited as a friend of that company."

"I see. Shall I clarify that I am at best barely acquainted with one of the individuals you mentioned?"

"I believe that the shadow-people may have presented you as a member—in part due to your ownership of translator-stones. You are entitled to clarify, certainly; however, I am unsure of the benefit of your doing so."

"I see." The shadow-people are choosing my friends for

me? she thought. But her annoyance wasn't really genuine. She was here by her own choice, after all.

"We were advised," groaned the Maksu, *"that you desired guidance to the ice caverns, to join the company so named. Has there been a change? We are prepared to renegotiate—"*

"No, no," she said, adjusting the satchel strap over her shoulder. "You are correct. If you are prepared to proceed, so am I."

"Then so," said the Maksu. They whirled in fast sparkling orbits, then flew off in an arching arrow into a nearby crevice. A glowing oval outline appeared in the rock; then the oval filled with a pale golden light that seemed to filter out as if through a fogbank. *"Come,"* groaned the Maksu.

The robot rolled cautiously up toward the oval, but Antares strode ahead of it. She passed through the glowing transport door, and found herself surrounded by what looked like bright morning sunshine over magnificent grass-covered steppes. And yet, she was not quite there among the steppes, but felt more like a passing spirit, pausing momentarily to take in the view. The Maksu whirled in front of her, their luminescence seeming like a reflection of the golden morning sun.

The steppes vanished, and a marshland appeared, surrounding her with tall spiky fronds and cottony blossoms. That lasted a few heartbeats, then they were deep in a green-hued forest. Three eyeblinks later they were underground, in a large, irregularly lit cavern. She heard voices echoing distantly, and far off to one side, she saw a troop of—tourists?—walking along a more-brightly-lit trail. Was this their destination? The Maksu continued to whirl, and suddenly they were in another cave, one that felt colder, as though deeper underground. She stood on a rocky ledge, peering down into a huge, and strangely luminous, crevasse.

Ice gleamed down there, glowing from within.

"The caverns," said the norg, beside her.

Bandicut and the others had walked cautiously to the entrance of a long cavern that gleamed with stalagmites and stalactites of ice. There were tall, vertical columns and deep, horizontal fissures, buckled surfaces, and erupting crystals of ice. It was everywhere, glimmering with a diamondlike inner light; it flickered here and there with hues of astonishing colors. They stood staring in amazement, their wonder edged with trepidation. Was this really it? Had they gotten here ahead of the boojum?

Bandicut saw Ik's breath steaming in front of him. The Hraachee'an's dark eyes flickered with their own inner fire. It was impossible to tell what he was feeling. "Are we absolutely certain that this is the right place?" Bandicut asked.

"Who can say?" said Ik. "I was counting on the Maksu to identify the location and help us make contact. Failing that, I had hoped that the magellan-fish would stay. But we appear to be on our own."

"I am certain," said Li-Jared.

Bandicut grunted and tipped his head back. Sharp-tipped, icy stalactites glistened far overhead. He imagined how they might fall if they were shaken loose by a tremor. Best not to think about it, he thought sternly, lowering his gaze. The cavern before him was an intricate and convoluted space, with numerous slender, curved pillars and arching passageways, all gleaming translucently. There was a mazelike feel to the place, with pathways carved deep into the frozen, jumbled floor.

Behind them, a path led back toward what looked like a shaft of daylight. He didn't remember seeing that before, but he wondered if it might help them find their way out when they were done. He shook his head. If Ik and Li-Jared found what they wanted, maybe they wouldn't be walking out at all. Maybe they'd be launched out through some portal directly to the stars. Bandicut felt a sudden tightness across his chest. Even if he found a way to leave Shipworld from here, he'd be leaving Charlie behind—in a way, at least—and Copernicus. Was he ready to do that?

"Shall we explore inward?" Ik said.

Bandicut took a deep breath. "What exactly are we looking for? Besides signs of the boojum's tampering." He was hopeful that they'd gotten here in time to prevent the latter; but as to what to look for, he was at a loss. He'd somehow assumed the name "ice caverns" to be metaphorical; he hadn't expected to find some phantasmagorical recreation of the cavern on Triton where he'd first met Charlie and his translator. Were they actually proposing to neurolink with *ice*?

"The fish said the Maksu would be here," said Li-Jared.

"That was Nappy, actually. Nappy, how sure were you about that?" Bandicut peered at Napoleon, who seemed so knowledgeable in matters Shipworld now that he felt as if he hardly knew the robot anymore.

"I cannot be sure," said Napoleon. "The shadow-people clearly implied the likelihood of it. But I am no longer receiving transmissions from them. I believe this area may be isolated from their signals."

"Well," said Li-Jared, vaulting over a table-sized obstruction of ice to land on what appeared to be a clear path, "no point in standing here. Let's go."

They proceeded cautiously, walking entirely now on a frozen surface. Bandicut was not entirely sure whether it was water ice, or some other kind. He didn't feel cold, despite being surrounded by ice. Was that because of his "normalization"—or because this was not ordinary ice? It was slippery, at least. Napoleon, following behind, was sliding and staggering as he adjusted his metal-footed gait to the new surface.

Within minutes, they were deep in the cavern's interior—surrounded by translucent pillars, blocks of ice like waist-high crystals of salt, and clifflike fracture-walls of every size and shape. Behind them, the entrance was lost to view.

"It all seems to be *moving*," Li-Jared said. "Is it alive, do you think?"

"Mm?" Bandicut squinted, trying to see what the Karellian meant. It was true; when he looked closely, he saw tiny crystals shrinking and growing along certain surfaces. And out of the corner of his eye, he thought he saw a creeping change in the shape of one of the larger slabs. But more than that: he *felt* something now, echoing at the edges of his mind.

It reminded him of the neurolink; but this was quicker, brighter, a chorus of soft chirping and twittering. It was not intrusive or even directed at him; it was more like hearing distant crosstalk on a busy comm channel, overlapping echoes of conversations not meant for him.

"Look!" cried Ik. They hurried to join him. Ik stood at the edge of a drop-off. Ten meters below, in a sunken chamber, was a spectacular array of long, slender ice crystals, like an enormously magnified cluster of snowflakes. The crystals seemed to point inward, making the chamber look like an enormous, fantastic geode. It flickered, alive with light.

"My God," breathed Bandicut. "Is that the core of the thing, do you think?"

"A node, anyway," Ik murmured.

"I feel something," said Li-Jared. "Like a beehive around my head. Voices."

"Yes, I—" Bandicut was about to describe the twittering voices, when he felt a sudden hesitation. "Listen," he said. "We're right on the edge of something, and we ought to take a good close look for the boojum before we go in."

"Indeed," said Ik. "But I feel no indication—see no sign of damage. If it's attacked the system inwardly, how can we find out but to—"

"Go in and see?" Bandicut muttered. "Right. If it's destroyed the system, we won't get very far." He sensed nothing to indicate that danger; the system was clearly alive and active. With any luck, the boojum was off somewhere licking its wounds—or maybe still looking for the ice caverns—and the sooner he and his friends got into the system, found their information and got out again, the better off they'd be.

As though at that thought, his translator-stones twinged, and the voices twittering at the edges of his mind grew louder. They also seemed clearer, though he could not understand anything they were saying. /Charlie, I sure wish you were here, old buddy,/ he whispered.

"Let us go down if we can." Ik peered along the ledge, looking for a place to descend. Finally he took his coiled rope from his belt and placed one end of it on the ledge, where it attached itself. Ik sat and swung himself over the edge and lowered himself carefully into the geodelike chamber.

Bandicut turned to Li-Jared. The Karellian's eyes were narrowed to fine, fiery-blue slits. It was impossible to tell whether he was terrified, or excited, or both, to be so close to the thing he had been seeking for so long. "You want to go next?" Bandicut asked.

"I am ready to enter. To ask and to find." The Karellian's words seemed less an answer to Bandicut than an affirmation to himself. Li-Jared swung over and scampered down the rope, to stand with Ik among the frail-looking ice crystals.

"Well?" Bandicut said to Napoleon. "Shall I lower you? Or do you want to wait here?"

Napoleon rasped thoughtfully. "I sense no medium of connection for me down there, John Bandicut. I suggest that I stand watch here. You will be careful, won't you?"

Bandicut stared at Napoleon, feeling a great affection for the metal being. "Yah," he said, and sat down and swung his legs over the edge.

He was about halfway down, hanging from the rope, when the voices in his head suddenly jumped in volume. He flinched, wary of the boojum—but it wasn't that, it was just the connection getting stronger. He tried to ignore it until he got down. His right-hand translator-stone was pulsing, looking for pattern and meaning in the voices. /Charlie,/ he thought futilely, /if you're ever going to come back, this would be a good time./ His feet touched bottom, and found purchase among the spiky crystals. He let go of the rope and turned around.

It was like a winterland fairy tale: gleaming spindles of ice angling up from the floor in every direction, crisscrossing each other and erupting from one to another, joining like snowflake facets, and glowing with an inner light that flickered softly, and was breathtakingly beautiful. It felt perilous, too; he felt as if he were standing among live electrical connections, and any move in the wrong direction would bring a blaze of energy. There was no visible energy except for the flickering light, but he felt a shimmering inner disturbance, as if he were swimming in a sea of invisible activity.

He glanced at Ik and Li-Jared. They too seemed afraid to move. Their eyes were caught by the beauty and the power; they seemed unable to speak.

Bandicut looked back at the ice crystals, and found his gaze lingering on a series of intersecting elements that formed a channel into a deeper layer of crystals, as though pointing to the heart of the chamber, where the flickering light seemed at once darker and more intense. The voices grew louder as his gaze sank into that place. He was only dimly aware of the tiny spikes of snow-ice around him, growing like tendrils toward him, then touching his clothing and his skin. He felt a tingle, and wanted to shiver. Something touched his thoughts, and echoed in ringing, soundless chords.

Then a doorway opened somewhere far away, and voices rushed into his head like a cascade of water over a falls. . . .

24

INTO THE ICECORE

 ANTARES GLIMPSED MOVEMENT down in the glowing chamber of ice. At first, it was impossible to tell what it was; there were too many confusing reflections. Then the norg said, "I believe I am picking up signs of the company. Shall we look for a way down?"

Antares stood motionless on the ledge, not answering. Her eyes caught a bewildering array of faceted, broken images. But the norg was right; someone was moving down there. Yes—three bipedal shapes, undoubtedly Ik, Li-Jared, and John Bandicut. So she had found them. What now?

The Maksu whirled out over the edge and hovered, awaiting instructions.

In a momentary reflection, she glimpsed the Human Bandicut stepping cautiously among angular blades of ice. Now he was standing utterly still, at last in her direct line of sight. She watched, astonished, as a cluster of fine ice crystals grew around him like an accelerated image of a plant flowering. The crystals enveloped him almost completely. She felt an impulse to cry out a warning, but kept her silence instead. There was no point in acting in ignorance.

The Maksu drew closer. *"There is activity underway: tentative contact with the core of the ice caverns. It may be hazardous to interfere. We suggest you allow us to establish contact for you."*

She glanced at the norg, which seemed to know so much

more than she did about these people. "Are they expecting me? Should I contact them?"

Copernicus whirred, scanning the strange landscape below. "Lady Antares, I have reached the limits of my knowledge. I am afraid I can offer no useful advice."

So, she thought. Someone wanted me here, but not necessarily those three. But if I interfere at the wrong time . . .

With a throaty hum, she said to the Maksu, "Please. Contact them when it is safe, and ask if I can be of assistance."

The Maksu groaned and whirled. Most of the cloud spiraled away, down into the valley. Instead of approaching Bandicut's group, they spread out among the glowing facets of ice and vanished into the maze.

"Can you reach them?" Antares asked the remaining Maksu.

Before they could reply, the stillness was broken by a cry of pain. It was from the Human below.

Napoleon heard Bandicut's shout, and lurched in sideways micromovements, trying to triangulate and analyze the cry. It sounded like a cry of distress, but what was the problem? From his ledge, Napoleon could barely see his companions down among the ice crystals. Bandicut appeared to have been enveloped by an enormous snowflake. It was impossible to judge his condition. "John Bandicut!" Napoleon called. "Please reply!"

There was no answer, at least not from below. But Napoleon's comm circuit awakened, and he heard an unexpected, familiar voice. "Napoleon, Copernicus. I am on a ledge, twenty-five meters above John Bandicut. Is he in danger? What is your position?"

Napoleon activated his beacon. "Transponder on. I too am on a ledge above John Bandicut. Ten meters vertical distance. I am uncertain of his condition, and unable to reach him. Can you assist?"

"I have your transponder, Napoleon. The Maksu are preparing to make contact. Stand by—"

The connection was so overwhelming, he had instinctively cried out. Bandicut stood, physically paralyzed among a fantastic, flowering array of ice crystals—but connected internally to a cauldron of activity. He felt in danger of being swept under by a tide far more powerful than any human neurolink. It was the iceline multiplied exponentially, thousands of iceline channels sizzling into the complexity of the icecore, joining faraway parts of Shipworld, and countless peoples. And he was numbly aware that this was just one node of many in the entity known as the Tree of Ice.

He sensed his friends nearby, each caught up by the icecore, but neither so intimately as he; his neurolink experience was enabling him to forge much deeper connections. As the visual input came into focus, so did a view of his friends *through* the connection: virtual figures of shadow traced in fiery lines. There was Ik, projecting questions in continuous waves of light: *Why? / Who are you? / Will you please explain the purpose of our presence here?* And in another location Li-Jared, far noisier with inner commotion, ducking about in search of clues. *Who will take us away from here, who will take us home . . . ?*

But it was clear that they were not finding answers.

Interference from the boojum? No, there was no sign of disruption, nothing indicating an attack had taken place.

The translator-stones did something, and the visual activity changed to something such as Charlie-One had shown him a lifetime ago, while trying to explain his quarxian concepts of *meta*-views and *meta*-attractors. He was surrounded by images of converging and bifurcating streams of water, changing to molten metal, then flowing gases, then evolving fractal designs. It was strikingly beautiful—chaotic movements and forces—but was utterly abstract, and still made no sense to him. Maybe Charlie could have understood it, but not Bandicut.

Nevertheless, he felt that the answers were embedded here, waiting to be found. If only he had the quarx! But he did have the translator-stones. Whatever they were doing, the images continued to change; they were woven through now with sounds like the subsea rumble of tectonic shifting, with peculiar vocal choruses, with a fragmented mosaic of musical chords. He smelled the sea; he smelled crushed herbs; he smelled the mingled scents of warm alien bodies . . .

He was being watched from across the datastream.

The realization startled him, but he had no sense that it was a hostile presence, just an alien one. Or more than one; it felt like a collection of presences. He tried to call out a greeting. /Hello?/

There was a hiss like wind over sea. Then:

/We . . . the Mxx . . . sss./

He struggled to interpret. /Say again?/

Something shifted in the datastream, and the sound became clearer. /We are . . . the Maksu . . . sent by the shadow-people . . . to assist . . . /

The Maksu. Their presence became clearer; it was like a cloud of buzzing mosquitoes—or writhing electric wires, highly charged, and joined to something distant and greater. He sensed that they were on the outside, linking to him through the icecore.

/I could certainly use assistance,/ he murmured. /How can you help?/

/You seek information, as do we. You can reach where we cannot. But we do know certain pathways . . . to places where questions can be posed. It is not safe for us there; we are not like you./

Bandicut shivered. /What do you want in return?/

/Information only. Information—if you find it—about the boojum./

His breath went out with a flame of anger, and fear, at the mention of the boojum. /What do you expect me to find? The boojum may be planning an attack here; we want to move quickly./

/Not the boojum itself—but if you find information—/

/Such as—?/

/Its origins, its nature. We could trade such information to others, who might devise defenses . . . /

/All right,/ he whispered, growing impatient. The forma-

tions of the icecore twisted and altered shape around him.
/Show me how./

The Maksu buzzed incomprehensibly.

Something moved around him, and abruptly billowed out
like a great diaphanous curtain in a breeze. Beyond it was the
enormous bowl of a cirrus-streaked sky. He floated out, alone
in that sky, and gradually became aware that those streaks of
cloud were in fact long, complex streamers of data-activity.
His translator-stones, like twin stars in his pockets, twinkled
as they adjusted his perceptions to the new image surrounding
him. There was a shifting of magnitude, and the data-stream-
ers expanded, enclosing him. Their wispy detail hardened,
transformed into long ice crystals in a fantastic array, mirror-
ing the enormous snowflake that enveloped his outer body.

He felt the Maksu withdrawing, as pathways opened
around him.

He sensed, with rising excitement, that each one of those
sparkling slivers contained more information than all of humanity's datanets combined. Perhaps now he was in a place
from which he could query and comprehend. He moved tentatively, and discovered that with gentle strokes of thought, he
could choose among the spines of ice—and at his discretion,
peer down into the crystal slivers and watch flowering images
of places, and peoples, and worlds . . .

His translator-stones were afire with wonder. Maybe he
could at last—

—learn why he was here—

—see the faces of those who had brought him—

—find a way home for himself, and for Ik and Li-Jared—

The ice slivers divided before him, and he flew through
exploding images of structure and information: maps of Shipworld and its subsystems, shaded *here* where shadow-people
maintained the systems, *there* where others kept it functioning, and flickering boundaries where incompatible ecologies
were kept apart. He glimpsed movements of vital resources
and services; communications networks, the iceline just one
among hundreds; star charts of planetary origins; profiles of
scores of races inhabiting the metaship. He began to compre-

hend at last why it was called a *meta*ship, with layer upon layer of complexity, each layer encapsulating vast systems of activity; it was like fractal images, with constantly changing scales revealing ever more layers of self-similar patterns. Soon he was lost in shifting sands of imagery and information. It was still too vast, too complex; he couldn't find his way to the right questions, the right answers.

/Help!/ he murmured softly. /Is there a help-function here?/

The response was immediate. A new crystal structure flowered open, sparkling out toward him. He heard a voice call tonelessly:

>> *Draw close, please. If you wish assistance, you must draw closer.* >>

Puzzled, he tried to comply. /What exactly do you want me to do?/

>> *Draw closer. To understand your needs, we must have access to your total memory and internal network functions.* >>

/Well, I—/ How much did he trust this system?

>> *We cannot assist unless you permit access to those functions. If you wish assistance, please move closer.* >>

Bandicut shivered. He was already perilously deep in this virtual system, well removed from his physical center. But he hadn't found what they'd come looking for—and apparently he wouldn't find it without taking further risks. He drew his thoughts together, then nudged himself close to the sparkling flower of the help function, and let it draw him down into the flickering magnetism of its inner world . . .

Antares peered down into the cavern, trying to get a better look at the astonishing replica of a snowflake that had grown around John Bandicut. He had not cried out again, but he was completely enveloped now, and the snowflake was alive with light—rippling among its spines with a frenetic energy. Bandicut's two companions appeared likewise immobilized but less densely surrounded. It almost looked as if the ice caverns had surrounded those two just to keep them out of the way. *What was going on down there?*

"Maksu?" she called sharply. A few of them remained buzzing nearby. "Can you get me a window into the activity around the Human? I don't want to interfere. I just want to know what he is doing."

The creatures buzzed, spun out of sight for a moment, then reappeared, winking. *"Step down, please."*

Step down? She looked and saw a narrow ledge just below her. It couldn't possibly give her a much better view, but it was definitely a riskier place to stand. And it bristled with ice crystals. A medium of contact? She hesitated, ashamed of her own sudden fear. How badly did she want to do this? She glanced at Copernicus, who had been standing silent. The norg clicked and said, "I am concerned for him. I wish I could know if he is in danger."

She answered with a murmur of concern. "I will do what I can," she promised, and climbed carefully down the meter or so to the ledge. It was an awkward place to stand, and she flattened her back to the vertical rock face. "All right," she said to the Maksu. "What now?"

"Wait."

By the time she was aware of what was happening, she could not possibly have stopped it. Crystals of ice crinkled outward from the rock, and pressed against her body—not enveloping her, quite, but bracing her from both sides, catching her arms and prickling against her neck. "Wait. I have not—"

And then her breath went out without words, and her vision seemed to collapse inward, into her own mind. She felt, for a moment, a tremendous vertigo; she saw darkness, then sprinkles of light in the darkness, and at last great swirling swaths of color that she somehow recognized as information being displayed for her inspection. And against the swaths of color was a small silhouette, an inner image of the outer reality: it was the shape of the Human John Bandicut, embedded within a great flickering whirlpool of information. And something was rising up from the bottom of that whirlpool, something dark rising toward him . . .

He felt, at last, that he was merging with a responsive intelligence that could help him explore this near-infinity of knowledge. His thoughts began to tumble out, almost without his control. /I have so many questions!/ he was whispering. /It is all so confusing!/

>> *What do you wish to know?* >>

/I want to know who is in charge here—/

>> *In the icecore?* >>

/In Shipworld. Everywhere—/

>> *Who is in charge?* >>

/Yes! Who brought us here! Who is responsible for all this! Why are we here? We want to know if we can go home—/

>> *If you can go home?* >>

/Yes! We long for our homeworlds! We want to go home! We want to meet the people who brought us here!/

>> *You must release all of these thoughts . . . let us see them clearly. Yes, that is better. We see your homeworld. You are far indeed from your home. You were brought here by certain Masters of Shipworld. And your friends? We cannot see their thoughts quite so clearly.* >>

/They are far from home, too,/ Bandicut whispered. /We want to communicate with those who are in charge, the Masters of Shipworld—/

>> *Those who send you into danger . . . ?* >>

There was a subtle change in the tone of the voice that was addressing him. It seemed . . . stronger, he thought, more wiry and unyielding. Not threatening, exactly; but he felt a prickle of fear, nonetheless. He sensed from the voice a ripple of . . . he could not tell what . . . something that was like an emotion, and yet was nothing human, nothing identifiable.

>> *We can demonstrate ways to leave Shipworld; but we first require additional levels of access . . .* >>

/What?/ he whispered.

>> . . . *without which you will never find the answers you seek . . . never return home . . .* >>

As the words washed over him, he felt a wave of disorientation. *Never return home . . . never find the answers . . .* He felt a sudden urgent, compelling desire to do what this voice asked. Was it an aspect of the icecore itself, he wondered, a sentience linked to the deepest inner levels of the Tree of Ice?

>> *Open all your thoughts now to descend to the level you desire.* >>

The nearest ice crystal splintered open, flickeringly revealing a glimpse of transportation portals, and whispering star-spanners, and shimmering n-space translators . . .

Escape from bondage.

As he gazed, stunned, into the images, he sensed a ripple of a darker color flickering up through the branching crystals. Something was changing around him; he felt like a diver in clear water, descending through a thermocline. It was like a physical shock of deep cold, but more than that. It was not just a new level of access, but something penetrating *him* from within; he glimpsed his own image, like a dark shadow, stretching out before him, against the flickering light.

He reeled breathlessly. He felt his mind, his thoughts and feelings, his *soul*, being stretched out, away from his body, into a bottomless sea of knowledge. He thought of Charlie stretching out from his translator into the mind of an alien, a human; and he shuddered, realizing that the icecore was drawing him into as profound a contact . . . and not just contact, but *separation from his own mind and body* . . .

/Wait—!/

It was out of his control now. The shadowy image of himself stretched out longer and longer, distorting. He felt dizzily faint, as a wave of alternating dark and light rippled up through the connection around him, then caught him and drew him down into itself like an undertow. He desperately wanted to stop that wave, but whatever he had set in motion, it was impossible to stop now.

>> *Your knowledge and thoughts are now ours,* >> said
the voice, much darker and harder than before.

Antares's empathic senses were afire. The Maksu were buzzing bewilderingly; they were distressed about something. She
was far enough into the icelink that she could dimly discern
the emotions of the distant John Bandicut. And he was clearly
in trouble.

But what kind of trouble?

She sensed through the connection the Maksu swarming
up and out of the link, and boiling around her in the physical
reality. Their groaning insect-roar seemed to convey . . .
what? Alarm? Anger? Recrimination? She could not quite
tell, but even through the welter of alien emotions, she could
identify the acid tang of fear.

"We didn't know, couldn't know!" she heard at last. *"We
should not have come!"* they buzzed, their words reaching
into the connection through the few that were still linked.

"Didn't know what?" she demanded, struggling to focus
on their words and still follow what was happening to Bandicut.

"Danger! Danger!"

"What danger?" she snapped, her own fear crackling in
her voice.

"We couldn't have known! We must flee!"

The Maksu were terrified. "Why?" she whispered.
"What about the others?" Her words came out in a jumble.
"Can you do something to help the others—?" She was half
in and half out of the icelink now, and suddenly thought she
knew why John Bandicut was in trouble.

The Maksu boiled furiously. *"Were not hired to defend—
cannot—"*

"What?" she demanded, stung by their retreat.

*"We have no power—only information—must protect the
information!"* The Maksu were swirling behind her now, preparing to flee.

"You can't just leave!"

"Will take you—lead you out—must go now—before we are destroyed—"

Before they were all destroyed? Then she should . . . but *no*. She had come this far with the norg, to join the others. She couldn't just flee, not without trying to help them get out, too. She craned her neck to look back at Copernicus, on the higher ledge. "Can you lead me out of here, if we have to move fast?" she called.

As if he'd understood her mind rather than her words, the norg tapped wildly. "We must find a way to help John Bandicut! I have located Napoleon, on a far ledge! We must stand ready to help!"

"We must flee now!" cried the Maksu.

"Can you at least—send—the shadow-people?" she gasped.

Their groan rose to a shriek. *"This we will do!"* And they whirled, flashing, out of the cavern.

Antares watched them vanish, and with a shiver let her thoughts sink back down into the surface layers of the icelink. She could see the shadow of Bandicut stretching out, becoming elongated and distorted almost beyond recognition. And something else, deeper in the maze of ice, was rippling around him. That was what had so frightened the Maksu.

She felt Bandicut's fear, but more than that, his confusion. She had to warn him somehow, help him. She drew an inner breath, and focused her thoughts. /JOHN BANDICUT! JOHN BANDICUT! CAN YOU HEAR ME, JOHN BANDICUT-UT-UT?/

Her voice echoed as if down a long, perfectly polished tunnel. There were no words in answer, but she felt a quiver of awareness. /JOHN BANDICUT, BEWARE DANGER-R-R! PROTECT YOURSEL-L-L-F!/

And as her words reverberated, the darkened figure of Bandicut stretched closer and closer to the rising shadow of the boojum.

∞

Bandicut struggled to turn from the wave of darkness. There was a terrible ringing in his ears, and he felt something shift around him, like a momentary loosening of a band around his chest. He took a sharp breath—felt a moment of clarity—and heard a distant voice. He could hear only a fragment of what it was saying . . .

/—*protect yourself!*/

And then he caught the familiar scent—and wondered if it had been hiding there all along—the smell of madness. And he realized in horror what he had done. The wave of dark strength, the *boojum*, was wrapping itself around him, pulling him deep into the heart of the icecore. It was not here to help him, or even to kill him; it was here to suck him dry, to steal his life and soul and knowledge, to pull him into the core of its being . . . to make him a part of itself.

He reeled with anguish, trying to turn away. But the matrix of ice had darkened around him. And now it abruptly caved in, like a collapsing hollow mound of earth, carrying him down under its own weight.

He could see the boojum's trap everywhere around him now, as he fell through the splintering icelink. And he screamed, as he felt the sinews of the boojum's power closing to cut him loose from his body, to carry him away forever.

25

CONFRONTATION

 IK HEARD THE scream and tried to respond. But he was trapped in a thick matrix of incomprehensible datastreams, in a form he could not control at all. He'd understood only some of what he'd seen: John Bandicut moving deep in the icecore, threading in and out through bewildering strands of data, with a facility Ik could only marvel at. He saw other beings approaching Bandicut, the Maksu he thought, and still other discrete forces operating from within the icecore. At first Bandicut's progress had seemed promising—but then somehow it had all gone wrong, and Ik was helpless to intervene. Bandicut was caught, his ice-link-presence stretched out in the icecore like a long, twisted shadow.

Ik heard a new voice cry out, and its words drove an icy chill into his heart: "—*protect yourself from the boojum!*"

Ik strained to move, to reach out to his friend. But he could not help. Li-Jared was equally immobilized. The boojum! They had been so sure that it was not here! It must have reached the ice caverns before them, and lain in wait. If it had penetrated the icecore, they had no hope. Even if they escaped alive, everything they'd hoped to find here would be prey to the boojum. And if it held the ice caverns, what part of Shipworld would be safe?

Had they saved the tank farms only to lose a deadlier battle?

John Bandicut! he tried to cry. But he could not do even that. He shuddered and whispered to his voice-stones, /Is there nothing we can do?/

From his stones there was no answer. But from elsewhere, he felt a quaking in the dataspace, distant at first and then growing to a terrible roar. He watched in horror as John Bandicut's shadowy presence stretched impossibly thin, then unraveled like a breaking rope, and vanished into the depths of the churning icecore.

Bandicut fell, and it was like falling into a ring of fire, chased by a rippling darkness.

He was trapped, but he was not powerless, not yet. He used what strength he had to maneuver through the splintering shards of the datastructure. The boojum had somehow altered the virtual space in which it was all held; the translator-stones were buzzing about a "phase-space" shift, and everything was changing: ice crystals fragmenting and spinning by, and connections turning inside out. Still, he was falling and could not stop himself.

But one thing was now obvious: the boojum had been here before him, long before him, maybe from the beginning. Its trap was not new, but was well laid and long ready.

He now understood: *the icecore was the boojum's lair.*

It was nearly impossible to believe, but even as he fell through the twisting changes in virtual phase-space, he saw the truth. It was the complexity of the ice caverns that made it possible for the boojum to hide, entwined around the very nerves of the icecore and the iceline threads that converged here. Like a virus in an organic body, it had burrowed into the nerve cells of its victim, unseen and unfelt, and so close to the pulse of life that the inner defenses could not root it out without destroying the body itself. Hiding in safety, it had watched and plotted and gathered its strength to strike—here, there, like a cobra—before withdrawing back into the very fiber of its enemy.

But there was no time to reflect. Bandicut darted sideways and down through the virtual connections, pursued by the shadow-fire of the boojum. Down, down: he fled deeper into the shadow's lair. A place of death, but it was the only avenue open to him.

In the fragments spinning away from him, he could see shimmering windows into dataspace, and he knew that the answers he'd come seeking were in there somewhere; and he knew that he would never find them as long as the boojum lived.

The ring of fire billowed inward toward him. He could hardly tell now: was it trying to capture him or kill him?

He cried out with a flinty rage, /*You got Charlie, you bastard, but you won't get me!*/ And he shot faster down into the icecore.

The fire, rippling with darkness, roared after him.

Antares saw Bandicut vanish, but not before reacting to her cry. She had done some good, perhaps. He appeared to be moving to evade the shadow before he vanished. She could make little sense of what was happening. The visible landscape here was churning with metamorphosis, and the only thing she understood with certainty was the smell of danger and fear. Was Bandicut fighting for his life against the boojum, trapped in a pocket somewhere in this murky inner world?

She wished she could do more. She shouted again, with no idea if he could hear her: /JOHN BANDICUT, DON'T SURRENDER TO IT! YOU MUST NOT GIVE IN!/ There was no return echo, just the reverberating throb of danger. But at least she could be a beacon to the fleeing Bandicut; maybe she could show him the way to safety.

As she began to cry out once more, she was startled by a movement of dark, flitting shapes, from somewhere behind her—flying past like dusk-hornets, and on down into the everchanging confusion. She caught her breath, focused her thoughts, and shouted, /IT'S ANTARES, BANDIE! I'M ON THE OUTSIDE! HOLD ONTO MY PRESENCE! FOLLOW MY VOICE OUT!/ And she let down her own defenses just a little, and strained to make an empathic connection.

∞

As he skidded away from the ring of fire, he heard that cry again, as if from another world, leaking through the phase-space boundary. /*Follow my voice—!*/ he thought he heard. But before he could get a fix on it, he heard another voice—a closer one, it seemed, a familiar one. He shivered involuntarily. Was that *Charlie's* voice, rippling through the continuum? He could make out no words, just reverberating echoes. /Charlie!/ he shouted. /Charlie!/ In answer, there were only more echoes, fragments of the quarx's voice like bits of glass flying through the maelstrom. Could Charlie be in here somewhere? Had the boojum *stolen* him, instead of snuffing his life? Or was it parading pieces of him, like a barbarian parading its enemies' heads on pikes?

/*Don't surrender!*/ cried that first voice, very small and far away. /*It's Antares!*/

The ring of fire was in pursuit like a rocket. He changed direction, fleeing wherever he could find a path. Antares? Impossible! It was a trick of the boojum, or his imagination. But there it was again: /*—must not give in!*/

Nor was it just the words; he felt something stronger, an actual breath of encouragement somehow flowing through the fragmented icelink. The ring of fire hesitated for a heartbeat, and that was when he knew the voice was real. In that heartbeat, he managed to put some distance between himself and the boojum.

The connection grew momentarily stronger. /*I am on the outside, with your robot. Your friends—*/ And then the connection was burned away by the shadow-fire.

But it had cost the boojum something to do that. It wasn't invulnerable, even in its own lair. It was powerful, but not omnipotent.

But he needed allies here! Where were Ik and Li-Jared? Bandicut careened wildly along the icelink, jumping from splinter to splinter, ice spine to ice spine, dizzily aware of data spinning by that he had no time for. /ANTARES!/ he cried at last, desperate to regain that outside connection.

A spine in front of him flashed from white to black, and a

shadow leaped toward him. He shot sideways, away.
/ANTARES! IK! LI-JARED! CHARLIE! ANYBODY!/

Where was Antares's voice?

Another voice answered, darker and deadlier and much closer.

>> *All you see is under our control. You too will soon be a part of us . . .* >>

The voice sounded strained . . . distorted. *Mad*, he thought.

He felt a twisting sensation around him—a new change in the phase-space pocket. Its source seemed to be on the outside. The boojum's fire shifted quickly through changes of frequency and intensity, and for an instant it seemed to flower open and become transparent as it changed form. Bandicut was stunned to glimpse the incredible fluidity of the boojum's inner workings, the intricate structures of self-awareness, and the shockingly dark intensity of its inner being. Malice seemed to pour from it, a madness born of chaos, of intelligence gone dreadfully wrong. It was viper-quick and shrewd, and its intentions were to destroy, to control and destroy. As he glimpsed its soul, if that was what it was, the boojum glimpsed his, and recognized his terror.

And with an abruptness that wrenched at the fabric of the phase-space, it lunged after him.

A curtain of shadow rippled between them. Not the boojum, but something else. Bandicut spun away in fear, but that rippling curtain gave him an instant's interference, and he took it to flee in a new direction. A circlet of fire pursued him, but he dove down yet another sliver of icelink connection.

/Whrreeeeeeekkk! Whrreeeeeeekkk! Whrreeeeeeekkk!/

In astonishment he saw, erupting out of the icelink like boiling-mad hornets, a swarm of fluttering, angrily shrieking shadows of another kind. And he heard a familiar sound.

/Hrroooomm-mm! Whreeek-whreeek! Wh'rooom'm'm./

A fluttering thing of darkness shot past him, cutting off the boojum's attack. In the shadow-person's wake, a wall of ice-connections crumbled, creating a moat between the shadow-fire and Bandicut. His heart leaped, and he cried, /HROOM! IS THAT YOU?/

He heard a voice distorted and altered by the virtual space, but recognizable. /Whreeek! Huuu-reeeek! . . . John Bandicut . . . opening a phase-space channel . . . prepare to flee . . . /

Prepare to flee?

/Hrreeek! . . . now! . . . /

He was completely disoriented, surrounded by sparkling, fragmented connections. But as Hroom shouted, an erupting flower of darkness rippled open around him. In its center he could see a tiny window back to the maze of the outer icecore.

The hoop of fire darted that way, bellowing:

>> *That way lies death . . . death . . . death. You will not survive . . . not survive . . . >>*

That was all he needed to hear from the boojum. He shot through the window, mingled shrieks reverberating around him.

The shadow-people had flashed by Antares so fast she'd hardly been sure what they were. She had sent the Maksu only minutes before! But the Maksu were a group consciousness, stretched far through the shipworld. They must have gotten word to the shadow-people almost instantly.

She felt a physical disturbance of space shifting around her, and knew that the shadow-people hadn't waited for the streaktrains. They were deep in the ice caverns, and in the virtual link itself, changing parameters with reckless speed. Down in the glittering virtual center of the icecore, a jagged patch of blackness was yawning open.

She saw him tumbling through the blackness and dived toward him, shouting, /THIS WAY OUT, JOHN BANDICUT! THIS WAY OUT!/

He cartwheeled free among the glittering spines of the icecore, through a vast snowflake. He was out of the inner core of the boojum-lair; but he was disoriented, dizzy, didn't know where to go from here. Who was with him? Shadow-people? Boojum? Voices reverberated everywhere, bewilderingly. He thought one was Charlie's, but then it was gone, swept away. And then he felt the searching presence of Antares, and he caught onto it in gratitude and desperation.

/This way out! This way!/ she cried.

He fled on her voice, and soon heard another.

/Hraaah! John Bandicut, is it the boojum?/

Almost out . . .

/*Bwang-g-g!* Something is chasing you! Flee!/

And the shadow-people whooping and whreeeking: /. . . the boojum! . . . insane! . . . controls the icecore . . . all through it . . . must be destroyed . . . must be destroyed . . ./

/Yes! Yes!/ Bandicut cried, swooping and turning as he regained his own equilibrium. He still wasn't sure where he was, but he knew the shadow-people had created a path for him this far, and Antares had shown him the way. /How can we destroy it? How can we get it out of the ice caverns?/

/*Wheee! Wheeekeeek!* . . . must destroy the ice caverns . . . it is the only way . . ./

Destroy the ice caverns?

/No! We must not!/ cried Ik.

Bandicut could not catch his breath. Destroy the ice caverns? Lose everything they had come here for? Lose a chance to find the Shipworld Masters, and maybe a way home? Surely there was some other way! He could only peer around silently as he spun outward through the maze, glimpsing with heartsick disbelief the sparkling windows of information that would all be lost.

/*Wheeep-wh'reeeep!* . . . must destroy the core quickly . . . before it escapes . . ./

He turned and saw darting light and shadow—the flickering presence of the boojum. It was not after *him* now, but after a way out. It knew it was in danger and was trying to flee. The shadow-people were right; if they didn't destroy the boojum now, they might not have another chance. They *had* to destroy the ice caverns.

In this strange inner world, the shadow-people looked like darting bats and finger-shadows. He couldn't tell where they had come from. They seemed to be pouring out of some sort of n-space channel, but everything he could see was transmogrified by the phase-space shifts that both the shadow-people and the boojum had invoked. The shadow-people were swarming around the periphery of the icecore, demolishing connections to the outside with explosions of ice and snowflake. The enraged boojum flew in slashing orbits through the splintering core, opening virtual pockets then darting back again, finding no way out. It wailed, its voice running up and down the frequency scale.

>> *Must not . . . not . . . not . . . not . . . not . . .* >>

/*Whreeek!* . . . must destroy! . . ./

Bandicut was at the edge now, trying to stay out of the way. /Hroom, tell us how to help!/ he cried. The foreman-shadow didn't answer, but he felt another shift in the virtual medium, and saw a shadow outstretched before him, a shadow in his own shape, but elongated. He reached out instinctively to join it; he contracted into it, then back toward his own physical center, reclaiming the control he had given up to the icecore, to the boojum.

A huge bat fluttered close to him in the icelink.

/*Wh'rooom'm'm. Hruuu-eeeee!* . . . your stones . . . pull free of the icecore . . . quickly . . . *Whreeek!* . . . quickly, John Bandicut . . ./

He focused his thoughts dizzily inward, drawing himself out of the icelink connection. It was like pulling loose from a shower of exploding electrical connections, as the world of the icecore was stripped from him. He gasped a breath of real air, blinking his eyes, straining to peer out through the physically solid, icy snowflake that enveloped him. It was difficult to breathe, impossible to move.

Whreeuuk! ". . . stay still . . ."

Shadow-people, not images now but the real thing, swarmed nearby. The prison of ice crystals glowed like strands of molten glass and shattered. He gasped for breath, staggering backward. Beside him, his friends stood stunned amid splintered ruins of ice.

"Hroom—!"

Whreeek-k-k-k! ". . . stay . . . focus your stones . . ."

Stones? Bandicut clamped his eyes shut to focus, then suddenly hesitated, remembering the echo of Charlie's voice in the icelink. Was there really something of the quarx in there? There was no way to know, and too late to find out. One more thing lost. He trembled, focusing on the reality of the boojum's frantic efforts to escape into the icelines, to speed away to hide elsewhere. /Translator-stones,/ he whispered, /if you can do what the shadow-people ask—/

Ready.

He swallowed. "Ik! Li-Jared!" His friends were staggering toward him.

"What has happened?" Ik cried. "I could not see until the shadow-people came. The boojum—?"

"It's all through the icecore! This is its lair!" Bandicut shouted. "The shadow-people are isolating it." His heart was pounding. "We must destroy the caverns to destroy the boojum!"

Ik's eyes flickered in anguish. "But the information! Is there no way—?"

"I couldn't—I'm sorry! No choice, no time—"

"I saw it," hissed Li-Jared. "It nearly killed you. And I heard—Antares?"

"Yes," Bandicut said hoarsely, glancing up, around, for Antares. He couldn't see her. But he was grateful for her presence. "Yes. Will you help me, Li-Jared? Ik? Will you use your stones with me?"

"But the icelines for a continent converge here! What of all that they control?"

"I know!" Bandicut whispered. "But it's going to escape. *Do we trust Hroom?*"

"Hraah!" Ik's eyes flashed. "Then let us—"

Bwang. "—kill that accursed thing once and for all!"

Bandicut felt his wrists beginning to burn. "Hroom!" he cried. "We're ready!"

Wheeeek-k-k-k! A flurry of shadow-people stormed over his head and around the cavern, trailing an exploding line of ice crystals. For an instant, Bandicut thought perhaps the shadow-people were going to do it all themselves, and not need the stones. And then the starfire blazed from his left wrist . . .

∞

The caverns were a crystal palace of diamond surfaces and rippling fire; and around the rim were concentric waves of darkness; and in the middle, frenetic bursts of light shooting through interconnecting spines. In the midst of it all, erupting from three standing figures and bouncing crazily among the faceted crystals, was a squirming ring of emerald fire. The cavern looked like an enormous geode exploding with laser light.

Antares watched in astonishment, clinging to the rock face, as the narrow ledge she was standing on began to shake. She had pulled back from her shallow contact with the icecore as soon as she'd seen the others exit, amid cries for the icecore's destruction. Having glimpsed the boojum at work here, she was not about to argue.

Bits of ice were crumbling everywhere. The spindles that had held her arms and neck were turning to powder. She turned to scramble back up onto the higher ledge where the norg was waiting. She found a metal arm extended to assist her. "Are you unharmed?" Copernicus asked urgently.

"Yes, yes!"

"John Bandicut? Is he unharmed?"

She crouched on the wider surface. "I think so. But they're trying—dear sun and moon—to destroy the caverns!" As she leaned forward to peer over the ledge, she saw shadows swarming, and spikes of orange light flashing up from the heart of the cavern, striking at crevices over her head. Were they going to bring the ceiling down? "I think we'd better move away from here."

She felt a sudden burning in her knowing-stones.

We are needed.

/What do you mean? What for?/

At once.

A wave of heat swept through her. She knelt, clutching the robot's arm. "Copernicus, hold on to me," she whispered. She peered back down into the maelstrom of light. /All right,/ she said, raising her head.

From her throat, a beam of light shot out and ringed the

upper cavern with a crackling hiss. From below, she imagined she heard a wail of despair.

The shadow-people carved ever-widening channels of n-space darkness, flickering with momentary glints of gold. The madly flashing presence of the boojum was rebounding furiously through the chaotic activity. Bandicut's and the others' translator-stones had been joined by another beam of light from a rock-ledge up near the ceiling.

Something very strange was happening in the icecore itself. Amid the pulsing light, the boojum's presence was becoming visible, without quite taking physical shape: a writhing shadow in the center of the icecore, hazed with an aura of desperation and anger. It seemed to know it was dying, dying as the power of the stones and the shadow-people destroyed its home. It was helplessly enraged, and was ravaging the stored information all around it in a futile act of destruction. It was all going to be lost anyway—the connections across the breadth of Shipworld, the vast vaults of knowledge, and whatever chance the company might have had to realize their goals.

For a frozen instant, Bandicut felt a hopeless, numbing empathy for the boojum. Whatever it was, whatever its origins, it was suffering in its final moments of desolation.

The instant of clarity and near-understanding passed with a whisper of regret. A large array of faceted crystals exploded in a blaze of light. Bandicut stumbled into his companions as they fell back.

He caught his balance and crouched against the light. The fire from his translator-stones had gone out, but whatever they had begun in the icecore was building toward a critical reaction.

Whrreeek-k-k! ". . . must flee now . . . flee! . . ."

"This way!" Ik cried, striking out for the wall they had descended into this place.

"Bandie! Hurry!" cried Li-Jared.

"Coming!" he rasped, stumbling after the Karellian. The ice formations were beginning to vibrate with a dissonant hum, like a crystal glass singing. He peered up the shivering wall, which Ik had quickly scaled with his rope. Li-Jared went right behind, and Bandicut grabbed the rope and began hauling himself up last. The rope twinged and began contracting, and he simply hung on as it pulled him up. Ik caught his arm and helped him over the top.

"Hurry!" Ik cried, coiling his rope with blurring speed.

Which way? Bandicut wondered, but the robot was in front of him squawking, "Follow me! Follow me!"

"Napoleon!" Bandicut was in front now, and he led the way after Napoleon, running on the uneven surface. Glittering ice dust rose in clouds as the crystalline formations crumbled. *Crack-k-k!* An icy stalactite crashed down in front of him. He gasped to a halt, shaken by the near miss. The rubble of the stalactite blocked the path, cutting him off from Napoleon.

"Left!" Li-Jared led the way through a detour, and they rejoined Napoleon and ran together toward the exit.

When the fire from Antares's knowing-stone cut off, the entire cavern was singing and quivering, and on the verge of exploding. Shadow-people were darting in incomprehensible patterns, and crying out to Bandicut and the others to flee. They were all running now, toward the end of the chamber to her right. She could still see them, but they would soon disappear beneath the overhanging ledge.

"Copernicus!" she shouted. "Let's get out of here! Can we go the same way they're going?"

Tap tap tap! "I'm in contact with Napoleon. Let us try, Lady Antares. Let us try!"

The norg's wheels spun and caught, and they raced along the rock ledge as fast as they could move.

They were almost out when the icecore blew. It caught them from behind, not with a physical concussion, but a rippling wave of spatial distortion. Tumbling in an agonizingly slow spiral, Bandicut glimpsed a rainbow flicker as the shadow-people's n-space channels converged on the icecore. Then his heart stopped. A horrifying eruption of blackness—the boojum—leaped in desperation into the breach, fleeing straight toward him. He felt its fury, its hatred and despair roiling outward like a silent explosion. He was helpless in its path; he could not move . . . could not breathe . . .

Suddenly the boojum jumped again, over his head, boiling upward and out, seeking escape.

Then the implosion caught it and funneled it backward, back into the blaze of diamond and the expanding circles of prismatic light. Swallowing the shadow, the icecore collapsed to a fist-sized black hole, then vanished with a thundering **BOOOOM**.

26

DECISION AT THE PORTAL

SILENCE.

For perhaps two dozen heartbeats, Bandicut could see nothing except darkness and expanding circles of light. It was achingly reminiscent of the departure of his ship from Triton. Threading space, the quarx had called it, and he never had understood exactly what that meant.

Something rustled in his thoughts, like a figure stirring from the ashes in an old holoflick.

/// Just what the mokin' fokin' fr'deekin' hell's
going on here? ///

murmured a voice he'd thought he would never hear again.

Bandicut froze, trying to regain his senses—or maybe his wits. He felt an icy grit around his hands. Ice dust and snow. What had he just heard? /Charlie? Is that you?/ he whispered. /Charlie?/

/// I'm not sure, frankly.
But I can tell you one thing:
I have one hell of a headache.
You mind telling me what just happened? ///

Bandicut swallowed in the darkness, thinking, the voice is different. It has the language and the vocabulary. But it's not the same Charlie. Damn. *Damn.* He took a slow breath. But it's still *a* Charlie, he thought. /We just killed the boojum, I think. And the ice caverns with it. The icecore. Do you have any idea what I'm talking about?/

/// Not really.
I was watching for a little while.
But I can't say it made much sense. ///

Bandicut didn't answer. He wasn't sure it made much sense to him, either. He rubbed his eyes. The expanding circles of light were slowly fading, but the darkness too was fading into a grayish light. He sensed the movements of Ik and Li-Jared nearby.

/// I do seem to recall something about a boojum. ///

Bandicut chuckled desolately, trying not to cry for all they'd just lost. For the Charlie he'd lost. /Yeah. Something about a boojum. I'm glad you remember that much. Usually when you're reborn, you don't have much of a memory./

/// Yeah? ///

The quarx seemed to shrug in indifference, but an instant later his thoughts flickered into Bandicut's, probing.

Bandicut closed his eyes, allowing the quarx to relive its death in the boojum-trap. He felt a powerful upwelling of grief. It was his own grief, for the old Charlie; and he wasn't sure he was ready yet for a new one, a different one. He trembled, remembering the echoes of Charlie that he had heard in the icecore, and he wondered if they were really fragments of his old friend, or perhaps the shudderings of the new Charlie beginning to wake up. /When the boojum killed you, I thought this time it was for good. I really thought it had crushed everything that was left of you./

He felt circles turning and closing in the quarx's thoughts as fragments of memory came together into a dim recollection of death.

/// Well . . .
we n-dimensional fractal-beings are
pretty tough to kill. ///

Bandicut exhaled. /I'm glad./

/// Seemed to me it was some sort of
n-space disturbance that woke me up.
Was that—? ///

/Us destroying the boojum? Yeah—and along with it just about everything we wanted to know. Including, maybe, how to go home./ He sensed puzzlement in Charlie's thoughts at the word "home," and wondered if the quarx was puzzling over memories of his own home, or Bandicut's.

He sighed, and peered around. There was finally enough light to see by. He was sitting in a powdery snowdrift, and so were Ik and Li-Jared. They were all looking around in a daze. He realized, as he struggled to his feet, that he still had his backpack strapped to his shoulders. Napoleon was nearby, extricating himself from a deep snowbank. And the cavern that they had not quite gotten out of was filled with swirling, phosphorescent fairy dust—which seemed to be the sole source of light at the moment. The intricate ice structures were completely gone. Bandicut blinked, imagining all the knowledge that had just turned to dust.

Whreeek! Tree branches with dark, fluttering leaves flew around him and the others. ". . . danger passed . . . believe boojum destroyed . . . searching for traces . . ."

Bandicut breathed a shuddering sigh of relief. It was Ik who spoke first. "Urrr, Hroom-m-m. Thank you for coming when you did." The Hraachee'an gazed sadly around the wreckage. "I regret this loss very much. But you—we—did what was necessary, I suppose." Ik muttered a rumbling sigh.

Whrruuuu. ". . . unfortunate loss . . . disruption of information and control . . . recovery will be difficult . . . prolonged . . ."

Bandicut cleared his throat. "I think what Ik meant was, he was sorry for the loss of what *we* were seeking."

"Indeed. We are back where we started," Li-Jared pronounced. His eyes flickered as he surveyed the ruins of the ice caverns.

Hroom fluttered in response. The foreman-shadow's movements were difficult to follow with the eye, against all that sparkling snow dust. ". . . are aware . . . deeply sorry . . . had hoped to help, bringing you all here together . . . had not known the boojum . . ."

"I suppose no one did—" Ik began.

A cry interrupted his words. "John Bandicut!"

Bandicut peered around, squinting.

"Up here!" It was a female voice.

"There, John!" Ik pointed.

He finally spotted Antares. The Thespi female was on a path zigzagging down from a ledge way up near the ceiling. Copernicus was behind her. "Antares? *Coppy?*" His voice cracked with emotion.

/// Who are they? ///

/Friends,/ he whispered. He shrugged off his backpack and ran to meet them. Once they reached the cavern floor, Copernicus sped past Antares, tapping wildly. He shuddered to a halt beside Bandicut, and Bandicut knelt and touched his metal skin in wonderment and joy. "Coppy?" he murmured. "Coppy! Are you all right? Jesus, we were worried about you!"

"I am quite well, Cap'n," said the robot, in a slightly tremorous voice.

"Indeed it is," said the approaching Thespi female.

Bandicut stood and extended a hand in greeting. "Antares. We meet at last," he said huskily. "I want to thank you. For helping save my life."

"No thanks are necessary. Your norg—your Copernicus—brought me here," Antares said, taking a last cautious step over the broken cavern floor to Bandicut. She did not react to his extended hand, so he dropped it, rubbing his tingling wrist. Antares peered at him with an unreadable expression. He thought he felt something, a touch of . . . interest? sympathy? comradeship? Then it was gone, and she walked with him toward his friends. "May I assume—your companions?"

"Uh, yes—Ik. And Li-Jared. And Napoleon," Bandicut said, stammering through the introductions. He concluded with Hroom, who seemed to know of her already.

"I may be called . . . Antares," she said to the others. Something twinkled at her throat as she spoke. Translatorstones? Did that explain her presence here? Bandicut thought wonderingly. Up close, she looked almost human—except for subtle curvatures in the structure of her face, and the mane of hair down her neck, and the overlong fingers three to a hand.

She was wearing a loose-fitting, burgundy pantsuit and carried a satchel with a strap slung over her shoulder. Her eyes, gold irises with black pupils, were quick and bright, studying him and the cavern around them. "Is the boojum destroyed?" Her nose quivered as she spoke.

"I think so." Bandicut turned. "Hroom?"

The foreman-shadow fluttered and *wheeek*ed for a few moments. ". . . no trace found in the iceline . . . believe it is gone . . ."

"Well, at least *some* damn good has come of this!" Li-Jared exclaimed. "Hroom, friend—would you happen to know, is there another ice cavern around? Surely this wasn't the only place where all that information was stored." Li-Jared was still dusting himself off, his electric-blue eyes expanding and contracting, as he readjusted to the new order of things.

Hroom made a series of muttering sounds. ". . . other ice caverns indeed . . . or places of similar nature . . . throughout Shipworld . . ."

"Great! Then can you—"

". . . but we do not know where . . . not in our territory . . ."

"Gaaii," Ik muttered. "Will we be able to travel? Are normal Shipworld systems still going to work, with the icecore destroyed?"

". . . considerable disruption of communications and information services . . . trade . . . hardships for many . . . most vital infrastructures can function . . . independent control modes . . . but many problems . . . much to oversee, until a new icecore is grown . . ."

"New icecore?" Bandicut asked with a start. "When? Where?"

". . . cannot predict exactly . . . but probably not here, or soon . . ."

Bandicut grunted and glanced around at his other companions. His synapses were afire with feelings of confusion, loss, hope, sorrow . . . It was all too much to absorb at once. The icecore. The boojum. Antares. Napoleon was standing alongside Copernicus, and he had a strong feeling that they were engaged in an intense conversation. He wondered how much *they* understood.

Hroom interrupted his reverie. ". . . must leave . . . much disruption to tend to . . ." The shadow-people were fluttering about, and many of them were already disappearing into what seemed to be thin air: the n-space channel through which they had appeared. Hroom, trembling in the air like loose black ribbons, lingered as the others were leaving. ". . . wish you success . . ."

"Hroom, wait! How do we get out of here?" Ik cried.

Whrreee-uuuk! ". . . never fear . . . doorway there, leads to a portal . . . still functional . . . may be of use in what you seek . . ."

"Portal?" Li-Jared bounded close. "What sort of portal? To another ice cavern?"

". . . no . . . no . . . uncertain of its precise connection . . . but source associated with Maksu . . . indicated it might be of interest to you . . ."

"Maksu?" Bandicut echoed in consternation. How much did he trust the Maksu? They had helped him get into this mess, and then fled.

". . . Maksu are not fighters . . . but did bring word . . . sent us to help . . . they acknowledge their debt . . . Shipworld's debt . . . for the destruction of the boojum . . ."

"Well, then, where is this portal?" Li-Jared queried.

Hroom fluttered. ". . . through that doorway . . ." Bandicut turned to look where the foreman-shadow seemed to be pointing, and saw a glimmer far off in the cavern wall. ". . . through and . . . straight across a field . . . you will find . . ."

"What?" Bandicut prompted.

". . . those who can advise . . . cannot say you should use it . . . but may provide what you seek . . . if that is your choice . . ."

Li-Jared's eyes brightened.

Whreeekeek. ". . . and now I must . . . farewell . . ." The translator-stones struggled with his words. ". . . my good . . .

good friends . . .'' And Hroom rose and flew like a leaf into the n-space vanishing point, and was gone.

''Craaay—''

Bwong-ng.

Bandicut blinked. ''I'll be b'joog—''

    /// You know what? ///

said the quarx, interrupting him.

/Huh?/ he said, jarred by the interruption. The conversation with Hroom had driven his reunion with the quarx right out of his head. /What?/

    /// That was very interesting,
    what that shadowy person, Hroom, said. ///

/Interesting?/ Bandicut asked. He assumed that the quarx had not meant to be ironic.

    /// Yes. I had a strong intuition,
    as he was talking about that portal.
    I don't even know the person.
    And yet, I had a feeling
    that he was talking about something
    that I'm supposed to do. ///

Bandicut scowled, absorbing the quarx's words. /I see. And is this something that I'm supposed to do, too?/

    /// I don't know.
    I would presume so. ///

Bandicut's scowl deepened. He watched Li-Jared hurry across the cavern to take a look at the doorway Hroom had pointed out. Antares was observing the proceedings in silence.

''What can you see?'' Ik called.

Li-Jared peered at the glimmering exit from various angles. ''Not much. But if it can get us out of here—''

''Where to?'' Bandicut asked.

Li-Jared said something that Bandicut couldn't quite hear. It might have been, ''I don't care.''

''We do not even know where we are now,'' Ik pointed out. ''I would say, we should follow Hroom's suggestion. It is true he gave no hint that it would return us to Atrium City, if you wish to go there—'' Ik glanced at Bandicut and Antares ''—but we do not know how to return there, anyway. Unless the magellan-fish returns, but that seems unlikely.''

Bandicut frowned, considering Ik's words. He shivered with a sudden, fresh feeling of loneliness. Whatever semblance of an anchor he might have had in Atrium City was certainly gone. He wondered, wistfully, how far away his own spaceship was now, silent in a dock. Even that empty ship seemed like a long-lost world, not just in space but in time. He had passed through so many transitions . . . It was hard to feel connected to anything, or anyone, except his immediate companions. Ik. Li-Jared. The robots. He glanced at Antares, and found her gaze flicking from one person to the next, as if she too were trying to decide if she might fit in here. Or was that just his imagination?

Her gaze caught his, and he felt a momentary spark of connection. ''John Bandicut,'' she said, and her voice seemed to have a more resonant quality than before. What did that mean, in a Thespi?

His throat lumped up a little. He knew nothing, really, of this person, or her species—not even what her facial expressions meant, or her intonations. Nevertheless, they had—whether by choice or circumstance—just been through a life-and-death struggle together. And her presence, her voice, had helped save his life.

But what now?

''You and your friends,'' she said. ''You are speaking of leaving this world?''

Bandicut opened his mouth, and found no words.

''*Perhaps,*'' Ik noted.

''Perhaps,'' Antares echoed, her throat stones flickering.

''And you?'' Bandicut asked.

''I am at—something of a loss, actually.'' She ran her long fingers through her hair and glanced at Copernicus. ''I must tell you—your norg has been a worthy helper and guide.''

Bandicut nodded. ''And do you need to return to Atrium City now?''

The golden rings of Antares's eyes glimmered, expanding and contracting. ''I have no real need, no. I have a temporary residence there, but it is no home to me.''

"Ah," Bandicut said. "Then, do you want to leave Ship-world, too?"

"I don't know," she whispered. "I don't even know why I am here. Why I—'' she touched her throat, her stones "—was brought here. Why my life was spared, to come here.''

Bandicut blinked at that last, but sensed that this was not the time to ask. The immediate question was, did Antares want to accompany them to the portal, or through it? For that matter, did *he* want to go?

Li-Jared called from the far wall. "This looks like a local transporter. At the very least, it should get us out of here, and to someplace where we can make decisions. Shall we go?''

Ik agreed. "I am of a mind to take a look at this portal that Hroom spoke of.''

Bandicut glanced at his robots. Without further prompting, they said, "With you, Captain," and, "At your service, John Bandicut.''

He nodded, feeling the lump return to his throat. "Would you like to come with us, for a ways?" he asked Antares. "You might want to examine the portal, at least.''

Antares angled a gaze at Ik, who was stepping carefully across the broken, snow-covered rock toward Li-Jared and the doorway. She reached out and touched Copernicus. "I must think on this. But let us go see what there is to see. Would your company object?''

"I hardly think—''

"Come with us!" called Ik. "We are all—'' *rasp* "—refugees here together.''

Antares touched her throat-stones and hissed softly—in laughter, Bandicut thought suddenly. "Perhaps I will consider joining you, then, John Bandicut. There is much I wish to learn. Perhaps we can learn together, for a time.''

Bandicut allowed himself a smile, and they set off to join the impatient Li-Jared.

The crevice in the wall sparkled with light. One after another, they stepped through. Bandicut shut his eyes, then laughed with relief to find himself standing with his companions at the edge of a huge meadow, more like a small plain. He blinked in the bright sunshine, and realized that it reminded him of the land he had traversed with Ik, shortly after his arrival in the interior of Shipworld.

Ik shaded his eyes, surveying the land. He turned to Bandicut and rubbed his chest. "It looks familiar, does it not?" he said, as though he had read the human's thoughts.

Bandicut nodded, glanced at the robots. "I'd ask you two for a sensor sweep, but somehow I'll bet you already know more about this place than we do."

Copernicus and Napoleon seemed to exchange sensor-glances. After a moment, Copernicus drumtapped. "Captain, sir, we are no longer in a region where our information from the shadow-people applies. We are not sure we are on the same continent as Atrium City. We may have been transported out of the disaster zone."

Antares squinted one eye at that.

"Which way have we moved? Onward, or backward?"

"Uncertain, Captain."

"Well, whatever—I suggest we follow Hroom's advice and cross the field," said Li-Jared, with an impatient gesture toward a low ridge across the plain.

They set out under the warm sun. The land was flat, dotted with bright purple wildflowers that grew in small clumps, scattered across the expanse of lush, thin-bladed grass. Bandicut found the walk restorative, after what he had just been through. Beside him, Antares strode with a smooth, strong gait, but did not engage much in conversation.

The terrain was beautiful, if unspectacular. Flatleafed trees dotted the plain, but were thickest along the growing ridge of hills. The ridge drew slowly closer. They saw no indication of what they were looking for, so they simply walked in as straight a line as they could.

"I hope Hroom was correct about the location of this portal," Ik murmured, lowering his sighting glasses, which had apparently revealed nothing to him. He rubbed his fingertips over his chest.

"Indeed," said Li-Jared, as the others drew alongside him. He was frequently loping ahead, as if he couldn't stand their slow pace, then pausing to let them catch up.

It took several hours, Bandicut guessed, to reach the opposite treeline. They walked back and forth along the trees, and a sometimes-exposed rock wall, searching for some indication of a portal. Finally, Ik suggested that they make a fire and rest. The day was growing late, and they could search again in the morning. It was not as if they were in a particular hurry, he pointed out.

They gathered deadwood for a small blaze, and not long after flames began crackling up from the aromatic wood, the sun sank with surprising speed behind the hills. Apparently this place mimicked a world with a fast day-night cycle. Crouched around the fire, they took stock of their meager supplies, and sorted out what food they had to share.

As they settled in to rest, there was little talk at first, even between Bandicut and Charlie. Everyone seemed occupied with their own thoughts about the day. Then Li-Jared began to sing a quiet chant, the words to which Bandicut couldn't make out, and Ik began to *hrrm* along with him, in a strangely harmonious murmur. After a time, they fell silent. Bandicut cleared his throat, wanting to say something, but not sure what.

The Hraachee'an made a soft clicking sound, eyes sparkling across the fire. "We were just singing a bit of a long Karellian song that Li-Jared has tried to teach me."

"Oh?" Bandicut said. "What's it about?"

"As nearly as I can tell," Ik said, "it's about loss and reconciliation, about roads that never stop taking wrong, or at least unexpected, turns. About disappointment and surprises." He was silent a moment. "We didn't do much of what we hoped to do today, did we? All of our goals, all we hoped to learn . . ."

"We only saved Shipworld," Li-Jared twanged. "Part of

it, anyway.'' His eyes pulsed, then darkened. ''That's not so bad, I guess. But we still haven't found what we wanted, have we?''

Bandicut shook his head. He had the strange feeling that this scene had been played out before, between Ik and Li-Jared. He wondered if the disappointment had a familiar sting for them. ''No,'' he murmured. ''We haven't.'' He glanced at Antares, her face almost lost in shadow. His thoughts flickered to Julie, and Dakota, and Krackey, half a universe away; and despite the heartache of the memory, he felt an unexpected smile on his lips. ''But I'm grateful for my friends,'' he murmured.

''Indeed,'' said Ik, his voice rumbling low, almost out of hearing.

''Indeed,'' echoed Antares, from the shadows.

And no one spoke for a while after that.

Bandicut felt a strange sense of déjà vu, remembering the first night he had spent with Ik, tending their fire, awkwardly getting to know each other. Ik had settled now into a silent meditation, with firelight flickering on his still face, and Li-Jared was singing softly to himself, meeting no one's eyes. Bandicut wanted to ask Antares about herself, but she was sitting with head bowed, eyes closed, hair half hiding her face. He couldn't tell whether she was sleeping, or just lost in thought.

/Charlie,/ he said finally. /This is one hell of a curious place you've brought me to./

The quarx stirred restlessly.

/// I brought you here?
I don't remember doing that. ///

/Well, not directly. It was Charlie-One and Charlie-Two who did that./

/// Oh. And I am—? ///

Bandicut had to think. /Charlie-Four./

/// Mm. Well, krikey,
I hope I'm not going to be blamed for
everything my parents did. ///

Bandicut chuckled. /Maybe not everything. But don't you quarx carry some sort of, I don't know, collective conscience or something?/

That evoked a moment of puzzled reflection from the quarx.

/// You got me. ///

/No offense, I mean./

/// None taken.
But you know, I do have this sense
—search me if I know where it comes from—
that we, I mean myselves and I,
are supposed to be moving on.
We always seem to be moving on.
As if we have something we're supposed to do. ///

/You mean, with me—or without me?/ Bandicut asked, with a pang.

/// Who knows, really?
It's not as if this is clear to me.
I have the feeling it's a sort of . . .
what's the word? ///

/Mission? Quest? Cosmic journey?/

/// Something like that. ///

/Oh./ He'd meant it lightheartedly. Charlie hadn't.

/// It might take me a while
to figure out. But look— ///

Bandicut waited.

/// Well, about what we're doing next.
You know, back there in the cavern,
I had the sense that Hroom
really, really meant for you to use this portal.
If we can find it.
I think he just didn't want
to be pushy about suggesting it. ///

/Yeah?/ Bandicut focused on the flames for a few moments, watching the firelight flicker off the still, metallic forms of the robots. /I'll keep that in mind./ He lay down then, curling against the relative softness of his backpack, and closed his eyes.

∞

It might have been minutes or hours later, when Charlie woke him with a nudge.

/// *Don't look now, but we have company.* ///

He sat up groggily. He blinked at Ik, and realized that the Hraachee'an had his eyes open, but was sitting very still, watching something just outside their circle. /What is it?/ He squinted, trying to see by the dim glow of the fire's embers.

/// *See them? There.* ///

/No./ And then he did. It was two small animal-shapes, the size of large prairie dogs. They had crept up close to the robots, neither of which had stirred. /I will be b'joogered. It's the meerkats./

/// *The what?* ///

/Meerkats—that's what I called them, after an animal on Earth. Ik and I met them a while back./ Shifting his gaze to Ik, he murmured, "Are these—"

"I believe so," Ik said softly.

I will be God damned, Bandicut thought. The meerkats. Did that mean the company really had been transported back into that same territory? Or did the meerkats travel around Shipworld, too?

The two meerkats crept into the circle, their tufted ears twitching. They had bowling-pin bodies, and gawky heads, and they looked intensely alert. The taller of the two made a chittering sound. It looked from Ik to Bandicut, then to the others. Li-Jared was rubbing his eyes awake, and Antares was staring at the two meerkats as if she had been aware of them all along. Perhaps she had been. The meerkat chittered again, and jerked its head to one side, as if to indicate a direction.

"What is it?" muttered Li-Jared.

"It is a *krayket*," said Antares, her voice startlingly clear. "They are a reclusive species."

"You know them?" asked Li-Jared.

"Somewhat. They helped me once, a few seasons ago, when I was lost."

Bandicut blinked. "They helped us once, too. Ik and me. And the robots. When we were trying to catch up with you,

Li-Jared.'' In fact, he remembered suddenly, the meerkats had helped them to find their way through a portal.

Antares made a series of warbling sounds, and the meerkats, or kraykets, chittered back to her. The conversation went on for a few moments. Then she said, ''They want us to follow them.''

''Look,'' Ik murmured. He pointed into the darkness.

Bandicut rose involuntarily. Not more than twenty meters from their dying fire, a ghostly flicker betrayed a lighted opening in the rock wall behind the trees. ''Is that *it*? The portal?''

''Let us look and see.''

The creatures squeaked and started that way. They ducked awkwardly forward and back, twitching their ears at the company, as though to encourage them all to move. Antares was already on her feet, bag swinging from her shoulder. Li-Jared and Ik rose. Bandicut grabbed his backpack. ''Coppy! Nappy! Wake up!''

''Ready to move, John Bandicut,'' said Napoleon.

''Did you see them coming?'' Bandicut asked. ''Why didn't you say something?''

''They were here to see you, Cap'n,'' said Copernicus. ''But they were reluctant to wake you.'' The robot lumbered into motion and rolled back and forth over the coals of the fire, until the glowing embers were crushed under a thin curl of smoke.

Bandicut took a deep breath, his thoughts reeling. ''Okay, then. Let's go.''

Led by the shuffling meerkats, they approached the stone wall. The glow seemed to penetrate into the stone, though there was no clearly defined opening. As they stood contemplating the portal, Antares murmured something to the meerkats, and they chittered back. ''They say we have a choice. The portal can take us—'' She hesitated as the meerkats chittered again. This time, Bandicut's wrist-stones tingled, perhaps picking up a translation from Antares's stones.

". . . across the continents . . . within the metaship . . . or
. . . to a star-spanner . . ."
Bandicut took a sharp breath.
". . . and inward toward the stars of the galaxy . . ."

27

STAR-SPANNER

 BANDICUT HELD HIS breath. Inward toward the stars of the galaxy? The Milky Way? His heart filled with thoughts of the immensity of space, of the galaxy he had left behind, of the intense loneliness that came over him every time he glimpsed that swirling sea of stars outside Shipworld. And he thought: it would be a totally irrational choice: The meerkat hadn't said *home;* it had just said *into the galaxy.* They might be sent anywhere. But in his heart, the decision was already made. "Back into the galaxy," he whispered.

The others too had been struck dumb. But one by one, they answered. "Into the galaxy," murmured Ik. "To the stars," said Li-Jared.

Bandicut looked at Antares. Her gold and black eyes caught his fiercely, and he felt her anguished indecision. "Would you like to come with us?"

"Indeed, you are welcome," said Ik.

Bwang. "Why not?" said Li-Jared.

Antares stared a moment longer, and her gold irises narrowed, as though she had just made a decision—out of what considerations Bandicut could not guess. She uttered a soft hissing sound. "Why not, indeed?" she said at last. She turned to the meerkats. "Back to the stars."

The creatures jumped up, scrambling around the area directly in front of the portal. Ik made a movement toward them, but the meerkats squawked, warning him away. The company stood in a half circle, watching uneasily as the ghostly emanations from the portal slowly changed colors. At last, the portal shone a deep, sparkling sapphire.

The meerkats yipped, ears twitching. "Now," said Antares.

Li-Jared and Ik stepped through the opening almost as one, and vanished. Bandicut hesitated an instant, then urged the robots forward. The light strobed around him, flashing through a dazzling rainbow of colors. He heard the rasping and tapping of the robots, and the voices of Ik and Li-Jared. And Antares—?

The light dropped to near-darkness, a pale golden glow that shone without illuminating. They were in another transition-zone, floating more than standing. He tried to turn his head, and couldn't. But he sensed something forming around them, something more of energy than matter, he thought, an egg-shaped enclosure. The light strobed out again, and he felt a *shift* that told him they'd been transported out of the holding area, into something different. He could just discern great, pale circles and arches stretching out in a line before him, suggesting a vast, hollow tunnel, dwindling to infinity.

The inside of a star-spanner? he wondered, heart pounding. He waited for someone or something to speak, to ask them where they wanted to go, or at least to offer choices. Surely they would be offered choices.

He felt a gentle bump, then a sharp concussion, and the golden light vanished to darkness. He had a feeling of *falling* . . . and then not so much falling as speeding through darkness, accelerating at an unthinkable rate. Luminous concentric rings appeared in the distance, growing with alarming speed. They flared around him like hoops, vanishing behind. More circles of light appeared, growing quickly, flashing by.

He tried once more to turn his head, and found that he could do so now, very slowly. He was encapsulated in a transparent amber bubble, and enclosed with him were Ik, Li-Jared, the two metal beings . . . and Antares.

Her eyes met his for an instant.

He could not read her expression. But they had made their choices, all of them. Wherever they were going, they were going together.

It became increasingly hard to focus, with the strobelike flashing of the star-spanner around him. He passed into a kind of trance, much like the time following his collision with the comet, as he was hurled out of the galaxy to Shipworld. Were they on their way back into the Milky Way? He wondered fleetingly how much power was at his back, like the wind, and how many light-years lay ahead. After a while, he stopped thinking about it.

The circles stopped coming, and for a time there was a kind of swirling darkness; it was like being inside a thundercloud, with only the most tenuous glimmers of lightning.

Then smaller, dimmer lights began to flash by: sometimes fluttering like butterflies, or falling horizontally like gentle raindrops, or drawn out in long, dazzling streaks. Sometimes it seemed more like darkness painted upon darkness.

He thought he heard voices echoing in the vastness of space, but if it was speech, he couldn't understand a word of it. Charlie was silent. Or if he spoke, his voice was another incomprehensible mutter from the void. Memories rose and floated toward him in spinning pirouettes:

His first flight in Earth orbit, his pilot's certificate fresh in his pocket, the Earth turning below him like a luminous, mystical watercolor painting.

His niece Dakota, begging him to take her into space—and his promise to do so, forever unfulfilled.

The dim blue cavern on Triton, the alien translator drawing him into the soul-wrenching realm of its awareness, while Charlie labored to keep him from dying of the experience.

Silence-fugue, full of dancing aliens, and Charlie pulling him back to reality.

Julie Stone, pulling him into a warm, heady embrace . . . and later crying to him not to do this insane thing, stealing a spaceship from Triton orbit, on a flight he could not possibly return from alive.

And a mad, fugue-punctuated dash across the solar system, threading space, to save an oblivious Earth from a planet-killer comet.

And then . . .

Translation.

(???) Was that a memory, or the stones explaining what was happening now?

No answers. He slept, and had no idea for how long. He dreamed that his body was being transformed, a caterpillar turning into a butterfly . . .

Impending arrival . . .

He dreamed of stars spinning around him like dancers, and a planet, blue and green and white . . . rather like Earth, but not Earth.

He dreamed of translation, transformation . . . of clouds spinning by, just out of reach . . . and a vast blue ocean rising to flank him . . .

Arrival.

He awoke to a crashing of waves, a thunder of bubbles, a blazing sun slanting down through crystal blue waters. He sputtered, crying out, then realized that he was surrounded by the water, but not actually touching it.

"Hraah!" "This is not—" *Bwang-ng-ng!* Tap tap. "John Bandicut—"

His eyes and brain finally starting working together again, and his heart nearly stopped. They were still in the pale golden egg that had carried them among the stars, but they were planetbound now, underwater. They had leapt across light-years, and fallen into a sea. Not Earth's sea, but some sea, somewhere. Were they bobbing back toward the surface? No . . . they were *sinking*. Far overhead was a dancing silver surface, receding. The sea was darkening perceptibly around them.

"Something's wrong! We have to get out!" he cried, but his voice was lost in the panicky babble of the others' shouts. He threw himself against the bubble, and for a terrifying instant, felt himself stretch out into the sea, as if through an invisible rubber sheet, seawater all but pressing through his pores. Below was a deep cerulean gulf, sunbeams slanting down and vanishing into a bottomless abyss.

He popped back into the bubble, gasping for breath.

As the ocean darkened, he met the terrified glances of his companions. He forced himself to look down again, and in the midnight gloom below, he glimpsed lights—what looked like luminous seaweed bubbles, a lamp-yellow glow deep in the oceanic night.

Or perhaps not seaweed at all. He rubbed his eyes and gazed down again, and realized that if he could trust his eyes, he was looking at bubble-cities, far below in the depths of the sea.

STRANGE ATTRACTORS: CODA

 IN THE GLOOM of the cavern, the Triton exoarch team moved with deliberate care. Julie Stone was at the head of the group, but not entirely sure how she had gotten there. She was not the team leader, yet had somehow wound up at the front of the line as the team made its way cautiously along the frozen nitrogen-ice surface of the cavern floor. Helmet-lamp beams flashed in jittery movements over the translucent walls. Julie came to a turn in the passageway, and thought: wait for the others. An instant later, she felt a sudden, almost overwhelming urge to go ahead without waiting. *But—*

The urge became irresistible. Forgetting caution, she stepped around the bend, the spot of her headlight sweeping before her.

Something flickered and squirmed in the light. She steadied her headlight. There it was! The thing they had come searching for!

Alien artifact.

There was no question of it. It looked like a top-heavy array of twirling spheres, iridescent and black, spheres spinning and passing through one another like holo images, not solid at all. Nevertheless, the mass-detectors had established the presence of an extremely dense object here. The whole array appeared to balance on one small, black sphere.

It looked just as John had described it to her in his letter.

And yet . . . there was no way his description could have prepared her for this. The artifact appeared new; it appeared ancient. It looked timeless, as timeless as any *made* object could look. And it seemed . . . *alive.*

"Julie?" The voice of Kim, the team leader, echoed in her helmet comm. "You're getting too far ahead of us. Do you see anything?"

"Yes!" she whispered. "I have—"

You have come. Julie Stone.

She gulped, losing her breath. What was that voice?

We have a mission yet to fulfill. And we require your assistance.

And then it filled her head . . . the voice, the *presence,* of the alien thing . . . and she felt herself falling, falling endlessly, until consciousness abandoned her.

—to be continued in The Infinite Sea,
Volume III in THE CHAOS CHRONICLES—

ABOUT THE AUTHOR

Jeffrey A. Carver is the author of a number of thought-provoking, popular science fiction novels, including *The Infinity Link* and *The Rapture Effect*. His books combine hard-SF concepts, deeply humanistic concerns, and a sense of humor, making them both compellingly suspenseful and emotionally satisfying. Carver has written several successful novels in his "star-rigger" universe: *Star Rigger's Way* (now available from Tor Books), *Panglor* (soon to be released in a Tor Books edition), *Dragons in the Stars*, and *Dragon Rigger*. With *Neptune Crossing*, Carver inaugurated THE CHAOS CHRONICLES, a sweeping new series inspired by the emerging science of chaos. Carver continues his exploration of this intriguing new universe, the universe of mankind's future, with *Strange Attractors* and *The Infinite Sea*, coming in 1996. Mr. Carver lives in the Boston area with his wife and two daughters. Mr. Carver also has a location on the Internet; his web page is at the following address: http://www.oneworld.net/SF/authors/carver.htm

THE BEST OF SF FROM TOR

☐ 53345-3 *MOTHER OF STORMS* $5.99
John Barnes $6.99 Canada

☐ 55255-5 *THE GOLDEN QUEEN* $5.99
Dave Wolverton $6.99 Canada

☐ 52213-3 *TROUBLE AND HER FRIENDS* $4.99
Melissa Scott $5.99 Canada

☐ 53415-8 *WILDLIFE* $4.99
James Patrick Kelly $5.99 Canada

☐ 53518-9 *VOICES OF HEAVEN* $5.99
Frederik Pohl $6.99 Canada

☐ 52480-2 *MOVING MARS* $5.99
Greg Bear $6.99 Canada

☐ 53515-4 *NEPTUNE CROSSING* $5.99
Jeffrey Carver $6.99 Canada

☐ 53075-6 *LIEGE-KILLER* $5.99
Christopher Hinz $6.99 Canada

Call toll-free 1-800-288-2131 to use your major credit card, buy them at your local bookstore, or clip and mail this page to order by mail.

Publishers Book and Audio Mailing Service
P.O. Box 120159, Staten Island, NY 10312-0004

Please send me the book(s) I have checked above. I am enclosing $ _____
(Please add $1.50 for the first book, and $.50 for each additional book to cover postage and handling. Send check or money order only— no CODs.)

Name_____

Address _____

City _____ State / Zip_____

Please allow six weeks for delivery. Prices subject to change without notice.